SEANAN McGUIRE

AN
ARTIFICIAL NIGHT

A TOBY DAYE NOVEL

corsair

First published in 2010 in the United States of America by DAW Books
First published in Great Britain in 2016 by Corsair

1 3 5 7 9 10 8 6 4 2

A CIP catalogue record for this book
is available from the British Library.

ISBN: 978-1-4721-1629-1 (ebook)
ISBN: 978-1-4721-2009-0 (paperback)

Printed and bound in Great Britain by
CPI Group (UK) Ltd., Croydon, CR0 4YY

Papers used by Corsair are from well-managed forests
and other responsible sources

MIX
Paper from
responsible sources
FSC
www.fsc.org FSC® C104740

Corsair
An imprint of
Little, Brown Book Group
Carmelite House
50 Victoria Embankment
London EC4Y 0DZ

An Hachette UK Company
www.hachette.co.uk

www.littlebrown.co.uk

For Vixy.
For always.

ACKNOWLEDGMENTS:

An Artificial Night is the third of Toby's adventures, and by the time I reached it, I had a decent idea of what I was doing ... or so I thought, before I was tackled by the fine members of the Machete Squad, who beat some sense into me and some awesome into the book. Big thanks go to every one of them for their tireless labors. Special thanks on this volume go to Deborah Brannon, Mia Nutick, Michelle McNeill, and Jeanne Goldfein, all of whom helped immensely with the process of hacking my way down into Blind Michael's lands. Mary Crowell took me down the scarecrow trail to show me a few things I'd missed when I was walking on my own, and Rebecca Newman was glorious, as always. A great deal of detail came from long discussions with Meg Creelman, who was a fantastic help. I couldn't have done it without all of them.

Chris Mangum and Tara O'Shea made sure my website was as awesome and low-stress as possible, thus allowing me to stress out over other things, like what my cats were doing. My agent, Diana Fox, was supportive and clever in all the best ways—it's good to have a superhero in your corner—while my editor, Sheila Gilbert, was a joy to work with. Marsha Jones and Joshua Starr at DAW answered my endless questions about this and the books before it, and made the process much closer to painless than it could have been. Here on the home front, Kate Secor, Michelle Dockrey, Brooke Lunderville, and Amy McNally kept me from losing my mind, and made the book better at the same time. Finally, a big, big thanks to Betsy Tinney, who rescued me from an emergency kitten shortage when she provided my latest family member, a blue classic tabby and white Maine Coon named Alice.

My personal soundtrack while writing *An Artificial Night* consisted mostly of *Archetype Cafe*, by Talis Kimberley, *Thirteen*, by Vixy and Tony, *Seven is the Number*, by Dave Carter and Tracy Grammer, and *Films About Ghosts*, by the Counting Crows. Any errors in this book are entirely my own. The errors that aren't here are the ones that all these people helped me fix.

Now breath in deep, and keep hold of your candle. It's a long way from here to Babylon.

PRONUNCIATION GUIDE:

All pronunciations are given strictly phonetically. This only covers races explicitly named in the first three books.

Bannick: *ban-nick*. Plural is Bannicks.
Banshee: *ban-shee*. Plural is Banshees.
Barghest: *bar-guy-st*. Plural is Barghests.
Barrow Wight: *bar-row white*. Plural is Barrow Wights.
Blodynbryd: *blow-din-brid*. Plural is Blodynbryds.
Cait Sidhe: *kay-th shee*. Plural is Cait Sidhe.
Candela: *can-dee-la*. Plural is Candela.
Coblynau: *cob-lee-now*. Plural is Coblynau.
Cornish Pixie: *Corn-ish pix-ee*. Plural is Cornish Pixies.
Daoine Sidhe: *doon-ya shee*. Plural is Daoine Sidhe, diminutive is Daoine.
Djinn: *jin*. Plural is Djinn.
Ellyllon: *el-lee-lawn*. Plural is Ellyllons.
Gean-Cannah: *gee-ann can-na*. Plural is Gean-Cannah.
Glastig: *glass-tig*. Plural is Glastigs.
Gwragen: *guh-war-a-gen*. Plural is Gwargen.
Hamadryad: *ha-ma-dry-add*. Plural is Hamadryads.
Hippocampus: *hip-po-cam-pus*. Plural is Hippocampi.
Hob: *hob*. Plural is Hobs.
Kelpie: *kel-pee*. Plural is Kelpies.

Kitsune: *kit-soo-nay*. Plural is Kitsune.
Lamia: *lay-me-a*. Plural is Lamia.
The Luidaeg: *the lou-sha-k*. No plural exists.
Manticore: *man-tee-core*. Plural is Manticores.
Naiad: *nigh-add*. Plural is Naiads.
Nixie: *nix-ee*. Plural is Nixen.
Peri: *pear-ee*. Plural is Peri.
Piskie: *piss-key*. Plural is Piskies.
Pixie: *pix-ee*. Plural is Pixies.
Puca: *puh-ca*. Plural is Pucas.
Roane: *row-n*. Plural is Roane.
Selkie: *sell-key*. Plural is Selkies.
Silene: *sigh-lean*. Plural is Silene.
Swanmay: *swan-may*. Plural is Swanmays.
Tuatha de Dannan: *tootha day danan*. Plural is Tuatha de
    Dannan, diminutive is Tuatha.
Tylwyth Teg: *till-with teeg*. Plural is Tylwyth Teg, diminu-
    tive is Tylwyth.
Undine: *un-deen*. Plural is Undine.
Urisk: *you-risk*. Plural is Urisk.
Will o' Wisps: *will-oh wisps*. Plural is Will o' Wisps.

ONE

September 7th, 2010

Away from light steals home my heavy son
And private in his chamber pens himself,
Shuts up his windows, locks fair daylight out,
And makes himself an artificial night.
—William Shakespeare, *Romeo and Juliet*

ONE THING I'VE LEARNED IN MY TIME working as a private investigator-slash-knight errant for the fae community of the San Francisco Bay Area: if something looks like it's going to be simple, it probably won't be. Some people might consider that an easy lesson. I must be a slow learner because it's been anything but easy. I've been turned into a fish, cursed, nearly drowned, impersonated, slashed, shot at, and had my car blown up—thankfully not while I was inside it, although it was a close call—and now I was chasing Barghests around Dame Eloise Altair's feast hall, trying not to get myself hurt. Also not easy.

"Toby! Duck!" Danny didn't sound particularly worried. Danny's also a pureblood Bridge Troll, which means he has skin that's as hard as granite and twice as difficult to damage. As a half-breed Daoine Sidhe, I'm a lot easier to hurt.

I ducked.

A Barghest sailed overhead, impacting the wall with a pained *thump*. Barghests are nasty semi-canine monsters with horns, retractable claws, and venomous stingers in their scorpion tails, but there's one thing they don't have: wings. I glanced over my shoulder long enough to confirm that the thing hadn't been killed by impact—it was still twitching, which made death seem unlikely—before turning to wrinkle my nose at Danny.

"Changeling, remember? Can you at least try not to hurl spiky critters at my head?"

"Sure thing," said Danny blithely. Too blithely. In my experience, people who sound that calm about requests that they not throw things have no intention of changing their behavior.

My name is October Daye; my friends call me Toby, largely because it's difficult to call a cranky brunette changeling with a knife October and get away with it. And this is not the way I usually prefer to spend my Saturday nights.

Every private investigator gets her share of weird calls, and the fact that I'm the only fae PI in the Kingdom means I wind up with more than most. Even worse, most of the weird calls come from the local nobility, which means I can't turn them down. Lucky me. I shouldn't complain. Work is work, and playing whack-a-mole with Barghests in Dame Altair's feast hall was better than going back to checking bags at the grocery store. Not that the grocery store was likely to rehire me, considering that I'd abandoned my job without warning when a friend of mine went and got herself murdered over ownership of a legendary fae artifact. Not the sort of thing I could explain to human resources. Stress on the "human."

Changelings rarely do well in jobs with fixed, dependable hours. We get that from the fae side of the family, while the human side makes us too stubborn not to try.

Dame Altair called on Monday to report that "something" was trashing her pantry, frightening her staff, and generally making life more complicated than she wanted it to be. By Wednesday, I knew that we were dealing with a Barghest infestation. I could try to claim the discovery was solely due to my awesome investigative skills, but that wouldn't be entirely accurate. The truth was, I stepped on one while I was searching the place.

The fact that it was "just" Barghests was a relief—for me, anyway. It could have been a lot worse. Dame Altair didn't seem particularly relieved, but they were nesting on her property, and that probably made them a lot more annoying. I explained the situation, requested the necessary supplies, and called Danny.

Danny McReady possesses a lot of positive qualities if you ignore his tendency to chuck Barghests at my head, but when it comes to monster hunting, "practically indestructible" is the one that counts. He's also a San Francisco taxi driver, which leaves him with a lot of pent-up aggression. The chance to spend the night playing whack-a-mole with Barghests was too much to pass up.

Dame Altair had evacuated the knowe by the time Danny showed up. We grabbed the enchanted rowan-wood crates she'd provided for us to stuff them into, paused while I pulled on my gloves, and marched back inside to deal with things.

There were a lot of things to deal with. Barghests breed about once a century, and like many of Faerie's more monstrous denizens, they balance a high mortality rate with a necessarily high birthrate. I'd counted at least eight before I gave up and asked the Dame for a bunch of boxes. She thought I was insane for not wanting to kill them on the spot, but even Barghests have a right to live. Just not in Dame Altair's feast hall.

Where we were actually going to put them was a problem for later; the problem for now was catching them without being seriously injured in the process. They were only pups, about the size of corgis. They were still equipped with multiple ways of killing a person, and they were absolutely *not* interested in coming quietly.

"This is the sort of thing I mean." One of the Barghests was chewing on Danny's leg, probably hurting itself in the process. "I ask what you're doing on a Saturday night, and you say 'hunting Barghests.' Forgive me for nagging, but you should maybe try getting a social life."

"I'm getting paid to be here, remember?" Another Barghest charged me with its tail raised in strike position. I parried with my butterfly net, almost managing to catch it before it popped its claws and ripped through half the mesh. Swearing, I tried to net the thing again before I added, "Besides, I have a birthday party to go to after this."

"The Brown kid, right?"

"Yeah." Mitch and Stacy's youngest son, Andrew, was turning four. "I promised to make it in time for cake."

"You'll make it."

"Starting to have my doubts," I muttered. One of the Barghests was slinking on its belly to my right. I leaned over, whapped it on the head with my net, and swept it into the first box. "Get that closed!"

"Got it." Danny plucked the Barghest off his leg, bowling it into the box after its sibling before slamming the lid. "That's two. I'm just saying you could benefit by going out sometimes. Live a little. In ways that don't involve maybe making yourself dead."

"But I'm so *good* at maybe making myself dead." I whacked another Barghest. "I wouldn't have taken this job if I'd known it was going to mean playing with poisonous things. Dame Altair thought the pantries were emptying due to theft."

"Well, they kinda were." Two more Barghests were industriously worrying Danny's ankles. A wide smile split his craggy face. "Aw, look at the cute little guys."

"They're poisonous monstrosities, Danny. That's not 'cute.'" I swung at another Barghest. It scuttled backward, barking at me.

"You get to keep that spiky thing, I get to think Barghests are cute," he replied philosophically and scooped up both Barghests, cradling them. "You think Her Lady-ship would mind if I took one or two of 'em home?"

"Spike's a rose goblin," I said sharply. "That's different."

"Maybe from where you're sitting."

I groaned, swatting another Barghest and sweeping it into a box before it could sting me. "There isn't a Barghest rescue society. I don't think Dame Altair is going to care what we do with them as long as they're gone when we're done here."

"Good," said Danny, dropping his two into a box and sealing it. "I'm taking them."

"What?" I turned to stare at him, sidestepping a Barghest intent on mauling my shins. "How many?"

"All of them." He grabbed another one. It twisted in his hands, ramming its stinger against his shoulder. He smiled indulgently. "I think he likes me."

"Danny . . ."

"I'll only keep a couple. If there's no rescue group, somebody's gotta look out for the little guys." He dropped the Barghest he was holding into a box, ignoring its ongoing attempts to sting him. "How about this: instead of splittin' the fee, you pay for my help by letting me take the Barghests."

"And here I thought my money wasn't any good with you."

"Poisonous monstrosities aren't money."

I had to laugh at that. "You win." We'd somehow managed to stun and capture the entire litter without serious injury. Putting my net down on the floor, I turned to peer at the boxes. "Looks like fourteen of them. They're not happy."

"You wouldn't be either," he said. "What do you think happened to their mama?" Barghests are notoriously protective of their young. A litter without a mother almost certainly meant something had gone wrong.

"Poison and claws don't protect you from becoming roadkill," I said. Barghests had an unfortunate tendency to play in traffic. Thankfully the night-haunts were always there to clean up the mess before the humans saw. "She's lucky she stowed them here, even if they did manage to cause a lot of damage before Dame Altair called me."

"It's a whole new world," he said sadly. There was no way I could argue with that.

A few millennia ago, when Faerie was still in its ascendancy, creatures like the Barghests would have roamed the moors, not afraid of anything but hunting parties and bigger predators. Things have changed since then. With Faerie in hiding and more of her creatures becoming extinct every year, the Barghests were probably lucky to have been captured. At least with Danny looking out for them, they might stand a chance.

Not all Faerie's denizens have fared as poorly as her monsters. Sure, the Barghests would have been free and happy to do as they pleased, but people like me and most of my friends would have been treated like lepers. Assuming we were allowed to live. As human civilization has taken over much of what used to belong to the fae, changelings have become more integrated into Faerie culture. Call it evolution in action. We're half-human, but our loyalties are to Faerie; that makes us useful tools in a world that includes things like iron and the Internet. Not that I've been able to figure out the e-mail account Countess April O'Leary set up for me, despite several telephone "tech support" sessions punctuated by April's muffled laughter. Missing fourteen years of technological advancement has left me a little behind the times.

Fortunately, most of Faerie moves slowly enough to make something as small as being turned into a fish for a decade and a half look positively inconsequential. Certain skills never become outdated, and that includes disposing of infestations of small, inconvenient monsters.

Danny started carrying boxed Barghests to his taxi while I tracked down Dame Altair to sound the all-clear and collect my fee. He was shoving the last box into the passenger seat when I emerged from the knowe, money safely tucked into my pocket.

I eyed the cab. It was completely filled with boxes, making it look like he'd decided to start moonlighting as a professional mover. "I hope you weren't planning on picking up any fares tonight."

"Nope." He grinned, dusting his hands together. "I'm gonna take the babies home and see about setting 'em up a kennel. She say anything about wanting the boxes back?"

"They're all yours." Dame Altair's knowe was tucked into an elegant Victorian house in a neighborhood nice enough that our cars stuck out like sore thumbs. "I'm gonna get going before I miss the party entirely. Call me if you need any help with the Barghests, okay?"

"Got it. And you think about what I said. Getting out more couldn't hurt."

"With who? Mitch and Stacy have kids, Kerry's always busy, Julie hates me, and you have a cab to drive."

He shrugged. "I don't know. How about you call that King of Cats guy I used to see you with? Take him out, get him drunk, and see if you can make him sing karaoke."

"No." My tone didn't leave any room for argument.

Danny blinked, looking startled. "Just think about it, all right? Open roads, Toby."

"Good night, Danny."

He was just trying to help, and I shouldn't be cranky about it. I told myself that half a dozen times as I got into my car and pulled out of Dame Altair's neighborhood, going more than a bit above the speed limit as I tried to make it to Andy's party on time. I glanced at the clock. Fifteen minutes to midnight. I could just make it, if I managed to avoid getting pulled over.

Human kids live their lives in sunlight. Staying up late is usually a treat reserved for special occasions. Fae kids live by a different clock. Almost all fae are nocturnal creatures, from Daoine Sidhe like my mother all the way down to the hearth-spirits and pixies. We don't like the sun; the sun returns the favor. Of Mitch and Stacy's five kids, only the oldest, Cassandra, was keeping anything like a human schedule. She was a freshman at UC Berkeley, and unfortunately, most of the required courses for a physics degree were held during the day.

The fae disdain for daylight made shopping for Andy's birthday present an adventure in and of itself. I'd finally managed to make it to a toy store downtown just before closing, where the clerk assured me that no four-year-old boy could ever have enough plastic dinosaurs. Since I'd been out of bed for less than half an hour, I was groggy enough that I would have agreed to buy the kid a box of plastic forks if it meant I could get out of there and go for coffee. The dinosaurs were in the back, in a bag covered with gamboling cartoon clowns. I hate clowns.

I was lucky: it was late enough that the roads between San Francisco and Colma were basically clear, and I pulled up in front of Mitch and Stacy's house with almost five minutes to spare. From the sidewalk, the house looked dark, silent, and totally deserted. Living in Faerie has taught me a lot about how deceptive appearances can be.

The edges of the lawn glittered as I walked toward the house, betraying the presence of an illusion spell. I stepped across the boundaries, and the house was suddenly blazing with lights, the air sharp with the smells of sugar and finger paint. Braziers were mounted on stakes all around the lot, with pixies fanning the tiny flames that kept the spell alive. Shouts and peals of happy laughter filled the air. The party, it seemed, was still in full force. I grinned and walked on, Barghests and Danny's attempt to meddle in my social life forgotten.

The side gate was open, invitingly decorated with a bouquet of bright balloons. I veered that way, ducking under a crepe paper streamer and into the backyard where chaos reigned.

At least ten kids of varying ages and species were racing around like they were jet-propelled. Most of their attention was on the jungle gym, where there was some sort of pirate game going on. It seemed to involve chasing each other up and down the slide while shouting, "Shiver me timbers!" A dun-colored Centaur cantered around the structure, crying, "Avast ye!" and trying to grab the others whenever they came into range. Jessica was directing the action, too absorbed by her six year old's autocracy to do more than wave distractedly at my arrival.

Cassandra was on the porch, struggling to read while children shrieked and zoomed around her. It seemed like a battle she was doomed to lose.

I walked over to sit down next to her, one eye on the wild rumpus. "Hey, puss."

She brightened. "Aunt Birdie!" Being nineteen and highly aware of her own dignity, she took great care in putting her book down before she hugged me. "You came! Andy's going to be thrilled."

"Couldn't miss the fun," I said, returning the hug.

Cassandra was the only one of Mitch and Stacy's kids born before my disappearance. She's the one who originally decided my name should be "Aunt Birdie," since she couldn't pronounce "October." She's short, plump, and pretty, and has her mother's gently pointed ears, tipped with tufts of black fur. She gets her coloring from her dad's side of the family, though, with Mitch's blue-gray eyes and unremarkable brown-blond hair.

It's hard to look at her and not see my own little girl, the one I lost when Simon cast his spell on me. I've been working on it. Cassandra deserves better than to be judged by who Gillian might have grown up to be.

Not that Gillian's been willing to let me see who she actually is. My daughter isn't dead. She just refuses to let me be a part of her life.

"Well, it's really good to see you," said Cassandra as she let me go.

I settled back in my seat. "Good to see you, t—"

My statement was cut short as Andrew slammed into me from the side and flung his arms around my neck. "Auntie Birdie!"

Cassandra laughed. "Aren't you glad I outgrew that?"

"You have no idea," I said, and ruffled Andrew's hair. "How's our birthday boy?"

"I'm four!" he said, showing me the appropriate number of grimy fingers. Towheaded, freckled, and filthy: all the ingredients needed for "ridiculously cute." Children shouldn't be allowed to be that adorable. There ought to be a law. "We're having a party!"

"I noticed."

Cassandra groaned, muttering, "People in Oregon noticed."

"We're gonna have cake, and ice cream, and presents, and—"

A rising shriek was coming from the direction of the swings. I shifted Andrew to my lap as I looked up. Cassandra rolled her eyes. "Incoming."

"Aunt Birdeeeeeeeeeeeeeeeeee!" Karen raced toward us. I braced for impact. At eleven, Karen never seemed to be able to make up her mind about whether or not she was too grown-up to tackle me. I got off lucky this time; she skidded to a halt and declared, "You came!"

"I did," I agreed. "You look like you've been wallowing in the mud."

She looked down at herself. She was coated with filth from the waist down, and muck caked her hair. "Wow. You're right."

"So what *have* you been doing?"

Gleefully, she crowed, "Wallowing in the mud!"

I sighed. "Right." Andrew was snuggling into my lap, getting dirt all over my jeans. I thought about moving him and decided not to bother. It was his birthday. He could get me dirty if he wanted to. "What's up?"

"We're playing pirates," she said. "I'm the first mate! Jessica gives orders and then I make bad people walk the plank."

"Good for you. So what's Andy?"

"He was my parrot, and then he was a shark. Now he's . . . what are you now, Andy?"

"M'a rowboat," he said sleepily.

"Do rowboats nap?" I asked.

"I wish," muttered Cassandra. "They've been trying to drive me crazy all night."

"Really? How are they doing?"

She flipped her ponytail over her shoulder, rolling her eyes. "Amazingly well."

"I see." I tickled Andrew until he stopped yawning and started giggling, then set him back on his feet. "Go be a rowboat." He laughed and ran for the swings, Karen close behind.

"How do they get all that energy?" I asked as I stood. "They never stop moving."

Cassandra grinned. "I have no idea. If I knew, I could skip freshman physics."

"I'm gonna go let your folks know I'm here. You need anything?"

"Can I have a tranquilizer gun?"

"No."

"Okay. Just tell Mom we need to cut the cake soon, or I may kill them all."

"Got it. Give the kids sugar before you kill them. Because *that's* gonna calm them down." I winked and turned to head inside.

If the party seemed hectic in the yard, it was even worse when packed into the confines of Mitch and Stacy's cluttered living room. School pictures and crayon art covered the walls, while toys, domestic mammals, and small children got underfoot when least expected. The furniture was covered with clear plastic sheeting, but that would just delay the damage, not prevent it.

Stacy was positioning chairs around a series of folding tables when I walked in. Anthony, their nine year old, was helping her, looking harried. The party was clearly getting to him, and just as clearly wasn't getting to his cheerful-looking mother. "Toby! Good, you're here," she said, unsurprised by my appearance. "Get the cake."

"Got it," I said, shaking my head as I moved toward the kitchen. If I'd been juggling that many kids, I would have demanded whiskey and duct tape instead of offering them things bound to make them even more hyper-active. But that's Stacy.

As a quarter-blooded changeling, Stacy was aging faster than any of us, but she wore it well enough that it didn't seem to matter. Her chestnut hair was pulled into a ponytail and a paint-stained apron was tied around her waist. All the kids take after her to some degree—Jessica looks like a miniature version of her mother—and they could have done a lot worse.

Mitch was in the kitchen unpacking the cake, a three-tiered monstrosity covered in sugar dinosaurs: clearly our friend Kerry's work. It would take hearth-magic to make realistic sugar reptiles that small. "Hey," he said. "Help me with this."

"Sure." I stepped into position, taking one side of the cake. "How many kids are here, anyway?"

"Nineteen." He laughed. "You should see the look on your face! It's a party, Toby."

"Most parties don't involve the entire kindergarten."

Mitch just laughed, muttering a quick charm to light the candles. We could hear Stacy's voice drifting from the living room, calling the kids to come in and sit down as we carried the cake through the kitchen door. A dozen different off-key renditions of "Happy Birth-day" promptly burst forth. The Centaur was singing in German, while a tiny Snow Fairy with ice in her hair joined in with what sounded like a Japanese pop song. Welcome to birthdays in Faerie.

Flanked by a Goblin and a Hamadryad and beaming from ear to ear, Andy leaned out of his chair to blow out the candles with one surprisingly strong breath. Every-one started to cheer. I clapped my hands, laughing.

Happy birthday, kiddo. Happy birthday.

TWO

THE BIRTHDAY PARTY was more draining than I expected. Too many memories of Gillian and the few birthdays we'd shared before I disappeared, too many little laughing ghosts waiting to ambush me. I got home a little after midnight and crawled straight into bed, where I lay awake, staring at the ceiling, until sometime after four. I'd been asleep for less than an hour when the telephone rang, jolting me awake.

I bolted upright, sending the cats tumbling off my chest as I groped around in the dark to find the phone. I glanced at the clock as my hand closed on the receiver. 5:34 A.M. Whoever it was had better have a damn good reason for calling, or they were going to suffer. *"What?"*

"Morning, Toby! I didn't wake you, did I?"

I suppressed the urge to swear. I only know one person who would risk physical harm by calling me that close to dawn. "What do you want, Connor?"

"Hey, nice voice recognition; you got it on the first try. How are you?"

"Do you know what *time* it is?" Most fae are notoriously late risers, as in "after sundown if at all possible." That's most of us, not all. Selkies are skinshifters. They don't have any real magic beyond some basic illusions and the power contained in their skins. Dawn messes with them just like it messes with the rest of us, but daylight doesn't bother them. Once the sun's up, they're fine. As a consequence, they have an annoying tendency to be morning people.

Exhibit A: Connor, who cheerfully said, "Half past five."

"Right." I groaned, wiping the sleep from my eyes. The cats had retreated to the foot of the bed, shoving Spike out of the way as they curled up in the warm spot it had created. Sadly chirping, Spike slunk toward me. "Now explain why I should let you live."

"I'm too cute to kill."

"Try again." Spike tried to crawl into my lap. I shooed it away as I swung my feet around to the floor. The rose goblin gave me a wounded look and began grooming its thorns.

"How about I say I'm taking you out for breakfast? My treat."

"Uh-huh." If Connor hadn't been married, that statement would have had me leaping for my clothes no matter what time it was. With things the way they were, I wasn't thrilled. "What does Raysel think of this plan?"

He hesitated before saying, "She doesn't exactly know."

I sighed. "Then I'm not going to breakfast with you. Raysel would kick my ass." Rayseline Torquill was Connor's wife, the daughter of my liege lord, and every interaction I had with her went a little further toward convincing me that she was certifiably crazy.

Raysel's madness wasn't her fault, which made it difficult to blame her for it, no matter how much it complicated things. She and her mother were kidnapped shortly before I was turned into a fish, and they were missing for almost as long as I was. They came back a few years before I made it out of the pond. Jin says they just appeared in the garden one day, returning as suddenly and unexplainably as they came.

If anyone knows what happened to them during

those missing years, they haven't told me. Luna came back quiet and a little sad, and Raysel ... Raysel came back broken.

Maybe it would have been different if I'd managed to avoid Simon's spell and keep myself from being transformed. Maybe, if I'd been just a little better at my job, they would have come home as healthy and happy as they left it. Maybe. Even in Faerie, time doesn't run backward, so I guess we'll never know for sure.

"It's not like we'd be doing anything wrong," he said, a note of pleading in his tone. "It's just breakfast and we've been friends since before Raysel was born."

"Skipping the part where you haven't exactly been subtle about liking me, that woman thinks I've done something wrong when I *breathe*." Raysel has hated me since I came back. The fact that there was a time when I'd have happily hopped into bed with her husband might have something to do with it, but it seems to go deeper than that. She acts like I'm her worst enemy, and I have no idea why.

"Please." Now the pleading was much harder to ignore. I hesitated. "What's the deal?"

"What's the deal?" He laughed. The sound was brittle. "I'm standing at a pay phone on Fisherman's Wharf because I spent last night sleeping on the beach. My wife is nuts, but it's a diplomatic marriage, so I can't leave her, and most of my friends from Roan Rathad are afraid to come near me because they're so sure she's going to kill them—and me—one day. I'm lonely. I spend all day, every day, watching my own back, and I'm *lonely.*" More quietly, he said, "I'm sorry about the kiss. It won't happen again. But I need a friend, Toby. I need a friend so badly you wouldn't believe it."

He sounded desperate. More, he sounded sincere. Connor's always been good at covering misery with apparent cheer, and I was starting to suspect that he'd been getting even better since he married Rayseline. Shoving my hair out of my eyes, I sighed. "All right, you win. We'll do breakfast. Where do you want to meet?"

"Mel's okay?" The change in his tone was immediate enough to make me feel bad for wanting to avoid him. Raysel wasn't that big a deal. I mean, if I can hang around with the Luidaeg, I can handle Rayseline Torquill.

"Mel's is fine." Mel's Diner in downtown San Francisco is a purveyor of classic Americana, from the ever popular fried egg sandwich to the fat-saturated roast beef platter. There are no surprises at Mel's. I like it that way.

"Meet you in an hour?"

"Better make it two." I stood, grabbing my robe off the floor. "I need a shower, and the sun isn't up yet. I can't go outside safely until it is."

"Oh, right. You're a wimp."

"And you're a skinshifting bastard."

"I love you, too. See you at Mel's!" The line went dead. Connor and I have been competing for the last word for a long time, and he's finally starting to catch up. I need to work on my phone-slamming skills.

I tied my robe and started for the hall, rubbing at my eyes. There was no way I was getting back to sleep. Spike and the cats followed me to the kitchen, where the astronomical calendar on the fridge informed me that dawn was scheduled for 6:13 A.M. I'd had to go to the Science Museum bookstore to find a calendar that listed times for sunrise and sunset, and it was worth the effort. Knowing exactly when the sun would rise meant I could have a cup of coffee without worrying about timing things wrong and scalding myself. I'd get through sunrise, take a shower, and meet Connor for a plate of something bad for me. It was starting to look like it might be a decent morning.

There was a knock at the door.

I turned, frowning. No one knocks on my door before dawn. Most of my clients are fae and wouldn't risk being caught out so close to sunrise, and I don't take human clients who seem likely to show up after midnight. "The hell?"

I started for the door, stopping as I caught a flicker

of motion out of the corner of my eye. The cats were huddled under the coffee table, tails bushed out and ears slicked flat. Spike had vanished completely. "Okay. That's weird."

There are certain basic rules of survival in my world. One of them is that you don't live to a ripe old age by ignoring the warnings you get from your pets. Cats who live with the fae tend to get a little touched by strangeness, and the things that get that kind of reaction from them are usually looking for worse reactions from me. Reactions such as screaming, running, or going for a weapon. Whoever or whatever was out there probably didn't intend anything good.

Feeling increasingly paranoid, I looked back toward the door as my visitor knocked again. I didn't want to deal with a potential threat before my morning coffee, but whatever it was wasn't going away. Just swell. I reached into the umbrella stand and pulled out my baseball bat as I approached the door. A girl can't be too careful if she's addicted to breathing, and I've found that being hit in the head with a stick of aluminum is enough to daunt most monsters, at least for a moment.

"Who is it?" I called. My mother's blood taught me about monsters, but both sides of the family taught me that I'd get smacked if I forgot my manners.

"Candygram."

I eyed the door. Whoever it was didn't just scare my cats, they also quoted bad comedy routines: truly the stuff of terror. Something about the voice made the back of my neck itch. I ran through a quick catalog of options in my head but couldn't connect it to anyone I knew. Shifting the bat behind my back in case it was one of my neighbors, I opened the door. And froze.

Considering some of the things—and people—I've found on my doorstep in the past, I didn't think I could be surprised anymore. I was wrong.

She stood about five foot eight, with long, almost gangly limbs and the sort of curves that get lost in anything shapeless. Her stick-straight brown hair fell to her shoulders, failing to conceal her dully pointed ears. She had the sort of pointed face that doesn't get called pretty, even on a kid. Striking maybe, or dramatic, but never pretty. Her eyes were beautiful, though, large and bright, with gray irises so pale they seemed to echo the colors around them. I knew those features pretty well. After all, I saw them in the mirror every morning. It was like looking at a photograph, only this photograph was answering my openmouthed shock with a smirk and a tip of an imaginary hat.

The only major difference between us was the clothes. She was wearing a long green skirt and a cream-colored sweatshirt that proclaimed, "Shakespeare in the Park: What Fools These Mortals Be" in faux-Gothic lettering. I was underdressed in bare feet and bathrobe.

"What the—"

"The name's May Daye," she said. "Pleased to meet you."

Not even shock can dim my eternally inappropriate sense of humor. "How cute," I said. Then I froze again, wondering what I'd just insulted. I'm normally pretty good at spotting the bloodlines of anyone—or any*thing*—I deal with, but painful past experience has taught me that I'm not always accurate. Especially when I'm dealing with shapeshifters.

"Really? I thought it was sort of trite myself, but what can you do? Post a complaint against the universe? Anyway." She brushed past me and took a slow look around the living room. "I like what you've done with the place. Hey, it's the cats!" She held out a hand toward Cagney and Lacey, who were still doing their best to disappear under the coffee table. "Here Cagney, here Lacey—" The cats bolted, vanishing down the hall.

May shook her head and dropped onto the couch in an easy sprawl. "Silly cats. Anyway, you'd better put that bat down before you hurt someone, like me. I'm allergic to physical pain. I'm pretty sure it gives me hives."

I closed the door without letting go of the bat, unwilling to take my eyes off her. She looked like me, she sounded like me; she could have fooled an uninformed observer. If she'd been willing to hold still and keep her mouth shut, she could have fooled my best friends. Even Devin's hired Doppelganger hadn't done its job *that* well.

May shook her head again. "Close your mouth. You look like a goldfish." The barb hit home. Anyone who knew me well enough to steal my face should have known better than to make cracks about the time I spent as a fish.

My notoriously short-lived patience was running out. I glared, demanding, "What the hell are you?"

"A Fetch. Your Fetch, to be exact," she said. "You know, the spirits that wear your face when they come to escort you to the lands of—"

"—the dead," I finished. "Little problem: *I'm not dead.*" A Fetch is a duplicate of a living person created when it's time for them to die. They're incredibly rare, and most people don't get one. I certainly never requested the honor.

May shrugged. "Mortality's a constant. I have time; I can wait."

"You can't be my Fetch! I'm not going to die!"

"Are you sure?" she asked, looking at me with renewed interest. "Did you go all pureblooded and death-proof when I wasn't looking?"

"Yes! I mean, no! I mean, yes, I'm sure!"

"I wouldn't be. I mean, you're not exactly Little Miss Caution. Look at this." She pulled down the collar of her sweatshirt, displaying a knot of scar tissue on her left shoulder. "Iron bullets? Yeah, *those* are a sign of good survival prospects. Or this?" This time she raised the bottom of the shirt, showing the curved claw-marks that crossed her stomach. I'd never seen those scars from the outside: they looked a lot worse from this angle. Some of those wounds should have been fatal.

May tugged her shirt back into place. "I'm sorry to be the one to tell you, but you're not exactly on the universe's 'ten longest projected life spans' list. I wish you were, because when you die, I die with you." She shrugged. "But fate doesn't have a suggestion box."

"Why are you trying so hard to make me believe that I haven't got much time before I—"

"—shuffle off this mortal coil? Because you don't, hon. I'm sorry, but it's true. And what's with the Shakespeare fixation? Didn't your mother know about Nora Roberts?"

"Well, first, my mother doesn't care about mortal authors," I said, slowly. Her rapid subject changes were confusing me. "Second, I was born in 1952. How was I supposed to find Nora Roberts? Borrow a time machine? And if you have issues with my Shakespeare fixation, why are you wearing that shirt?"

She glanced down at herself. "It's what they had in the Goodwill donations box. I didn't manifest with clothes on. Do you have any idea how hard it is for naked people to go shopping?"

"I've never shopped naked," I said. "I thought you were my Fetch. Aren't you supposed to know these things?"

"Of course. I know everything there is to know about you, right up until the universe decided you were destined to die and created me to be your guide."

"Everything?" I didn't like the sound of that. There are some things I don't want *anyone* to know.

"Everything. From what you got on your sixth birthday to what kind of flowers you leave on Dare's grave. I even know what you were thinking about Tybalt after you saw him in those red leather pants—"

I held up my hand. "Stop. I believe you."

"I thought you might." She smirked, adding, "I didn't even need to get *detailed*."

"Trust me, I don't want you to." Raking my hair back with one hand, I gave her a long, hard look. It was like looking into a strange, hyperactive mirror. Your reflection doesn't usually start to fidget and study its nails while you're standing still.

"Why now?" I asked, finally.

May sobered, giving me the first serious look I'd seen

from her. "I guess someone feels you've earned yourself some time to settle your affairs before you go. I'm your wake-up call. Don't put anything off, because you may not be around that long."

"I'm not ready to die!" I protested. My mind was racing. What was it going to be? Simon and Oleander coming back to finish what they'd started? Or something simpler, like a drunk driver who didn't hit the brakes in time? There are a lot of ways to die, and I'd never really thought about them before. I was pretty sure I didn't want to be thinking about them now.

Death omens aren't a blessing, no matter what people say; they make you nervous, and that can get you killed. Maybe it's just me, but I dislike self-fulfilling prophecies. They're too much like cheating.

"I don't know much about how people really think, since all my memories are borrowed from you, but I'm pretty sure no one's ever ready to die." May rose from the couch, moving with an easy, artless grace that finally confirmed she wasn't a Doppelganger playing tricks.

When shapeshifters copy a person, they copy them exactly, body language and all. I've seen Fetches before. I would have known what she was the moment I saw her if I'd been willing to believe it. Fetches don't have time to learn little things like motor control, so they come complete with the knowledge of how to move and comport themselves. May was created from fragments of me, but she moved like a pureblood: all fire and air and unconditional grace. She moved like something I'd never been and never would be.

"Anyway, I'm just here to do my job," May said, and then grinned, solemnity abandoned. "I just want you to know what's coming down the pike, so to speak. Now that you do, I'm going to go try that twenty-four-hour Chinese place down the block. I remember that you like kung pao chicken. I wanna see if I do, too."

Dazedly, I said the first thing that popped into my head: "If you had to steal clothes from the Goodwill, how are you planning to afford Chinese food?"

May laughed as she crossed to the door. "Don't worry about it." Putting her hand on the knob, she paused. "I'll be around, and when the time comes, I'll be waiting." Then she stepped out the door, whistling. I can't carry a tune; neither could she, and that made it all real. I'd believed her, but I hadn't really understood what she meant until I heard her mimicking my utter inability to whistle. I was going to die. I couldn't stop it.

I was going to die.

She paused to wave. I grabbed a plate off the coffee table, flinging it in her direction. Her eyes went wide before she slammed the door. The plate hit it and shattered.

"No!" I shrieked, regardless of whether or not she could hear me. I was screaming at the universe as much as I was screaming at her, too angry to think straight. "I will *not* lie down and die because you say it's time! Do you understand me? I *refuse!"*

There was no answer but the sound of my own breathing. The cats crept out of the hall with their ears pressed flat, growling in the backs of their throats. Spike slid out from behind the couch, stalking stiff-legged to sniff at the doorjamb. The threat was over from their point of view; it was safe for them to come out and make a show of being brave.

I really wished that I could say the same. I've never been the most safety-oriented person in the world. I know I take too many risks. But I've always been able to promise myself that I'd stop, that tomorrow I'd settle down and stop playing with fire. Only now it looked like there wasn't going to be a tomorrow. And it wasn't fair.

Spike was pacing in front of the door, making an angry keening noise. "Aren't you a little late to play protector?" I asked. It rattled its thorns. With a sigh, I moved to lock the door. Fragments of plate crunched underfoot, cutting my feet. I didn't care. It didn't matter. When you're waiting to die, you have bigger things to worry about than a little bit of blood.

I clicked the lock home, shuddering, and turned away.

Dawn was coming; it was time to get ready for breakfast with Connor. If there's one thing I know about destiny, it's this: it doesn't give second chances, and it doesn't believe in waiting for you to be ready. If it was coming for me, it was already too late. All I could do was try to make sure it didn't catch me sitting still.

THREE

"**E**ARTH TO TOBY. You in there?"

"What?" I stopped mashing my eggs into my home fries to blink across the table at Connor. He was leaning on his elbows, watching me. It's always hard to adjust to seeing him with a human disguise—I deal with him mostly at Shadowed Hills, and he has no reason to hide himself there. His hair was supposed to be speckled with gray, like his pelt in seal-form, not a standard shade of brown. His hands look weird without webbing, and I'm not used to seeing whites or definite pupils in his eyes.

Those eyes were fixed on me now, and his expression was one of earnest concern. "What's wrong?"

"What do you mean, what's wrong?" I put down my fork and brushed my hair back, trying to look casual. It wasn't working.

"You've barely touched your breakfast."

"I'm not hungry."

"Your coffee cup's been empty for five minutes, and you haven't threatened to track down and gut our waitress." Connor shook his head. "I know you. What's *wrong*?"

"Nothing," I said. "I'm just tired." I didn't want to tell him about May. I didn't want him trying to help; I just wanted to have it left alone until I was ready to deal. That might not be until after I was dead, but it was my choice, not his. I try to be straight with my friends when I can, but there are times I make exceptions. Right after I've had my death predicted by the fae equivalent of a singing telegram is one of those times.

Connor sighed, turning his attention to his own breakfast. "Have it your way." After a pause, he added, "If this is about my wife . . ."

"It's not. I haven't given her a reason to kill me this week, and I'm not intending to give her one, either." I smiled faintly. "I'm over you."

"My heart bleeds."

"It would if I weren't over you and Raysel found out." I took a bite of my eggs. They were cold and gummy, but I swallowed them anyway before I said, "Your heart, my heart, a lot of other body parts . . ."

"You give her a lot of credit."

"For potential mayhem? Yeah." I put my fork down. "She worries me. There's something not right about her."

"You know, most guys just have to deal with their ex-girlfriends being jealous of their wives. Not coming up with elaborate conspiracy theories about them."

"I was never your girlfriend."

"The point stands."

"Tell me I'm wrong."

He sighed. "I can't." Glancing to the clock, he added, "I should be getting back to Shadowed Hills. I've got to attend formal audiences today."

Sometimes I wonder if the essentially diurnal nature of the Duchess of Shadowed Hills is the real reason she married her daughter to a Selkie: she was looking for moral support. "I need to get going myself," I said, leaving my mostly untouched breakfast behind as I rose. Connor eyed my plate. "If you want a doggie bag, get it yourself."

"It's okay," he said, his tone making the words into a lie. He clearly wasn't happy about my failure to eat, but I decided to let it go. I didn't have the energy.

We paid our check and exited the restaurant. Connor, ever the gentleman, held the door for me. My fingers brushed his before he let it go, and I pulled away. Wanting each other wasn't allowed to matter anymore.

There was a chill in the air outside, and the sky was solid gray, warning of rain. I looked up, frowning. "Weather's taking a turn for the worse."

"Guess so." Connor stepped closer. I stepped away, and he stopped, not bothering to hide the hurt expression that flashed briefly over his face. "Toby . . ."

"Just don't, okay? Please." I shook my head. "Just don't." I hadn't been so quick to pull away when we were in Fremont together, trapped in a knowe with a killer stalking the halls. I kissed him there, tasted the salt on his lips, remembered why I'd ever wanted him as more than a friend.

Oberon help me, I couldn't risk that happening again.

Connor sighed. "Right. Well. Later, Toby."

"Open roads," I replied.

Treating Connor like that makes me feel low, but until he stops trying to get closer, I don't have a choice. He's married, and I have principles. I'm also smart enough to be afraid of his wife, which means I need to be even more careful about how close I am to him. Raysel strikes me as a serial killer waiting to happen. I don't intend to be in front of her when it does.

The phone was ringing when I got home. I ignored it. I'm not normally fond of the answering machine, considering that Evening Winterrose used it to cast a binding spell on me from beyond the grave, but it has its uses. Taking calls I'm not in the mood to deal with falls into that category.

I was hanging my jacket when the machine picked up and Stacy's half-hysterical voice poured from the speakers. "Toby, it's me again. I'm sorry, I know I said I'd wait for you to call back, but I *can't* wait, I *can't*. Are you there? Please, oh, please be there—"

I vaulted the couch and ran down the hall to snatch the phone. "Stacy? What's wrong?"

"Oh, thank O-Oberon you're there," she sobbed. "I was calling and calling, but you weren't h-home . . ."

"What's going on?" Stacy's one of the calmest people I've ever met. She could look a dragon running rampant in a school zone in the eye and swat it on the nose with a rolled-up newspaper. She doesn't panic, ever.

"It's Andrew and Jessie," she whispered.

I froze. "What about them?"

"They're gone." Her voice quavered. "I went to check on the kids and make sure they'd slept through sunrise without any problems. Andy and Jessie weren't there."

Oh, root and branch. "When? What about Karen and Anthony?"

"An hour ago, and Karen and Anthony were still in their beds."

I glanced at the clock. It was a little after eight. "Have you checked the backyard?"

"We checked the whole neighborhood." She sniffled. "We even called Cassie at school, to see if she took them to class for some reason. They weren't there. She's on her way home."

Great—we could get everyone in the same place for the nervous breakdown. "You're sure you've looked everywhere?"

"We've looked everywhere. Toby, Andy's only four! He can't cast his own illusions!"

"Oh, oak and ash," I muttered. That explained why Stacy was calling me instead of the police: she couldn't involve human law enforcement even if she wanted to.

It takes children a while to grasp controlled illusions. There's a brief period where things like that are automatic, but our reflexive magic fades as we get older, making everything a matter of focus and intent. Disguise spells take time to learn and some kids learn faster than others. Unfortunately, Andrew was one of the slow ones.

"Can Jessica hide them both?"

"For a little while. Toby, please come. We have to find them."

"Shhh, I know. I'm coming." I was fighting not to let her panic infect me. The kids were probably sitting under a tree in someone's yard while Jessica showed her brother the finer points of a don't-look-here illusion. "Just stay calm until I get there, okay?"

"I'll try."

Something else was wrong. Stacy shouldn't have panicked that fast, even when two of the kids might be missing. "What else is going on?"

"I . . ." She hesitated. "We can't wake Karen. Mitch even poured a glass of ice water over her head, and she didn't move. I'm scared, Toby. I'm so scared . . ."

My heart lurched. "Stacy, slow down and stay with me. Is she breathing?"

"Yes."

"Good. Make sure she's comfortable." If Stacy had something to do, she might not do anything foolish. "No more water. Just wait for me."

"Hurry." She was sobbing as she hung up. I stared at the receiver before slamming it down and bolting for the bedroom. First a Fetch, and now something was messing with Stacy's kids. This wasn't shaping up to be a good day.

Silently thanking Connor for getting me out of the house long enough to eat *something,* even if it wasn't much, I started yanking drawers out of my dresser and scattering clothes across my bed. The cats slicked their ears back and fled the room. "Oak and ash and stupid, rotten pine," I swore, digging through the mess. It was juvenile, but it made me feel a little better.

"Ow!" I moved my hand back, putting it on the handle of my knife rather than the blade as I pulled it from the tangle of T-shirts. The sheath was a foot away, buried under a drift of socks. I pulled it free as well, slid the knife into it, and clipped it to the inside of my jeans. I try not to go into danger unarmed these days; I've learned my lesson and I have the scars to prove it. And I've gotten smarter about my weapons. I started wearing a sheath after the incident at ALH Computing, where I nearly gutted myself rolling away from my exploding car with an unsheathed knife tucked into the waistband of my jeans.

Life has been interesting lately.

Returning to the living room, I grabbed my jacket off the floor and pulled my hair into a loose ponytail that would hide the tips of my ears. Disguises are for times when subtlety is required; I wasn't intending to deal with anyone besides my friends, and I wasn't going to waste the magic unless it was absolutely necessary. I might need it later. I turned to head for the door.

Claws drove themselves into my calf. I stopped, looking down to see Spike clinging to my leg with both forepaws. "Spike, let go. I need to leave." It yowled, not releasing my leg. "What do you want?" It looked toward my shoulder. I sighed. "You want to come?"

Spike took that as consent, withdrawing its claws and scrambling up my side to perch on my shoulder. I shook my head and left the apartment. No more delays.

Despite Spike's tendency to ride pressed against the windshield, I didn't need to worry about it being spotted; rose goblins have instinctive glamours that keep them hidden from anyone they don't want seeing them. Control erodes natural magic. The better any race of fae gets at "using" magic, the less instinctive magic they have left. Some things come easier to certain races—like blood magic to the Daoine Sidhe—but a lot of the natural talents common to the smaller fae are almost missing among the races that can pass for human. Spike can do pretty much whatever it wants without fear of being noticed by the human world.

The drive to Mitch and Stacy's felt like it took no time at all. Panic does that, cramming weeks into hours and hours into seconds. Devin used to call it "running on changeling time," his way of referring to that state where time runs too fast and no matter how much you have, it's not enough. All I could think about while I drove was how losing Gillian had nearly killed me. I couldn't let that happen to Mitch and Stacy. I just couldn't.

Mitch met me at the car. "Mitch," I said, and hugged him. He clung for a moment before I pushed him to arm's length, looking him in the eye. "Where's Stacy?"

"Inside," he said. His voice was shaking as much as he was. "She won't let the kids out of her sight. She even had me move Karen downstairs so she could watch her sleep."

"Okay. Can you answer a few questions before I go in?"

He stared long enough that I was afraid he didn't understand me. Then he nodded, saying, "I can try."

"Stacy said Andrew and Jessica were missing." He nodded. I continued, "Did you see them go to bed?"

"Yes. They were there, and Cassie says Jessica was in her bed when she left."

"Good to know." That was when Spike leaped from the car roof to my shoulder, anchoring itself through my leather jacket with a full complement of claws. I flinched. Cats are blunt instruments compared to rose goblins.

Mitch stared. "Toby, why is there a rose goblin on your shoulder?"

"Spike wanted to come, and I didn't have time to argue." Spike sniffed the air and growled. I frowned. "It's never done that before. Spike? What's wrong?" That was all the warning it gave before it launched itself from my shoulder and raced for the house, claws churning divots out of the lawn. It looked enraged, like it was running to defend its territory against an unwelcome invader. I glanced at Mitch, snapping, "Go to Stacy," and followed Spike.

I almost caught up with Spike on the run across the yard, but it jumped through the window to the living room while I was forced to take the door. It beat me to the stairs by leaping over furniture while I had to weave past Stacy and the kids. We paced each other to the upstairs hall where it began to circle, thorns rattling angrily. It was making a low, almost subsonic snarling noise, like something about the hall offended it. That didn't bode well. Spike originally belonged to the Duchess of Shadowed Hills. It usually had a pretty good idea of what was and was not dangerous, and if it was unhappy about the hallway . . .

I drew my knife, holding it against my hip. "Which way?" Spike looked up and hissed. I sighed. "That doesn't help."

There were six doors. One led to the linen closet, and the one next to it led to the bathroom. The door to Cassandra's room was ajar, showing a tangle of papers and discarded clothes on the floor, and the door to Mitch and Stacy's room was open, displaying the characteristically unmade bed. Mitch works nights; Stacy must have woken him when she found the children missing.

The first door led to Jessica and Karen's room; the door to Anthony and Andrew's room was across the hall. Both rooms were cluttered, verging on messy—nothing out of the ordinary, considering the age of their inhabitants. I started toward the girls' room, scanning for signs of a struggle. It was in disarray, but not beyond the normal limits of a room shared by two preteen girls. Whatever happened, Jessica left without a fight.

A hand on my shoulder stopped me as I started to step across the threshold. I stiffened. Only the knowledge that Anthony and Cassandra were in the house kept me from swinging around blade-first. Sometimes I think I'm getting trigger-happy. Then I think of how many things have tried to kill me and I wonder why it's taken this long for the paranoia to kick in.

"Aunt Birdie?" Cassandra whispered.

I relaxed, looking over my shoulder. "Yeah, puss?" Spike was still turning in slow circles, growling. I wasn't sure what had it so pissed, but I wasn't going to get in its way.

"Did you find them?"

"Not yet. I'm sorry."

"Oh," she said, face falling. "Mom's not doing so good. Will you come down?"

The tone of Spike's snarling changed, becoming more insistent as it stopped circling and began advancing, stiff-legged, toward the boys' room. "Not yet," I said. "Keep your mother and everyone else downstairs, all right?"

"Okay," Cassandra said dubiously, looking at Spike. "Your rose goblin is growling."

"I know. Go downstairs, Cass. I'll be there soon." *Or I'll be dead,* I added silently. I try not to ignore warnings, especially ones I don't understand. Spike could be freaking out over a mouse, but it might also be reacting to a threat I couldn't see. Assuming the worst is a good way to keep from being surprised.

She looked at me, frowning. Then she turned and went downstairs.

I waited for the sound of her footsteps to fade before following Spike into the boys' room. Half of it was Anthony's, decorated in spaceships and astronomical posters; the floor was marginally cleaner on that side. Andrew's half was done up in dinosaurs and clowns, all bright colors and rounded angles. The dinosaurs I gave him for his birthday were on the shelf beside his bed, seeming small and somehow sad. The boy who loved them wasn't here.

Spike stopped in the center of the room, tossing back its head and howling. The sound scraped at my nerves, leaving them raw. I flinched and stepped past it, moving to study Andrew's bed. It didn't look like there'd been a struggle: the sheets were thrown back and the blanket was shoved to one side, but that was normal. Kids sleep hard. If Andrew was taken from the bed, he either didn't wake up, or he went voluntarily. Considering Faerie, both were options. I knelt to check under the bed before moving to poke through the closet.

Nothing looked out of place, and yet, despite the outward lack of disturbance, there was something in the air that made the room feel like it was somehow wrong. Sliding my knife back into its sheath, I closed my eyes and took a deep breath. There were other scents under the expected odors of sweat and small boy. I started focusing on them, shutting out everything else.

The smell of blood came first. Of course it did; I'm my

mother's daughter and if there's blood I'll find it. I identified it as Andrew's almost without thinking, spending just enough time feeling it out to be sure that he'd been the only one to bleed, and that his wounds had been superficial at worst. There were other things layered in an undefined pattern beneath the blood, and so I pushed it aside to study them more carefully.

Mold; old, dry dust. Ash. Fire. Steel. They were faint, nearly overwhelmed by the smells of blood and plastic and fabric softener and finger paint, but they were there. And I had no idea what they meant.

Eyes still closed, I stretched my arms out in front of me and began following the scent trail, ignoring the plastic dinosaurs squeaking underfoot. The scents were stronger close to the bed. My hands hit the window, and I stopped, pressing my palms against the glass as I tried to sort through the increasingly disparate scents.

There was a distinct tang of candle wax, freshly burned and not quite dry, hidden under the stronger scents of blood and fire. "Candles?" I said, bemused. Spike snarled again, the sound climbing to a roar as the smell of ash became overwhelming. The glass beneath my hands was suddenly searing-hot, and I jerked away, opening my eyes. "What the *hell*—?"

The window looked normal, showing nothing but the front yard and street beyond. I glanced at my hands. They were already starting to blister.

I had my answer, after a fashion; the kids hadn't run away. They'd been taken by something that made glass burn and left the scent of ashes and candle wax in its wake. Unfortunately for all of us, I had no idea what it was. The only thing I was sure of was that it was going to take more than a few missing-child flyers to get them back.

"Spike, come." I turned away, beckoning for the goblin to follow as I left the room. Surprisingly, it came. I closed the door behind us, ignoring the pain in my hands, and turned to at least look into the girls' room. It was much the same: messy, cluttered, and with no signs of a struggle. Their window was open, and the fresh air had wiped away any traces of the scent trail I'd followed in the boys' room, if it was even there to start with.

Shaking my head, I walked down the stairs to where Stacy waited. There was no way I could tell her I was done, even though I knew damn well that we wouldn't find the kids without a lot more power than I had. You don't tell a panicking mother that her children have been taken by something you can't identify or name; it doesn't work that way. So I did the next best thing.

I lied. I told her I thought they might have wandered away on their own. I made a lame excuse about hurting my hands by picking up Spike the wrong way and bandaged them myself in the downstairs bathroom. The rose goblin didn't notice or care that I'd defamed its character; it was perfectly willing to follow me through the house, although it refused to calm down. It kept stopping and snarling at nothing, rattling its thorns in challenge. I took note of the places where it stopped and didn't touch any more windows. I *can* be taught.

Stacy stayed in the living room, clutching Karen's hand. She'd stopped crying about twenty minutes after I arrived, but she didn't look like she felt any better; shock can take an awful lot of forms. I was in shock myself—fortunately for me, my version of shock normally manifests as anger. Anger, I can use—I understand it. Sometimes it can even help keep me alive.

We didn't find anything. I hadn't really been expecting that we would, since judging by the traces upstairs, there was nothing for us to find. Anthony didn't even put up a pretense of searching; he just followed me, trusting that I would protect him. Cassandra at least tried, but she eventually went to join her mother in the living room, taking Stacy's free hand and sitting in silence.

Mitch stayed with me to the bitter end, combing the house for some sign that his children had left under their own power. When we'd emptied the last drawer and searched through the last closet he turned to me, expression begging for some sort of reassurance. "Toby?"

"Yeah?"

"They're not here, are they?"

I looked down before my face could give me away. "No, Mitch. They're not."

"Where are my children, October?"

"I don't know." I looked up. "But I'll find them."

"I believe you're intending to try—and that's not enough. In a minute, we're going to have to tell my wife that they're missing. I saw your hands."

"What?"

"Your hands were fine when you got here. How did you burn your hands? *Where are my kids?*" That last statement was delivered with such vehemence that I realized for the first time in years just how large Mitch was. He doesn't usually go in for violence, but he still has eleven inches and at least a hundred pounds on me.

Sometimes honesty is the best policy, especially when you're dealing with someone who could break you in two without blinking. "I don't know, but they aren't here," I said. "I don't think they're anywhere this side of the Summerlands."

The look on his face was beyond broken; he'd passed all the way into bereft. "Can you find them?"

"I can try," I said.

"And Karen?"

Oak and ash, Karen. "I don't know what's wrong with her. But I can take a look." I'm not a miracle worker; I'm just a half-blood with a talent for not getting killed. So far. The problems start when people assume that if I can survive, I can do anything. I wish they were right. It would make my life a lot easier.

Turning, I walked back to the stairs without another word. I was halfway down before I heard him following me.

Stacy looked up as we approached. She was still clinging to Karen's hand. Cassandra was sitting on the other couch with her arms around Anthony, her chin resting lightly against the crown of his head. The pressures of the day had been too much for him, and he'd fallen asleep. Anthony nestled closer to his sister as I watched, whimpering in his sleep.

"Did you—" Stacy began. I shook my head. She pressed her free hand against her mouth. I'd never seen her look so old. I always knew her thinner blood meant she'd age faster than the rest of us, but it never seemed real before. She'd seemed too alive to show the signs of mortality. Now her children were in danger, and she was showing those signs in full. Looking at Stacy, I wasn't sure she'd ever recover the vitality her fear had leeched away.

She still looked better than her middle daughter. Karen was practically a wax statue of herself, all the color bleached from her skin and hair. It was like looking at a corpse with faintly pointed ears, and my stomach lurched before I glanced away, trying to compose myself. Faerie corpses are supposed to be impossible. Unfortunately for my peace of mind, I know that's not the case; it's possible to keep the night-haunts away, if you really try. I don't advise it.

Spike rubbed against my leg, whining in the back of its throat before leaping onto the couch next to Karen and curling up by her head. I knelt, studying her carefully.

Karen wasn't dead, just so asleep she couldn't find the way home. Her pulse was strong, if slow. I leaned forward to hold my cheek near her mouth and felt the unlabored movement of her breath. There was nothing physically wrong with her. She just wouldn't wake up.

"She's asleep," I said, sitting back on my heels. "I don't know why."

Stacy stared at me, eyes wide. "Well, c-can't you wake her?"

"Not alone." I paused. What I was about to ask might be too much, but I didn't see another choice. "I may know someone who can. Will you let me take her with me?"

"No!" she cried, moving to shield her daughter with her body. I rose and backed away, not arguing. Mothers aren't always logical. I should know. I used to be one.

"Stacy—" Mitch stepped forward. "We need to let Karen go with Toby."

"No! She's our daughter—Mitch, how could you?" She clung to Karen like a drowning man clings to driftwood. It made sense; in her own way, she was going under. "We can't just let her *go!*"

"Toby will be with her," he rumbled. "Toby? Where do you want to take her?"

"The Tea Gardens. The Undine who guards them may know how to help." Undine are regional fae and, once they merge with a place, they can never leave it. Lily hasn't left the Japanese Tea Gardens since she came to America.

"If that doesn't work?" He was talking to me, but his eyes were on Stacy; he was trying to make her understand. Good man. He knew as well as I did that unless we found out what was wrong with Karen, we might never get her to wake up. That's how it is with enchanted sleep.

"I'll take her to Shadowed Hills. Jin may be able to do something."

"Let her go, Stacy. Let Toby take her." Mitch knelt and put his hand on her shoulder, engulfing it. "She'll bring them home to us. She'll bring them all home." Sobbing, Stacy sat up and threw her arms around Mitch's neck, burying her face against him.

Mitch nodded toward Karen. I moved behind them and scooped her into my arms, ignoring the pain in my hands. "I'll call you," I said. Cassandra stayed silent the whole time, smart enough not to interfere.

"Please." Mitch kept his arms around Stacy, reassuring and restraining her.

Spike was sitting by the front door, thorns sleeked down. It seemed to have calmed down. I was glad one of us had. "Don't let Anthony go back into the bedroom. It's dangerous. And keep your hands off the windows."

Mitch frowned. "He can sleep in the room with us for now. He won't like it, but he'll do it, and it might make Stacy feel better."

"Good. I don't know exactly what's wrong with his room, but I don't want him near it." I looked down at Karen. "It's not safe."

"Are *any* of us safe?"

"I don't know," I said. Mitch watched blankly as I turned and walked away. There was nothing left to say; even good-bye would have been too final. Spike dogged my heels as I walked to the car, Karen cradled in my arms. Inside, Stacy started to wail. I flinched, but no one came out of the house.

It took ten minutes to strap Karen into the passenger seat; the bandages made my hands clumsy, and the pain was getting worse. Burns hurt for a long time. And still no one came out of the house. Spike jumped into Karen's lap once she was settled, and I got into the car and drove away.

FOUR

FINDING DAYTIME PARKING in Golden Gate Park isn't easy. I finally had to park behind the snack bar, wedging my car into the space between the dumpsters and the side of the building. I tried to be careful, but I still hit the wall at least twice. I'm hard on my automobiles. The latest was a battered brown VW with a bumper covered in political stickers that were outdated well before I disappeared. At least the new dents were unlikely to show.

I got out of the car, locking my door before turning around. I wasn't expecting anyone to be standing there, so I didn't have time to stop before I collided with Tybalt. He grabbed my shoulder, steadying me until I no longer looked like I was going to fall.

I stepped backward, yanking myself out of his grasp. "Tybalt."

"October." His expression was composed to the point of being unreadable. "This is an interesting choice of locales. I was unaware of your love for the smell of rancid grease."

"Nowhere else to park," I snapped, pushing past him. Opening the passenger side door, I began trying to undo Karen's seat belt. Spike was curled on her lap. It chirped at me before jumping down to the pavement, rattling its thorns at Tybalt. "What do you want?"

"Isn't the pleasure of your company enough?"

I looked up, eyes narrowed. "Hasn't been for a while now, has it?"

"You know, in that brief absence, I'd almost forgotten how much you frustrate me." Tybalt sighed. "I had my reasons. I apologize if my disappearance troubled you."

Given the amount of time I've spent avoiding Tybalt over the years, I couldn't think of a good response to that. I settled for placing one hand on Karen's shoulder and glaring.

When he worked at it, Tybalt could be the most infuriating person I'd ever met. Being a cat, he worked at it a lot. He was pureblooded Cait Sidhe, powerful enough to hold his position as the local King of Cats—not an easy thing to do, given the literal viciousness of Cait Sidhe politics. He might have been less annoying if he wasn't every bit as good-looking as he thought he was. Black streaks in his brown hair suggested the stripes on a tabby's coat, and his eyes were a deep, clear green, made slightly alien by feline pupils. He had a cat's casual elegance and an athletic build, combined to irritatingly good effect with the sort of face that made women give him pretty much whatever he wanted. It wouldn't have been so bad if he'd had the decency to freckle or at least tan, but I guess freckling is beneath the Cait Sidhe.

Tybalt and I have a complicated relationship, and it seems to get worse as often as it gets better. He was civil, even friendly, when we were tracking a murderer through Tamed Lightning . . . and he disappeared as soon as we were done. I hadn't seen him since, despite spending several nights wandering the alleys of San Francisco searching for the Court of Cats.

I tried to tell myself that I just wanted to give him back his jacket. I've never been good at believing my own lies; I wanted to see him, nothing more or less than that. It was ironic, in a way, because if somebody had asked six months ago how I'd feel about Tybalt deciding to mind his own business and leave me alone, I would have answered "relieved." When he actually did it, I was hurt. I wasn't sure how to deal with that, so I went for the easy option. I got pissed.

He looked at my expression and sighed again. "I take it my apology isn't accepted?"

"Was there a particular reason you decided you needed to vanish?" I finally got Karen's seat belt undone and hoisted her out of the car, trying to balance her against my side long enough to let me lock the door. Spike barely jumped clear fast enough to avoid being stepped on.

"I had business to take care of." Tybalt moved almost too fast for my eyes to follow, suddenly taking the bulk of Karen's weight. "Let me help you with that."

I eyed him but didn't object as I finished locking the door. "What do you want?"

"Do I have to want something?"

"You haven't spoken to me in more than two months, so yeah, you have to want something."

"Good to see you haven't changed," he said, the ghost of a smile tugging at his lips. He eased Karen fully into his arms, holding her easily. "Where are we going?"

"There's no 'we' here, Tybalt. Karen and I are going to see Lily. You can go wherever it is you go when you're not bothering me."

"And here I thought you'd missed me." His smile remained, growing a bit more solid as he said, "You're still wearing my jacket."

"Yeah, well. It was the only thing I wasn't worried about damaging." I forced myself to keep looking at him, denying the urge to blush and look away. "What do you *want*, Tybalt?"

He looked at me, smile fading. "I need your help."

I hadn't expected that. I blinked. "What?"

"I need your help." He looked down at Karen like he was addressing his words to her instead of me. "Five children vanished from the Court of Cats this morning." His tone was infinitely weary. I stared. "Three were changelings living with their fae parents. One was a quarter-blood living with her changeling mother. The last was pureblooded." He glanced up at me, and now the weariness was in his face as well as in his voice. "It's my brother's son. The only royal Cait Sidhe born in my fiefdom in the last sixty years."

"They just vanished?" My mouth was suddenly dry. Spike rattled its thorns, almost like it was punctuating the question. Cait Sidhe tend to be even more nocturnal than most fae; their feline natures usually keep them unconscious through the days. "Are you sure?"

"The quarter-blood is the youngest—she's only six, and she's still living as a human. Her mother woke to find her missing and notified the Court, thinking we might have taken the girl. That was enough to make us check on the others."

Oh, oak and ash. Pushing the panic down to keep it out of my voice, I asked, "Why are you coming to me with this, Tybalt?"

"I could say a lot of pretty things that don't mean anything, but the fact is, you're the only person I could think of." He kept looking at me gravely. "You're good at this sort of thing, October. And more . . . you owe me a debt."

I blinked. "What?"

"Asking you doesn't put the Court in a position of owing one of the local nobles." Another smile—a bitter one—ghosted across his lips. "There's only so much my subjects will tolerate. It's my responsibility to get the children back, but I can't endanger our sovereignty to do it. Please. Do this, and there are no debts between us. Everything is paid."

Tybalt had helped me hide a very powerful artifact after the woman who owned it died. He'd held me in debt ever since. For him to offer my freedom . . .

"Help me get Karen into the Tea Gardens, and we'll talk," I said, raking my hair back automatically and wincing as the gesture pulled on my bandages.

Eyeing my hands, Tybalt asked, "What have you done to yourself now?"

"I touched a window," I said. "Come on."

We had barely left the shadows behind the snack bar when I felt a spell settle over us, accompanied by the musk and pennyroyal signature of Tybalt's magic. I gave him a sidelong look and he smiled, a bit more genuinely this time.

"I thought it best that we not be seen," he said.

"Fair." I might have been annoyed at him for using magic on me without permission, but I was too relieved that he'd noticed the need. I was more relieved not to have been the one to cast the don't-look-here. I was starting to think I'd need all the resources I could tap.

We made a strange, ragtag little procession as we crossed the courtyard to the Japanese Tea Gardens: me in the lead, Tybalt behind me carrying Karen, and Spike running circles around all three of us. I tried to ignore the throbbing in my hands as we walked up to the gates. Spike traipsed at my heels, occasionally scampering off to scatter the pigeons. The birds were pretty blasé about being chased by an animate cat-shaped rosebush; I guess living in Golden Gate Park has gotten them used to the bizarre. I can understand that. It's a pretty strange place.

The park sits in the middle of San Francisco, squarely in the private holdings of the Queen who rules Northern California. Despite that, it swears no fealty, serving instead as home to dozens of independent Courts. They have their own hierarchy and etiquette. More traditional nobles have learned—to their dismay—that interfering in the Golden Gate Courts is a good way to get hurt. Lily's Court is one of the oldest and best known of the independents. She sets the law in the Tea Gardens and that shapes the law of the park all around her. None of the fae living there would intentionally go against her wishes. Since they obey her, she never orders them and, since she never orders, they obey. It's a circle that's served the park well for a long time.

The girl at the ticket booth looked up at our approach, blinking. "Whoa," she said, in an exaggerated California drawl. "It's, like, Toby Daye and Tybalt." She was every inch the Valley Girl, from her feathered blonde hair to her pink tank top. Her makeup was an expertly applied mix of pale green and bubble-gum pink; she looked like she wouldn't recognize a changeling if it bit her. It's a good cover. After all, it fooled me the first time we met.

"Hey, Marcia." She looked human, but she wasn't quite. Somewhere in her family tree was just enough fae blood to pull her over the line into a world where glass burned and children vanished in the night. A pale gleam surrounded her eyes, betraying the amount of faerie ointment she was wearing. With blood as thin as hers, she needed it.

She squinted at Tybalt, making an effort to see through the don't-look-here he had covering Karen. Her faerie ointment was good enough to tell her he was carrying something, but not good enough to see through it. She finally gave up, asking, "What are you two up to?"

"Just stuff," I said. "What's the admission today?"

"Is Lily expecting you?"

"No." I rarely phone ahead. It's not that I enjoy surprising everyone I know; it's more that I almost never know where I'm going before I actually get there.

"No charge." She grinned. "Lily complains all the time that you never come to visit."

"Uh-huh." Between the missing children and my burned hands, I didn't feel particularly social. Judging by Tybalt's expression, neither did he. "We'll go on in."

"Any time." She waved us through before resuming the intent filing of her nails. Like most people who live on the outskirts of Faerie, she knew a "thank you" when she didn't hear it. One of the stranger tenets of the fae moral code says that the phrase "thank you" implies an obligation beyond the acts already performed and is thus to be avoided at all costs. Faerie is fond of avoiding obligations. I guess that's part of why the mortal world has always dismissed us as flakes and tricksters; we only thank you if you owe us.

The Tea Gardens are always beautiful in the fall. The Japanese maples turn pale shades of orange, red, and gold, dropping the occasional leaf into the koi ponds to float decoratively on the water. The lilies are in bloom, and you can see the shining shapes of the fish darting beneath them. Wooden trails wind between high, elegant bridges. Unfortunately, wood is slippery when wet, and the trails get wet a lot. If I'd been carrying Karen, odds are good that we'd have ended up in a pond. Tybalt didn't miss a step, making his way quickly down the paths to the base of the moon bridge that marks the entry into Lily's knowe.

The moon bridge is built in an almost perfect semicircle, rising steeply into the air. Its apex vanishes behind a curtain of cherry branches, making it look like it goes on forever. The illusion is more accurate than most people realize.

Tybalt continued up the bridge without a pause, not even hindered by the fact that his arms were full of an unconscious child. I muttered, grabbing the rail and beginning the climb. The moon bridge has *never* been my favorite part of the Tea Gardens, and I'm usually making the climb with unburned hands. Spike bounded ahead, chirping as it raced for the top.

The branches grew more and more tightly interlaced overhead, filtering out the sun until the sky was gone, replaced by a woven willow ceiling. Fireflies and pixies glittering with a dozen shades of pastel light illuminated the air. I took another step. The bridge dissolved, leaving me on a cobblestone path winding through a marshy fen. We had entered Lily's knowe.

Faerie knowes are little pieces hewn out of the Summerlands, carved to fit fae needs and desires. They generally reflect the personalities of their keepers. Some knowes are hollow hills and some are castles; one, in Fremont, is a labyrinthine computer company where the floors blend in an endless series of cubicles and hallways. Lily was an Undine, a river spirit bound to the waters of the Tea Gardens, and her knowe mirrored her nature. It was a twisting realm filled with moss and small streams, entirely at ease with itself.

Tybalt knelt on the nearest patch of relatively dry land, settling Karen on the moss. She was still asleep. He rose and stepped back as I hurried over to them. Dropping to my knees, I pressed my hand against her cheek to check her temperature. She was cold. I shrugged out of Tybalt's jacket, spreading it over her. Maybe it wouldn't do any good, but I didn't see where it could do any harm, either.

"October—"

"Don't." I kept my eyes on Karen, not looking at him. If I saw pity in his face, I was going to scream. "Just don't."

An awkward silence fell between us. There were never silences like that before he followed me to Fremont. There were never silences at all. He insulted me, I sniped at him, and things stayed simple. Things didn't feel simple anymore—my feelings were a long way from simple, and his feelings could be just about anything— and I had no idea what to do about it.

The sound of gentle splashing from behind us was a relief. I turned to see a column of water lifting itself out of the pond. "Hi, Lily," I said.

The water flowed closer to the land, resolving into the diminutive form of the Lady of the Tea Gardens. The air around her molded itself into a dark blue kimono that gleamed like rain-wet stones. A series of jeweled pins secured her long, dark hair, trapping it in an ornate bun.

"October, Tybalt," she said, sounding surprised. Her accent was thicker than usual; she'd just gotten out of "bed." Undine are normally bound to their places of origin. Lily originated in Japan. One of these days I'm going to get her to tell me how she managed to move herself to San Francisco. "I wasn't expecting you."

"Sorry I didn't call," I said, rising. "Things have been a little hectic." Tybalt snorted at the understatement.

Lily looked at Karen and frowned, the scales around her mouth tightening. "You have a sleeping child. Have I missed something?"

"She won't wake up," I said. "Her mother called me, and she—"

Lily raised a hand, cutting me off. "What have you done to your hands?"

"That's what I'd like to know," said Tybalt.

"I burned them," I said, grimacing.

"And how did you do this immensely clever thing to yourself?"

"I touched a window."

Lily sat, gesturing for us to do the same. "Now, explain. When you're done, I may ask you to explain again, this time using actual words, but we'll see. Perhaps you'll surprise me."

"Gee, that's sweet." I sat, all too aware of Tybalt sitting beside me and began the story. He interjected from time to time, providing the information on his Court's missing children. Lily sat at attention throughout, hands folded in her lap.

When we were done, I asked, "Is that clear enough?"

"Quite," she said. "Give me your hands."

I frowned. "What?"

"Come now; you're occasionally oblivious, but I've rarely seen you stupid." Tybalt snorted. Lily merely shook her head. "Those burns need tending."

"Oh." Shooting a sharp look toward Tybalt, I scooted forward and offered her my hands. She took them gently.

Pulling the bandages back hurt more than I thought it would, probably because the burns were worse than I'd assumed. Tybalt went stiff when he saw them, swearing under his breath. I shared the urge. The skin was blistered and cracked, revealing the raw flesh underneath. If I hadn't known better, I would have thought my hands had been thrust into an open fire and held there for several minutes. Unfortunately, I *did* know better. I would've been happier with a fire. Fires are supposed to burn. Windows aren't.

Lily shook her head, sighing. "I think I may wear myself out repeating this, but I still feel compelled to try: stop hurting yourself."

"Please," said Tybalt.

I cast a startled look in his direction, feeling my ears go red. "Trust me," I said, scrambling to regain my composure. "I really don't mean to."

"This time, I believe you. Judging by your story, you had little choice." My attention returned to Lily in time to see her pulling a chunk of moss from the ground. "What you have encountered, I cannot say. But I will say this: what the waters cannot tell you, you should perhaps ask of the moon."

I blinked at her. "What?"

She looked at me, eyes unreadable. "There are things I may not speak of. You know this, yes?"

"Of course," I said, frowning. Undine are even more easily bound by chains of protocol and politeness than most fae races. I'd tripped over a few topics she wouldn't—or couldn't—discuss over the years.

"This is such a thing. Where children go, why glass burns, how far you can get by the light of a candle— these are not topics for me to discuss. But if you were to ask the moon, well, the moon might give you answers." She began kneading the moss, her other hand holding mine.

"And Karen?" My attention was on Lily's hands. There was a good chance that moss would be in close contact with some rather tender skin in the near future. I wanted all the warning I could get.

"Why a child would sleep without signs of waking, I do not know."

"Right." I paused. "What do you mean, 'ask the moon'?"

Lily shook her head. "If you can't answer that, you haven't been listening to anyone for years."

"I guess." I watched her fingers. I was sure whatever she was planning would hurt, and I'm not fond of pain.

Ironic, considering how often I put myself through the meat grinder.

Tension puts you off-balance. I was so busy watching what she was doing that I wasn't prepared when she dropped the moss, grabbed my wrists, and yanked me forward. There was time to yelp and catch my breath, then I was falling through a curtain of water, with Tybalt shouting in the distance. After that, I was just falling.

FIVE

I HIT THE GROUND HIP-FIRST, rolling to a stop before I sat up. I was dry despite my fall through the water, and my hands didn't hurt anymore. I looked at them and laughed as I saw that the skin was whole and smooth again. Well, I guess that's one way to heal someone, assuming you go in for slapstick. "Lily, that wasn't—" I stopped, blinking. "—funny?"

The knowe stretched out around me in an array of ponds and flatlands, all connected by narrow bridges. Lily, Tybalt, and Karen were gone. "Tybalt?" No one answered. I stood, automatically reaching up to shove my hair back, and stopped as my fingers encountered a tight interweave of knots and hairpins. I pulled one of the hairpins free and glared at it before shoving it back into place. Jade and dragonflies. Cute.

My frown deepened as I looked down at myself and took in the whole picture. Lily apparently extended her services to healing my fashion sense as well as my hands: my T-shirt and jeans were gone, replaced by a steel-gray gown cut in a vaguely traditional Japanese style and embroidered with black and silver dragonflies. A black velvet obi was tied around my waist, my knife concealed underneath a fold of fabric. It wouldn't be easy to draw, but at least she hadn't left me unarmed. Pulling up the hem of the gown exposed one battered brown sneaker— she'd left my shoes alone.

"Not funny," I muttered and started down the nearest path. We were going to have words if she'd vaporized my clothes.

Finding your way out of Lily's knowe is easy, as long as you don't mind walking. The boundaries of her lands are flexible—sometimes there are miles between landmarks, at others it's only a few feet—but all paths eventually lead to the moon bridge. I'd gone about a quarter of a mile, grumbling all the way, when a throat was discreetly cleared behind me.

"Yes?" I said, turning.

A silver-skinned man was standing on the water, the gills at the bottom of his jaw fluttering with barely concealed anxiety. He was wearing Lily's livery, with slits cut down the sleeves and in the legs of his pants to allow the fins running down his calves and forearms the freedom to move. "My lady has . . . sent me?" he said, uncertainly.

"I can see that. What did she send you to say?"

"She wishes me to tell you she is . . . waiting in the pavilion? With . . . the King of Cats and . . . your niece?"

"Good to know," I said, bobbing my head. "Which way to the pavilion?"

"Go as you are and turn . . . left . . . at the . . . sundial?"

That seemed to be the end of his instructions. I was turning when he spoke again, asking, "Lady?"

I glanced back over my shoulder. "Yes?"

"May I . . . go?"

"Yes, you may," I said. He smiled and dissolved into mist, drifting away across the water. I shook my head and resumed walking. Naiads. If there's a way to make them smarter than your average rock, nobody's found it yet.

The rest of the walk was uneventful. A flock of pixies crossed my path at one point, laughing as they tried to knock each other out of the air. I stopped to let them pass. Pixies are small, but they can be vicious when provoked. Several flocks inhabit the park and are currently at war with the flock in the Safeway where I used to work. I've been known to supply the store pixies with weaponry—usually in the form of toothpicks or broken pencils—and I didn't need a flock of park pixies descending on me seeking retribution. I started again after they passed, crossing several more small islands and mossy outcroppings before I reached a sundial in the middle of an otherwise featureless patch of ground. It cast no shadow. I rolled my eyes, wondering why Lily bothered, and turned left.

There was no pavilion before I turned. As soon as I finished turning, it was there: a huge white silk pavilion decorated with a dozen coats of arms I didn't recognize and anchored to a raised hardwood platform by golden ropes. Its banners and pennants drifted in a breeze I couldn't feel. Apparently, "turn left" didn't mean "keep walking."

Lily was kneeling on a cushion, pouring tea into rose-colored china cups that rested on a table so low to the ground that kneeling was the only option—not that she'd provided chairs. Lily can be a bit of a traditionalist when she wants to be, and that's most of the time. Tybalt sat across from her on a similar cushion, looking entirely at ease with his surroundings. That's another infuriating thing about him. He's so damned self-confident that he could probably have dinner with Oberon himself and not feel like he was outclassed.

Karen was asleep against the pavilion wall, pillowed on a pile of cushions with Spike curled up on her stomach. It looked like she'd taken her own trip through the amazing Undine car wash and healing salon. She was wearing a white robe embroidered with cherry blossoms and her hair was combed into a corona around her head. She was just as pale as she'd been before Lily pulled her little stunt and, somehow, I didn't think she'd woken up. Her original clothes were folded on the floor next to her, along with mine.

"I see you've found us," said Lily. She waved a hand toward the other side of the table, indicating the place next to Tybalt. "Please. Sit."

"You could have warned me, you know," I said, walking over to settle as directed. My knees complained when I tried to kneel, so I sat instead, sticking my legs straight out in front of me. Tybalt appeared to be kneeling as comfortably as Lily. I shot him a dirty look. Show-off. "Was there a reason you needed to shunt me halfway across the damn knowe?"

"Yes," she said, continuing to pour. That was really no surprise. I rarely get out of the Tea Gardens without stopping for a cup of tea with Lily, no matter how urgent my business seems to be. Still . . .

"I'm not sure we have time for this, Lily," I said. "We should be looking for the kids."

"There's always time for tea," chided Lily, placing a cup in front of me. "I 'shunted you,' as you so charmingly put it, because you needed to be healed. The damage was magically done, which made it fixable, if I was willing to be firm with it. As for why I didn't warn you, your dislike of water is difficult to miss. I thought you might resist if you knew what was intended." A small smile creased her lips. "A certain resistance to getting wet is a trait you share with our royal friend here."

Tybalt made a face. "I don't consider avoiding pneumonia to be a bad thing."

"If you can contract pneumonia in the waters of my land, you have more troubles than a touch of moistness," said Lily. Sobering, she looked toward me. "I am sorry, October, but I can't wake the child. I tried. I can keep body and spirit together for the time being, but I fear that may be the extent of my capabilities."

"But what's *wrong* with her?"

Lily raised her teacup, using the habitual gesture to try to conceal the worry flickering in her eyes. "I don't know."

"Should I take her to Jin?" Jin was the Court healer at Shadowed Hills. She wasn't in Lily's league—almost no one who isn't an Undine even comes close—but she was good, and her skills were somewhat different. The Ellyllon aren't environmental healers, like the Undine; they work with charms and potions, and that can make them try harder. They aren't limited by what the water can do.

"I don't think so," said Lily. "Moving her before we know the source of her condition may do more harm than good. You did well to bring her here. I can watch over her until more is known."

"So we don't know why Karen won't wake up, we don't know what happened to the missing kids—I don't even know where I should start with this one."

"Ask the moon," said Lily.

"You keep saying that," Tybalt said, with a frown. "Perhaps you'd like to translate it."

"I can't," said Lily, calmly meeting his eyes. "If you wish to find your answers, you'll need to begin thinking, not merely reacting."

"Thinking," I said, and turned toward him. "Tybalt, when you went looking for the missing kids, did you notice anything unusual about the places where they normally slept?"

"Beyond their absence?" His frown deepened. "The air was sour. It smelled wrong, like things that shouldn't have been there."

"Things like what?" I asked, a grim certainty growing inside me.

"Blood and ash. And candle wax."

There was a crash from the other side of the table. We turned to find Lily picking up the pieces of her teacup with shaking hands. I stared. I'd never seen Lily drop anything before.

"I'm so very sorry," she stammered, rising. "Please move away from the table . . . I'll clean the mess directly . . . I am so sorry . . ."

I started to scoot back, but froze, staring at the tea leaves smeared across the table. There were shapes in the mess, almost clear enough to understand. Three loops, like arched gateways; a wilted rose; a tall, slim column tipped with a triangular smear. A candle . . . ?

Lily's hand reached across the table and grasped my chin, turning me to face her. Her eyes seemed darker, less like eyes and more like pools of water. "It's time to go," she said. "I'm sorry, but the leaves have spoken. He's too close for the safety of me or mine."

"Lily, what—" Tybalt began. Lily shot him a sharp look and he quieted.

"You have business to conduct, both of you, although the weight of it stands on Amandine's daughter," she said. "You must speak to the moon, October. Leave the girl in my keeping. Perhaps I can wake her, perhaps not, but she'll be safer with me than she could be on the road with you."

"But—"

This time the sharp look was for me. "You know there are things I can't discuss. I'm sorry they touch on your affairs. I can tell you this much only: you must ask the moon, for you'll find no answers here, and you must leave the girl behind."

"I can't just leave her!" I protested. "Her parents trusted me with her."

"Have you had an unexpected visitor?" she asked. I froze. She continued, "One who belongs to your line even as mistletoe belongs to the oak? You can't lie to me. I know you."

"How . . . ?" I whispered. Tybalt was frowning, but I didn't care. If Lily knew about my Fetch, what else did she know?

Her smile was sad. "There are always ripples on the water. Some of us just watch them more closely. Leave the child and go. You have miles yet to travel on this road."

"Lily, I—"

"There's nothing else to say. You will go on your errand, and Tybalt's, and all the others who haven't time to reach you. You will go, because you must. Go *now*, October." She looked at the mess on the table. "You have little enough time to find your way. Go."

I stood. "You're not telling me anything else, are you?"

"There's nothing else to tell." She crossed to Karen, picked up my clothes, and offered them to me. "You may keep the gown. It suits you."

"Guess I don't have time to change." I took the bundle. "How do we get out of here?"

"Leave the pavilion and turn right."

"Got it." I turned to walk away. Spike leaped off of Karen, following at my heels, with Tybalt just a few feet behind, his footsteps silent on the pavilion floor. It was oddly comforting not to be leaving alone.

There was a moment of disorientation as we stepped down from the pavilion to the mossy ground. The landscape fell into place around us and we were back in the Japanese Tea Gardens, standing outside a door marked EMPLOYEES ONLY. There was a tingle in the air and the smell of jasmine tea. I reached up and touched one ear, feeling the illusion-rounded angle of it.

"Isn't this fun," I said, darkly. I realize most purebloods have absolute control within their knowes, but that doesn't mean I need illustrated examples. I can't *stand* other people throwing my illusions on for me. It makes my ears itch. Area illusions like Tybalt's don't-look-here were annoying enough, and they didn't actually touch my skin.

"You look very nice," said Tybalt.

I eyed him, unwrapping his jacket—unwrapping *my* jacket—from around the bundle of clothes and shrugging it on. The battered leather made an odd contrast against the formal silk gown. I didn't much care. "I look like a geisha."

A small smile tugged at his lips. "As I said, you look very nice."

"Uh-huh." I snorted and turned to head for the exit. Looking amused, Tybalt followed. The second time I tripped on the hem of my dress, he reached over and took the bundle of clothes from my hands. I blinked, but didn't say anything.

Neither did he, until we were almost to my car. When

he did speak, his voice was uncharacteristically soft. "I didn't mean to upset you."

"What?" I glanced toward him.

"I said, I didn't mean to upset you. I didn't realize my absence would be a problem." His smile widened slightly. "It seemed you were eternally trying to be rid of me."

"Yeah, well." I stopped next to the car, taking my clothes out of his hands. "I guess I wasn't expecting it to be quite that abrupt. Did I piss you off?"

"Piss me off? No. You didn't. I've been . . ." He paused, sighing. "I've been looking for someone. There are questions that trouble me and I'd like to find some answers."

"Anything I can help with?"

The question was casual; his response was anything but. Going still as a cat stalking a mouse, he studied my face, eyes darting back and forth as he considered me. Finally, almost wonderingly, he said, "No. No, I don't think it is." He looked oddly relieved. "My apologies for my absence. Clearly, you've been lost without me."

I blinked, digging my keys out of the pocket of my jeans and checking the backseat for intruders before unlocking the car door. "You're very strange, Tybalt," I said. "But I guess I knew that. Do you need a lift anywhere?"

He paused, looking thoughtful. "What did Lily mean? The mistletoe and the oak?"

In for a penny, in for a pound. If he was trusting me to find his Court's missing children, I might as well trust him with the realities of the situation. Squaring my shoulders, I met his eyes and said, "My Fetch showed up this morning."

"Ah," he said, softly. "I should have known it would be something of the sort." Before I had a chance to react, he stepped forward, kissing me on the forehead. "I have to return to my Court and let the parents of the missing ones know that you've agreed. I'll come to you later."

I stared at him, stunned. "What . . . ?"

"Open roads, Toby. Find our children." He hesitated like he was about to say something else, but he didn't; he just turned and walked to the edge of the parking lot.

"What . . . ?" I repeated, standing there with my keys dangling in my hand.

Looking back over his shoulder, he smiled, almost shyly, stepped into the shadows, and was gone.

"This is officially getting strange," I said, as much to hear my own voice as anything else. Missing children, a Fetch on my doorstep, Lily being freaky, and now Tybalt was deciding to redefine "acting weird"? The day wasn't getting any better. I got into the car and started the engine.

I needed coffee, and I needed it now.

SIX

I ARRIVED HOME HALF AN HOUR and a McDon-
ald's drive-through later, with most of an extra-large
coffee doing its best to settle my stomach. It was failing. The failure became more profound as I approached
the apartment and got my first look at the front porch.
Quentin was sitting there with his arms wrapped around
his legs and his chin resting on his knees, looking for all
the world like an enormous kicked puppy.

At least he'd had the sense to put on a human disguise, blunting the points of his ears and making his features a little more believably attractive. Daoine Sidhe
are gorgeous, but it's not a human beauty. With the
disguise, he could have been a teen idol; without it, he
would have started riots. He was wearing blue jeans and
a black T-shirt that proclaimed YOU'RE JUST JEALOUS BE-
CAUSE THE VOICES TALK TO ME. It didn't look like his corn
silk–blond hair had been combed in days, and one of his
sneakers was untied.

The only time I'd ever seen him look that untidy was
right after he'd been shot. Something was wrong.

He scrambled to his feet when he saw me, almost
stumbling over his shoelaces. "Toby," he said, voice
cracking. "I—"

Loose lips sink ships and panicked kids say things

they shouldn't. I live in a decent area, but I have neighbors and neighbors hear things. "Wait until we're inside. You want to get the door?" I tossed him the house keys, getting a better grip on both my bundle of clothes and my skirt in the process. "I do *not* like walking in this thing."

"So why are you wearing it?" He caught the keys, frowning quizzically.

"It's a long story." I snapped my fingers, muttering a quick snatch of "Mary Had a Little Lamb." The wards around the doorframe flared red and released. "Just open the door."

Lucky for me, that boy has been schooled in obedience since the day he was born. He shrugged and turned, unlocking the door. His courtly manners even carried over into holding it open for me before he followed me inside, where he collapsed onto the couch and dropped his head into his hands. I had to admire that—like most teenagers, regardless of breed, he had an almost instinctive grasp of the theatrical.

"Tie your shoes," I said, dropping my bundle of clothes on the bookshelf before locking the door and turning to head for the kitchen. I needed to make a pot of coffee. He'd talk when he was ready, and most of my cheap fast food coffee was long-since gone.

I was filling the filter when he said, tentatively, "Toby?"

Jackpot. "Yeah?" I turned. He was standing in the kitchen doorway. "You going to tell me why you were camping on my porch?"

"Katie's gone."

I put the filter down. "You want to try that again?"

"Katie's gone. She disappeared this morning."

The name was familiar, it just took a moment to figure out who he meant. Oh, no. "Your human girlfriend." He nodded. There was a sudden sinking feeling in my stomach. *Please let him be here to tell me they broke up . . .* "When you say gone, what do you mean exactly?"

"I don't know. Away." He looked down at the floor,

continuing in a monotone, "She didn't come to school this morning."

It's getting harder for the purebloods to pretend that the mortal world doesn't matter, so they've started sending their kids to school—human school. Call it the hot new way to play faerie bride. I'm not sure what I think of the idea of a bunch of pureblood kids getting the human childhood I never had, but my opinion won't reverse the trend. Quentin was in his second year at the human high school near Paso Nogal, and he was doing surprisingly well, all things considered.

I leaned against the counter. "She could be sick. Humans get sick."

"I know that," Quentin said defensively. "I went to her house at lunch to check on her."

"And she wasn't there?"

"No. Her mom said Katie was gone when she got up. She didn't take her shoes or her bag or anything." He swallowed hard before continuing, "I asked if I could look around her room to see if she left a note or something. You know. Investigating, like at ALH."

"That was clever of you." The sinking feeling in my stomach was getting worse. "What did you find?"

"No note," Quentin said. "But . . ." He paused. "Don't laugh, okay?"

"I won't laugh," I said quietly. Somehow, laughter was the last thing on my mind.

"The air in her room tasted funny. Like . . . well, like blood."

"And candle wax," I muttered.

"What?"

"Nothing. Did you touch the windows?"

He frowned. "Of course not. Why would I touch the windows?"

I held up my hands. Lily did a good job, but I could still feel the burning if I thought about it too hard. "I don't know. But if you had, you'd probably be in a world of pain."

"What are you *talking* about?"

"Finish your story, then I'll tell you mine." He eyed me, and I added, "Promise."

"All right." He sighed. "Her mom came in and said I needed to leave. She was pretty worried." He bit his lip. "So am I."

"Understandably." I picked up the filter and slotted it into place, then turned on the coffee maker. I needed more caffeine before I tried to deal with any more of this.

"Are you going to tell me what's going on now?"

"I probably should," I said, and sighed. "Come on." I pushed past him into the living room, not waiting to see if he was following; it's not that big of an apartment. I sat on the end of the couch, tugging the hem of my skirt until it was even.

Quentin followed, sitting on the other end of the couch. Spike leaped into his lap, and he started scratching the rose goblin behind the ears. "Why would the windows hurt me?"

"Because Katie's not the only one that's gone," I said. "Stacy Brown called this morning because her two youngest children were missing. When I searched their rooms, I found the same scents you found in Katie's. I've also spoken to Tybalt, and he says five children disappeared from his Court last night."

"Same smell?"

"Same smell," I said. "I touched a window when I was following the scent trail. It burned my hands."

"But they don't look—"

"Lily healed them. Katie . . ." I sighed. "She's pure human, right? Not thin-blooded or a merlin?" Humans with very small amounts of fae blood are sometimes still capable of working magic and perceiving the fae world; it's rare, but it happens. We call them "merlins," and we avoid them when we can. They're dangerous, in their way.

"She's human," Quentin said, glaring.

I winced. "I didn't mean to imply anything. But Quentin—whatever this is, it's snatched purebloods, changelings, and now a human girl. What does that mean?"

"It means we have to get her back," he said, jaw set in a hard line.

"Right," I said, pinching the bridge of my nose. "Does anybody know you're here?"

"Not exactly. I came straight from school."

"So kids are disappearing and you just *ran out?* Did you at least tell Sylvester and Luna you'd be home late?" Quentin's parents fostered him at Shadowed Hills to be trained in the courtly arts. I've never met them, but they must have been fairly minor nobility to place him in a court as unfashionable as Sylvester's. Judging by the slight accent Quentin displayed in times of stress, they were somewhere in or near Canada. The Torquills are both his liege lords and his parents now, at least until the fosterage ends.

"No . . ."

"Maeve *wept,* Quentin." I stood. "Stay where you are. Understand?"

He nodded as I stalked back to the kitchen, where I grabbed the phone and dialed the number for Shadowed Hills. The phone rang twice before a man's voice came on the line, saying, "Shadowed Hills. How may I assist?"

I paused, amazement overwhelming my annoyance. "Etienne, is that *you?*"

"Oh, blast. Hello, Toby," he said, wearily. "Please don't start."

"Was the phone in danger? Did they have to get a big, brave knight to guard it?" Etienne is one of Sylvester's most reliable knights. Pureblooded Tuatha de Dannan and so honorable that he squeaks—in short, boring as hell. I respect the man and even like him in the abstract, but when it comes to actually spending time around him, well, let's just say that we've devoted a lot of time to driving each other crazy.

"Melly is out, so someone had to mind the phone. What's going on?" It was impossible to miss the disapproval in his tone. I'm a lot more likely to just show up, trouble following on my heels, than I am to call ahead.

"Right. Sorry." I sobered, saying, "Quentin's at my place. He's fine, and I'm about to bring him back to the knowe."

"Quentin's *there?* Why in the world would he be—"

"He came on his own, Etienne, I didn't steal him or anything." His answering silence betrayed how close I'd been to guessing what he was thinking. I sighed. "Please let people know that Quentin is safe and will be there shortly for you to yell at in person."

"Of course," he said, stiffly. "Open roads."

"Kind fires, Etienne," I said and hung up the phone.

I was smacking my head rhythmically against the wall when I heard Quentin clear his throat behind me, saying, "Toby? What's wrong? Who was that on the phone?"

I stopped banging my head and straightened, turning to face him. "Come on. We're leaving."

He followed me to the front door, asking, "Where are we going?"

"I'm taking you back to Shadowed Hills."

"What?" He stopped, staring at me. "Why?"

"This situation is too dangerous. I'm not going to risk your life again." The last time Sylvester sent me on a job, Quentin came along to watch and learn. He learned, all right. He learned what it's like to get shot and nearly die, and what it's like to bury your liege lord's only niece. There are some lessons I really don't feel like reinforcing.

"But—Katie!" Quentin protested.

"I'm on it. I don't need your help." I'd risk my own life to bring the children home, but I wouldn't risk anyone else. Nobody was going to get hurt on my watch; especially not Quentin. I'd already hurt him enough.

He stared at me, looking like I'd just slapped him. "But she's my girlfriend. You're supposed to . . ."

"To what? Let you help?" I shook my head, doing my best to sneer. It hurt, but not as badly as the thought of his broken body. "Haven't you been paying attention?

When people get involved with me, they *die.* I'm not taking you on this case."

"I have to find her. *Please,* Toby, she's just human; she doesn't know—"

"You're not trained and you're not coming." I was being cruel, but there was no other way. Not unless I wanted my Fetch to stand for his death as well as mine.

Quentin recoiled, eyes wide and hurt for an instant before his expression hardened. He nodded curtly. "Fine. I'll find her on my own."

"No, you won't. Come on."

"What?"

"Like I said, I'm taking you back to Shadowed Hills." He glared. I glared back. I've had more practice, and he looked away first, hunching his shoulders. I briefly considered changing my clothes, but dismissed the idea. Quentin might sneak out if I left him alone. I wanted him where I could see him until I got him back to the knowe.

"Toby . . ."

"Come on." I grabbed his arm and tugged him outside. Spike followed, darting between my feet and nearly tripping me. Letting go of Quentin, I stooped and scooped up the rose goblin, dropping it into his arms with an unceremonious, "Hold this."

Quentin frowned, automatically cradling the rose goblin to his chest. Spike chirped, compacting itself and beginning to make the weird grating sound that served as its purr.

I ran my fingers down the sides of the door, muttering fragments of nursery rhymes under my breath. The smell of copper and cut grass rose around me as the wards flared red, reactivating, and a bolt of pain hit me behind the temples. The spell worked, however much good it was going to do. Mitch and Stacy kept their house warded, too.

Lowering my hands, I turned to Quentin. "Let's go."

He handed me Spike without saying a word and stalked off toward my car. I sighed, but didn't object. If he wanted to play silent treatment, I could play silent treatment. It might even be easier that way.

The drive to Pleasant Hill seemed to take forever. Quentin sat in the passenger seat glowering and refusing to look at me, while Spike had decided to ride in my lap rather than in its usual spot on the dashboard. I don't know whether it was trying to comfort me or be comforted, but between that and my skirt, it was pretty hard to shift. My thoughts kept creeping back to Karen. I wanted to believe she'd wake up on her own. Somehow, I just couldn't.

Especially, said a nagging voice at the back of my mind, *if Quentin's girlfriend and the Cait Sidhe kids vanished the same way Andy and Jessica did.* I shivered. Something was starting that I didn't like at all and, by the root and branch, I didn't see any way to stay out of it.

The sun was descending into afternoon as we pulled into the parking lot at Paso Nogal. "Come on. Let's go."

Quentin looked at me solemnly. "Please change your mind. I want to help."

"I'm not getting you hurt again. Now get out of the car."

Quentin glared but opened his door, obviously intending to stalk away. One problem: I didn't trust him to actually stalk back into the knowe. I got out of the car and walked around the car to meet him, offering a sunny smile as I grabbed his elbow.

"Let me walk you home."

"That isn't—" He tried to pull himself loose and scowled. "That isn't necessary."

"Funny thing is I think it is. Now come on."

It was a good thing the park was basically empty, because anyone who saw our progression up the hill would have had good reason to call the police and report me for kidnapping. Quentin didn't struggle, but he didn't help, either; he just let himself be half led, half dragged through the complex series of steps that opens the door to Shadowed Hills. Completing the steps with him in tow took most of my attention. There was no way to keep my skirt from getting torn. I gave up trying after the third time it snagged on the hawthorn bushes. It wasn't like I paid for the damn thing.

Quentin tried to jerk free again as the door into the knowe finally swung open. This time, I let him go. I wasn't willing to let him risk his neck if I had any say in the matter, but there was no reason to embarrass him on top of everything else.

Spike darted past us as we stepped into the entrance hall, nearly sweeping me off my feet. Its ears were pressed flat against its head, and it was running fast enough that it was out of sight around the corner almost before I realized it was moving. Visions of its strange behavior at Mitch and Stacy's place flashed through my mind. "Quentin, stay here!" I snapped, and took off after it.

It's hard to get purchase on a marble floor while wearing sneakers. I careened around the corner in the direction Spike had gone, already stumbling as I pursued it into the next hall.

The hall was already occupied. Luna was sitting on a low velvet couch about twenty feet away, expression distant as she arranged dried roses in a vase atop a cherrywood table. Spike raced ahead of me and jumped into her lap. She looked down at it for a moment before she raised her head, taking note of my approach. Twitching one silver-furred ear, she tucked her feet beneath her body, letting go of the vase.

"Hello, October," she said mildly.

"Uh . . ." I tried to bow and stop running at the same time. The skirt snarled my legs, my feet slid out from under me, and I landed flat on my back.

Luna watched my descent, apparently unperturbed. It's hard to fluster Luna. She's a three-tailed Kitsune who voluntarily married into one of the most frustrating noble families I've ever dealt with. Someone like that is either crazy or patient as a rock. I sometimes suspect that Luna might be both.

She waited for me to slide to a stop before asking calmly, "New dress?"

"Lily," I said, by way of explanation. Sitting up, I rubbed the back of my head with one hand. "Well, that was a little overdramatic."

"But funny, which forgives many sins." She stood, cradling Spike against her chest. "The return of Quentin is appreciated. He'll need to be spoken to, of course. I'm sure Etienne will cherish the opportunity."

"Better him than me."

Luna laughed, offering her hand. "Come on. Sylvester will want to speak with you."

"I do so love meeting with my liege when I'm dressed like an idiot and just concussed myself on the floor," I grumbled, letting her pull me up. "Still, that's a good thing, because I want to speak with him, too."

Her laughter died, taking the light in her eyes with it. "I rather thought you might," she said, quietly. "I'd hoped that someone else would . . . but it's no matter. Come along."

Still holding Spike against her chest, she turned and walked away down the hall, clearly trusting me to follow. Perplexed by her change in moods, I did exactly that. Sylvester needed to know what was going on.

SEVEN

SHADOWED HILLS IS THE BIGGEST KNOWE
I've ever seen and it's easy to get lost there. I'm not
sure whether it actually rearranges itself when no one's
looking, but I wouldn't be surprised. After all, we're talking about a sprawling Summerlands estate large enough
to hold Sylvester, Luna, their daughter and her husband,
their fosters, the staff, an entire Court, and all of Luna's
gardens. It's a wonder the place isn't bigger than it is.

Luna led me down the hall into a room with walls
made of falling water. She didn't say a word, cradling
Spike against her chest and looking fixedly ahead, like
she was afraid her head would fall off if she turned it.
Even Spike seemed subdued, lying passively in her arms
with its head down and its thorns slicked flat against its
back. That didn't strike me as a good sign.

"Luna . . . ?"

"Please, October." She glanced back over her shoulder, expression pained. "Just give me a moment. Please.
Everything will be explained."

That answer just worried me more. Still, I quieted, following her out of the waterfall room and into a vast hall
filled with darkness. There was no visible floor. Doors
hung suspended in the air, scattered with no regard
for where the room's walls might have logically fallen.

Luna walked to the nearest door, opened it, and stepped through, vanishing into the nothingness on the other side. Swell. I swear, if anything will eventually condemn Faerie to becoming nothing but a world of fantasy and kitsch, it's the pureblood obsession with special effects. Hoisting my skirt around my knees, I followed her.

The darkness broke into shards of yellow and turquoise before resolving into the lush green of an English country garden. Luna and I were standing on a narrow cobblestone path that wound off in a multitude of directions, branching around trees and statuary. Ferns arched overhead, casting lacy shadows on the stones beneath our feet. Like a proper English garden, it was so artfully tended that it looked like it had never been tended at all. Fat gardenias and gladiolas nodded their heads in the shade of climbing ivy and honeysuckle vines, while morning glories twined around the arms of a hanging loveseat. Marble statues peeked out of the corners, nearly buried in the heavy greenery.

"This is new," I said, looking around.

"This is very, very old," she corrected. "I sealed it for some time, to let the trees grow. It seemed appropriate for today."

I gave her a sidelong look. "Luna, what's going on?"

"Just come," she said, and started down the nearest branch of the path. Spike looked over Luna's shoulder at me, clearly expectant. With a sigh, I followed.

The odds are against me ever having a knowe of my own—changelings don't usually get that kind of real estate—but if I ever do, I'm posting maps with arrows saying YOU ARE HERE on every corner. I'd be completely lost if I let Luna out of my sight, and that didn't seem like it was going to help with the quest at hand.

We didn't go far. After circling an ornamental birdbath ringed with rosebushes, we found ourselves facing an elegant picnic spread beneath a weeping willow. All the dishes came from the garden: salads, platters of fresh vegetables and cut fruits, jars of jam and honey. Harvest food. Sylvester was sitting on the blanket, slicing into a blackberry pie. Looking up, he smiled.

"There you are! Etienne said you'd be coming to return Quentin. Come on, have a seat. You look like you could use some lunch." His smile faltered, melting into confusion. "Luna? What's wrong?"

"Everything. Nothing." Luna laughed—a thin, brittle sound, like fingernails on a blackboard—and moved to drop almost gracelessly onto the blanket next to him. Her tails were lashing madly, tying themselves into complicated knots that untied just as quickly. Spike jumped free of her arms as she sat, and it ran back to me, flattening itself against my ankles. Luna didn't seem to notice. "The hills are on fire, Sylvester. The candles are going out."

His hands slowly stilled, the pie apparently forgotten as he stared at his wife. Finally, he turned to look at me, and said, in a voice that had gone almost flat, "Why don't you sit down, October, and tell us what's been going on?"

"I'm not completely *sure* what's been going on, Your Grace, but I can try," I said, walking over and sitting carefully. I still didn't trust my skirt. "This morning—"

"Eat."

I looked toward Luna, blinking. Sylvester did the same. She had snatched the knife he'd abandoned, using it to slash the pie into ragged, uneven slices. Her hands were shaking as she lifted the first slice onto a plate and thrust it in my direction.

"Eat," she repeated. "You have to eat something." She forced a wavering smile. "You're too thin."

"No, I'm not," I said automatically as I reached out and took the plate. Blackberry juice leaked from the sides of pie, forming a viscous purple slick. "Luna, are you okay?"

"Oh, no, dear. No, I'm not okay at all." Her smile was beatific and almost dazed. It was a madwoman's smile. My mother used to smile like that in the years just before I disappeared. "I'm so many miles from okay that I don't even know where it is anymore. Eat your pie."

I glanced to Sylvester. He nodded. Taking that as instruction of a sort, I picked up a fork and prodded at the pie before taking a cautious bite. It was excellent pie. The crust was light and flaky, and the blackberries were perfect, managing to be sweet and tart at the same time. It was even still warm. Too bad I was too wound up to enjoy it.

Sylvester cleared his throat after I'd taken two bites, saying, "I do appreciate your returning Quentin. His parents would be rather put out if I lost track of him."

"I bet," I said, taking that as a sign that I could put my plate aside. "How long is he fostered here, anyway?"

"Oh, we're to have all of his training. We'll be assigning him a knight soon enough, getting him started on his time as a squire." Sylvester's smile was almost nostalgic. "I was squired to Sir Malcolm in Gray Fields. That was how he met my sister. I'm not sure our parents ever forgave me." He glanced toward Luna. "Parents so rarely do."

"I never asked them to forgive me," said Luna. "I only asked them to leave me alone."

"Um, guys?" I raised a hand. "Can we get back to why Quentin was on my doorstep this morning? I can't stay for long. I have to go take care of things."

"You have no idea what you're trying to take care of," said Luna, in that same sharp tone. "You have no idea at all."

Spike rattled its thorns, chirping at her.

Luna's attention switched to the rose goblin. "I don't believe that's relevant."

Spike chirped again.

I blinked at the pair of them. "Luna? Do you understand what it's saying?"

The strangeness cleared from her expression for a moment, replaced by perplexity. "Well, yes. Didn't you know?"

"Uh, no, I didn't."

"You're not surprised when Tybalt talks to the cats, are you?"

"No; he's their King." Tybalt's kingship meant he could probably get running updates on how I was doing just by coming by the apartment and talking to Cagney and Lacey. I tried not to think about that too much.

"By that same logic, you shouldn't be surprised that I can talk to my roses." She looked back to Spike, the darkness returning to her face as she said, "Although there are times I wish they had less to say."

"Luna." Sylvester leaned over, placing a hand on her arm. "Please."

She sighed deeply, seeming to pull the sound up from the very center of her being. "I don't want to," she said.

"I know." He turned toward me. "Toby?"

I know a cue when I hear one. Taking a deep breath, I said, "Stacy Brown called me this morning. Two of her kids went missing sometime right around dawn."

"How old were they?" asked Luna. There was no surprise in her words, only sorrow.

"Jessica is six, and Andy just turned four."

"Such perfect ages," said Luna, and closed her eyes. "How many others?"

"Five from Tybalt's Court," I said, slowly. "Quentin's girlfriend, Katie, is missing, too, but I'm not sure whether it's connected or not. She's mortal."

Luna's answer was a bitter laugh. Shaking her head, she said, "Oh, no. She's the proof. Without her, this still might be something other than what it is. At least eight in a single night, with two more nights to go? How many haven't called for help yet? Always take them just before dawn. That leaves the most time before they sound out the alarms."

"I have no idea what you're talking about," I said. That didn't stop her words from upsetting me.

"Oh, you will, soon enough. Are there any others?"

"Mitch and Stacy's middle daughter, Karen. She's eleven. She isn't missing, but she won't wake up, no matter what we do. Lily has her now."

"That should do for the time being." Spike rattled its thorns again. Luna looked down at it, frowning. "Really?" Her attention swiveled back to me. "What time did she arrive?"

Somehow, I knew which "she" Luna was talking about. "A little bit before dawn."

"Who?" asked Sylvester.

I sighed, looking down at my partially-eaten pie. "My Fetch."

Silence fell among the three of us, broken only by the sound of leaves rustling in the wind. Even Spike had stopped rattling. When the silence got to be too much, I raised my head and found myself looking into Sylvester's eyes.

"Really?" he asked, in a dangerously soft voice.

"Really," I said, swallowing. Forcing a smile, I added, "She said her name was May."

"October ..."

"Her Fetch came when he was taking the children from their beds like a farmer taking apples from his tree," said Luna. Sylvester whipped his head around to stare at her. She met his gaze without flinching. Her expression was more than solemn—it was sad and frightened and wounded, all at once. "He Rides, Sylvester. He Rides, and she's bound to go following after."

"Amandine—"

"Isn't here," Luna said, quietly. "Hasn't been here. Won't be here again anytime soon. Those roots fell on shallow ground, and you know it. Now will you keep him from our gates and let me tell her what she needs to know?"

Sylvester's expression hardened. The look he turned on Luna was colder than any I'd seen him cast her way. Standing, he crossed to me, pulled me to my feet, and hugged me, almost hard enough to keep me from noticing that he was shaking. Then he released me and strode away down the garden path without a single word. He didn't look back.

I was staring after him when I felt Luna's hand on my

shoulder, and turned to see her standing next to me. "He needs to warn the Court. It's his duty and his privilege, because . . . because of who he is." Her voice faltered. "I need to talk to you. Alone."

I couldn't take it anymore: the demand burst out of me, born of fear and frustration. "Oberon's *teeth,* Luna, what's going on?"

"You've been to see Lily." It wasn't a question. "She told you to ask the moon."

"Did Spike tell you what color my underpants are to-day, too?" I scowled. "I have no idea what she was talking about."

Luna didn't answer. She just looked at me.

"Oh, *damn." Ask the moon.* There were a couple ways to interpret that, and the most obvious—the one I should have thought of first—was *ask Luna.* She was the only moon I knew who could answer questions. "What's going on, Luna? What do you mean by 'He Rides'?"

She sighed. "Toby, if I say challenging him is futile, that you'll change nothing and only grant the omen you saw this morning power over you . . . if I say you can save your life and your heart by walking away from this, will it matter?"

Part of me—most of me—wanted to say, "Yes, it would matter; please tell me to stay here. If you tell me, I'll stay." I didn't want to go. I'm not a hero; I never have been. I just do what has to be done.

But when you get right down to it, isn't that the defi-nition of hero?

"No," I said. "It won't."

Sounding resigned, but not surprised, she said, "His name is Blind Michael."

"Blind Michael?" I frowned. "But that doesn't make sense. He and his Hunt only harass you if you go into the Berkeley Hills on the full moon. They—"

She looked at me. I stopped, biting my lip. After a moment, she continued; "His name is Blind Michael. His mother was Maeve and his father was Oberon. His domain was wider once, but none of us are what we once were." Her smile was brief and bitter, gone in an instant.

"He's *Firstborn?*"

"Yes." She nodded. "He saw the races of Faerie born, yours and mine alike."

"What does he have to do with this?"

"Have you never wondered where he gets the members of his Hunt?"

"What?" That wasn't a question that ever occurred to me. Blind Michael and his Hunt were part of the landscape, like the trees or the rocks. They didn't need to come from anywhere.

Her voice was calm and measured as she continued, like she was reciting something she'd memorized years before, something painful. "He rides them hard. Night after night through the darkest parts of the Summerlands, where there are still monsters, and old magic—he brings the madness with him. He rides them, and there are casualties. There are always casualties. Where do you think he finds his Riders? Who would willingly bow to such a fate?"

I stared at her, trying to ignore the sinking feeling in my stomach. It wasn't easy to do; I'm not stupid. Damn it. "No one."

"No one," she agreed. Her eyes were too bright, but she wasn't crying. Yet. "And when there are no willing Riders, the unwilling will suffice."

"The children."

"Yes. Once a century. Fae children to be his Huntsmen; human children to be their steeds. No locks can keep him out. No door can bar his way. He's too old and too strong, and he follows the laws of Faerie too closely to be caught that way."

I shook my head to clear away my growing horror, asking, "What does he do to them?"

"Do?" She cocked her head. "He takes them and he binds them. Fae children ride, so they grow strong and fierce; human children are ridden, so they learn the ways of hoof and bridle. And they are changed. Beware Blind

Michael's children, Toby—beware *all* his children, no matter how honest or honorable they seem. I can't stop you from trying. Heroes never listen. That's why they're heroes."

"Luna—"

I don't know if she heard me; she just kept talking, words falling together like stones constructing my tomb. "You, at least, I can still warn: beware his children. They're too lost. There is no peace for them. There is no salvation. There is nothing but the Hunt and the darkness and the hope that, one day, death will claim them." She shivered and turned her face away. "Be wary, beware Blind Michael's children and come back to us. Please."

Slowly, I asked, "Where did Sylvester go?"

"There are ways to keep him out. Not gates, not locks or bars, but laws and rituals that make him less than welcome. Sylvester has gone to warn the Court so that we can keep the dark at bay a little longer." She shook her head, ears flattened. "It's all we can do. It's not enough."

I shuddered. Her words were taking on two meanings in my head. Neither of them was good. Maybe that was all *they* could do, but I had to do more; staying safe was a luxury I couldn't afford. I wanted to ask Luna how she knew so much and why her eyes were so far away, why she was almost crying. I didn't. I didn't have that luxury either.

"How do I find Blind Michael?"

She glanced back toward me, expression bleak. "There are roads."

"Can you tell me how to find them?"

"My roads are Rose Roads. If you seek darkness, ask the darkness. It can help you."

"Luna . . ." I shook my head, biting back a groan of frustration. "What do you mean, ask the darkness? I'm getting tired of being told to talk to things that won't talk back just because people don't feel like saying, 'Hey, go ask Bob, he knows what to do.'"

She sighed. "I've sent you to her before, when I

thought we might lose you if I didn't. Now I'm sending you again. This time, I'm afraid you're already lost."

I froze. "Oh. No."

"Yes," she said. "You have to go to the Luidaeg. Tell her he Rides."

Oh, Lord and Ladies. The Luidaeg and I may be the equivalent of old Scrabble buddies these days, but there's a big difference between visiting a friend and asking a favor from one of the Firstborn. The latter is a lot more likely to get you killed. And that was exactly what Luna was telling me to do.

EIGHT

I WALKED TOWARD THE EXIT with Spike riding on my shoulder. I'd finally given up on fighting with my skirt, hacking it off above the knees before letting Luna lead me out of the garden. It was a relief to walk without constantly feeling like I was going to trip myself. That was the only thing that gave me relief.

Once I called the Luidaeg, everything would be in her hands, not mine. Luna was right. The situation called for extreme measures, and the Luidaeg is about as extreme as you can get.

The Luidaeg's Firstborn, like her brother, and she hasn't lived this long by being kind. None of the Firstborn have. Maybe more important, the Luidaeg is one of Maeve's children, and there are very few of them left. Cruelty always came easier to the children of Titania; the only survivors of Maeve's line are the ones who let themselves learn how to become monsters. Titania's children are cold and hard and beautiful. Maeve's children are hot and strange and come in every shape imaginable. Oberon doesn't claim most of his descendants, leaving them to the mercies of their mothers. Those few races that he does claim . . . those are Oberon's children. And Oberon's children are heroes.

The Luidaeg has lived in San Francisco for a century

or more, and familiarity has bred a certain degree of contempt. You can spend your whole life in this city and never see her; fae parents use her as a threat for kids who won't mind their manners or eat their vegetables. Some people think she's dead, or just gone, but I know the truth. She's real, she's dangerous, and she's the single crankiest person I've ever met.

The first time we met, we played a game of questions that ended with her in my debt by a single answer. She swore she'd kill me when that question was asked, and I believed her. I kept her in my debt as long as I could, but circumstances conspired to cost me my last question . . . and she didn't kill me, largely, I think, because I didn't poke at her. I showed up on her doorstep a month afterward, and she demanded to know where the hell I'd been. I started visiting again. We played lots of chess, and I didn't ask for anything. I'd almost stopped flinching every time she raised her voice. And now it was time to bring it all back.

The park was empty. I went down the hill at a run, not particularly caring who saw me. I was dressed idiotically but I looked human, and that was what mattered. People can justify almost anything as long as it doesn't come equipped with pointy ears.

My car was just a few yards from the phone. I dropped Spike on the hood and trotted over to grab the receiver, not checking for a dial tone before dialing the numbers in a clockwise spiral. "Jack Sprat could eat no fat, his wife could eat no lean." A sharp pain shot through my forehead, telling me the spell was cast. In magic, it's not the words that matter, but the belief behind them. I believed the Luidaeg would hear me.

The line filled with hissing and the click of relays being established between networks that had no real reasons to meet. The hiss faded, replaced by the sound of a distant heartbeat. The Luidaeg is obsessively fond of sound effects. I keep thinking one day I'll call her and wind up hearing bongo drums and Tarzan yells. The heartbeat cut off in midthrob, replaced by silence. I started wondering whether she'd changed the number. Can you change a number that doesn't technically exist? The spell was obviously working, but that didn't mean it had to connect me to the Luidaeg.

I was about to hang up when the line shrieked and a familiar voice demanded, "Who are you and what do you want?"

"Luidaeg, it's Toby."

"What the hell are you doing on my phone? Did you forget the bagels again?"

"I'm not supposed to come over until tomorrow, Luidaeg." That was where my courage failed me—or tried to. I closed my eyes, saying, "This isn't about me coming over, at least not like that. I need your help."

She was silent long enough that I was afraid she'd hung up. Then, quietly, she asked, "Why? You know I promised to kill you after last time." Was it my imagination, or was there regret in her words?

"I know."

"And you still want my help. Why are you that stupid?"

The moment of truth. "Because Luna Torquill gave me a message for you." If Luna was wrong about asking the Luidaeg for help, I was a dead woman. I wondered vaguely whether I'd have time to call the night-haunts before she could get to me. They'd be pleased to hear of my impending death; they did me a favor not long ago, and from what I've seen, they're fond of visceral paybacks.

"A message from Luna?" She sounded interested despite herself. "What is it?"

"He Rides," I said, and waited. The next words had to be hers.

"How many children?" she asked, after a long pause. Resignation hung heavy in those words.

"At least eight. Maybe more."

"Damn it!" Her voice rose in a shriek. I heard things shattering behind her, but couldn't tell whether she was throwing them or whether they were breaking out of sympathy. "Damn it damn it *damn it*—why the *fuck* is she sending you to me?"

"Because she thought you might be able to help." *Because it takes darkness to understand darkness.*

She sounded heartbroken when she spoke again. "Why me? Why can't you people just leave me alone?"

"Because we need you, Luidaeg. Because *I* need you."

She caught her breath and held it for a moment. Then, slowly, she said, "I can help."

"I know," I lied. I *hadn't* known. I'd hoped. After what Luna said to me, hoping seemed like the best course of action I had.

"I don't come cheap. You're willing to give me a blank check?"

I winced. "Yes. I am."

"You're still an idiot," she said and laughed, low and bitter. "It's good to know some things never change. You're at Shadowed Hills?"

"Yes."

"Hang up and get over here before I change my mind. I need you to do exactly what I tell you to. Can you handle that?"

"I think so."

"You'd better *know* so, or we're finished before we start. Leave now. Don't go home. Once you're on the road, don't stop, don't look back. Have you eaten today?"

"Not much. I've had about half an egg, some home fries, two bites of blackberry pie, three cups of coffee, and some tea at Lily's."

"I can work around that. Get your ass over here."

The line went dead. I hung up and turned toward my car, massaging my throbbing temple with the palm of my hand. I didn't look back—something that became increasingly difficult as I got into the car and pulled out of the parking lot. I eventually decided that "don't look back" was a literal command, and I'd be fine as long as I didn't actually turn my head to see what was behind me. It was a cheat, but it was the best I had.

The drive to the Luidaeg's took more than an hour and a half, thanks to that famous San Francisco traffic. She lives next to the docks; it's not easy to get there even when the tourists aren't out in force. Fill the streets with idiots who want to see Pier 39 "one more time," and you're lucky if you can get anywhere near the water without getting stuck in stop-and-go traffic. My headache had developed into a full-grown migraine by the time I reached her neighborhood.

The brightly colored tourist traps gave way to crumbling, half-decayed buildings that looked like they were longing for an excuse to collapse. They pressed in on each other, creating a corridor of close-set looming walls. The air stank like stale water and rotting fish. I've gotten used to it—visiting frequently makes it easier to bear—but that didn't keep me from wondering how she could live with it every day. I guess the answer is simple. The Luidaeg was born to the marsh and fen, the places where land and sea meet, mate, and destroy one another. She lived there still.

Spike huddled in my lap, watching the landscape and occasionally letting out a small, frightened whine. Judging by its reactions, it knew who we were visiting, and it didn't approve. It doesn't like the Luidaeg. It never has.

"It's all right, Spike," I said. "She's not likely to rip off your head and show it to you." That pleasure was reserved for me.

I slowed as the Luidaeg's building came into view on the left. It was a heap of crumbling brickwork and peeling paint that looked like it was going to collapse any day. I think she's the only tenant—at least, I hope she is. No one should live that way unless it's by choice. I pulled into the first available space. Whimpering, Spike followed me out of the car. I couldn't reassure it. Hell, I couldn't even reassure myself.

The Luidaeg's door was set deep in the shadows, sheltered by a rickety fire escape. The frame was darkened and warped by years of neglect. There were no wards; she didn't need them. Raising one hand, I knocked.

"It's open!"

Great, a self-service portal to hell. Just what I always wanted.

The door swung silently open when I turned the knob; the Luidaeg likes special effects, not clichés. I stepped inside and choked, trying not to gag on the mixed smells of seaweed, mold, and rotting fish. The dark hallway was filled with clutter and half-seen obstacles; a light flickered at the other end, very far away. Spike flattened itself against my ankles before climbing my side to huddle on my shoulder. Giving it what I hoped was a reassuring pat, I began picking my way through the garbage on the floor. Things moved in the darkness near the walls, scuttling and hissing, and I was suddenly glad my night vision isn't as good as my mother's. Spike hissed. I stroked its head with one hand and kept walking.

The Luidaeg was in the kitchen, rummaging through a water-stained cardboard box. Gas lamps filled the room with a shifting, unsettling glow. She looked up as I entered, asking, "Did you look back?"

Sometimes I think the Luidaeg never ends a conversation; she just puts them on hold until you come back into range. "No," I said. "And if you think that was easy at rush hour, you're nuts."

"I never said it would be easy."

"I know." I thought about adding "but I don't understand," and decided against it. I wanted her to help me. Pissing her off would be a bad idea.

She put her hands on her hips, eyeing me. I waited. Never rush anyone who's personally witnessed continental drift.

The Luidaeg doesn't use glamours to make herself look human; she's a natural shapeshifter, and she's as human as she wants to be. Freckles and a peeling tan warred for dominance over her features, and a piece of electrical tape barely held her oily black curls in a rough ponytail. She was wearing stained coveralls and heavy dock boots, leaving her arms and upper chest bare. She could have been in her late teens or early twenties.

There was nothing fae about her, and that was scary as hell. She's Firstborn and incredibly powerful, but she can hide so well I'd never see her coming. There are a lot of things I'd rather face than the Luidaeg on a bad day. Like Godzilla.

"Did Luna tell you what was going on?"

"Some." I found a reasonably clean spot on the counter and leaned against it, trying to ignore the cockroaches scuttling away. "She said Blind Michael was riding because he needed new members for his Hunt."

"Pretty much." She snagged one of the larger roaches and popped it into her mouth. I winced. Swallowing, she continued, "He Rides once a century. Before that happens, he sends his Huntsmen to bring him suitable children. They find the kids, catch them, and bring them to him."

"Why children?"

"Because they're young enough to become his." She shook her head. "He can't have a Hunt without Riders."

"Why haven't we killed him?" I blurted and instantly regretted it. Blind Michael was the Luidaeg's brother; her sisters died at the hands of Titania's children a long time ago, and she's never forgiven Titania's line for their deaths. Considering my own heritage, reminding her that Firstborn can be killed didn't seem like the best possible idea.

She narrowed her eyes, pupils thinning to serpentine slits. "It's been tried. Once it was even tried by my sisters and I—we belong to Maeve, but that doesn't make us monsters. Remember that, child of Oberon: even we can tell the difference."

The Daoine Sidhe are claimed by Titania, not Oberon. This didn't seem like the right time to point that out. "Why didn't it work?"

"Because there are rules, and they weren't followed."

I frowned, reaching up to stroke Spike. It huddled against my neck, whining. "What do you mean?"

"Have you ever *seen* Blind Michael?"

Blind Michael was part of the local landscape. Everyone knew his name, everyone had seen his Hunt riding the Berkeley Hills in search of prey. Smart people kept their distance; if you weren't careful, you might end up on the wrong end of their spears. I'd seen Hunt leaders, and I'd seen Hunters. Had I ever seen their lord? "I don't know. I think so?"

"You haven't. You'd know. Blind Michael doesn't leave his lands, because as long as he stays there the rules protect him, and he's safe. That's why my sisters and I couldn't kill him. You can't hunt him in his own halls, you can't follow him into his own darkness."

"But I've seen his Hunt."

"They ride when the fancy strikes them. He Rides only when there are children to be claimed. He's vulnerable one night out of every hundred years—the odds are against you. No one stops him."

"I will," I said with a confidence I didn't feel.

The Luidaeg shook her head. "This isn't another crazy changeling, Toby. This is *Blind Michael.* He's stronger than I am. I couldn't stop him. What makes you think you can?"

"Nothing," I said, with complete honesty. It pays not to lie to the Luidaeg. She might take offense and rip off one of your limbs. "I'm probably going to die horribly."

"Glad to see you haven't lost your fatalistic outlook on life," she said, clapping her hand down on another cockroach. "It's always been one of your best features. Why bother going if you know you're going to fail?"

"I have to."

"Why?" she asked, popping the roach into her mouth. "It's pointless. If you're that anxious to die, just say the word. It would save us all a *lot* of trouble."

"I don't want to die." That's why I was negotiating with a woman who'd threatened to kill me at various points in the past. Sometimes my life seems devoid of any logic whatsoever.

"Then *why?*"

"I have to," I repeated. "He took two of my best friend's children, and there's a third who won't wake up, no matter what we do, and that doesn't even touch the kids he took from the Court of Cats. I have to try. How could I live with myself if I didn't?"

"I see." Almost gently, she said, "If I help you—and you *need* me to help you—you'll owe me. Can you live with that?"

"Yes."

"Are you sure?"

"Yes, Luidaeg. Three times asked and three times sure." I shook my head. "You want my word, you have it. Now please. Tell me what I need to know."

"Fine." She crossed her arms, leaning against the cutting board. "You have to move fast; he'll have started to change the children, but he hasn't had them long enough to do any permanent damage. Wait too long and you won't save any of them. You'll go tonight, and you'll go alone, and you won't look back. Because the rules say so." Her smile showed the edge of a single scrimshaw fang. "It's the beginning of September. He'll hold them until Halloween night, changing them to suit his whims, and then they'll Ride. It's his way of remembering our mother. Her Rides were always held on Samhain night."

I nodded, feeling the first flickers of hope. "So there's a chance."

"The rules let you try, right here, right now. I don't know if you'll succeed." She yanked open a drawer, digging through it. "The rules require me to warn you, just so you know."

"Warn me?"

"You go alone. You can take any help you find, but you can't ask for it. You fight with what you have and what you're given; neither steal nor buy any weapon of any kind. You can take each road once, and only once, and some roads not even that often. You go *now*. Are you ready?"

"Do I have a choice?"

"Not really. Do you know where you have to go?"

"Blind Michael's lands."

"No." She shook her head. "If that's all you know, you're finished before you start. Stop, think, and ask again." She straightened, a paring knife in one hand. The handle was made of pearl and abalone, and the blade was a curl of silver barely wider than my finger. It looked like it could cut the air.

I kept my eyes on her face, trying to ignore the knife. It wasn't working. "Just once, I wish you'd speak English like a normal person."

"What would be the fun in that? Give me your hand." I blinked, automatically holding out my left hand; she grabbed it, raking the blade across my palm. It cut deep, but there was no pain. Yet.

"Hey!" I yelped, yanking my hand away.

She looked at me impassively. "Give me back your hand."

"No!"

"We can do this the easy way, or we can not do it at all. You can wander the hills looking for Blind Michael and never see him coming . . . or you can give me your hand, and I can give you a road to follow." She shrugged. "It's your call. You owe me either way."

Great. Rock? Meet hard place. I extended my hand, trying not to think about what I was doing. Spike jumped down to the counter where it crouched, rattling its thorns.

The Luidaeg looked at it, amused. "Fierce protector."

"It does its best," I said, watching with sick fascination as the blood started to flow over my palm.

"You'd be surprised at how deep rose thorns can cut. They're pretty, not safe." She wrapped her fingers around my wrist, turning my palm toward the floor. Blood spattered on the dirty linoleum. The Luidaeg dumped a handful of tarnished silver coins into a baby food jar and shoved it under my hand, saying, "Hold this. We only need a little blood."

"Why do we need *any?*" I was trying not to be sick.

I've never liked the sight of my own blood. If I get hurt in the line of duty, I can usually handle it until I'm out of the path of certain doom. Standing in the Luidaeg's kitchen with no visible dangers—except maybe the Luidaeg herself—was forcing me to fight the urge to stick my head between my knees and pass out.

"Because there are no free roads, moron," she said, sorting through the mess on her counter. "You should know that by now." She turned back to me, holding a length of filthy, off-white twine. "You're going to need a map. The blood pays for it; proves you mean it."

"A map *where?*"

"Back in time and just around the corner. You're going to visit my brother, and he's choosy about who he lets through the door. Give me that." She took the jar from my hand. "Silver that's come a long way already, the iron in your blood . . . it's going to have to do. Go ahead and run your hand under the tap, but don't bandage it. The wound's not going with you."

"What are you talking about?" I turned on the faucet, looking dubiously at the cloudy water, and then stuck my hand under it. The cold registered a moment before the pain. I shrieked and jumped back, turning to glare at the Luidaeg.

She shrugged. "I'm the sea witch, remember? Were you expecting fresh water?"

I shouldn't have been, but I was. I'd stopped worrying about the Luidaeg and started thinking only about her brother; that was a mistake. "No," I said, quietly. "I guess not."

"Good girl." She dropped the twine into the jar and screwed the lid on before shaking it. The coins rattled, and the blood sloshed against the glass. I looked away. "Wimp," she chided. I looked around to see her uncap the jar, pouring the contents into a wax mold, and topping them with salt water from the tap.

"What are you doing?" Blood rituals are dangerous. If I was going into one, I wanted to know.

"Making your map." She lifted the mold and shattered it against the kitchen counter, easily catching the candle that fell out of the shards. "Perfect."

I stared.

The candle was a foot long, made of multicolored wax. Swirling streaks of moon white, copper red and pale straw gold mingled together in long, lazy spirals. The wick was a deep, rich brown, like long-dried blood. "What the—"

"There are three ways I could send you to my brother." She turned the candle in her hand, making the colors in the wax seem to dance. "There's the Blood Road—you could take it, but you don't want to. Not if you want a chance to come home alive. There's the Old Road, but even with my help, you couldn't find the door as you are. You're too much of a mongrel."

"What does that leave?" I asked. Spike was still rattling its thorns, growling. It didn't like this. Neither did I.

"The last road." She held up the candle and smiled, almost sadly. "The road you walk by candlelight. It's not going to be easy—it never could be—but you have iron, and you have silver, and you can get there and back if you hurry."

"How do I get started?"

"Did you jump rope when you were a kid?"

I stared at her. "What?"

"Jump rope. Did you stand on the playground jumping over a piece of moving rope and chanting? Cinderella dressed in yellow, Miss Suzy's steamboat?"

"Of course."

"Blind Michael is a child's terror. When you're hunting bogeymen, you look for the nets you need in the stories you've almost forgotten." Her eyes flashed white. "Look where the roses grow. You need to take a walk to my brother's lands. Do you remember the way?"

"I never knew it!"

"Of course you did. You've just forgotten. How many miles to Babylon?"

"What?"

The Luidaeg sighed. "You're not *listening*. How many miles to Babylon?"

The phrase was familiar. I paused, searching for the answer in the half-forgotten memories of the childhood I'd long since left behind, and ventured, "Threescore miles and ten?"

She nodded. "Good. Do you know how to get back again?"

"You can get there and back by a candle's light." I could remember holding hands with Stacy while we jumped and Julie and Kerry turned the rope, certain we'd be young and laughing and friends forever.

"Even better. Are your feet nimble and light? For your sake, they'd better be." She opened the refrigerator, removing a brown glass bottle capped with a piece of plastic wrap and a rubber band. "But there are ways to fake that sort of thing. Here." She held the bottle out to me.

I looked at it dubiously. I could hear the stuff inside it fizzing. "What am I supposed to do with that?"

"Did someone hit you with the stupid stick this morning? You're supposed to drink it."

"Do I have another option?"

"Do you want to come back alive?"

I sighed, reaching for the bottle. "Right." The plastic wrap disintegrated where I touched it. "How much do I need to—"

"The whole thing."

There was no point in arguing. I lifted the bottle, swallowing its contents as fast as I could. It was like drinking mud mixed with battery acid and bile. Gagging, I wrapped my arms around my waist and doubled over. Spike jumped off the counter and bristled at the Luidaeg, howling, but I was too busy trying to make the world stop spinning to care. I didn't want to throw up on the Luidaeg's floor. There was no telling what she'd do with it.

"If you throw up," she said, sharply, "you *will* drink it again."

The reasons not to be sick got better and better. Still gagging, I forced myself to straighten. The Luidaeg nodded, apparently satisfied. Spike kept howling, thorny tail lashing.

"You and me both," I mumbled. My throat felt charred, but the pain in my hand was gone. I glanced down. The wound on my palm was closing. Somehow, that just seemed like the natural progression of events.

"Now," said the Luidaeg. "Come here."

One day I'm going to learn not to listen when she says that.

I stepped forward. She reached out, grabbing my chin and forcing my head up until our eyes met. Her pupils and irises dwindled, filling her eyes from top to bottom with white. I froze, unable to move or look away. She's older than I am, much, much older, and catching me doesn't even challenge her.

She smiled again. The expression wasn't getting any nicer—practice doesn't always make perfect. "How many miles to Babylon?"

I swallowed. "Threescore miles and ten." The air felt thick and cold. I was losing myself in the white of her eyes, and I didn't know whether I'd ever be found.

"Can you get there by candlelight?" She forced the candle into my hand. I clutched it, feeling the blood it was made from singing to me, even though I was barely feeling my own skin. This wasn't good at all, but the further I fell, the less I cared. "Can you, October Daye, daughter of Amandine?"

"Yes, and back again."

"If your feet are nimble and light, you'll get there and back by the candle's light." She leaned down, placing a kiss on each of my cheeks. I blinked at her, puzzled. She was too tall or maybe I was too small, and the world was falling away. "You have a day. Do you understand?"

"Yes," I said. My voice sounded thin and far away, and a pale mist was blurring my vision, leaving only the whiteness of the Luidaeg's eyes. I could still hear Spike howling, but I couldn't see it.

"I hope you do." She tapped the wick with one finger, and it burst into dark blue flame. The light pulled the color out of the world, leaving me alone in a sea of mist. The Luidaeg had vanished with everything else, and the sky above me—sky? When did I go outside?—was endless and infinitely black.

"Luidaeg?" I called.

Her voice chanted from the middle distance, light and faded as a memory or ghost. "How many miles to Babylon? It's threescore miles and ten. Can I get there by candlelight? Aye, and back again. If your feet are nimble and your steps are light, you can get there and back by the candle's light." She paused, voice changing cadences. "Children's games are stronger than you remember once you've grown up and left them behind. They're always fair, and never kind. Remember." Then she was silent, leaving me alone in the seemingly endless mist.

"Luidaeg?" I shouted. I didn't want to be there; more, I didn't want to be there alone.

The candle's flame jumped and surged in time with my panic, a tiny light beating against the darkness. A wave of dizziness hit me, and I staggered, dropping the candle. It hit the ground and rolled several feet, blue flame burning away the mists as it touched them. At least the blood that it contained kept singing to me, keeping me from losing track of its location. I scrambled after it, realizing dimly that I wasn't wearing the dress anymore. Then I reached the candle and curled myself around the light, and wept until the dizziness passed.

NINE

THE WORLD SEEMED TO KEEP SPINNING for the better part of forever. I stayed huddled on the ground, sobs fading into dry coughs. Disorientation actually rates somewhere below all-day court cases and shopping for shoes on my personal scale. You won't catch me on many roller coasters.

I didn't move until I was sure I could stand, and even then, it took a surprisingly long time for my equilibrium to return—I normally bounce back pretty fast, but my body was still reeling from whatever the Luidaeg had done to me. The taste of the Luidaeg's potion coated the inside of my mouth, making it feel like something had died in there. One thing was sure; she wasn't going to be giving Alton Brown a run for his money anytime soon.

The mist was gone, leaving the land around me visible. Looking around, I found myself almost missing the gray.

I was in the middle of a vast plain. Dry, cracked earth stretched out in all directions, studded with jagged rocks and snarls of hostile-looking brambles. Mountains cupped the plain on all sides, looming over the land, and the sky overhead was solid black without a star in sight. Only a few thin clouds broke the darkness, shoved along by a wind I couldn't feel. The air on the ground was chilly but motionless.

Shivering, I wrapped my arms around myself. I don't normally mind the dark. The fae aren't fond of the sun, and the Summerlands exist in a state of near perpetual twilight. There are always shadows in Faerie. It's just that they're normally warm, open shadows, the kind that create a welcoming sort of darkness. This wasn't a warm night. It was a night for endings, and for monsters.

There was something wrong with the perspective. The problem didn't seem to be with the land around me, hostile as it seemed—it looked entirely proper when I didn't try to think too hard about what I was seeing. There was something wrong with the way I was looking at things, like I was somehow out of proportion with the landscape. Something—

The candle blazed abruptly upward, forcing me to flinch to keep from setting my hair on fire. I wound up holding it at arm's length, watching the blue flame burn higher and higher. The Luidaeg said the candle was my map; if it burned out, I might have problems a little more pressing than my slightly warped perspective. I tried blowing on it and shaking it, but there was no change. Finally, desperately, I said, "All right! I won't think about it! Okay?"

The flame immediately dwindled to an ember. Whatever was wrong, the Luidaeg—or at least her candle—didn't want me thinking about it. I glared at the candle. I hate riddles, and I hate them even more when I'm forced to play along. I've always preferred the direct method: hit the riddler upside the head until he gives you the answer. Maybe it's more likely to get you hurt, but it's also a lot less confusing. Still, if they wanted me to play, I'd play. It wasn't like I had a choice.

I turned in a slow circle, studying the landscape. A forest stretched off toward the mountains some distance behind me, made up of the sort of tall, gnarled trees that act as a natural barrier against the world. It managed to look even less welcoming than the plains, and that meant it was probably where I needed to go. Sometimes dealing with fairy-tale clichés is even more annoying than dealing with fae manners. If I ever meet any descendants of the Brothers Grimm, I'm going to break their noses and possibly a few other convenient body parts.

Maybe I had to play along with this stupid scenario, but that didn't mean I had to like it. "I am so tired of this gothic crap," I muttered. "Just once, I want to meet the villain in a cheerful, brightly lit room. Possibly one with kittens."

Blind Michael's lands seemed unlikely to supply me with anything resembling an airy sitting room, and any cats I encountered would probably be of the four-hundred-pound, man-eating variety. I was willing to bet that a cat the size of a Sherman tank would bother even Tybalt. I shook my head, trying to make the image go away. Blind Michael's realm was obviously in the Summerlands. It was probably an Islet, a bubble of space anchored between the Summerlands and one of the deeper, lost realms. Reality is malleable in the Islets. You can't change it with a casual thought, but fears and phobias have a distressing tendency to come to life. If Blind Michael didn't have giant attack-cats, I didn't want to be the one who gave them to him.

The feeling of wrongness was still clamoring in the back of my mind. I didn't know why, and the Luidaeg's spell obviously didn't want me to. I took a deep, slow breath. She didn't do freebies. Whatever she'd done, it was probably intended to keep me alive, and if that hinged on not understanding, I could play dumb for a little while.

At least her spell had been kind enough to trade my cut-down dress for jeans and a bulky green sweater. It made a certain sense; she wanted me to get back alive, and jeans were more useful than a skirt while crossing the wasteland. A thin leather strap secured my knife to the belt, and a similar leather strap was holding my hair away from my face. If I screwed up, it wouldn't be due to interference from my wardrobe.

Finally, lacking any better options, I started for the forest.

The plains were wider than they looked. I had barely covered half the distance to the trees when my legs informed me that I needed to take a break, now, and that if I didn't find something to sit on, they'd be fine with dumping me on my ass. Choosing rest over close contact with the treacherous surface of the plain, I walked to the nearest rock and sat. My candle was burning steadily. That was good. The spell that brought me to Blind Michael's lands was tied to the candle, and I probably wouldn't survive for long if the candle went out. If I was lucky, losing it would kill me quickly. If I wasn't . . .

The Luidaeg called Blind Michael a child's terror. He wasn't likely to be happy with an adult intrusion into his lands. "Great," I muttered. "Damned if you do, damned if you don't." It helped to hear my own voice, but something was wrong with it. I stood, trying to make sense of the conflicting messages my senses were delivering. The candle blazed again, illuminating the land around me as the Luidaeg whispered on the edge of my hearing, *Don't think about it, don't stop, just keep moving keep on keep going keep—*

Hunting horns blared in the distance as the flame turned orange and dwindled to a pinprick. I took a step backward, confusion forgotten in the face of panic. I knew what those horns meant; there was only one thing they *could* mean. Blind Michael's Hunt was riding.

Taking another step back, I started to run.

My breath was harsh and loud as I ran, but nowhere near as loud as the horns sounding on the other side of the horizon. They were coming and there was nothing I could do to stop them. A thought struck me as the horns sounded again, a thought that seemed almost brilliant in its clarity. If I stopped, they might listen to reason. They'd take me to Blind Michael, and he'd understand;

he'd return my children without complaint. He was a good man at heart. He—

The candle flared, splashing wax down the length of my arm. The pain was stunning, knocking me out of a haze I hadn't even felt coming down. The bastards were blowing enchanted horns. Of course they wouldn't listen! Blind Michael's Hunt has never had a reputation for mercy. I'd die if I stopped. I might die anyway, but at least if I ran, I had a chance.

Even without their suggestive power, the horns were getting louder. I wasn't going to reach the forest before the Hunt reached me. Still running, I started scanning for a place that I could hide.

There was a tangle of brambles up ahead that looked promising. I ran toward it, grimacing as I saw the length of the thorns. They didn't look like pleasant bedmates. I was considering looking for another place to hide when the horns sounded again, closer now than ever. Right. Gritting my teeth, I dropped to my knees and began squirming into the shelter of the thorns.

I stopped once there was a concealing wall of brambles between myself and the plains, tucking my candle down behind my knees to hide its light. I could hear hooves pounding the earth as well as the trumpet of the horns; they were getting closer. I scooted backward, heedless of the thorns. A little blood was a small price to pay for staying alive.

Holding my breath, I waited for the Hunters.

They didn't appear. A girl ran into view instead, crying as she raced for the woods. Her dress hung in bloody tatters, and more blood matted her curly brown hair. I opened my mouth slightly, breathing in the balance of her heritage. Hob half-blood, probably no more than fourteen. She was barefoot, but she ran over the stony ground without stopping. Something worse than death was following her, and she knew it. She was clutching a half-grown Abyssinian cat against her chest. A thin haze of magic surrounded the cat, rebounding randomly off the shadows around them and shattering them without doing anything productive. Cait Sidhe almost certainly; they specialize in moving through shadows, opening portals to take them from here to there. But the shadows here were Blind Michael's, and the poor kid wasn't getting a foothold.

The girl closed her eyes, finding a last burst of terrified speed as the horns sounded again. The cat in her arms went still, eyes fixed on the forest's edge. The Cait Sidhe tend to be realists, and that cat knew as well as I did that they'd never get there in time. I stayed where I was, biting my lip. I wanted to tell them to hide while they had the chance, and I couldn't. The Riders were too close. There was nothing I could do but watch, and remember, and take whatever I saw home to tell their parents.

Whatever happened would be my responsibility, because I didn't save them. Sometimes doing nothing is the hardest thing of all.

The horns sounded a final time, and Blind Michael's Hunt poured over the hill. There were at least a dozen of them, dressed in mismatched armor and mounted on vast horses whose hooves ripped the earth as they ran. They looked like they'd been snatched from different armies and thrown together by an indifferent general, one who only cared that his soldiers be menacing. Their weapons were as mixed as their armor, but that didn't matter; all that mattered was that each of them was well-equipped to kill.

The girl must have heard them, because she did something that surprised me so much that I nearly threw myself out of the bushes to shield her: no one that brave should have to die. She tripped and fell in what was obviously a staged maneuver, "accidentally" flinging the Cait Sidhe away. It twisted in midair, landing a few feet from my hiding place.

That was my chance. Praying I wouldn't be seen, I scooted forward and snatched the cat, yanking it back into the brambles. It writhed, sinking its teeth into my arm. I've lived with cats for a long time. I didn't scream or let go, but shifted my grip to the scruff of its neck, giving it a solid shake before whispering, "Tybalt sent me." It stopped struggling. Trusting it not to attack, I gathered it against my chest and turned back to the scene outside.

The Hunters hadn't noticed me. I wasn't counting on that to last once they realized the Cait Sidhe was missing, but for the moment, they were focused on the girl. Weapons drawn, they formed a circle around her. She didn't even try to rise as the nearest Huntsman prodded her with his spear, saying something I couldn't make out. The kitten understood, because it flattened its ears, growling almost silently. Two more Riders dismounted, picking her up and sliding her onto the back of the nearest horse. A Rider mounted behind her, turning the horse back the way they'd come. Through it all, she never made a sound.

The other Riders stayed behind, fanning out in an obvious search pattern. I held my breath, but none of them approached our hiding place. They circled farther and farther away, looking behind stones and through the sparse underbrush. I clutched the kitten to my chest, trying to come up with a way out. The forest was less than a hundred yards ahead of us. If the Riders went far enough, we'd have a chance.

In the end, we didn't need it. The horns began to sound, and the remaining Riders turned as one, galloping out of sight. The sound of hooves faded before the horns did, but eventually even they were gone. I pulled out my candle and was reassured to see that the flame had gone back to a steady blue, flickering upward. I relaxed, assuming that meant we were as close to safe as we were likely to get.

The cat squirmed loose and ran to the edge of the briar, where it stopped and eyed me suspiciously. I didn't try to stop it. If it wanted to run away, it could take care of itself. "Go ahead," I said. It flattened its ears and hissed. I sighed. "Okay, whatever."

Bracing my elbows in the dirt, I crab-walked my way back into the open and stood, holding up the candle and beginning to pick thorns out of my knees with my free hand. The cat crept out after me. I watched it out of the corner of my eye while continuing to remove the thorns from my jeans.

After sniffing warily at the ground, the cat stretched and reared up onto its hind legs. The air crackled with the smell of pepper and burning paper, and the cat was gone, replaced by a gangly teenage boy with bruises covering the left side of his face. He looked like a small fourteen, dark-skinned, with glass green eyes and hair that was the same russet red as his fur. His pupils were thin black slits, and his ears were more feline than human, tipped with fringes of black fur. Cait Sidhe pure-blood. "Who are you?" he demanded.

"October Daye," I said, tucking the thorns I'd collected into my pocket. You never know what you might need later. "Yourself?"

He narrowed his eyes, looking at me disdainfully. I recognized that look; I got it from Tybalt all the time. "My name is Raj. I am—"

"You're the local Prince of Cats," I said, cutting him off. "Yeah, I know."

He wasn't expecting that. His eyes widened, wariness returning. "How did you know?"

I sighed. I didn't have the heart to tease him—not after seeing his companion taken. "Like I said, Tybalt sent me. He's . . ." How could I describe my relationship with the King of Cats? I finally settled for saying, "A friend of mine."

Raj frowned, eyes narrowing again. "That's not possible."

I frowned back. I was too tired to put up with adolescent royalty. "So we're not *friends* as much as we're enemies who haven't killed each other yet. Does it matter? He sent me to save you."

"You? Save *us?*" He laughed bitterly. No child should ever laugh like that. "Come back when you're older."

"What?" The disorientation rushed back, trying to keep me from putting the pieces together. Unfortunately, ignorance was becoming a luxury I couldn't afford. Fighting the impulse to ignore what Raj had said, I looked down, already nearly sure of what I'd see.

Just once, it would be nice to be surprised.

Most people know the shape of their own body. They may have little illusions about it—how thin they are, how fat, how good they look in that black velvet dress—but the essential topography is ingrained. The length of a hand, the texture of skin, the slope of a breast; it's all there, and when it changes, it usually does it slowly enough that your mental map changes with it. I've lived with myself for a long time now, and the years I spent as a fish just made me more aware of the shape I'm supposed to be. I lost myself once, and that made me pay a lot more attention when I got myself *back*.

The body I was wearing wasn't mine—or rather, it wasn't mine anymore and hadn't been for a very long time. I'd been whittled down, curves smoothed away. I turned to the hand that held the candle, finally really looking at it. The fingers were too short, and the nails were too broad. Not an adult's hands. Reaching up, I felt the outlines of my face, still round with the remains of baby fat, and pulled the band from my hair. The strands that promptly fell across my eyes were an indeterminate ashy blonde, the color my hair had been until the time I was about twelve. Putting what I could see and feel together, I'd have guessed my age at somewhere between eight and ten, probably on the higher end of the scale. It was hard to tell. Changelings age oddly; I was a child for a long time.

Raj's eyes remained narrowed as he watched my slow self-examination. He was frightened but hiding it well; I hoped my own fear was as well concealed. I doubted it.

"Oberon's *balls*," I muttered, and flinched from the sound of my own thin, too-high voice. How did I miss that before? Easy: the Luidaeg made me. "Luidaeg, what did you *do?*" The answer to that was pretty easy, too. I just didn't want to think about it.

Blind Michael was a child's terror. The Luidaeg said

that there were three ways to reach him, that one would kill me and that one was hidden ... but the third way had to be open to children of all races and types, or he wouldn't be able to take them. She'd done what I asked. She'd found a way to get me into Blind Michael's lands. It just didn't come with full disclosure.

Silently, I resolved to kick her ass after I got home and she'd given me back my real body. Assuming I made it home in the first place.

Raj's eyes widened and he looked around wildly, like he expected the Luidaeg to appear and make things worse than they already were. "Why are you calling *her?*" The royalty was gone; suddenly, he was just a frightened teenage boy with no way home.

"Because she's the one who did this to me. I think she thought she was helping. 'You can get there and back by the light of a candle.'" I kept talking, too angry to stop. "Why don't people ever say things the way they mean them? 'You can get there, but if you lose that candle you're screwed, and by the way, you're going to have to be nine. Hope that's not a problem.'"

"What?"

"Hang on ... sorry." I sighed, forcing myself to calm down. "Let's try this again. Tybalt really did send me. I'm here to rescue you. The Luidaeg turned me into a kid so I could get on the road, but if you'll just trust me, I—"

He stared at me. "You're insane! You're working for *Him!*" It was clear from his tone of voice that he wasn't talking about Tybalt.

"No, I'm not! It's just that—"

"They took Helen, and you didn't stop them!" His voice was getting louder. I glanced around, wondering how far sound carried on the plains. "You're already His! You want to take me back! Well you can't! I won't go!" He turned toward the forest and took off running.

"Raj, wait!" I bolted after him, and I might have caught him—panic is a great motivation—but he had an advantage I didn't. The air shimmered around him, and

I was suddenly chasing a half-grown Abyssinian. Four feet are more stable than two and faster over short distances. His lead was increasing rapidly.

And far behind us, the hunting horns began to sound.

Raj reached the edge of the wood and leaped, vanishing into the trees. I followed him without a pause. Better the forest than the Hunt. The day had started badly and kept getting worse, and now here I was, nine years old and alone in a dark forest with Huntsmen on one side and the unknown on the other, and nothing but a candle to light my way.

Some days it really doesn't pay to get out of bed.

TEN

BRANCHES SNATCHED AT MY HAIR as the trees closed around me, blocking my view of the plains. I ducked away from them, walking deeper into the wood. It didn't seem like the smart choice—going deeper into the dark, foreboding forest so rarely is—but if I'd wanted the smart choice, I wouldn't have come to Blind Michael's lands in the first place. At least my fae blood gives me pretty good night vision—between that and the glow of my candle, I was able to see well enough not to fall. The candle's flame was burning a steady blue, which I chose to interpret as a good thing. It turned orange when the Hunt was nearby, and if I was lucky, it might keep acting as an early warning system. Frankly, I needed the help.

I continued to pick my way through the trees, trying to avoid the rocks and trailing roots that turned the already uneven ground into a maze of obstacles. Branches kept snarling in my hair, pulling me to sudden, unexpected stops, and my patience was running out. I was bruised, scratched, and frightened, and in an incredibly bad mood to boot. I was also no closer to my goal. The Hunt came from the mountains and rode back the same way. I didn't know where the boundaries of Blind Michael's lands were drawn, but the geography seemed to be at least semilinear. I wouldn't find the kids by walking away from them.

The forest was far from silent. Owls hooted in the distance, and small creatures rustled through the underbrush, rattling the leaves. The faint chorus almost made me feel better—you're not likely to find many monsters in a place where there's still wildlife. Of course, that could just mean nothing in this forest was harmless, but I was trying not to think about that. Vampire bunnies did *not* appeal. It seemed to be getting darker as I walked, the glow of my candle nearly vanishing into the shadows. The sounds around me faded out as well, getting softer and softer until they were gone. I didn't like that at all. If King Kong came bursting out of the bushes, I was going to be pissed. Swallowing hard, I continued to walk.

No giant apes appeared. Instead, the trees opened up into a clearing. I stopped, leaning forward as I tried to catch my breath. I'd forgotten how much longer distances were to a child. My legs hurt, my knees hurt, and all I wanted was the chance to curl up somewhere and sleep it off. And there was no way in hell that was going to happen.

Something snapped in the brush. I straightened, eyes flicking automatically to my candle, which was still burning a serene blue. That might mean I wasn't in danger, but it could also mean the spell only reacted to Blind Michael's Hunters, and I didn't want to take that chance. Whirling, I darted across the clearing to a hollow, half-rotten tree, dropped to my knees, and squirmed inside. It was surprisingly easy to wedge myself there; I'd forgotten how small I was. Then I waited, half holding my breath, to see what would happen next.

The snap was repeated, followed by rustling that continued for several minutes. I stayed frozen in my hiding place, managing not to scream as a figure stepped out of the trees directly ahead of me. My candle was still burning blue. Swell. Either whoever it was wasn't a danger, or I couldn't count on the candle to act as an early warning system. Watching whoever it was approach, I didn't have a clue which it was.

The figure was thin and hooded, its outline obscured by an ankle-length cloak. It held a lantern in one hand; the light filled the clearing with a dim white glow. It drifted to a stop, raising the lantern to head height. One hand was lifted in a beckoning gesture. A branch swung toward it, stopping as it brushed the outstretched fingers.

"Ah," the figure said, in a voice as soft and dry as dead leaves on the wind. Despite the rustling thinness of the voice, I could tell it was female. "I see." She lowered her hand, rubbing her fingers together. "We have a visitor."

Oh, oak and ash. I scrambled farther into my hiding place, cupping one hand around the candle to block the light. It burned my fingers, and I still wasn't sure she couldn't see it.

"Come out," she called. She turned in a slow circle, pulling back her hood. "This is my wood. Come out and let me see you." Lantern light fell over her face as she moved, bringing her into harsh visibility.

Her skin was daffodil yellow. Tendrils of brown and gold hair snaked around her cheeks, so matted and snarled that they looked almost like thin tree roots. They writhed constantly, twisting themselves into knots and curls. Her eyes were long and narrow and the color of brass from end to end; her pupils were thin silver lines visibly contracted against the light, like a cat's, or a serpent's. I'd never seen anything like her.

I shivered, wishing the Luidaeg was there. She'd have known what to do. There was something painfully ironic about that desire; I wasn't a child, but I looked like one, and I was wishing for the sea witch to come and save me.

The woman frowned, eyes narrowing as I failed to appear. "I know you can hear me; the trees felt you pass. They can't tell me where you are, but they know you're here. Come out before you make me angry." Her features were generous and well-formed, with a nose that was a little sharp and a lower lip that was a bit too large. Still, she was pretty, or had been once—a heavy scar ran from just under her left eye to her chin, pulling the side of her mouth into a permanently puckered scowl. There's only one thing that can scar a pureblood like that. Iron.

And she *was* a pureblood. I could taste the purity of her blood like fire on my tongue, almost hot enough to actually burn. Whatever she was, it was strong. Strong enough that she might be Firstborn. The Luidaeg is the only Firstborn I've ever dealt with on a regular basis, and her power is subtle, damped down until she can seem human to the casual observer. This woman's power wasn't hidden at all. It blazed all around her, seeming brighter than the lantern light. And something had been fast enough and strong enough to run a scar down her face. Whatever it was, I hoped it wasn't in the forest with us.

I stayed huddled in the dubious safety of my hiding place, shivering harder. My heart seemed impossibly loud to my terrified ears, and for an illogical moment, I was afraid it would lead her to me. It was so loud. How could she miss it?

She lowered the lantern, frown deepening. "My name is Acacia, and these are my woods," she said. "If you seek Blind Michael, go toward the mountains; if you seek me, come out now. If you seek neither of us, go home by whatever road you choose. But do not hide from me in my own places, or it will not go well for you, no matter what your quest may be." She paused, waiting. I didn't speak. "Very well. Never say you had no choice."

The branches bent to allow her passage as she turned and walked out of the clearing, her cloak billowing behind her. I've seen Luna get similar treatment from her roses, but never on such a grand scale; this woman seemed to be in command of the entire forest.

I stayed where I was for what felt like an eternity, listening to the silence. Her footsteps had faded; she was gone. At least I hoped she was—she could be lurking in the underbrush, waiting for me to come out. Why hadn't she seen me? The forest obviously obeyed her, and my candle wasn't that well hidden. If she was in control of the trees, they should have led her straight to me. So why hadn't they?

The sounds of the forest slowly returned, and I started to breathe again. Uncurling cautiously, I stuck my head out of the hollow tree and looked around the empty clearing. If I ran, I might make it back to the plains before she found me. The threat of the Hunters had dimmed before the threat of the forest. They would just take me to Blind Michael. This woman might do anything.

Something brushed against my shoulder. I flinched, somehow managing not to scream. When I made it home—*if* I made it home—I was going to allow myself the luxury of a long, unhurried panic attack, but this wasn't the time. Taking a deep breath, I asked, "Who's there?"

For once, luck was with me. An anxious, familiar voice answered, "It's Raj. I . . . the forest is very dark."

"Yes. It is." I looked to the right and saw Raj crouched beside my tree, making himself as small as he possibly could. "How did you get away from Acacia?"

"The yellow woman?" He snorted, arrogance returning as he said, "She asked the trees about invaders, but not about animals, so they didn't tell her. Trees aren't very smart."

"Clever." I meant it. When I was fourteen, I thought trees were things to climb, not things you could trick. "Why did you come back?"

"Because of her." I looked at him blankly, and he said, "She was looking for you. I don't think she'd have been looking for you if you worked for Him." He paused. There was no trust in his eyes, but there was something else: the first flickers of hope. "Are you really the October my Uncle Tybalt knows?"

I sighed. "Yeah. That's me."

Raj frowned. "My father says Uncle Tybalt's friend October is an adult." He paused. "And a hussy."

"I usually am. An adult, not a hussy." Hussy? What the hell was Tybalt telling his Court? The King of Cats and I were going to have a long talk when I got my own body back.

"But you're younger than I am!"

"Courtesy of the Luidaeg," I said. Raj flinched at her name. More quietly, I said, "Your uncle asked me to get you and the others out of here, and the Luidaeg put a spell on me to make it possible."

"You let the sea witch cast a spell on you?" The wariness vanished, crowded out by awe and fear. "And you survived?"

"She'll kill me eventually, but not today. Today I'm going to get you out."

"How?"

Good question. We were crouched in the middle of an enchanted forest with nothing but a hollow tree for cover, and I still had no idea where the other kids were. For that matter, I didn't know how I was going to get them out when we found them. All I had was a knife that was too big for my hands, a candle I didn't dare to put down, and a half-grown Cait Sidhe who kept fluxing between terrified and arrogant. There have been times when I had to work with less, but root and branch, you can only count on a miracle so many times before reality puts its foot down.

Not that there was anything else I could do. It was time to roll the dice against that miracle one more time.

"You were running from the Huntsmen before," I said. "How did you get away?"

"It was Helen," he said, sounding ashamed. Of course he was ashamed—no teenage boy wants to admit that he was saved by a girl. "She found a way out of the room we were locked in. None of the others would follow her. But I . . ."

"You thought it might be worth trying."

"I thought I could find the trail they brought us in by." He looked away. "I thought I could get us out, and Uncle Tybalt would come, and we'd destroy them."

"How far did you get?" I asked. I hated to do it; his posture told me he was on the brink of tears, and pushing him over that edge might make him useless. I didn't really have a choice. I needed to know whether I had any hope of saving the others.

"A long way," he whispered. I waited, but he didn't say anything else. He just huddled, ears pressed flat, shaking.

Right. I rose, offering him my hand. "Come on. We're going now."

"Where?"

"Away from here." I didn't know how I'd get him out without going through Blind Michael, but that could wait. He needed to be moving more than I needed to have a plan.

He looked at me warily, then slid his hand over mine, covering it to the wrist. The reality of what the Luidaeg had done was sinking in. How was I supposed to save the kids and defeat Blind Michael when I was just a kid myself? Raj was watching me with an anxious sort of trust. I sighed. Whether I stood a chance or not, I had to try. I hate being the last resort.

It took us longer to fight our way out of the woods than it had taken to enter; the branches snagged at our clothes, and the roots tangled around our feet until it seemed like the trees were actively working against us. But the candle was steady and blue, and I found that if I watched the flame rather than the landscape, I could walk without stumbling.

"You can get there and back by the candle's light," I murmured.

"What?" said Raj.

"Nothing. Just a rhyme." A thin, steady light in the distance marked the edge of the trees. "It looks like we're almost out."

Raj tightened his grip on my hand, clinging to me like I was his only connection with home. Maybe I was; he didn't exactly have any better options. "What comes next?"

"I don't know." I gave him what I hoped was a reassuring look. "I won't leave you."

I hate it when I lie by accident.

We stepped into the open, turning toward the mountains, and started to walk. Eventually, Raj let go of my hand, choosing to walk a foot or so ahead of me. Nothing disturbed us as we walked out across the plains, outside the range of any reasonable cover. There was nowhere left to hide when the flame of my candle suddenly flared upward, burning a bright, furious orange.

And the Huntsmen came. They boiled up out of the ground, surrounding us in an instant. There was no time to run and nowhere to run *to;* all we could do was stand our ground and wait to be taken. Their attention was fixed on Raj, but I didn't expect that to last. I reached out and grabbed for his shoulder, even though I didn't know what good it would do. It was instinctive. I suppose what happened next was instinctive, too. Cornered tigers will fight, after all.

Raj lunged for the nearest Huntsman, shifting into feline form in midair and going for the eyes. He was making himself a distraction. I had to admire the effort, even as I started after him, screaming, "Raj, no!"

Whatever illusion was protecting me wasn't strong enough to hide me from my own stupidity. The nearest Huntsmen turned toward my voice, eyes wide and startled, like they were seeing me for the first time. The one Raj was lunging for swatted him away. He fell without a sound, landing in an unmoving heap as the others closed in on me, weapons drawn.

I was so busy watching their weapons that I never saw the one who hit me. There was a sudden, sharp pain in the back of my head, and I was falling again, back into mist and candlelit darkness. And there was nothing.

ELEVEN

I AWOKE FACEDOWN in the middle of a marble floor that had been white once, before it was buried under years of mud and gore. My head was throbbing in time to an unseen samba band. I took a brief mental census, confirming that my aching head was still attached to the rest of me before pushing myself upright.

I could feel the blood the Luidaeg used to make my candle even before I realized that my fingers were still wrapped tightly around it. The flame blazed up as soon as I looked at it, growing until it was a foot high and burning brilliant red. That couldn't be good. Raj was nowhere in sight. That could have meant he'd managed to escape the Hunt, but I didn't think so. There was probably some ceremony he'd already gone through that I still needed to undergo in my new role as one of Blind Michael's captive children. There are always ceremonies in Faerie, even in the parts that we'd rather ignore.

The room I was in was probably a ballroom before it became a prison. The walls had been shattered about ten feet up, and the roof was entirely gone. Brambles boiled over the walls on three sides, obscuring all the doors. Tattered tapestries hung between the loops of briar, their patterns worn away by dirt and time. The sky had grown even darker while I was unconscious, but there were still no stars. No stars at all.

Shadows too dark for changeling eyes to pierce pooled at the base of the walls, and I could hear giggling and rustling noises coming from inside them. That wasn't promising. I've learned to never trust the laughing ones; they're either insane or genuinely glad to see people frightened and in pain, and either way, they're likely to cause problems.

I stood, trying to ignore the shivering weakness in my knees. The Rider that knocked me out had obviously done it before, because I wasn't dead—it takes skill to knock someone out from behind without smashing their skull. If I was lucky, the pain would pass before I needed to run. I seemed to be counting on luck an awful lot.

It took a moment to be sure I wasn't going to fall down. When I was confident my balance would hold I called, "All right, I know you're there. Now come out where I can see you." My words almost echoed Acacia's, and that coaxed a small, wry smile from my lips, even as I wondered whether May knew where to find me. What good is a Fetch if she isn't there when it's time to die?

My voice echoed against the walls. As the echoes faded, the children came creeping into the open. At first they came in little groups—two and three at a time, staying tight and close together—but the groups grew larger as they got bolder, until they were approaching in clusters of five and six and even eight. They ranged from toddlers to teenagers on the edge of adulthood, and there were a lot of them, moving too quickly for me to count. I froze, watching them. They were wrong. The children were . . .

The children were wrong. It was hard to tell their breeds or make my eyes define what I was seeing. Some of them were easy to identify—he was Daoine Sidhe, she was a Bannick, he was a Barrow Wight—but subtly changed, until they looked more like parodies of their races than actual fae. Others were strangely blurred and blended, twisted into strange mockeries of what they should have been. Pointed ears and cat-slit eyes, scales and fur, wings and long, thrashing tails were combined without any visible logic, creating things that were entirely new, and entirely wrong.

There was a Tuatha de Dannan, perfect and unaltered, except for the streaky brown feathers that turned his arms into ragged wings. Behind him was a Centaur with the hindquarters of a small Dragon. He had iridescent green scales in place of fur, and his hooves were more like talons. A Piskie with webbed hands and legs that tapered to fins straddled his back, her snarled hair tied out of her eyes with a strip of dirty linen.

I opened my mouth to test out their bloodlines, and gagged on the impossible mixture that hit the back of my throat. Their blood might remember how they started, if I had the time to taste them out one at a time, but in a group, they were smothering. He hadn't just changed them on the outside. He'd changed them all the way down to the bone.

Faerie has her citizens and her monsters, and sometimes the two are the same, but it's by design, not accident or malicious alteration. We are what we were meant to be, and every race has a role to play. The Daoine Sidhe are beautiful and fickle and so tied to blood that our hands are never clean. The Tuatha de Dannan bridge the gaps between our varied lands, gatekeepers and guardians. The night-haunts may be monsters, but they perform a service the rest of us can never repay; they eat our dead and keep us hidden. We do our jobs.

Even the Firstborn, unique as they all are, have a role to play. They give us legends and night terrors; they give us things to aspire to and avoid, and without them, Faerie would lack focus. There would be nothing for the heroes to hunt for or the villains to aspire to become. We need them as much as we need each other. But these children had no purpose anymore. The things they'd become were nothing natural, even on the strange shores of Faerie. It didn't matter how it had been done, or why; all that mattered was that it was too late to save them.

All I could do was hope the children I'd been sent to save weren't already among them.

"New girl," said a Urisk with long antennae growing in front of his stubbed and broken horns. He was wrapped in a stained muslin sheet, toga-style, with slits cut for his gauzy locust's wings. The hair on his goatish legs was sparse and matted.

"New girl," said the Centaur. The Piskie on his back smiled, baring a mouthful of unnaturally angled fangs.

"New girl," she said.

The others took up the cry, whispering, "New girl, new girl," as they crept closer. I stood my ground, fingers clenched white-knuckled around my candle. Luna warned me about Blind Michael's children, telling me to beware and be wary, but I couldn't. I couldn't be afraid of them. I could pity them, and I knew better than to trust them, but I couldn't fear them.

The Piskie reached out and tweaked a strand of my hair, twisting it between heavily webbed fingers. Her expression was politely fascinated; she was probably somewhere near ten years old. "Human blood," she said finally, and yanked, hard.

I jerked away, clapping my free hand against my scalp. "Hey! That hurt!"

She ignored me, laughing as she held up the strands of hair she'd stolen. "Rider or ridden?" she demanded. "How strong?"

This seemed to be a great question, and an even better game. The children began to skip in a circle around me, chanting, "Rider or ridden, Rider or ridden," over and over. They stressed the second syllable of each word, making it a singsong rhythm that clashed with the pounding in my head. I was uncomfortably aware that at least half of them were bigger than I was, and that the ones who weren't either came paired with larger friends or had some sort of natural weaponry. All I could think of was the Jabberwock, with its claws that catch and teeth that bite. Me, I had my knife and my candle, and that was it.

The flame was burning higher and higher, and it seemed to be doing some good—only the Piskie had touched me. The circle they'd formed around me would draw in close and then spread out again, like the children were trying to stay out of the candlelight. I waited for the circle to close again and then thrust the candle out at arm's length to test my theory. The nearest of the children shied back, nearly breaking the line.

"How many miles to Babylon?" I asked, half whimsically. The entire circle staggered back, so fast that some of the smaller children fell. The youngest I could see was a tiny Roane with raw-looking gills fluttering in the sides of his neck. He looked like he couldn't have been more than three years old when he was taken. Oberon only knew how long ago that was; the Roane have been all but extinct for centuries. Oak and ash, how many lives had this man destroyed? Why hadn't anyone stopped him?

There'd be time for hatred later. Right now, getting out was what mattered. I took a step forward. "Don't you remember the answer? It's threescore miles and ten." The children moved back again. One of them hissed. "Can I get there by a candle's light? Oh yes, and back again." I was passing them, and they weren't stopping me in their haste to get away from the light. All of them were fleeing now, all but that little Roane boy who couldn't seem to get back to his feet.

Pausing, I offered him my free hand, heedless of the danger. It wasn't his fault. None of them had chosen this. He raised his head and looked at me, eyes wide and empty. I jerked away instinctively just before he lunged, leaving his razor-sharp teeth to close on empty air. They opened a wide gash in his upper lip, and it began oozing blood that was practically black.

That would teach me not to reach out to the monsters. I stepped backward, holding up my candle like a shield. "If your feet are nimble and your heart is light, you can get there and back by the candle's light," I said, as fast as I could. "How many miles to Babylon? It's threescore miles and ten—" I kept chanting, backing toward the wall.

The children were slinking back into a group, watching me with angry, empty eyes. It's always nice to feel loved. I kept backing up, chanting the rhyme over and over until my shoulders hit the wall. I glanced from side to side. There were no doors. No way out.

Emboldened by my sudden stop, the group of children began creeping closer. They surrounded me in a loose semicircle, stopping well out of reach. The Piskie looked at me, saying, "Oh, you won't go." She seemed to be the unofficial spokesperson for the group. Most of the others didn't say anything more complex than "new girl" without being prompted. "There's no leaving before it's time."

"I see," I said, not moving. "That's good to know."

"Good and bad don't matter—there's no point in running. Rider or ridden, it's not your decision, and if it's the second, to the stables you'll go. If the first, you'll join our company . . . for a time." There was no softness in her smile. "Making enemies of the only friends you'll find here isn't wise."

"Maybe she wants enemies," said the Centaur.

"No one smart wants enemies," replied the Piskie.

Considering that I'd voluntarily entered Blind Michael's lands, I wasn't sure I qualified as smart. "What happens now?" I asked, keeping my voice steady. They were avoiding the candlelight, but candles can't last forever. Eventually, the wax would burn down, and they'd take me.

"Now we wait," said the Piskie.

"We wait for Him," added the Urisk, in a hiss.

"He'll come."

"Because you're here."

"New girl."

"New blood."

"Rider or ridden."

"And maybe he'll take one of us when he takes you."

"To the Ride—"

"—the Hunt—"

"—to where the darkness waits—"

"He'll take us home." This last was from the Roane, who popped his thumb into his mouth as he finished speaking. His fangs fit neatly around it, barely grazing the skin, although the blood from where he'd bitten his own lip made that difficult to see.

"How long have you all been here?" I asked, keeping my shoulders pressed against the wall. I'd been distracted by their seeming innocence once, and I wasn't going to risk doing it again. In this place, innocence could kill.

The answers came from all around, called out too quickly for me to see who made each one. "A long time."

"Long time."

"Many new children."

"I was new once."

"We were all new once."

The Piskie hugged herself, saying, "Sometimes He comes and picks one of us, even when there aren't any new ones. He takes us away to join Him, and we never come back here again."

"Where is here?" Children like to talk—even monster children. If I could keep them talking, they might tell me something I needed to know.

"Home," said a voice from the back of the crowd. The Piskie scowled over her shoulder before looking toward me again, eyes narrowed.

"The Children's Hall," she said. "It's where we wait. You'll wait, too, if you're a Rider."

"And if I'm not?" I was certain I wouldn't like the answer.

"If you're not a Rider, you're ridden," said the Centaur, smiling thinly. "You won't come back here, if you're ridden. You'll go to the stables, and do your waiting there."

That didn't sound promising. "What—" A heavy grinding filled the air as the flame of my candle turned a brilliant white, blazing up another foot. The children stepped back, laughing, suddenly at ease. "What the hell?"

"You'll understand now," said the Piskie, through her laughter.

And everything changed. The walls of the Children's Hall dropped away, transforming the shattered ballroom into a clearing ringed by warped, almost menacing trees. Riders lurked in the shadows of their branches. The candle flame abruptly dwindled to a tiny blue spark, and just as abruptly the children were upon me, pinching and shoving as they surrounded me on all sides. They pulled me back when I tried to break away, jeering at my distress.

A deep voice rumbled in the distance, drowning out the voices of the children: "Send me the intruder. Let her be seen."

Still laughing, the children pushed me forward, and I saw Blind Michael.

He was tall—no, he was more than tall; he filled the sky. His arms were tree trunks, and his feet were the roots of the earth, and standing in front of him, I was less than nothing. I was dust and dry leaves skittering across the sky, and my only hope was that he would open those arms and let me hide under them until the world ended. His smile was the smile of a benevolent god, kind and merciful and willing to forgive all my sins. Only his eyes broke the illusion of peace: they were milky white, like ice or marble, and seemed almost as cold. I snapped back to myself for a moment, almost remembering who I was and why I was there; for that instant, I knew what I was looking for.

And then the glamour slammed back over me in a wave of glory, and He was my entire world. The children moved out of the way as I stepped forward, letting me pass. I wasn't theirs to torment anymore—I belonged to our mutual god, and I was His and His alone. I was barely breathing as I realized the magnitude of my devotion. I would live for Him. I would die for Him. I would kill in the name of His glory . . .

A sudden wind whipped through my hair, snarling it around my face as the candle blazed white again. The air was abruptly filled with the sharp, ashy stink of burning hair. I jerked the candle away from myself, ready to throw it aside—I didn't need it anymore, I was home—when a thin line of wax blew free and spattered on my lip, filling my mouth with the taste of blood.

There wasn't much blood in the wax, but there was enough to let me break the glamour he was throwing over me. Blind Michael wasn't a god; he was just a man sitting on a throne carved from old wood and decorated with yellowing bones. He couldn't block the sky if he tried. Oak and ash, what had I been about to do?

I sucked in a breath, almost choking on the taste of burned hair, and said, "No." My head was pounding, but there wasn't time to deal with that now. I could have a migraine later, when it was safe to collapse. "I'm not yours. You don't get to take me that easily."

"Don't I?" he rumbled, and his magic rolled over me again. For a moment, His voice was the shaking of mountains. The moment passed, and the glamour passed with it; it's harder to catch someone after they've escaped you once, even if they only made that escape by accident. Thank Oberon. "I am older than you can dream, child. All things are easy to me."

"Actually, I doubt that," I said. When there's nowhere left to run, take refuge in cockiness. "I dream some pretty old dreams."

"Do you?" His illusions were gone, and I could see him properly now. He was tall and thin, with skin streaked white and tan like ash bark, amber-colored hair, and ears that were forked like a stag's horns. Just another fae lord, no less strange than the Luidaeg and maybe stronger than she, but not the world wearing flesh. He wasn't a god, and I was glad. I can handle purebloods and Firstborn. I can't handle gods.

"I want my kids back," I said, keeping my voice steady. Even if he wasn't a god, the Luidaeg was afraid of him, and I respected that. I respected getting out alive even more. "Give them to me, and I'll go."

"Your 'kids'? You seek playmates? Come now, the best games are here. The best toys are here." He dipped a hand behind himself, pulling out a crystal globe with a yellow swallowtail butterfly trapped inside it. The butterfly was frantic, beating its wings against the glass. "Stay."

"I can't," I said, with level courtesy. "I have a job to do."

"They thrust you into service so young? Poor thing, you've forgotten how to play. I can teach you. Stay."

"No."

"Well, then. If you're so set—which of my new friends are 'your kids'?"

"Stacy and Mitch Brown's children. The children of the Court of Cats." I paused, remembering Raj, and added, "The Hob, Helen. They're my responsibility, and I'm not leaving without them. Give them to me, and let us go."

Blind Michael laughed, sounding honestly amused as he tucked the crystal sphere away behind him. "Why should I?"

Good question. "Because I'm asking so nicely?"

"You're in my lands, little girl. Why should I let you go, much less let you take any of my new family?" He kept turning his head, like he was seeing me from multiple angles. I glanced to the right and saw that the children on that side were watching me intently; they weren't looking at their lord all. The Riders, on the other hand, were only looking at Blind Michael—I might as well not have been there. Interesting.

"Because I'm under your sister's protection." I held up my candle. The flame had died back to a glowing ember, but it was still burning. I tried to take comfort in that. "The Luidaeg promised me passage."

"And passage you have had. Passage through my

lands and through my consort's wood. Now you are come to me. My pretty sister cannot guarantee your safety in my Court."

Damn. "Because it's no fun for you if you don't let us go?"

"Hmmm. Almost a point, child—but you aren't a child, are you?" He leaned forward, frowning. "You're not mine. You should be. What are you, little girl that isn't mine?"

"I'm here under your sister's guardianship. Nothing else about me matters. Now let me go, and let me take my kids. You admit that I'm not yours."

His frown deepened for an instant, becoming cold and puzzled. "You're Amandine's daughter, aren't you? You are. I can smell it on you. Why are you *here?* She never came, and once a road is set aside, no other feet should claim it."

"For my kids," I repeated. I could worry about how he knew my mother later.

"Take them," he countered. "Play a game with me, and save them if you can."

Something in his words clicked. I straightened, hoping he wouldn't hear the excitement in my voice. "I'm your prisoner. That's not fair." He was a child's terror, and that implied a certain reliance on games. More important, it implied a dependence on being *fair.* Children don't care about good or evil; all that matters is that you play fair and follow the rules. If Blind Michael followed children's laws, he'd have to play fair with me, or winning wouldn't count.

Root and branch, I hoped I was right. Blind Michael nodded, turning sightless eyes toward the trees. "It's not, and games must be fair," he said. "Shall we have a wager, then?"

"What kind of wager?" I asked cautiously. The fae may not have souls to gamble with, but there are other things that we can lose.

"My Hunters cannot see you while you hold my sister's mark." He gestured toward my candle. Bingo. They couldn't focus on me directly. The children still could. That's why he was watching me through them. "I'll give you a head start before I loose my Hunters. If they can find you, if they can catch you, you belong to me, forever. If you can free your children . . ."

"If I can free them, you don't follow us out of your lands."

"Agreed. The children you have claimed can go with you, if you can escape me."

I had to be missing something, but there wasn't time to argue. "Deal."

His expression sharpened. "So run, little girl, as far as your candle will take you. You have until I order my Hunt to follow, and my patience is not long." He settled back in his throne. "Go."

There was a rustling behind me. Turning, I saw that the children had moved aside, opening a clear path to the plains beyond the line of trees. I took off running without a backward glance, clutching the candle close to my body to shield it from the wind. Blind Michael's Court howled and catcalled behind me, trying to break my focus. I just kept running until I was through the crowd, through the trees, and the sounds of the Court vanished behind me. I was suddenly on the plains where I'd started, surrounded by empty wasteland and miles away from my goal.

Only now Blind Michael's entire Court knew I was here. And they would be coming after me. Just great.

TWELVE

THE LANDSCAPE HADN'T CHANGED since my arrival in Blind Michael's lands; even my footprints were intact, marking my point of arrival. I turned to face the distant mountains. That was where Blind Michael and his Court were waiting, and that was presumably where he was holding the kids. Somehow my panicked flight had carried me back to the start of my journey, with no ground lost or gained . . . but now Blind Michael knew I was coming. I had to go back to his Court, steal my children, and escape, all without being seen.

Planning has never been one of my strengths—I'm better at leaping before I look—and I know when I'm outmatched. Blind Michael was bigger, meaner, and stronger. I needed to have some sort of plan before I approached him again, or I was going to wind up joining the misshapen throng that haunted the Children's Hall. I suppressed a shudder. Death would be better than transformation and eternal enslavement to a madman who thought he was a god, and that was probably exactly why he'd do his best not to let me die. People like that like to keep their toys, no matter how broken those toys get.

That just meant I couldn't let him catch me. I turned

away from the mountains, looking toward the forest. It was closer than the mountains. I could reach the edge of the trees in less than an hour, if I hurried.

"Blind Michael said the woods belonged to his consort," I muttered, thinking of the yellow-skinned woman. She hadn't looked very friendly. I'm normally willing to forgive first impressions, but if she was Blind Michael's consort, I probably didn't need to. The Luidaeg's spell hid me from her. I doubted that made her an ally. "Let's not go that way." "Don't go to the wood" was the first part of a plan. Now I just needed a way to get back into Blind Michael's Court, rescue the kids, and get them out of his lands without being caught by any of his legion of heavily armed, extremely faithful servants. Why is nothing ever easy?

My candle burned a reassuring blue as I started toward the mountains. I found myself moving in an uneven line, always staying in easy reach of cover. It wasn't a conscious decision, and it was still the best idea I'd had all day. The Riders couldn't see me very well—the Luidaeg's spell made sure of that—but they'd spotted me when I drew attention to myself. Walking straight for Blind Michael's throne would probably count as drawing attention.

The sky was somehow managing to get darker, and a thick mist rose from the ground as true night approached. At least my candle was burning as steadily as ever, the wax still refusing to melt. That was for the best. Being trapped here without the Luidaeg's gift to protect me would be a bad thing. A very, very bad thing.

The hours passed slowly, marked by the darkening sky. My legs ached, and my knees were burning, but I didn't seem to have gained any ground; the mountains were as far away as they'd been when I started. I turned around, suddenly suspicious.

The forest hadn't receded at all.

"Oh, Maeve's *bones*," I moaned. Of course the land was working against me. We were deep enough in the Summerlands that the entire Islet was like one gigantic knowe, bound to the will of its owner. Blind Michael's word was law here, and he didn't want me to get away.

I stomped my foot, fighting the urge to scream. Maybe it was childish, but if you can't be childish when you *are* a child, what's the point? I'd been walking for hours. My headache wasn't going away; if anything, the long walk without water or aspirin had made it worse. It felt like little men with jackhammers were trying to rewire my brain. My knees hurt. My legs hurt. I was so thirsty that swallowing scraped the back of my throat, and all I wanted was the chance to curl up somewhere and sleep until everything was better. I forced myself to take a deep breath. There had to be a solution, somewhere. I just needed to force myself to see it.

I walked to the nearest bramble thicket and dropped to my hands and knees, crawling inside. I stopped once I was past the first row of thorns, staring. I wasn't the first one to use this as a hiding place; someone had cut away the branches on the inside, opening a path. The cuts didn't look fresh, and the ground was undisturbed—whoever created this hidey-hole hadn't been back in a long time. Looking more closely, I saw that the brambles had been twisted so that they'd grow back into the main body of the briar, making the shield of thorns on the outside thicker and more secure. No one would be able to see me from the plains. Those same careful cuts made the narrow tunnel self-sustaining. It could probably go unused forever.

That decided me. Secret places in bushes and quarries are generally the property of children, and this one had likely been cultivated by some long-forgotten child who'd managed to escape the Hunt, at least for a little while. If it was at all like the hiding places I shared with Stacy and Julie when I was a kid, no adult had ever seen it: they could walk right by and never realize it was there. I crawled deeper, careful of the thorns.

The path wound inward until it met the main trunk, where it widened to become a clear bubble of open space. Whoever made the path also dug a shallow dip in the soft earth, making just enough room for a small person to sit upright. Any vague hopes for alliance were dashed when I saw that indentation judging by the way the brambles encroached on its edges, whoever created this little hiding place had been gone for a very long time. Just another casualty of Blind Michael's lands.

I scooted into the scrape and braced myself against the trunk, relaxing slowly. I just needed a little rest and time to think before I had to start moving again. Holding my candle away from the dry wood all around me, I closed my eyes.

I was only supposed to be there for a few minutes. I didn't mean to fall asleep. That part just came naturally. And I dreamed . . .

The world was blue and gray and amber, ringed by mist that never fully lifted. Sometimes it retreated into the stones, sometimes it hovered among the trees, but the mist itself was eternal. Smudged charcoal lines defined the landscape, sketching the outline of endless plains broken only by mountain's stone and dying forest.

Dying? No, living. The mist retreated as I moved closer, leaving behind a wood I didn't recognize. The trees were lush and healthy, green and gold and springtime yellow. Willows stood sentry, reaching out with hungry fronds to grab intruders. This was Blind Michael's land. It changed, but the heart of it remained the same. The heartbeat of the land . . .

The land's heartbeat wasn't mine. Who was I? I fought to remember my name, my purpose, anything. The mist twined around me in a lover's embrace, trying to pull me closer, taking me farther and farther in . . .

"Aunt Birdie?"

I knew that voice, and because I knew it, I had to know myself: one demanded the other. I shrugged the mist away, turning. "Karen?"

She was standing in the trees, still wearing the robe she'd gotten from Lily. Yellow and brown butterfly flowers were twined in her hair. She looked frightened. "It's not safe to dream here, Aunt Birdie. You shouldn't. He'll know if you do."

"Baby, you're awake!" I started toward her. The ground snatched at my feet, but I wrenched myself free and kept walking. *"We've got to get you out of here. It's not safe—"*

"I know, Aunt Birdie," she said, moving to reveal a small girl crumpled by the base of the nearest willow. *"It never was."*

The little girl couldn't have been more than ten years old, dressed in a tattered nightshirt, feet bloody and bare. She was obviously of Japanese descent, slat-thin and used too hard. Her long black hair was knotted at the base of her neck. Tears had washed streaks through the dirt on her face. Three silver-furred tails were curled behind her, and silver fox ears were pressed flat against her skull. Kitsune.

She wasn't breathing, and I realized with slow dread that the grass around them was dead, crumbling into dust. *"Karen, your friend—"*

"Her name is Hoshibara. This is her place."

"Honey, she's not breathing."

The look on Karen's face was infinitely sad. *"I know."*

"Karen—"

"Aunt Birdie, you have to listen now," she said. Somehow her voice filled the world, and I stopped, watching her. She shook her head, something ancient and tired lurking in the faded blue of her eyes. *"I'm not really awake. I can't wake up while he has me. Something's wrong, Aunt Birdie, something's very wrong. You have to find her before it's too late."*

"Find who?"

"The rose's daughter, the woman made of flowers who wanted to be a fox instead. The Blodynbryd queen."

"Karen, I don't understand. I need to take you home. Your parents are worried."

She tilted her head to the side. *"Home? You can get there and back by the light of a candle, they say. Where's yours?"*

My candle? I realized that my hands were empty.

Where was it? We couldn't get home without the candle. I turned, looking for the familiar flame, and found it on the horizon, far away and moving farther. I shouted, "Wait here! I'll be right back!" and ran after it. The years fell off me as I ran, until I was a child again, as lost as the rest of them, and I ran . . .

. . . and ran . . .

. . . ran . . .

Night had finished falling while I slept, and shadows filled my hiding place. I snapped awake to the sound of footsteps and caught my breath, confusion seared away by the sight of my candle. It was burning an almost lambent red, flame licking high against the brambles. I was half afraid it would set the bush on fire. That was really the least of my worries, because if Blind Michael's Riders took me, a little fire wouldn't matter at all.

They would find me. They had to. The light would lead them to me if nothing else, and then the game would end, with Blind Michael taking the checkmate. It was only a matter of time before one of them realized I was there and shouted for the others.

But they didn't. The footsteps faded, leaving me alone with the frantic beating of my heart. The flame dwindled to normal, calming a lot more quickly than my nerves. "What did you expect me to do, Luidaeg?" I muttered. "Walk up and take them away from him?" I could still see Blind Michael when I closed my eyes, tall and vast against the sky. He was willing to be my god. All I had to do was let go of the candle and let him in.

No way in hell.

He was blind but saw everything in his lands— everything but me. He wouldn't have agreed to my little game if he didn't have to, because victory is always better than playing fair. He couldn't see me, he couldn't hold me, and so I was almost safe. But why was I so special? Why should a candle matter so much? I paused, reviewing. The Luidaeg gave me the candle and sent me into his lands. She said I could get there and back by the light of a candle.

Of course: we were in a child's land, playing by children's rules. Blind Michael would catch me if he could, because that was how the game worked, but he couldn't stop me or see me as long as I kept my candle burning. That would make the game unfair.

"Just great," I said. I was trapped in the realm of a mad Firstborn who obeyed the laws of children's tales, and my only hope for escape was pinned on a candle flame. It hadn't been able to hide Raj from the Riders, and I wasn't counting on it to be able to hide any of the other children, either. The Luidaeg and I were going to have words when I got home.

And then there was the dream. I've always been a vivid dreamer, but this was different. It felt almost real, and it felt like it was important. Like it was something I needed to remember. Not that I could have forgotten the look in Karen's eyes, even if I wanted to.

My thoughts distracted me enough that I didn't hear the rustling until something grabbed my shoulder. That's the kind of mistake you only get to make once, because afterward, you're generally dead. I whirled as far as the bush allowed, ignoring the thorns raking my cheek as I pulled back my free hand to strike my attacker. Whatever it was might be disoriented enough by prey that fought back for me to get out of the brambles and run.

I started to swing and froze, staring. Quentin stared back. The brambles had forced him to his hands and knees. Mud was caked on his face and hair, making him look more like an extra from *Lord of the Flies* than a well-groomed courtier. Spike was on his shoulder, looking unperturbed by the situation. I guess when you're made of thorns, a few more don't hurt.

"Quentin." I slowly lowered my hand. Spike gave me a wounded look, and I added, "Spike. What are you two doing here?"

It took Quentin a moment to find his voice. He just gaped, still staring, before he stammered, "T-Toby?"

"In the flesh." I glanced down at myself and grimaced. "So to speak. How the hell did you get here?" Don't you know you're going to get yourself killed? Did you think for a *second* before you did whatever it took to follow me?

Idiots. Idiots, children, and heroes.

"I—the Luidaeg said you'd be here. She told me to look for the candlelight." He pointed to my candle. "But I didn't think . . ."

"Yeah, it's a little weird from this side, too. I ask again, what are you doing here?" He'd gone to the Luidaeg. Oh, root and branch. The Luidaeg can be kind when she wants to, but her gifts are never free. What had he paid to find me?

Quentin stiffened, looking away for a moment before he turned back to me and said, "I'm here for Katie. You're going to let me help," in what was probably supposed to be a commanding tone.

I've been commanded by a lot of people in my time. Some of them were pretty good at it, and a few were even good enough to make me listen. Quentin had heritage and history on his side, but he didn't have the practice, and when you're trying to make me do what you want, practice is what counts. It also helps if you're not down on your hands and knees.

I snorted. "I'm sorry, but no. Go home. It's too dangerous."

"I don't care. They have Katie. I'm not going anywhere until we get her out."

"There's no 'we' here, Quentin. You have to go."

"Why? This can't be worse than when we went to help Jan, and I was good enough to go with you then. I'm staying. You can't make me leave."

How the hell was I supposed to tell him about Blind Michael? No one could have warned me about him. You can't describe something so vast and old that it blanks out the sky; the words just aren't there.

"Quentin, look at me," I said, "Really *look* at me. This isn't some kind of illusion—this is real. This isn't the world you're used to. We're on an Islet. What does that tell you?"

"That things work differently here," he said. Spike leaped off his shoulder, padding over to lean against my knee. I automatically started scratching under its chin. My pets have me well trained. Undaunted, Quentin said, "The Luidaeg warned me. I'm not scared."

Of course he wasn't scared. The fear comes later, after the hurting starts. "You need to go home."

"Not without Katie." His voice seemed to echo through the brambles and out to the plains. I cringed. He didn't have a candle; Blind Michael could see him. If we kept fighting, I might be responsible for getting him caught.

"Fine, whatever," I hissed, "But I'm in charge here, understand? You listen to me."

"Of course," he said, and smiled. My giving the orders and his taking them was a familiar pattern. Hopefully this time we could skip the part where I almost get him killed.

I gave him a bleak look and shook my head, turning to crawl out of the brambles. "Follow me."

Getting back into the open was easier for me than it was for him: sometimes size really does matter. He had to back out, while I was able to crab-walk, only touching the ground for balance. Spike rode on my shoulder, pressed flat. It crooned as we moved, obviously glad to see me. I was glad to see it, too. I knew Spike could take care of itself, and having it along meant that if something happened to me, Quentin wouldn't be alone.

Quentin stayed close, swearing when thorns caught in his clothes and hair. I didn't feel sorry for him. He'd followed me into Blind Michael's lands of his own free will, and I'd send him back if I could. We'd been through too much together. I didn't want to see him hurt again. And he'd made sure that there was nothing I could do about it. Damn it. Why are we always so stupid when it comes to our own survival? How much of that was he learning from me?

I straightened once I was clear of the thorns, leaving Quentin still struggling to get free. The night seemed even darker without the brambles making a ceiling overhead to trap the candlelight.

Quentin finally got loose. I grabbed his sleeve, hushing him. I'll give him this much: he froze, waiting for my signal before he did anything else. I couldn't hear anyone coming—yet. That didn't mean they weren't on the way. "Quentin?"

"Yeah?"

"Run." We bolted from cover together, my shorter legs pumping madly as I fought to keep up. The forest was a smudge on the horizon, holding darkness and shadows and Blind Michael's lady. There was nothing there with reason to be friendly, but the Riders hadn't been willing to follow me past the trees when I hid there before. We'd be safe a little longer if we could make it that far. Having Quentin along changed everything. He had no candle to hide him and no weapons I could see; he was defenseless, and it was up to me to get him out of the way as quickly as I could. We were almost there. All we had to do was keep running.

I shouldn't have been surprised when the Riders stepped out of the fog at the forest's edge. I really shouldn't have. Quentin stumbled to a stop, and I pulled up a foot behind him, barely avoiding a collision. Spike dug its claws into my shoulder and hissed, starting to make a low, almost subsonic snarling noise.

The nearest Rider leveled his sword at Quentin, ignoring me entirely. "Tag," he said. "You're it."

"Toby, run," Quentin whispered, drawing himself up to his full height. Oh, sweet Titania. He was going to try to be a hero so that I could get away. "You have to save Katie."

I've never been any good at playing the damsel in distress and no matter how young I looked, I was way too old to start. "Like hell," I snapped, shoving myself in front of him and looking up at the Rider with a brilliant smile. "Hey, asshole. Can I help you?"

The helmet swung toward me. "You're it," he repeated, sounding somewhat unsure.

"You said that already." I tried to ignore the Riders circling us. My small, screaming urge toward self-preservation wasn't making it easy. Everyone has a little voice that tells them when they're doing something stupid. I've gotten very good at ignoring mine over the years. Spike's hissing was harder to ignore. Well, Spike could take care of itself. "So what now? Are we supposed to start hunting you? If that's the case, I want your horse. My feet are tired."

"What are you doing?" hissed Quentin. "Stop teasing them and run! I'll hold them off!"

"Sorry, but no," I said. If I was going to die, I wasn't going to do it cringing. Not in the middle of my most spectacular failure yet. "You couldn't hold off my cats. What the hell are you doing coming here unarmed, anyway?"

"But—"

"No buts. Here." I turned, pressing my candle into his hands. The Riders saw him when he wasn't the one holding it. Hopefully, this could change the game. "Hold this for me, okay?"

"What are you—"

"You can get there and back by the light of the candle. Remember that." The Riders had shifted focus, becoming less concerned with Quentin and more interested in Spike and me. The candle was working, thank Oberon. "Well, boys? Are we gonna party or what?"

"You will come with us," their spokesman rumbled.

"That's a good line. I'll have to remember that." I had them confused; they weren't used to having children talk back without tears. I might be able to get past them if I ran now. That wouldn't help Quentin unless I could count on the candle, and I had to be able to count on the candle. If he didn't move, he should be all right.

"One more thing," I said, trying to project a bravado I didn't feel. The Rider leaned forward, and I bolted, running for the gap between the two nearest Riders as fast as I could. They turned, but not fast enough to stop me; they were used to defiance, not actual, coherent thought.

I shoved past their horses and ran for the forest, not looking back. If I could reach the woods, I might survive. If I survived, there was a chance. If there was a chance, everything could still come out okay.

The hoofbeats began almost immediately. It sounded like they were all following. Good. That would give Quentin time to get away and finish what I'd started. He was a smart kid, and he did well in Tamed Lightning, and he could do it, if he was clever. He could get out. You can get there and back by the light of a candle, after all. The first spear thudded into the dust a few feet in front of me. I stumbled but kept running, forcing myself toward the forest. Blind Michael probably wanted me alive but that wouldn't stop them from hurting me. Changelings can survive a lot of damage, and fae magic can heal almost anything. I didn't trust them to play nice.

The second spear hit me in the back of my left thigh. The momentary pain was followed by a disturbing numbness that spread down my leg, locking my knee into place. Suddenly off-balance, I staggered and fell.

Spike jumped off my shoulder and turned to face the Riders, rattling its thorns and keening in a high, warning tone. It was a display as brave as it was stupid. They would crush my poor goblin and take me anyway. I wanted to tell Spike to run, but I was so tired all of a sudden; the numbness was spreading upward, making it hard to think, move, or breathe. Poison. Damn it, Luidaeg, is there a law that says the Firstborn can't play fair?

The Riders formed a half circle around us, weapons at the ready, and stopped. Only a half circle? I forced my head up, and found myself looking into the trees at the forest's edge. We'd almost made it. Oak and ash, I'd been so *close* . . .

I let my head fall back down, closing my eyes. I was tired. I was so very tired, and the weight of the spear jutting out of my leg seemed great enough to crush me. I heard Spike running past me into the trees, thorns rattling. Good. At least one of us was going to get out of this alive. It was making a shrill keening noise as it ran, like it was calling for help. A pity that help wasn't coming.

The numbness had spread through most of my body before I realized the Riders weren't moving. They had me surrounded, but none of them were coming to grab me. Why the hell not? They'd already won. All they needed to do was come and claim their prize. At least none of them was holding Quentin. The candle had spared him that much. For now.

Then I felt hands on my shoulders, and someone was lifting me. I forced my eyes open and found myself looking into a scarred, yellow-skinned face. Acacia. Blind Michael's lady.

"You sent the goblin. Do you know my daughter?" she said. Her voice wasn't kind, but it wasn't cruel; just bemused. "Did she send you? Where is she?" Raising her head, she scowled at the Riders. "Go away and tell my lord that this one reached the wood. That makes her mine, not his, and I will not cede her. Run your races somewhere else."

One by one they turned and rode away. Acacia shook her head, sighing as she watched them go. Her arms seemed too fragile to support my weight, but she held me without trouble. There was a thin mewling noise. "You may come too, if you insist," she said. I heard the rattle of Spike's thorns and closed my eyes again. My leg was burning, even through the numbness, and I could feel the blood soaking through my jeans and running down my thigh. Quentin; I was leaving Quentin alone. I was . . .

I did what any sensible person would have done under the circumstances. I fainted.

THIRTEEN

*T*HE MISTS WERE HEAVIER NOW. I tried to stand
and couldn't. The earth had closed around me, covering my feet. "Hello?" I shouted, and winced as the echoes
returned my voice. I spoke as an adult; the echo answered
as a child. "Hello?"

"I'm here, Auntie Birdie, it's all right." I felt a cool
hand on my forehead, and Karen whispered, "You have
to wake up. It's not safe."

"Karen. I found you." I knew she was there. I just
couldn't see her.

"No, you didn't. You can't find me yet; it's too soon.
You have to get out of here, and you have to find her.
Please!"

"Find who?" I shook my head. "Sweetheart, I'm here
to save you. You and the others."

"No one came to save her, and so she had to save her-
self. She's sorry, but you have to find her. It's important.
It's very important." She pulled her hand away. The smell
of roses hung heavy in the air; not the perfect roses of
Evening's curse, but a richer, earthy midsummer scent.
"You can't find us if you don't find her. Wake up, Aunt
Birdie. Wake up . . ."

I opened my eyes and promptly wished that I hadn't.
My lower body was numb, and my head felt like it was

on fire—not a good combination. If I squinted I could force the shadows above me to resolve into a canopy of branches and dead leaves . . . the woods. I was in the woods. If I was in the woods, what I remembered happening after the Riders shot me wasn't a dream. Acacia saved me because she thought I knew her daughter. No matter what this meant, it probably wasn't something I was going to like very much.

Spike was sitting in the middle of my chest. It gave a triumphant squeak when it realized I was awake, beginning to make the rasping, scraping noise that served it as a purr.

"Hey, Spike," I whispered, forcing myself to smile. "You been there long, guy?" It chirped. "Right. I'll just pretend I understood that, okay? I missed you." Fighting my natural inertia—once at rest, I tend to stay at rest—I raised a hand and scratched the top of Spike's head. "That's my good Spike."

I continued to scratch as I took slow stock of my body. My throat was burning, and it felt like I'd been sucking on sandpaper. More, my head was pounding, my back hurt, and I couldn't feel my legs. Whatever I was lying in swayed with the motion of my hands—a hammock. I couldn't see past my chest; for all that I knew, my body ended just past the point where Spike was sitting. That probably wasn't the most comforting idea I could have come up with. Damn. I spent an unknown amount of time trying to twist around so that I could see myself before exhaustion overwhelmed me and I fell into an uneasy doze.

Maybe my body got some rest out of that unplanned nap, but my mind didn't. It kept racing, generating countless nightmare scenarios beginning with what Blind Michael would do when he learned I couldn't run and going downhill from there. I woke to find Spike sniffling at my face, attracted by my whimpering.

"It's okay, Spike," I said, stroking its side. "You'll be okay." It whined but subsided, and I returned to my unhappy napping.

I don't know how long that went on before foot-steps in the dark heralded Acacia's return, snapping me awake. I tried to twist toward the sound, half hopeful, half afraid, but I couldn't even move that much. I was more than trapped; I was helpless. Spike jumped to its feet, chirping at whatever it saw in the shadows. That re-action may have been the only thing that kept me from freaking out completely. Spike is usually a pretty good judge of character. It wasn't worried—why should I be? Unless, of course, this was the one time it happened to be wrong.

Clearing my throat, I said, "Hello?"

"Good; you're awake." Acacia stepped into view, the light from her lantern filling the clearing and finally let-ting me see without squinting. It was a small comfort—there was nothing but the trees. "I was starting to worry." She didn't sound it. If anything, she sounded bored.

I looked at her, taking a moment before I spoke. Except for the scar that cut down the side of her face, her skin looked almost impossibly smooth, like she'd been carved from living wood and the knife had slipped. Only one bloodline had skin like that. "You're a Dryad." That explained why the forest was willing to obey her: Dryads are the spirits of trees, and they're halfway to being plants themselves. None of the Dry-ads I'd met had that sort of control over plants, but that didn't make it impossible. Dryads are strange, even for fae. What I didn't understand was what she was doing there—why would a Dryad choose to live where all the trees were dying? Especially a Dryad as powerful as Acacia appeared to be.

"In a sense," she said, with a small, bitter smile. "You're quite observant. It's a pity you don't pay closer attention to thrown weaponry."

"It's hard to pay attention when it's behind you." She had to be talking about the spear that caught me in the leg. The only question was how bad the damage was. As calmly as I could, I said, "I can't feel my legs."

"That's to be expected; poison will do that." She

shook her head, tangles of rootlike hair snaking down her shoulders. "The potion on that spear was well brewed. You should be a tree by now, rooted and growing to grace my forest. It's a mercy, of a sort, to grant my husband's victims that much freedom."

I paled. "Then why . . ."

"I stopped it. I brewed it to begin with; it was bound to listen to me." She tilted her head in a curiously familiar gesture. "I wanted to talk to you. Are you well enough for that?"

"I guess I can make an effort." Inappropriate humor—the last resort of the terrified.

"Good." She reached toward me, and for a horrible moment I was afraid she was going to pick me up again. Instead, she stopped her hands a few inches from my chest, and Spike stepped into them. She smiled, cradling it close. Spike chirped, beginning to purr. I gaped at them, stunned and bizarrely hurt. Maybe she was a Dryad, but this felt like a betrayal.

"Where did you get this?" Acacia asked. Spike nudged her fingers with its head, eyes narrowed to content slits. Her smile warmed for a moment, then faded as she raised her head and looked at me.

"It used to belong to a friend of mine," I said guardedly. I didn't want to say Luna's name until I knew more about Acacia.

"I see." She frowned, pulling the scar on her face into a sharp line. "How did it come to belong to you? It's yours now. I can tell that much."

"I named it by mistake."

"Names have power. It's been with you since then, I suppose."

"Yes."

"You've treated it well." She ran a hand down Spike's back, not seeming to mind the thorns. "Rose goblins are hard to care for."

"It's pretty easy. I just give it water and sunshine, and sometimes fertilizer."

"We used to have them in these woods. But they died.

All of them." Acacia sighed, hands stilling. "All the roses that grew here died a very long time ago."

For a moment, there was nothing frightening about her; she was just a woman, lost and a little bit lonely. I almost wanted to comfort her. I didn't know how to begin. "I'm sorry," I said finally, aware of how lame the words sounded.

"They had to die." Her voice was filled with the sort of distance people create to keep themselves from crying. "What good would they have done? The sun never shines here, and roses never bloom in darkness. Better they should spread their wings and fly away."

"Roses like the sun," I said, parroting one of the few gardening tips Luna had been able to drum into my head.

"Yes, they do," Acacia said. "Where is my youngest rose now?"

"I don't know what you're talking about."

Her eyes narrowed. "You carry a rose goblin bred of her lines. I know the cuttings that sprouted your companion; I nurtured their parents and originals. You can't lie to me. I won't allow it. Now tell me: where is my daughter?"

Oak and ash. "Your daughter?" I was stalling and I knew it. Hopefully she wouldn't.

Hope doesn't always cut it. "Her name is Luna," she said. "Where is she?"

"I don't have to tell you."

"Don't you?" she asked. She shifted Spike to the crook of one elbow and raised her hand.

There may be words for the pain that swept through my midriff and torso, consuming what was left of my lower body and racing upward until it was almost to my chest. If there are, I don't have them. The numbness followed close behind it, dulling the pain and replacing it with something a lot more chilling: utter nothingness. I screamed. I couldn't help it.

Lowering her hand, Acacia smiled. "I think you *need* to tell me," she said. I stared at her, fighting to breathe.

"Unless you want to be a part of my wood forever. If it progresses far enough, not even I can free you."

Wood. The poison turned flesh to wood. I twisted my neck as far as it would go and stared down at myself. The edge where flesh and wood collided was visible now as a ridge just below my ribcage, tendrils of bark weaving through my sweater. I caught my breath, suddenly aware of how little of my body I could feel. "Oberon . . ." I whispered.

"My father won't help you," Acacia said. "Where is my daughter? Where is Luna?"

I shifted to stare at her, wide-eyed. "Your *father?*"

"Yes," she said. "My father."

"But . . ."

"My mother was Titania of the Seelie Court; my father Oberon, King of all Faerie."

Firstborn. Another Firstborn. Bitterly, I said, "Can't you people just leave me alone?"

"You came to me, changeling, carrying my half sister's candle and stalking my husband's subjects. There's no reason for me to leave you alone. Quite the contrary: there's every reason for me to kill you where you lie and collect my lord's bounties for it." She paused. "Every reason but one."

"What's that?" I said, fighting to keep the terror from my voice. She'd hear it; she'd have to hear it. The Firstborn are good at that sort of thing. They're legends—they're practically gods—and they're supposed to have the decency to be dead or in hiding. Why the hell was I suddenly running into them around every corner?

At least this one hadn't mentioned my mother.

"You know where my daughter is."

I closed my eyes. So that was it. Voice numb, I said, "After you kill me, let Spike go. It didn't do anything to you."

"Are you refusing to tell me?"

"My lady, you're bigger and meaner than I am. I know that. But I can't save my kids like this; I'm going to die here, whether I tell you what I know or not." I sighed. "I can be a coward sometimes, but not today. If I'm going to die, I'm not betraying Luna while I do it."

"But I'm her *mother.*"

"You don't look a thing like her." I forced myself to relax. If I was going to die, I could at least pretend to do it with dignity.

"I see," she said, after a long pause. Her cloak rustled as she leaned closer, and then her hand was pressed against my cheek. Her skin was as cool and smooth as willow wood. My headache faded under the touch, and I sighed inwardly. I hate it when the villains tease.

"Just get it over with," I said. I felt the prickle of Spike's claws as it jumped onto my chest, still "purring." At least one of us was happy.

"And so I shall." She placed her other hand on my opposite cheek and leaned down to kiss me on the forehead. Dignity suddenly wasn't an option. I screamed.

It felt like I was dying. Worse than that, it felt like I was being born. Every muscle in my body was pulled tight, flayed open, and made new again. It seemed to last forever, and part of me wondered through the screaming if this was the true effect of the poison; not to kill or to change, but to hurt. Forever.

Then the pain stopped, replaced by the tingle of pins and needles in my reawakening flesh. Acacia pulled her hands away, sounding slightly bemused as she said, "You can open your eyes now, daughter of Amandine. It's over."

"How do you know my mother?" I asked, and opened my eyes. Spike climbed up to my shoulder as I sat up, looking down at myself. My legs were flesh again: sore, aching flesh, but flesh all the same. I ran a hand down my side. There was no lingering roughness; even my headache was gone. "Everyone seems to know her, but no one tells me why."

"She was very . . . visible, once. A long time ago, before her choices were made. You have her heat in you. I should have seen it sooner. I would have, but I was unaware she had a child. I thought her line had ended." I looked up to find Acacia watching me, half smiling. "Believe me, I've left you no surprises; you are as you were when first you snuck into my woods. I couldn't stop the scarring, but the wound is healed."

"Why?" I asked, bemused.

"You wouldn't betray my daughter." She shook her head. "She must be a good friend."

"She is."

"Is she . . . well?"

Maybe it was the longing in her voice; maybe it was the fact that I know what it feels like to lose a child. If someone had offered me information on Gillian, the chance to know that she was thriving . . .

Whatever it was, I believed her. However strange the idea might seem, she was Luna's mother. I couldn't trust her with anything important, but what harm could a little news do? Acacia spared my life—hell, she *saved* my life. I owed her that much. "She's good," I said. "She's married now; she has a daughter."

"A daughter." She rolled the words on her tongue like wine. "What's her name?"

"Rayseline."

"Rayseline—rose." Acacia laughed. "She named her daughter 'rose'?"

"Yes."

"Is she still in the Duchy of Roses?"

"The . . ." I paused. Some people call Shadowed Hills the Duchy of Roses because of Luna's gardens. I don't know any other place with that name. "Yes. She's still there."

"I thought she would be." She lowered her lantern, smile fading into something sadder. "I don't know where else she could have gone. She could never leave her roses."

"I don't understand how she can be your daughter," I said, risking honesty. "Luna isn't . . . she's not a Dryad."

"She never was. She wore a Kitsune skin when she

left me, but you could see the truth of her if you knew to look. Who she was, where she began, it was always there. It always will be."

"I don't understand." The Kitsune aren't skinshifters—you either are one or you aren't. They're not like the Selkies or the Swanmays, who can give their natures away.

"That's all right, you weren't meant to. Just believe me when I tell you she is my daughter, and that she lived here with me once, before she left to live where roses can grow."

I slid out of the hammock, catching myself on the netting as my feet hit the ground. My legs were full of pins and needles, but it was a welcome sensation; it meant they were mine again. "I need to go. I have to save my kids."

Acacia nodded. "I understand. Children are important. Where is your candle?"

"I . . . oh, root and *branch*." I gave my candle to Quentin. There was no telling where he—or it—had ended up. "Quentin has it."

"The little Daoine Sidhe? Ah. He's at the edge of the woods; he thinks he's hidden." Her tone was amused. "I haven't cared to dissuade him."

So my candle hadn't hidden him completely. That made a certain sense; the Luidaeg used my blood, not his, when she made it. "I—" I stopped, aware of how close I'd come to saying thank you. There are some things Faerie etiquette won't forgive. "Can I go to him?"

"I won't hold you." She raised her lantern again, silver-shot eyes solemn. "But I'll ask a favor, if you'll indulge me."

Titania's daughter, one of the Firstborn of Faerie, was asking *me* for a favor? Every time I think the world can't get weirder, it finds a way. "What do you need?"

"A gift." There was a rustle of fabric, and she was holding a rose out to me. The petals were black tipped with silver, as soft and weathered as ancient velvet. "For my daughter."

"You want me to take it to her?"

"Please."

"Is it—"

"It isn't poisoned. I would never do that to her. *Please.*"

I paused, frowning. She let me go; she didn't have to, and she did. What harm could a rose do? "All right," I said. "I can take it to her."

Acacia didn't speak—what could she have said without thanking me? She just nodded and handed me the flower. I nodded in return, tucking the stem into the curls behind my right ear. I just had to hope it would stay put.

She raised one hand and pointed toward the edge of the woods, saying, "Go that way, and you'll find him. And when you see my daughter, tell her that I miss her."

There was nothing more to say. Gathering every scrap of courtly etiquette I'd managed to pick up in my years as a hanger-on at my mother's side, I dropped into a deep, formal bow. Acacia's expression when I straightened up again was worth the effort; she looked shocked and gratified, like a woman who'd just received an unexpected gift. I smiled, turned, and walked away. The light of her lantern faded behind me until there was nothing but the darkness of the trees. And I walked on, toward the distant calling of my candle.

FOURTEEN

QUENTIN CROUCHED AT THE EDGE OF THE FOREST, staring at the plains like he expected them to rise up and attack at any moment. Considering everything that had happened so far, I wouldn't have been surprised if they had. My candle was in his right hand; the flame was burning a soft green that shifted to a cobalt blue as I approached. Apparently it also reacted when allies came closer—good to know.

He was so fixated on the horizon that he didn't hear me coming. I put my hand on his shoulder, saying, "Quentin." He jumped back to his feet but managed not to scream as he whirled to face me. Good; he was learning.

Folding my hands behind my back, I grinned. "Hi. Miss me?" Spike chirped a greeting, rattling its thorns.

"I—you—I—" he gasped.

"Yes, I snuck up on you, and you let me get away with it," I said, trying to conceal how glad I was to see him alive and unharmed. "If I was something hostile, you'd be dead by now. Have you forgotten everything I taught you? Now give me back my candle."

He stared at me, eyes wide, before flinging his arms around me and hugging me so tight I was afraid he'd break something. Like my neck. "Whoa! Quentin, hey, come on, let go—"

"I thought you were *dead!*" he wailed. "You fell down, and then that woman came out of the woods, and I tried to follow you, but the trees kept closing in, and I couldn't see—"

"Oh, Quentin." I wrapped my arms around him as well as I could, given our relative sizes, and I held him until the shaking stopped. "It's okay. I was scared, too." He was a brave, cocky, annoying, headstrong kid that had been through a lot with me, but he was still a kid. If he needed a few minutes to calm down, he could have them. Even if I *had* told him to stay at home.

Eventually he pulled away, wiping his eyes. I looked at him, asking, "You okay?" When he nodded, so did I. "Good. What happened? How did you get away?"

"Once you gave me the candle, it was like they didn't see me anymore."

"Good. That means the Luidaeg's spell doesn't just cover me; if anything happens, you can take the candle and get home."

"Not without you," he said stubbornly, "and not without Katie."

"Right," I said, smothering a sigh. There's nothing more stubborn than youth, with the possible exception of old age. "Still, it's good to know that you can, if it's necessary."

"Are you hurt? You were hurt. I saw." Quentin twisted around to look at my leg, using the movement to cover his clumsy change of subject. I decided to let it go as I snatched the candle out of his hand. "Hey!"

"Hey yourself," I said. "It's my candle, and I'm fine. Acacia healed me."

"Acacia?"

"The one you saw carry me away. She healed me and told me where to find you."

"But why?"

"So we could save the others. Come on. If we follow the trees for a bit, we'll have a better shot at getting across the plains without being seen." I started walking, hoping the activity would be enough to kill the conversation, at least for now. If he questioned me too deeply I might tell him what I'd learned about Luna, and that really wasn't mine to share.

Whatever Acacia was, I knew enough to be worried. I knew she was Firstborn; she was old, possibly as old as the Luidaeg; and she called one of my best friends daughter. The implications of that hurt my head. I tried to remember what little I knew about Luna's past—where she came from, who she was before I knew her. There wasn't much. Popular legend says she was waiting when Sylvester came to establish the Duchy of Shadowed Hills, already tending her roses. When he arrived, she smiled and said nothing more complex than "you'll do." They were married the day the knowe was opened.

Was there anything else? She'd mentioned her parents once or twice, but she'd never said anything specific about her past. It was always just "I was the youngest, the others were grown when I arrived" or "my mother taught me about roses." She'd never mentioned Japan, not once, even though the Kitsune were born there. She wasn't fully Japanese, either; Luna was the only half-Caucasian Kitsune I'd ever seen. Lily served a perfect tea service, but Luna never did. She served rose wine, yes, and milk with honey, but never tea.

"Maeve's bones," I muttered. "She never had to lie."

"What?"

I looked over my shoulder. "Nothing. Just plotting the things I'm going to say to the Luidaeg when we get home."

"Oh," he said, drawing up alongside me. "Yeah."

We walked in silence for a while before I said, "What did she charge you?"

"Charge me?" he asked, sounding too innocent.

"Yes. Charge you." I kept walking. "The Luidaeg never works for free; I don't think she *can*. You said you'd do what I told you to if I let you stay, and I'm telling you to answer me. How did you find her, and what did you pay her?"

"Oh." The candlelight played across his cheek and

forehead, turning him into a ghost out of someone else's memory. Not mine. For that moment, he wasn't mine. "I followed you when you left Shadowed Hills."

"You followed me? How? You don't drive."

"I swiped your spare car key while you were on the phone." He had the good grace to look embarrassed, ducking his head as he said, "I hid in the backseat and cast a don't-look-here to keep you from seeing me."

I stopped to stare at him. "You hid in my car so I'd take you to the Luidaeg?" I demanded, following the question with, "You *stole* my car key?" I wasn't sure which was pissing me off more.

"Pretty much," he said, wincing. "I'm sorry."

"You realize how stupid that was, right?"

"I figured it out. But I didn't have a choice."

"There's always a choice, Quentin. I told you I'd take care of it."

"You didn't even care that I love her! How was I supposed to trust you to bring her home?" He looked at me, expression pained. "I had to."

"Quentin . . ."

"I know you're a hero. Does that mean no one else gets to even try?"

"I'm not a—"

"You can deny it. I don't care. Do you even care anymore about what happens? Or are you just here because you think you have to be?"

"Quentin, are you seriously standing with me in the middle of Blind Michael's realm and asking if I care? Because if you are, you need serious help."

"Do you really want to know what she charged me?"

Narrowing my eyes, I nodded. "Tell me."

"Fine." His face was filled with a grim determination that I recognized even as I tried to reject it. "I get out *with* you. Not before, not after; *with*." He paused before adding, more softly, "Not without."

I stared at him. "That isn't funny."

"I'm not kidding. That was the price for her showing me how to follow you. She gave me my passage in, but I don't get out without you. You're my ticket home." His chin was set, making him look very young, and very scared. "I'm on the Children's Road, just like you, but I don't have a candle. I have to make it home by the light of yours."

"Oh, root and *branch*." I stared at him, fighting to keep my hands from shaking. "That's what you agreed to? That's what you paid?"

"That's what she asked for," he said. "I didn't have anything else."

"So you came to save Katie without knowing whether or not I was alive."

"And because you needed me." He looked at me, expression an odd combination of determination and hope. "You *do* need me, you know."

I paused, and then nodded, slowly. "You're right. I need you." I offered him my hand. "Come on. Let's go." After a moment, he slid his hand into mine, squeezing my fingers. I smiled at him, and we turned together, stepping out of the shadow of the woods.

And then we stopped, staring.

The landscape had shifted, but the changes weren't apparent until we left the shelter of the trees. The mountains were barely a half mile away, glowing purple-gray against the sky. I could see the rough shapes of Blind Michael's halls scattered around the base of the mountain like abandoned building blocks. They all seemed to have shattered walls or broken turrets, outward signs of their decay.

Quentin's fingers tightened on mine as he asked, "Is that—?"

"It's Blind Michael's place," I said. "Come on." I took note of the location of the one solid building—it would make a good prison—and then we started across the plains.

I never want to have another hour like the one that followed. We crept across the ground like invading soldiers, trying to stay low. The light of my candle offered some protection, but I didn't know if it could cover us both, and I didn't want to find out what would happen if we pushed it too far. Spike raced ahead in a blur of gray and green, waiting behind each new obstacle until we caught up. Quentin had taken the first steps toward knighthood in Sylvester's Court; he knew how to be silent and patient. My training has been less formal, but it's had a lot of the same results, and I can keep my peace when I need to. Somehow, trying to hide in plain sight in the lands of a mad Firstborn was really driving that need home.

We stopped when we reached the walls of the first building, sliding behind a pair of water barrels and sinking to the ground. The wall was hot, like there was a fireplace behind it. "All right; here's the plan," I said, voice pitched low. "The kids are in one of these buildings. We find them, we grab them, and we go."

"And Katie?"

"Katie . . ." Getting her first might be the easiest way; she wouldn't be with the others, so we could hide her in the woods while we went back for the others. If she would stay hidden. Terror is an unpredictable thing, and Katie was human. She had less experience with monsters than her fae counterparts.

Katie's humanity raised another issue. The twisted children I'd encountered said the human children would be ridden and changed, becoming horses. If she wasn't herself, I didn't want Quentin to see her until we'd already done everything else we had to do. "We may have a problem there." When his eyes widened, I raised my hand, saying, "I need you to stay calm while we go over this, okay?" He nodded. "Okay."

Lowering my hand, I explained what I'd seen during my brief time as one of Blind Michael's captives—and what they'd said to me. Quentin's eyes narrowed as I spoke, and when I finished he asked, coldly, "Why didn't you mention this before?"

"Because there wasn't time. I'm sorry, and you can hate me if you want, but even if I'd told you before, it wouldn't have changed where we wound up, which is here, needing to rescue *all* of the captives. All right?" He nodded, reluctantly. "Okay. We go for the others first."

That was the wrong thing to say. He sat bolt upright, quivering with fury. "We aren't abandoning her just because she's human! We—"

"Be quiet!" I hissed. "We need to go for the others first because there are more of them, and they're a lot less likely to be traumatized by all of this. You said yourself that Katie doesn't know about the fae. How do you think she's handling this?" He sagged, expression going bleak, and I nodded. "Exactly. We get the others first, because they might be able to help us find her, and if not, at least they're less likely to make things more difficult."

"Fine," he muttered.

"Hate me later," I said. There'd be time to worry about Katie after we found the other children—but that was the real problem. How were we supposed to find them? I turned the candle over in my hand, muttering, "You can get there and back by the candle's light . . ."

"Toby?"

"Just thinking out loud about how we do this. We don't want to open the wrong door."

"No," he agreed. Neither of us wanted to see what skeletons Blind Michael might be keeping in his closet.

I shook my head. "There has to be a way to find them. Blind Michael has to play fair."

"Why?" Quentin frowned. "What's going to make him?"

"The rules. This is a kid's game, and they're always fair—that's what makes them worth winning." I turned the candle again. "There has to be a way."

"Oh." He sighed. "I don't really hate you."

"I know." I paused, eyes widening as I stared at the candle. The game was fair. The game had to be fair. "Hang on a second."

"What?"

Shushing him, I raised the candle. The Luidaeg used my blood to create it, and it sang to me. More and more,

I've been finding that most of my strength is in my blood; there had to be a way for me to use it. Everything in Blind Michael's lands seemed to be based off broken, childish logic, all doggerel and jump rope rhymes. If the rhyme said that I could get there and back by the light of a candle, I probably could, as long as it was the right candle. It was the only lead I had. I might as well try taking it.

"How many miles to Babylon? I fear we've lost our way," I chanted, ignoring Quentin's quizzical look. "Can we get there and back by the candle's light . . ." I tapered off, cursing inwardly. Rhyming has never been one of my strengths.

"Before the break of day?" Quentin finished, putting his hand over mine. I flashed him a grateful look as the flame changed colors, going from blue to a hot amber gold.

That wasn't the only change. Runnels of wax began dripping down the sides, streaking the previously smooth surface. There was no actual blood, but I could feel the tingling burn of blood magic taking hold around me. "That's our cue," I said, standing. "Come on."

"Where are we going?"

"If this is working, to the kids." *And if it's not,* I added silently, *straight to hell.*

The flame brightened as we raced from building to building, trying to outrun the wax and our unseen pursuers at the same time. The flame dwindled whenever we took a wrong turn, guiding us along and consuming wax at a frightening rate. We ran until I wasn't sure I could run anymore, and I was about to call for a stop when the flame flared, turning blue again. I skidded to a halt. Quentin wasn't quite as fast; he caught himself on my shoulder, nearly knocking us both over. "Hey!" I protested. "Remember, you're *bigger* than I am!"

"Sorry," he said, straightening. "Why did you stop?"

"I think we're here." I gestured toward the nearest door. It was made of rough wood shoved into a badly assembled frame, and the walls around it were more intact than those of the other buildings. The wax had stopped melting. I was taking that as a good sign.

"Now what do we do?"

"We break in. Here, hold this." I handed him the candle and turned to examine the door. Just for fun, I tried the handle. It was locked. I hadn't expected anything else. Drawing my knife, I inserted it into the keyhole and twisted until it had gone as deep as it would go.

"What are you doing?" asked Quentin.

"Hang on." Devin had taught me a lot of things, including opening locked doors. He said I was one of the best students he'd ever had. I jiggled the knife a bit more, getting it exactly where I wanted it, and smacked the pommel with the heel of my hand. The lock gave way, leaving the door to swing easily open.

Quentin gaped. I stood, shoving the knife back into my belt, and reclaimed the candle. "One of the many skills you can learn from a wasted youth," I said and stepped inside.

The room was dark and square, filled with rustling noises and small, huddled shapes that seemed to be trying to crawl into the walls. I held the candle up in order to see what they were, and a small voice from the back of the room asked, "Toby? Is that you?"

Oh, thank Maeve; we were in the right place. "Raj?" I called back. "Come on out, kiddo. It's me."

The shadows rustled again, resolving into children. They were clinging to each other, obviously terrified, and I couldn't blame them. One stepped forward, holding his head high as he tried to look like he hadn't been afraid. I lowered the candle to keep the light from hurting his eyes, but even in the dimness, it was impossible to miss the bruises covering his face and shoulders. The Hob he'd escaped with before was leaning on his arm, limping; she looked like she'd been beaten worse than he had.

Raj stopped, looking at me gravely. "October. You came."

"I came," I said. Quentin stayed silent behind me, watching.

"Auntie Birdie? Is that really you?" The voice was soft and anxious, like it expected to be silenced at any moment. I froze. Jessica has always been one of the most confident children I've ever known. Hearing her sound like that ...

Blind Michael was going to die. There wasn't another option.

"Yeah, baby," I said. "It's me."

That was all the confirmation she needed. Jessica came running out of the back of the room, towing Andrew along with her, and flung her arms around me. My height—or lack thereof—didn't seem to matter; I'd said the right words. She buried her face against my shoulder, sobbing, "I was so *scared.*"

"I know, baby," I said, stroking her hair with my free hand. I looked down at Andrew, who had switched his grip from Jessica's arm to my belt. "You okay?"

"We gonna go home now?" he asked. "No more bad mans?"

I nodded. "Yeah. We're going home. We're all going home." I looked up, asking Raj, "How many of you are there?"

"Many," he said, not even trying to hide his exhaustion. "Five from my uncle's Court, and more that I don't know."

"There's at least twenty, Auntie Birdie," Jessica whispered. "They're real scared."

Oh, root and branch. My bargain with Blind Michael only covered my kids; that was all he'd promised me. And there was no way in hell I could leave the others behind.

"Everyone get up and come on," I said. "We're getting out of here."

Children are children whether or not they have pointed ears, and sometimes the illusion of authority is all they need. They broke away from the walls and walked toward us, sniffling and crying as they came. Jessica was right; there were more than twenty of them, a mixed bag of changelings and purebloods. They were alone, and justifiably terrified of what was going to happen. I couldn't have left them behind if I wanted to.

"Quentin, Raj, each of you take a group of about ten," I said, looking to the two who seemed least likely to fall apart. "I'll take care of the rest. Spike, keep an eye out for guards, okay?" The rose goblin rattled its thorns and leaped from my shoulder, streaking out of the hall.

That was the only real precaution I could take. Offering a silent prayer to any gods who might have time to listen to a changeling who didn't know when to quit, I turned and led our motley group out into the shadows of Blind Michael's artificial night. If we were lucky, we'd live to see another dawn.

FIFTEEN

THE SMALLEST CHILDREN WERE THE FIRST
TO TIRE. They faltered and fell, and the larger kids
picked them up and carried them without needing to
be told. They knew that unless we worked together, we
were lost. I surveyed them grimly as we walked across
the plains. Most were barefoot, and more than a few
were wounded; they'd never survive any kind of real
journey. I had no idea how I was going to keep them
calm and moving long enough to get them home. For
the moment, that could wait. My main concern had to
be getting them out of the open and out of the reach of
Blind Michael's men.

Just as a precaution, I made everyone hold hands,
forming clumps that led, eventually, to leaders holding
onto my belt. If the candle could do anything to cover us
all, it would be a blessing.

The forest seemed to reach out to meet us as we made
our way across the plains. Whatever power Acacia had
in her husband's lands was working for us, thank Maeve,
and as the trees grew closer, Quentin, Raj, and I urged
the children to walk faster, moving them toward safety.
It wasn't until the last of them was under cover that I
really started to breathe again. The hard part was still
ahead of us, but we'd cleared the first hurdle.

Helen—the Hob who escaped with Raj—was one of the worst off. Her leg was sprained when the Riders took her back, and after watching her walk, I was afraid her ankle might be broken. Despite that, she'd shown a real gift for calming the smaller children, and once we were in the trees, she settled down with half a dozen of them, humming lullabies in an attempt to get them to sleep. I hoped she'd succeed, because they'd need the rest. We had a long way to go.

Quentin and Raj approached as I stood at the edge of the trees, moving up from opposite sides. Raj was walking more easily now that we were away from the hall, and some elements of natural Cait Sidhe cockiness were creeping into his gestures. Good. I didn't know him well, but no kid deserves to be broken, especially not by a monster like Blind Michael.

"How is everyone?" I asked, looking to Quentin.

"Shaken, but holding together," Quentin said. "Most of them seem to think they've already been rescued, and that this is just the break before we head home."

"Encourage that; I'd rather they were optimistic than hysterical." I looked to Raj. "Helen's pretty hurt. There weren't any healers in my group or Quentin's—how about yours?"

"No, and I'm not sure how much farther she can go," Raj said, expression grave. "How far are we from the exit? We may need to carry her."

"Damn. Is she strong enough to do some basic sewing-magic?" Hobs are hearth-spirits; their magic focuses almost entirely on cleaning and patching things. They can wash and darn a sock with a wave of their hand, using stitches too small for the human eye to see.

"I think so."

"Good. Get any clothes the other kids have to spare—socks, jackets, whatever they can afford to give up—and see if she can sew it into a litter. We'll drag her if we have to."

"Can't we just use some branches?" asked Quentin.

I eyed him. "Do you want to explain that to Acacia?"

He paled. "Okay, no."

"Good." I looked back to Raj. "Can you keep everyone calm until we get back?"

His eyes widened, pupils narrowing in surprise. "Get back? Where are you going?"

"To get my girlfriend," Quentin said. His voice was sharp but calm.

"Your girlfriend?" Raj glanced toward Helen, almost automatically. "Why wasn't she with the others?"

"Because she's human," I said. Raj turned to stare at me, ears slicking back. "Blind Michael takes fae kids to be his Riders. He takes the mortal ones to be his horses."

"That's not going to happen to Katie," Quentin said.

I shook my head. "No, it's not. But that means we have to leave for a little while. Raj, can you watch things here?" Even though I barely knew the kid, he and Quentin were the closest thing I had to lieutenants. I couldn't abandon the children if Raj wasn't willing to take care of them, but I couldn't let Quentin go after Katie alone, either.

Much to my relief, Raj nodded. "I think so. Almost everyone is tired. They should sleep for a little while."

"Good. Just don't let them leave the trees. Do you remember the lady of these woods?"

"The yellow woman?" he asked.

"Yes, her. Her name is Acacia. If anything happens, go to her. Tell her I couldn't make it back, but that Luna is expecting you. She'll help you." *I hope,* I added silently. I had to give Raj something to cling to; if I was leaving him in charge, he had to hold things together. That meant he needed to believe he had a way out. "If we don't come back . . ."

Raj nodded. "I understand."

"Auntie Birdie?"

I winced. "Yes, puss?" I said, as I turned.

Jessica was behind me, expression pleading as she grabbed my arm. "Please don't leave me. Please don't go. I'll be good. Just please, please, don't go."

"Oh, sweetheart." I hugged her tightly, careful to hold my candle away from her hair. "I'm sorry. I have to."

"Will you come back?"

I pushed her out to arm's length, expression grave. "I'll try, baby." Looking back to Raj, I said, "If we don't come back, find Acacia. She'll get you out." If she could.

"All right," Raj said.

Jessica made a soft mewling noise, beginning to cry. I gave her a final hug and pried her hands off my arms as I turned to walk out of the woods, Quentin close behind me. Spike trailed us to the edge of the trees before stopping, clearly intending to stay where it was most needed. Good. Between Spike and Raj, I could almost believe the kids would be all right without us.

"Toby?" Quentin said.

"Yeah?"

"I . . ." He stopped, searching for words. He couldn't thank me.

I smiled wryly. "I know. Come on." I offered my hand. He took it, and together, we stepped out onto the plains.

The distance between the forest and Blind Michael's village hadn't increased while we were in the trees, a small blessing, and one we needed very much. We crossed the plains quickly, moving with more confidence now that it was a familiar journey. That was good, because the stakes were higher, and this was our last try. We'd get Katie and get out, or the odds were good that we wouldn't get out at all. My candle burned clean the entire way, and that made me nervous. Blind Michael had to be expecting me. Either the Luidaeg's protections were working better than I'd dared to dream, or we were walking into a trap. I honestly couldn't have guessed one way or the other. All we could do was keep going.

We saw no one as we entered the village and began moving from building to building, searching for something that could make a feasible stable. Blind Michael's horses were alive and mortal. That meant they'd need food and water to survive, as well as enough space to stay healthy. There should be a paddock of some sort, and a place where they could be exercised . . .

I stopped, sniffing the air. Everything in Blind Michael's lands smelled foul and rancid, but this was something different, something under the decay.

I smelled human blood.

"Come on," I said, turning to head deeper into the village. "This way."

Looking puzzled, Quentin followed as I moved deeper and deeper into the cluster of ramshackle buildings, letting the distant smell of blood serve as my guide. It was human; I was sure of that now, and so strong that it was practically visible. I glanced to Quentin, who was pacing me with a look of grim determination on his face, but no outward signs of knowing where we were going. He was Daoine Sidhe, and the smell of mortal blood was strong enough to be almost choking. He should have smelled it before I did. So why didn't he?

Before I could follow that train of thought any further, the trail ceased to be a trail, resolving instead into a thick miasma of blood, manure, and spoiled grain, surrounding a rickety building whose walls were patched with a dozen types of decaying wood. A second roof had been constructed beneath the shattered remains of the original. Lanterns hung from each corner, casting pools of sharply delineated light and shadow across the ground. There was no door, just a broad, open archway leading to the inside. There was no point in locking the stable. Who would be stupid enough to steal these horses?

I waved for Quentin to stay back. He obeyed, scowling. His posture told me that he wanted to bolt inside, but his training was stronger. He'd been hurt before. He wasn't going to get hurt again just because he didn't listen to me.

Already dreading what we were going to find, I approached the archway. If it was too late to save Katie, none of my efforts to keep Quentin safe would be any good, because it would break him. He was too young to be hurt that way and not be changed by it. Maybe we're always too young for that.

"Toby . . ."

"Come on." The candle was still burning blue. I started forward, motioning for him to follow.

Inside, the stable was just one long, low room, lit by lanterns like the ones we'd seen outside. They cast a sickly white light, making it harder to see, rather than easier. Rotting straw covered the floor, and strange things I assumed were used for the care and tending of horses hung on the far wall. I recognized the saddles. And the whips. Stalls lined the walls on either side, their doors sealed with gates of brambles and twisted wire. Wails and whimpers came from inside, muffled and modulated into high, nickering screams. They didn't sound like children. They barely sounded human.

Horses, I thought numbly. *Faerie children are his Riders, and the human-born are his horses.* I'd been warned, but somehow knowing that it was real made it worse. There are few things I can think of that are worse than unwilling transformation.

Quentin stopped beside me and tensed, taking a sharp breath. I put a hand on his arm, keeping him where he was.

"We're taking this slow, Quentin. All right?" He blinked at me, expression betraying no understanding. "All right?" I repeated. He nodded. I relaxed marginally, taking my hand off his arm. "Good. Follow me." I started down the length of the room, keeping close to the wall. Quentin followed, his footsteps sounding dangerously loud even through the muffling straw.

Now we just needed to figure out which stall Katie was in without opening every door. Filling the stable with panicked human children would be a fast way to bring the guards down on our heads—if they weren't already en route.

Blind Michael's lands followed their own rules, but those rules had been consistent and thus technically fair so far. What worked once should work again, unless the rules had changed, and changing the rules was cheating. I raised the candle, saying, "How many miles to Babylon? It's three-score miles and ten. Can we find what we seek by the candle's light and still get out again?"

The flame blazed upward. I jumped, nearly losing my grip. I think I would've dropped it if I hadn't internalized the rhyme so intensely: I could get there and back, yes, but only by the light of a candle. If we lost that light, none of us would be going anywhere. Slowly, the flame shrunk, becoming brighter until it was nothing but a small, nearly blinding spark. The wax was melting twice as fast as it had been before. Damn. We needed to hurry, or the wax would run out and our problems would get a *lot* worse.

"Toby, what—"

"We're just gonna follow the candle." I stepped forward and the flame dimmed, almost going out. I stepped back, and the flame brightened again. Quentin followed as I walked to the mouth of the stable, and we began making our way down the middle of the room, both of us watching the candle.

We were halfway to the back wall when the flame turned red. There was only one door nearby. It was rough wood behind a gate of wire and brambles, just like all the others. I walked over to it, reaching out and trying the handle. It was locked.

"I can't break this with a knife, and I don't have my lock picks. We need to find a key." I let go of the handle. A loop of thorns immediately snarled my fingers, holding them in place. "Oh, crap." I pulled, trying to free my hand. The brambles tightened. "Quentin, it's got me."

"What am I supposed to do?" he asked, eyes wide.

"Get me loose!"

"How?"

"Cut it!" The thorns burned cold, freezing all the way down to the bone. "Fast!"

Quentin jerked the knife from my belt and swung it toward the briar. I gritted my teeth, doing my best to hold still. Having a killer thorn bush attack my hand was bad; accidentally losing a couple of fingers would be worse.

Then the blade hit the brambles.

The vines themselves seemed to scream, a thin, keening noise that came from everywhere and nowhere at once as they tightened, writhing and burying themselves more deeply in my hand. I shrieked before I could stop myself, crying, "Quentin, *stop!*"

His hand shook as he pulled the knife away. The thorns stopped screaming, but didn't let go. I stood there blinking back tears, listening for sounds of alarm. We couldn't afford to attract attention to ourselves. If we got caught . . . I shivered. If they caught us, we were worse than dead.

Fine: we couldn't cut through the thorns. What else could we use to open the door? Blood obviously wasn't the answer; it had plenty of my blood already. I could try a spell, but I don't know any make-the-living-lock-let-go spells. I might have been able to manage an illusory key, but I didn't know what it needed to look like, or how to make the lock believe it was real. Quentin wasn't going to be any help until he calmed down, and the candle flame was so high that it was almost scorching my skin. I paused. Everything in Blind Michael's lands had been affected by the candle. Why should the lock be any different?

I brought my free hand up and around, shoving the candle into the brambles. The vines wrapped around my hand let go, and I staggered backward, swearing. The cuts they left behind were small but deep and ran across the length of my hand.

"Are you okay?" Quentin asked, moving to brace me.

"I'm fine," I said. The vines were continuing to retreat. The flame returned to its normal height as the last bramble pulled away, dimming to a placid blue. It looked like we'd reached our destination, whatever it turned out to be. "I think it's safe to go in."

"Are you sure?"

"No." Unsurprisingly, the door wasn't locked anymore. I pushed it open, stepping through into a narrow stall full of dusty straw and strange, unpleasant shadows. A trough stood along one wall, half-filled with murky liquid. It was too dark to see anything clearly. I lifted the candle almost without thinking about it, letting it illuminate the area.

The light wasn't merciful. I closed my eyes, whispering, "Oh, sweet Maeve . . ." Quentin stepped up next to me and stopped, putting his hand on my shoulder. I could feel the tension in his fingers, and so I opened my eyes, trying to make sense of what I was seeing. It wasn't easy.

Katie was in the far corner with her back pressed against the wall, watching the open door with obvious terror in her face. She wasn't visibly injured, and her clothing was mostly intact; she hadn't been beaten or raped. That was a point in Blind Michael's favor. It wasn't nearly enough.

There's an art to transformation. Lily once described it as being a sort of sculpture, using flesh instead of wood or metal: you take something that *is* and turn it into something that *isn't*. Like any art it takes talent and practice. Someone truly skilled in the transformational arts can finish a change in an instant or stretch it out into a year. It all depends on the work itself . . . and on how cruel the artist wants to be.

Streaks of white radiated through Katie's hair, longer and visibly rougher than the human hair around them. Her ears had grown long, flexible and equine, sprouting a fine covering of short white hair and moving up the sides of her head until they were clearly more horse than human. She flicked them back as Quentin started to approach her; it was an instinctive gesture, and that, in and of itself, was chilling—how much humanity had she already lost? Her hands were splayed on her knees, like she was trying to force the fingers to stay apart, and her fingernails had spread to cover the first knuckle, taking on a dark, glossy sheen as they warped into hooves.

Her face was still human, even framed by horse's ears and the beginnings of a mane, and the terror in her eyes told me that her mind was equally intact. Blind Michael was taking his time, making every inch hurt. That was the best way to get what he wanted; when the change was done, her spirit would be broken, and she'd be ready to obey. Bastard. Silently, I swore he'd die for what he'd done. It wasn't the first time I'd made that promise. I was pretty sure it wouldn't be the last.

Quentin dropped to his knees in front of her, reaching out as if to pull her into his arms. She whimpered and jerked backward, almost falling. The reason for her oddly formal posture became apparent as she moved: her skirt had been split up the back and tied together with a dirty shoelace. A fully-formed horse's tail protruded through the hole she'd made there, matted with muck and straw from the stable floor. It would've been pretty, if it hadn't been attached to a panicked human girl.

"Katie—" Quentin said helplessly, and reached for her again. This time she screamed. It ended in a high-pitched, inhuman whinny. Things were changing inside her as well as out.

"Quentin, move away from her," I said.

"But—"

"Look at her. You need to move away." Katie looked toward me and cringed, falling silent. She'd already learned the value of obedience. I guess terror is a good teacher.

Quentin rose and walked back to me, shivering. "What's wrong with her?" he asked.

"Besides the obvious?" I gestured toward my ears, then his. "We're what's wrong with her. She's already confused, and she thinks you're human. Right now, you look like another part of this nightmare."

"I—" he began, and stopped, staring at me. "Oh, root and branch." He looked back to Katie, who was trying to vanish into her corner. "She thinks I'm one of them."

"Yes, she does," I said, gently. "You can't go to her. She won't let you."

"But ..."

I put a hand on his shoulder. "Let me do this?"

Quentin bit his lip, nodding. I could see how much the gesture had cost him.

The scratches on my hand were still bleeding, and that was a good thing; blood always makes things easier for me when there's magic involved. I walked over and knelt in front of Katie, holding my candle between us. "Hello," I said. She whimpered. I ignored it, continuing, "My name's Toby. I want to take you home. Do you want to go home?" She burrowed farther into the corner, flattening her ears. She wasn't going to believe a word I said, and that was fine; it just meant I'd have to work without her permission. With fresh-drawn blood on my hands, the lack of permission wouldn't stop me.

"'If we shadows have offended, think but this, and all is mended,'" I said. The smell of copper and cut grass rose around us, damped down and made small by the alien nature of Blind Michael's lands. "'That you have but slumbered here while these visions did appear ...'" The spell wasn't taking hold. I needed more blood; I wasn't strong enough to catch her without it. I've never been strong enough to work without the blood.

I raised my wounded hand to my mouth and sucked at the deepest of the scratches. The blood was hot and bitter. "'And this weak and idle theme, no more yielding but a dream.'" The smell of copper burst around us, leaving me with a pounding headache. Magic takes strength, and I was running out.

Katie's face went slack as the spell took hold. I shook my head to clear it and said, "Katie, you don't feel well. You have an upset stomach, and you want to go home. You don't see anything strange, you just feel a little sick. Your boyfriend is going to walk you home. Do you understand?" She nodded, expression unchanging. I patted her hand, and she didn't pull away. "Good. Quentin will be here in a moment." She nodded again and smiled, settling in to wait. She'd wait until Quentin came or the spell ran out, whichever came first. As long as nothing broke my illusions, she'd be fine, but any major shock could jolt her back into the present. I needed to keep her away from mirrors and away from Blind Michael.

I stood, breathing unevenly. "Quentin, hurry. You need to get her out of here."

"Are you all right?"

"It's just a little magic burn. I'll be fine. Now hurry."

He nodded and walked back over to Katie, kneeling in the straw. "Kates? You okay?"

She smiled. The spell was working; thank Maeve for that. "Hi, Quentin. I've been waiting. Are you gonna take me home now?"

"Yeah," he said, and smiled back. I don't think she could see his tears through the illusions clouding her eyes. "I'll take you home. Are you ready to go?"

"Oh, yeah. I just don't feel good." She stumbled as she stood, and Quentin caught her. The tail was throwing her off-balance. Katie frowned. "I think I need to lie down."

"It's okay," he said, leading her toward the exit. "I'll get you home."

I followed as fast as I could, trying to pretend that it didn't hurt to leave the other locked doors behind. There were more children behind those doors, changing into something they didn't understand, and I couldn't save them. That much magic wouldn't just hurt me; it might kill me, and then what would *my* children do? Blind Michael was going to pay for everything he'd done, but most of all, he was going to pay for making me walk away and leave those children behind. I'd come back for them if I could, but my kids needed me first. And it wasn't fair. Life so rarely is.

Just once, I'd like to find a real hero, someone who can save the day, because I'm obviously not cut out for the job. I followed Quentin and Katie out of the stable, half blinded by pain and anger, and once we were safely hidden by the shadows of the plains, I let myself cry. I'd have to stop before we reached the forest—the kids needed me to look strong—but for the moment, it helped.

Where the hell's *my* hero?

SIXTEEN

JESSICA CAME RACING OUT OF THE TREES as we approached, already sobbing. She slammed into me and buried her face against my shoulder. I managed to brace myself enough to absorb the impact without falling over, but it was a close thing; we were too similar in size for that kind of collision to be comfortable. "Aunt Birdie!" she wailed, voice muffled. "I thought you weren't c-coming back!"

I sighed, letting go of Quentin's hand and stroking her hair. "I've been getting that a lot lately." Spike came slinking out of the woods and sat by my feet, thorns bristling as it whined in the back of its throat. I understood the warning it was giving us; we couldn't afford to dawdle. Blind Michael promised safety once we were out of his lands—or at least he'd promised safety for the kids I'd bargained for, and I didn't want to consider what that might mean for the rest—but he'd never said anything about leaving us alone inside his borders.

"Are you back for keeps? Can we go home now?"

"I'm back." I looked over Jessica's head to watch Quentin guide Katie the last few yards.

Katie had fallen into brittle silence as we walked, using Quentin as much for guidance as for balance. The spell clouding her vision could only take so much abuse, and she could keep it alive longer if she refused to see what was going on. Smart girl. I wondered numbly whether Quentin realized she'd lost a shoe, and whether, if he did, he realized that it was because her feet were already broad and blackened, more than halfway to being hooves. The changes were continuing. They were slow, but they weren't stopping.

"Come on," I said, shifting Jessica so that she was just clinging to my arm. "We need to get back to the others."

"And then we'll go home?" whispered Jessica.

"Yeah, baby. Then we'll go home." I started walking, heading toward where we'd left the rest of the children. The word "home" seemed to give Jessica some of her confidence back, because she let go of me after a few steps, darting ahead and vanishing into the trees.

Raj and the others had been hard at work while we were away. Five of the older kids were busy lashing bundles of sticks together as they finished Helen's litter, and there were sentries posted in the trees, almost invisible through the leaves until you walked under them. I smiled faintly. "Leave it to the Cait Sidhe to take to guerrilla warfare without blinking," I said.

"What?" asked Raj, appearing accompanied by the smell of pepper and burning paper.

Quentin jumped, nearly knocking Katie over. I just shook my head. One good thing about spending years being tormented by Tybalt: I don't surprise as easily as I used to where the Cait Sidhe are concerned.

"I was just saying that you seem to have things pretty organized," I said, taking a better look around. The kids that Raj didn't have on sentry duty or building a litter had mostly gone to sleep, pillowed in the leaves and clinging to one another. Those that were still awake but unoccupied were sitting with Helen, listening raptly as she spoke. From the way she was moving her hands, I guessed she was telling them a story, and for a moment, I almost envied her. Whether we lived or died, the pressure wasn't on her. She was taking care of the children and leaving the heroics to Raj—and to me. Lucky us.

"Busy is easier than idle," he said, one ear flicking back. Turning, he looked at Quentin and Katie, and frowned. "Is this your friend?" he asked.

Quentin nodded. "This is Katie."

"I thought you said she was—"

"That's enough," I said. The spell I'd cast on Katie was keeping her from noticing the changes in her body—and don't think I didn't see the irony, considering what the Luidaeg had done to me—but it wasn't going to stand up to someone questioning her humanity where she could hear it. "Raj, is the litter ready?"

"Almost," he said, looking bemused.

"Good." Andrew rose from the group around Helen when he heard my voice, walking over to take hold of my sweater. I sighed and stood a little straighter, sliding my arm around him. I had to be their hero whether I liked it or not; I was the only option they had. "Quentin, Raj, leave Katie with me and start collecting the others. We need to move."

Helen looked up, eyes going wide. "But everyone's exhausted!" she protested. "We can't move yet."

"If we don't move, we risk being caught. If anyone wants to stay behind, they can, but we're moving now." It wasn't a nice to thing to say, and I didn't care. I couldn't risk everyone because a few were unwilling to move. It would kill me to leave them behind, but I'd do it. I knew that as surely as I knew I'd die before I let the Riders take back Jessica and Andrew. Maybe that made me a bad person. Maybe it didn't. Either way, it was time to go.

My words had the desired effect. The children who were awake moved to rouse the others with a speed that bordered on panic as the sentries dropped out of the trees, rejoining the group. Several of the larger kids hoisted Helen onto her litter. The buddy system seemed to have become a religion—everyone had someone's hand to hold. No one wanted to face the plains alone. Their eyes were blank and hollow, like the eyes of ref-ugees running from a war they didn't understand and couldn't escape. There were no tears. The time for tears was past. It was time to go, and none of us knew what was coming.

I led the way onto the plains with Jessica on my arm and Andrew clinging to my shirt, the hand-holding chains re-forming behind them. Quentin walked beside me, supporting as much of Katie's weight as he could. I'd been more concerned about Helen, but I'd also underestimated how quickly Raj would be able to find the strongest among the children: six of them traded off dragging the litter, taking turns so that no one got too tired, while the youngest took turns riding with Helen. It was a good system, and it kept us moving faster than I'd hoped.

Spike stayed near the back of the procession, whining and rattling its thorns as it urged us to keep moving. Blind Michael couldn't miss us forever. Worse, my candle was still melting; it was barely half the size it was when the Luidaeg gave it to me, and I didn't know how much longer it would last.

Raj wandered up to the front after rotating the litter-bearers, glancing back over his shoulder. "Where are we going?" he asked, voice low. "Everyone is getting tired. We'll have to make Helen walk soon."

Sometimes you have to admire the bloody-minded selfishness of cats. It was obvious that he didn't care about most of the kids, but Helen was his. He wanted her to be safe.

I was too tired to lie. "I don't know."

"What?" he demanded, ears flattening. Even Quentin turned to stare at me, his arm tightening around Katie.

"We can get there and back by the light of a candle." I shrugged. "We have the candle. Now we just need to find the way out."

"Didn't you get a . . . a . . . a tracing spell, or a map, or something?"

"I got a candle." The instructions said to get "there and back again." That meant I needed to exit where I'd started, if I was going to exit at all, and that meant the plains.

"What if it's not enough?" he asked. Jessica raised her head, eyes wide. I glanced around. Several of the other children were staring at us, expressions troubled. He was scaring them.

Right. I glared, saying, "That's enough. Raj, please don't make this worse than it is. I'll get us out of here. I promise." Me and my big mouth. Promises are binding; I need to learn to stop making them. The Cait Sidhe looked at me for a long moment before turning and walking back to Helen's litter, posture telegraphing his displeasure. I couldn't blame him—I wouldn't have been any happier in his place—but we needed to keep moving.

We walked for what felt like hours before the landscape began becoming more familiar. The rocks began to look less random and more like landmarks. I stopped when I saw the first footprints. Waving the group to a halt, I knelt, studying the ground. "Quentin, Raj, come here."

Quentin reluctantly handed Katie off to one of the litter-bearers and walked over, reaching me just as Raj did. "What's up?" he asked.

I indicated the footprints. "Are these mine?"

"They smell like you," Raj said.

Quentin's answer took more time as he looked from my reduced feet to the marks in the dirt and back several times. Finally, he nodded. "Yes."

"Good." I rose. This was where I'd entered Blind Michael's lands. If there was a way out, we'd find it here. "We rest here."

The children dropped where they were, forming loose circles as they flopped on the stony ground. Quentin led Katie to one of the larger rocks, helping her settle. The tail was a problem; she wasn't aware of its existence, but she couldn't sit on it without hurting herself. Quentin finally reached around and moved it out of the way, pulling his hands away from the silky hair like he'd been burned.

Katie smiled glassily. "Will we be home soon?" The

changes were continuing; thin lines of white hair now ran down her cheeks like a parody of sideburns.

"Sure, Kates. Sure." He gave me a pleading look. Of course. Leave it to Toby—she needs another ulcer.

My candle was dwindling, still burning a steady blue. We were safe, but for how much longer? I was afraid to risk another invocation. The two I'd done already had used up most of the wax, and we couldn't afford a failure.

Oh, well. Third time's the charm, especially in Faerie. "Luidaeg?" I said. "Luidaeg, if you can hear me, we're scared, and I don't know how this works. We need to come home now. I've got the candle, Luidaeg, you said I could get there and back . . ." The flame sputtered and turned crimson, surging upward. I jerked it away from myself, nearly dropping it, and a hunting horn sounded in the distance.

More horns followed, and more, and more, until the air rang with them and the sound of hoofbeats began to rumble through the ground. Blind Michael's men were coming, and my candle couldn't cast enough light to hide us all.

And everything started to happen at once.

The children jumped to their feet, clustering around me in uniform silence. They knew that screaming would destroy any chance of escape. Not that silence was going to save us: the hoofbeats were getting closer, and there was no place to hide. It was finished. It had to be.

I looked at the candle in my hand and at the knife at my belt, and wondered how many of them I could kill before the Riders took us.

"Aunt Birdie! This way!"

I turned toward the voice. Karen was standing behind me, pointing toward the nearest briar. Her robe was dark with dust. "Karen?" None of the others had turned. It was like they couldn't hear her calling.

"You have to hurry! Go through the thorns—you'll need the blood! *Hurry!*" She gestured frantically, and I realized with dim horror that I could see through her. In my experience, see-through people are usually dead.

I was raised a daughter of the Daoine Sidhe; we listen to the dead, and there'd be time to grieve after I'd
gotten everyone else out alive. I grabbed Jessica's hand,
tucking Andrew up under my arm, and sprinted for the
briar, calling, "This way!" There was a pause, and then
the shell-shocked children followed, hauling each other
along as they hurried to catch up.

The horns were getting closer. Blind Michael's men
were faster, armed, and on our trail, while all I had was
a candle and the word of the ghost of a girl I hadn't seen
die. Not great odds.

I skidded to a stop at the edge of the briar, searching for an opening. There didn't seem to be one. Karen
said we needed blood; fine. Blood was something I could
manage. I thrust the hand that held the candle into the
branches, ripping my skin in a dozen places. There was
an instant of perfect silence, like the world had stopped.
Maybe it had.

And a door opened in the air.

The Luidaeg was on the other side, white-eyed and
frantic, with ashes in her hair. Her panic barely registered in the face of my own. "Hurry!" she shouted in
an eerie imitation of Karen's tone. "You let it burn too
long!"

I didn't pause to think. I pulled my hand out of the
thorns, grabbed Andrew and shoved him at her, then
pushed Jessica after him. Raj and Quentin seemed to
get the idea, because they started herding the children
toward the door. Katie and Helen were among the first.
Then the Riders came over the hill, and there was a mad
rush as children raced for freedom. In no time at all, it
was just Raj, Spike, and me, standing on the wrong side
of a door between the worlds.

"Toby, come on!" shouted Quentin, reaching back
toward us. I looked over my shoulder, shoving Raj into
his arms. The weight of the Cait Sidhe knocked Quentin
backward, leaving me with a clear escape route. Spike
jumped after him, hissing as it went.

That was it. "Toby!" the Luidaeg shouted. I jumped, reaching for her—

—and a hand grabbed my ankle, dragging me back. I screamed, scrabbling for purchase in the thorns.

"The candle!" the Luidaeg called. "You don't need it anymore!"

The candle? I twisted around and flung it away as hard as I could, catching a glimpse of darkness and horns as it hit the Rider holding me. He let go of my ankle, falling back with a scream. Then the Luidaeg had me, pulling me through the hole in the world. Everything went dark. There was a boom, like something sealing itself, and the light returned in a flash.

I was on top of the Luidaeg in the middle of her kitchen floor, surrounded by frightened, crying children. I blinked at her, trying to figure out what had happened.

"Are you done, or do you need a nap?" she demanded. "You're heavy. Get off."

"Sorry." I pushed myself away from her, wincing as I put pressure on my sliced-up hands. The kitchen seemed too large, and the children were still too close to my height; leaving Blind Michael's lands hadn't broken the spell. Swell. "Is everyone here?"

"All of us," Raj called, helping one of the others stand. "We're all here."

"Alive," added Helen. I looked around anyway, reassuring myself. The kids were frightened and crying, but none of them looked any worse than they had on the plains. Katie was seated in one of the few intact chairs with Quentin behind her. He was stroking her hair, wincing when his fingers hit a patch of white. My spell was holding; she was smiling, oblivious to it all.

"Oh, thank Maeve," I breathed, looking back to the Luidaeg. "Your gifts worked." Thanking her mother was as close as I could get to thanking her.

She smiled, the brown bleeding back into her eyes. "I knew they would. You made it."

"Yeah, we did." I paused. "Luidaeg . . . I'm still a kid."

"And a cute one at that." She grinned. "Bet your mom could just eat you up. You're a bit pointier than you used to be, but that's what you get for wrestling with thorn briars."

"How long is this going to last?"

"Not long." She sobered, shaking her head. There was something I didn't recognize behind the darkness in her eyes. I didn't like it. "Not long at all."

"Luidaeg?"

"What?" She frowned, the strangeness fading. "You need to get these brats out of here. I can't stand kids."

"Of course." I make it a rule not to push the Luidaeg when she doesn't want to be pushed. I don't want to be a snack food. "Can I use your phone?"

"Why?" she asked.

"I can't exactly drive like this." Although the idea of a car full of kids careening down the highway was amusing, it wasn't practical. For one thing, I wouldn't be able to reach the pedals. "We need someone to pick us up, unless you want to drive us."

She wrinkled her nose. "Me, play taxi? No."

"Thought so." Andrew and Jessica were still clinging to each other as I slipped out of the kitchen, heading into the living room. The phone was on an end table next to the couch. I walked over to it, ignoring the crunching sounds underfoot, and paused.

Who was I supposed to call? Tybalt didn't drive, and I didn't want to explain the current situation to Connor. Mitch and Stacy didn't need the added stress, especially not given what I thought I'd learned about Karen. There would be time to tell them that their daughter was probably dead later, after I'd managed to get the rest of the children home.

The Luidaeg's phone had a dial tone; that surprised me. It implied a more solid connection to the real world than I'd expected. I dialed Danny's number from memory. Six rings later, Danny's voice announced jovially, "You've reached Daniel McReady—"

"Danny, great! It's Toby. I—"

"—and I'm not available to take your call right now, on account of I have a job. If you're calling about breed rescue, please leave a detailed message, including your name, address, and how many you want." Something barked in the background. Muffled, he shouted, "Tilly! You stop biting your sister!" before returning to say, more normally, "Everybody else, you can leave a message, too, and I'll call you just as soon as I can. I gotta go break up a fight in the kennel. Later." With that, the connection was cut, leaving me groaning.

Danny wasn't available. Now who was I supposed to call? Santa Claus? He could fly through the city dropping us down chimneys . . . no. Not Santa, but someone almost as good. I dialed again, quickly, and waited.

The phone was answered immediately. "You've reached October Daye's place, this is Toby."

"No, it's not," I said. "If you were me, you'd know I never sound that happy when I answer the phone."

"Toby!" said May, delighted. "Where are you?"

"At the Luidaeg's; I need a ride. Can you take a cab over here? My car's here, but I can't drive it right now."

"I guess. Where did you *go?* Don't you know you're not supposed to leave without telling me? I can't do my job if I don't know how to find you!"

My Fetch was yelling at me for ditching her. Surrealism lives. "I'll keep that in mind, okay? Just get over here."

"Sure thing, Boss," she said, and hung up. I shook my head, putting down the receiver as I rose. Doesn't anyone believe in saying good-bye anymore?

Of course, the fact that May existed meant I'd be saying some final good-byes in the near future. I walked back into the kitchen, almost grateful for my exhaustion. I was too tired to get as upset as I wanted to.

The Luidaeg was leaning against the refrigerator,

keeping a wary eye on the children. Most were asleep in piles on the floor; the ones who were still awake were sitting with Helen. Raj, back in feline form, was dozing in her lap. Quentin was still behind Katie, unmoving.

"Well?" said the Luidaeg. "Who did you call?"

"No one," I said, kneeling to pick up Spike and pressing my face against its thorny side. "Just Death."

SEVENTEEN

MAY ARRIVED ABOUT HALF AN HOUR LATER. Most San Francisco taxi drivers are barely this side of sane and drive like they expect scouts for the Indy 500 to be hiding on every corner. When you add that to their creatively broken English, you've created a taxi experience everyone should have once. Just once. Only once. Unless you're in such a hurry that you're considering grabbing the nearest Tylwyth Teg and demanding a ride on a bundle of yarrow twigs, wait for the bus. If that's too slow for you, you may want to look into the local availability of yarrow twigs, because splinters in your thighs are less upsetting than taking a San Francisco taxi.

The Luidaeg answered the door in her customary fashion: she wrenched it open, snarling, "What do *you* want?" Then she froze, staring. Nice to see I wasn't the only one who reacted that way. "What the fu—"

May waved, a grin plastered across her face. "Hi, I'm May. Is Toby here?"

The moment was almost worth the entire situation. I'd never seen the Luidaeg flustered before. It only lasted a few seconds before she narrowed her eyes. "Whatever you are, you're not Toby." Her voice was suddenly pitched low, and very dangerous. "You smell wrong. What are you?"

"I should smell wrong—I just doused myself in strawberry eucalyptus bath oil. It's disgusting!" Her grin broadened. "Is Toby here? She told me to meet her here. This is the right place, isn't it? You are the Luidaeg, aren't you? You look like the Luidaeg ..."

"Yes," said the Luidaeg, not relaxing. "I am. Now who the hell are *you?*"

"I already told you." May blinked, smile fading in confusion. "I'm May Daye."

The Luidaeg stiffened. I stepped forward, putting my hand on her arm. "Luidaeg, wait." Somehow I didn't think letting her gut my Fetch would prevent my impending death. Pity. "She's my Fetch."

"What?" The Luidaeg turned to stare at me, eyebrows arching until they almost hit her hairline. There was something in her eyes that looked like fear. Why would the Luidaeg be afraid of my Fetch? May was there for me, not her.

"Fetch," said May, cheerful as ever. My sudden second childhood didn't seem to be bothering her. It wasn't surprising her either. I really should've paid more attention when my mother taught me about Fetches. I knew May was created with my memories, but I didn't know how much she'd know about what happened to me after she was "born." "I'm here to escort her into the valley of the damned. Only first I'm going to give her a ride home. And maybe stop for Indian food."

I smiled wearily. It was hard not to admire her enthusiasm, even if she existed because I was about to die. She'd go when I did, and I couldn't have been that cheerful if I had that short a time to live. Oh, wait. I *did* have that short a time to live, and I wasn't that cheerful. "Hi, May."

"Hello!" she said, waving again. "Could you do me a teeny little favor?"

"What's that?" I asked warily. Call me crazy, but I'm not big on granting my personal incarnation of death little favors, no matter how much I like her attitude.

"Tell me before you run off to get yourself killed,

okay? It would *really* help me do my job." She looked at me pleadingly.

How was I supposed to answer that? I struggled for a moment before settling for sarcasm. "Far be it from me to hinder your efforts to carry me off into the great beyond."

"Great!" she said, grinning again. She was apparently invulnerable to sarcasm. Her smile faded as she realized that the Luidaeg was still blocking her way. "Um, can I come in?"

"Luidaeg?" The sea witch was looking between us, eyes narrowing. I could almost see her losing her temper. "Can she come in?"

"Sure," she said, tone tight as she stepped aside. "I'm always glad to invite death into my home."

"I'm not death," said May, stepping into the hall. "I'm just part of the auxiliary plan."

She obviously didn't get my survival instincts when she inherited my memories. I would never have brushed the Luidaeg off like that, at least not if I wanted to keep my head attached to the rest of my body. "May—" I began.

"Oh, don't worry," she said. "She can't hurt me."

"She's right," snarled the Luidaeg. The look in her eyes was more than angry—it was furious, and I suddenly wondered whether she'd be the one who killed me. "You're her target. I can't hurt her unless I do it by hurting you."

I frowned, trying to conceal my worry. "So what, she can get away with anything?"

"Just until you die," said May, in a tone that was probably meant to be reassuring.

Rolling my eyes, I turned and walked back to the kitchen. May waved to the Luidaeg one more time and followed, staying close at my heels.

I should have thought about what would happen when I walked into the kitchen with my adult double, but I was tired and scared and worn down, and I didn't even consider it. Most of the kids stayed where they were, huddled together and more than half-asleep. They'd never seen what I really looked like, and my former adulthood was just a story to them.

I have to give Quentin credit—his hands tightened on the back of Katie's chair, but he didn't move. He just waited for my signal, ready to attack or run on my command. The kid was learning. Jessica was less discreet. She looked up and screamed, shielding her head with her arms as she tried to hide behind Andrew. Katie jerked, the spell that was keeping her calm visibly weakening. The other children were awake and scrambling to their feet in an instant, eyes wide with panic. I ran across the room to Jessica, pulling her arms away from her head and making shushing noises. There'd been too much screaming already.

Andrew frowned at his sister and looked solemnly from me to May, taking his thumb out of his mouth. Jessica kept screaming, screwing her eyes shut until I slapped my hand over her mouth in exasperation. That got her attention. Her eyes snapped open, staring at me.

"Jessie, you need to calm down, please," I said. "It's okay. She's not here to hurt us." The screaming stopped, but her breathing didn't slow. I took my hand away from her mouth and wrapped my arms around her.

Andrew studied me, then looked to May. "You're not my auntie," he said gravely.

May nodded. "You're right."

"She is," he said, and pointed to me.

"Right again."

"Okay." He put his thumb back into his mouth. The discussion was finished: as long as May knew she wasn't his aunt, he didn't care whose face she wore. Sometimes I envy kids for the way they dismiss the things that don't matter. They still get bogged down in details, but at least they're different details.

Keeping my voice low, I said, "Jessica, this is my cousin May. She's here to give us a ride home." I don't normally lie to kids, but somehow, I didn't think telling them their rescuer was doomed to die soon was exactly going to help. "You want to go home, don't you?" Jessica sniffled and nodded, clutching me more tightly. "That's my good girl."

The Luidaeg was leaning in the kitchen doorframe, arms crossed over her breasts. She was clearly doing a slow burn, almost radiating anger.

Letting go of Jessica, I straightened, saying, "Luidaeg?"

"Yes?"

"I need to get the kids home. But my car . . ."

"You want me to cast an expansion spell on that junk heap you insist on pretending is a car? Blood and thorn, Toby, when you decide to go into debt, you don't screw around." She snapped her fingers. "It's done, and yes, it comes with a don't-look-here to keep your idiotic ass out of sight. Now get the hell out."

"Luidaeg . . ." I wanted to thank her, but it wasn't allowed. Why aren't things ever simple?

She smiled bitterly. "Just get out. That's what you want, isn't it?"

"I'll get everyone out of here," said May with sudden, aggressive cheerfulness. Maybe she was smarter than I thought. She started gathering children out of the corners, herding them toward the door.

"Raj, Quentin, get Katie and Helen and go with May," I said, keeping my eyes on the Luidaeg. They didn't argue. Raj slid back to human form, and the kitchen was filled with scuffling, hisses, and whines for several minutes as they led the assembled children and cat-form Cait Sidhe into the hall. Spike got a running start, leaping first to the counter and then into my arms. I clutched it, glad for the contact. Spike hadn't changed. I needed that.

When the kitchen was empty I said, "Luidaeg, what's wrong?"

"Wrong?" The color bled out of her eyes as she looked at me, leaving them white and angry. The lines of her face had sharpened, becoming alien. She was losing her grip on her human shape, and that was a little scary.

What had I said that upset her that much? "Why would you think anything was wrong, October Daye, daughter of Amandine? I swore I'd see you dead. It just looks like I was right."

Oh, oak and ash, I hadn't warned her about May. "Luidaeg, I—"

"Is that why you were willing to come to me? Because you already expected to die?" Her voice was rising. "I never took you for a coward. Now get out of my house."

"Luidaeg—"

"Get *out!*" Her hands were curling into claws. I'm not stupid. I didn't want to leave while the Luidaeg was mad at me—dangerous though she can be, I consider her a friend—but I also didn't want her to kill me for pushing my luck. Keeping Spike clutched against my chest, I turned and ran into the hall, then out the door.

The sunlight was an almost physical shock. I stumbled, and the doorknob hit me in the side as the door slammed behind me. Spike jumped out of my arms, running to where it wouldn't be hit if I fell. Then an arm slid under mine and Raj was there, holding me up.

"Clumsy half-blood," he said, scornfully.

I smiled, hoping it would hide my panic. "Just pissing off the Luidaeg. No big."

"Clumsy *and* stupid," he said, with a note of respect in his voice. He let go of me, walking over to my car. May was leaning against the hood, and the children were inside. *All* the children. When the Luidaeg bends space, she doesn't screw around.

You can fit four people in a VW bug if they're friendly; you can manage five if you don't need oxygen inside the car and six if no one cares about having feeling in their limbs. That's it, period, you've reached the limit. I never got an exact count of the children I'd rescued from Blind Michael, but there were more than twenty, and all of them, except for Raj and Quentin, were in the backseat. I knew my car wasn't big enough. My eyes were telling me it was.

Never argue with reality when it's working for you. I walked over to open the passenger side door, saying, "Okay, everybody in."

Quentin and Raj climbed into the back, Quentin pausing to squeeze my shoulder. I settled in the front, barely flinching as Spike jumped onto my lap with all claws extended. "Is everybody okay back there?"

There was a mumbled chorus of assent. May walked around and sat in the driver's seat, fastening her seat belt. "Everyone buckled up?" The chorus mumbled again. "Good!"

I gave her a sidelong look as I fastened my own belt. "Worried about safety?"

"Yup. No one's immortal." She winked. I suppressed a shudder. "Where to?"

"Shadowed Hills."

"Whatever you say, Boss!" She slammed the clutch back, and we were suddenly hurtling down the street at a speed fast enough to make me grab the dashboard and gape at her. Not being able to see through the windshield didn't help. I'd forgotten how scary it is to be a kid in a car. You don't know where you're going, you don't know how you're getting there, and you don't know whether you're going to survive the trip.

May's driving wasn't helping. She didn't turn the wheel; she *attacked* it, like she was wrestling snakes instead of steering the car. Some of the kids roused themselves enough to treat it like a roller coaster ride, cheering as we careened around corners and through stop signs. I just closed my eyes and waited for the inevitable crash.

Shadowed Hills is normally more than a thirty-minute drive from the Luidaeg's place. I didn't open my eyes until I felt the car bump to a surprisingly gentle stop, and even then I only looked up cautiously, half expecting to find us dangling over a ravine or something. Instead, we were parked in the Paso Nogal parking lot, well clear of any other cars.

May grinned, looking pleased with herself. "As requested, Shadowed Hills."

"Peachy," I said dryly, climbing out of the car and pulling the seat forward to let the others out. Quentin and Katie came first, the young Daoine Sidhe guiding his half-crippled girlfriend with almost painful care. She stumbled as she walked; her knees were trying to bend the wrong way. The changes were still accelerating. That scared me. That scared me a lot.

I stepped over and slid my arm under Katie's, helping to hold her up. "Watch the kids," I said to May, more sharply than I meant to. It wasn't fair to blame her. That's never stopped me before. "I'm going to help Quentin get Katie inside."

"You don't need to," Quentin said. He sounded exhausted. Worse, he sounded broken. I wasn't willing to accept that. No more losses, damn it. I wasn't giving anyone else up.

"I want to," I said. Katie leaned on my arm, still oblivious to her surroundings. Quentin finally nodded, and we started up the hill, guiding her along. Spike followed us, stalking along at my feet as we walked slowly into the trees.

EIGHTEEN

THE DOOR IN THE OAK SWUNG OPEN under my hand. We stepped into the receiving hall, still supporting Katie between us like a broken doll. Luna and Sylvester were standing just inside the door, clearly waiting for us; someone must have spotted us coming up the hill. Sylvester's jaw dropped when we came into view, and he stared at me with openmouthed dismay. Luna didn't match it; she didn't look surprised at all.

"Toby," she said, smiling sadly.

"Your Grace." I helped Quentin guide Katie to a seat before turning and walking back to them, folding my hands behind my back. Spike sat at my feet, trilling. "I got them back."

"I see that," she said. "How much did it cost you?"

"Enough."

Sylvester finally closed his mouth, swallowing before he said, "October? What happened?"

Forcing myself to look up and meet his eyes, I said, "The Luidaeg did it so I could get into Blind Michael's lands on the Children's Road."

"The Luidaeg." Anger sparked in his eyes. I braced myself, waiting for him to yell. Instead, he turned toward Luna, words laced with a cold fury as he said, "You sent her to the Luidaeg."

"I did." She looked at him with a brittle, resolute calm. "You knew I would. You knew it was the only way."

"You could have—"

"No." The word was flat, carrying a world of finality. "I couldn't."

"We'll discuss this later," he said, and looked back to me, asking, "Did you go alone?"

It took me a moment to find my voice. I was too stunned by Sylvester's anger at Luna. Finally, I said, "Yes. I did."

"I followed her," said Quentin, still standing with his hands on Katie's shoulders.

His words didn't seem to register with Sylvester, who was shaking his head, anger fading into exhaustion. "Oh, Toby, Toby, Toby. You went to the Luidaeg and then to face Blind Michael alone." He sounded utterly resigned. Somehow, that was worse than anger would have been. "Why did you do that?"

"Because I had to." Because that madman took my kids, and my Fetch was already here, so there was no point in not going. Because I had debts to pay and no one else would do it for me. "You knew I was going after him. What did you expect me to do?"

"I was hoping you'd find a safer way." He cast a sidelong look at Luna, who glanced away, looking ashamed. "If that wasn't possible, I hoped you'd take someone with you."

"Got any suggestions?" I sighed. "Quentin followed me, or I wouldn't even have taken him. I try not to risk anybody's neck but my own."

Sylvester shook his head. "You never think about keeping yourself alive, do you?"

"Well, if you listen to what people keep telling me, I get that particular tendency from my mother," I said. "I get it from you, too, you know."

"You don't get a bit of it from your mother," he said, reaching out to brush my hair away from my face. "She never would have gone. Now stop it. You don't want to be a hero."

"Never said I did," I replied, with a sigh. "Forgive me?"

"Always." He dropped to one knee and hugged me. I wanted to stay there and let him hold me for a little while—he's the closest thing I have to a father, and I needed the reassurance—but Quentin needed me as much as I needed Sylvester, and I had duties to fulfill. I slipped out of his arms with a murmur of apology, walking back to where Quentin was waiting with Katie.

Quentin was stroking Katie's hair with the back of his hand, staring into her wide, empty eyes. I wasn't sure he'd even heard my conversation with Sylvester after his interjection; he was far away, wrapped in his own potential loss.

I put my hand on his shoulder. "How is she?"

He turned to look at me, expression pleading for me to tell him that everything would be okay. I could see it in his eyes. And I couldn't do it. "What did you do to her?"

"It's just a little confusion spell—it's all I was strong enough to cast. She's sinking all on her own. I can't stop her." I looked back to Sylvester and Luna. "Can you help her?"

"Fix what's been done?" Luna shook her head. "I can't . . . we can't . . . no. There's nothing we can do for her."

Why didn't I believe her? Keeping my eyes on Luna, I asked cautiously, "Blind Michael's that powerful?"

She chuckled without a trace of humor. "You have no idea."

"Yeah, well. There's no field guide to the Firstborn." Quentin shivered under my hand. I tightened my fingers. "I just keep tripping over them."

Luna made a small, pained sound, visibly forcing herself to keep her composure before she asked, "How many . . . how many of the children did you get out?"

"The ones I went for and as many of the others as I could manage. About twenty, all told." I kept watching her. "Katie's the only human kid I got out."

"You *stole* twenty children from my—from Blind Michael?" asked Luna, eyes going suddenly wide.

"They weren't his to have," I said simply.

"Oh, Toby. Oh, my dear." She shook her head, eyes closing. "Do you know what you've done?"

"What I had to." I turned toward Sylvester. "Can they stay here with you? I have to finish taking care of the others."

"Of course," he said. "They'll be safer here than they could be anywhere else."

That was one less thing for me to worry about. "Great."

"Are you hurt?"

"Not really. A little scraped up, and I could use some Band-Aids for my hands, but I'm mostly just stressed and exhausted." I looked back toward Luna, very deliberately removing the black rose from my hair and holding it out to her. "I brought you a present."

She paled, staring at the flower like she expected it to bite her. It was like she hadn't seen it until it was offered. "Where . . ." she began, in a stunned whisper, and faltered before saying, "Where did you get that?"

"From your mother," I said, calmly. "She misses you."

"Oh, Toby, what have you done?" She sounded like she was somewhere between choking and crying. Not taking her eyes from the rose, she said, "Sylvester?"

"It was bound to happen one day, Luna," he said wearily. "I'm honestly amazed that it's taken this long. Maybe if Amandine hadn't stood aside—"

"But she did," said Luna. Her tails were lashing, stirring her skirt into a wild tangle. "Please, Sylvester."

He sighed. "What would you have me do?"

"Take Quentin and his . . . his friend . . . to the Children's Hall and get them settled comfortably. Bring them drinks and go down to collect the others." She glanced at him, then away, as if the sight of him hurt her eyes. "I'll be there as soon as I can."

"This is your garden as much as any other, Luna. You

planted it. I love you. But don't you dare try to deny the need to harvest." Sylvester gave Luna a disgusted look, helping Katie to her feet. She stood without protesting, moving easily on legs that now bent the wrong way and tapered into dainty, fully formed hooves. Her glossy smile didn't change as Quentin slid his arm through hers; I wasn't even sure she knew he was there.

Luna closed her eyes, standing silent as the three of them made their way out of the hall. Tears began to trickle down her cheeks, flowing freely by the time she sighed and said, eyes still closed, "So you've met my mother."

"You could've warned me."

"No, I couldn't. I might have tried, if I thought you'd reach her forest alive, but I didn't think you'd make it that far." She made the admission without flinching. When I left for Blind Michael's lands, she didn't expect me to come back. Opening her eyes, she looked at me sadly, and asked, "She gave that to you?"

"She asked me to bring it to you."

"Did she tell you why?"

"Because she misses you and remembers that you like roses? I don't know. Luna, what the *hell* is going on here?" I glared at her, not bothering to hide my frustration. "I'm a kid, Katie's turning into a horse, my Fetch is waiting with the car, you sent me off to die, and I'm pretty sure Blind Michael's your—"

"He's my father." Her voice was calm now; resigned. "I said to be careful of all his children, you know. You never listen. I watched you walk out of here, and I knew you wouldn't be back, and I didn't tell my husband, because he wouldn't have let you go. I love you, Toby. I always have. But I hate my father more, and when you offered the choice of your life or my own, I took the one that kept me safe. You should have listened when I said to be careful. He has you now, whether you know it or not, and I don't know if you can be saved."

I froze. "What?"

"How many times do you need me to say it? Yes, he's

my father, and yes, I sent you to die. At least Mother's always said he was my father, and I believe her. She's never broken free of him." She smiled bitterly. "They re-created Faerie more accurately than they dreamed; she doesn't love him and hasn't loved him in centuries, but she orbits him like the moon orbits the earth. He knows it and hates her, and they'll never leave each other. Habit holds them."

"But . . ."

"But what? I was the last of their children, born when they still thought they could love each other. When he still allowed the sun to rise." Her smile faltered, fading. "There was sunshine then, and rainbows. We lived in his halls once; I remember that. But things changed. They fell out of love. The sun stopped rising. It was too late for us to leave his lands—my siblings were gone, scattered, and they couldn't hide us—so Mother and I ran to the forest. The trees were strong because Mother was strong, and the roses were strong because I was there. I used to watch the Hunt sweep the moors searching for children . . . for me." She shook her head. "I'm part of what he's looking for. His lost little girl. And I will *not* go back."

"How did you get away?"

"I escaped. Isn't that how one always gets away? One escapes. One takes whatever route is open and gets out. The methods don't matter."

"Sometimes they do."

"No, they don't." Her expression hadn't changed, but her voice . . . she was begging, and I didn't know what she was begging *for*. "Please, October, believe me. They don't matter."

I looked at her. There were a hundred questions I wanted to ask, and years of history telling me I shouldn't. Why should I care where she'd come from? She was my friend and my liege, and Sylvester loved her. And she sent me to my death.

There were reasons to ask. There were reasons to keep my peace. Answers are bitter things, and once you get them, they're yours and you can't give them back. Did I want to know badly enough that I was willing to live with whatever answer she gave me?

No. I didn't. Swallowing hard, I said the first thing that came to mind: "Well, I guess that explains Raysel."

"Yes, it does. Blood will tell. I tried to pretend it wouldn't, that we could change, but blood always tells. We carry the burdens of our parents." She sighed, holding out her hand in an easy, imperious gesture. "My rose, if you would?"

I considered arguing. Then I saw the look in her eyes, all bitter sorrow and broken resignation, and handed it to her without a word. She curled her fingers around the stem and heaved a deep, bone-weary sigh, closing her eyes as she whispered, "Hello, Mother."

The rose began gleaming like a star, getting brighter and brighter until everything was obscured save for Luna and the rose. There was a flash of black and silver light, burning pink around the edges like a sunset, and Luna was gone, replaced by someone I didn't know.

She was taller than Luna, with marble white skin and hair that darkened from pale pink at the roots to red-black at the tips. It fell past her knees, tangling in the rope of briars that belted her grass green gown. She looked like nothing I'd ever seen, and it hurt my heart until I stepped away from her, holding out my hands in the mute hope that I could push her away. She was beautiful, but she wasn't mine.

"Mother, please . . ." she whispered. The voice was still Luna's.

I bit my lip. "Luna?"

The rose woman opened her eyes. They were pale yellow, like pollen. And then she was gone, leaving Luna standing in her place. Luna's ears were pressed flat, and her tails were wildly waving. Blood ran between her fingers where the barbed thorns of the rose had broken her skin. They were long and wickedly sharp; I couldn't see how I'd managed to avoid them.

That was easy to answer: the thorns weren't there

when I held the rose, because it wasn't intended for me. "Luna—"

"She wasn't trying to hurt me." She walked to the nearest vase, tucking the bloody rose among the more mundane flowers with exquisite care. "She just forgets what I am these days."

"What are you?" I could taste her blood on the air, but it didn't tell me anything that I could understand. Her heritage wasn't Kitsune. It was nothing that I knew at all.

She looked to me and smiled, sadly. "Who I've always been: Luna Torquill, Duchess of Shadowed Hills. I'm Kitsune, for all that I have a few more ... unusual traits than most. I'm also my mother's daughter, but I'm not as strong as she remembers me. Much of my strength is spent in staying as I am."

"What *were* you?"

"Something else, when the world was younger and had more room for roses."

"Oh," I said. What else was there? It made sense the same way everything in Faerie does: sideways and upside down, like looking in an underwater mirror.

Luna lifted her wounded hand, studying it. "I paid for the right to bleed when something cuts me. Mother won't understand that, and I can't expect her to. It's not in her nature."

"What isn't in her nature?"

"Bleeding." She closed her hand.

I looked at her, shivering, and said, "Now what?"

"Now you take the rest of your children home." She smiled wanly. "Sylvester and I will ... we'll make our peace. We'll do what we can for the children staying here, and for Quentin's lady love. There must be a way around what Father did to her. Spells can always be broken."

"All right," I said, nodding. "I'll be back as soon as I can."

"Are you sure?" Her smile faded. "My father knows your name, and you've chosen Death for your driver.

I'm sure she's a sweet death, and one who wears your face most prettily, but she's Death all the same. I'm sorry to be part of the reason that she's here, but if you come back, it will be a miracle."

"I'll be back."

"As you say." She looked down, watching the blood trickling down her fingers. "You should go. The day is waning."

I knew a dismissal when I heard one. I bowed and turned toward the door, shivering despite the warmth in the hall. Nothing was what it was supposed to be; I wasn't sure I even knew who Luna was anymore. I certainly didn't know who I was, and now I was going to die. The week just kept getting better.

I stepped back into the mortal world, closing my eyes as the door swung shut behind me, trying to reorient myself. The shock of transition is always there when we move between worlds; just another little consequence of being what we are.

For some reason I wasn't surprised when I heard a familiar voice behind me, sounding amazed and a little frightened. It had been that kind of week. "That wasn't you, was it?" I opened my eyes and turned to face Connor. He stared. "I saw your car, and you were with it, but you looked right through me. I thought you were mad, but you're not, are you? That wasn't you."

"I don't know what you're talking about." Oh, there was a clever lie.

"Of course not. Toby."

"Why are you calling me that?" My voice sounded childish and shrill, even to my own ears.

He shook his head, walking toward me. "Did you think losing a few years would fool me?"

"I sort of hoped," I said, shoulders sagging.

"Wrong answer. I knew you when you were a kid, remember? You tried to drown me in your mom's garden pond and got angry when I wouldn't die. I used to spend hours watching you chase pixies in the hedge maze. I know you, October Daye, and you can't hide from me."

He paused. "I'm sorry you feel like you need to. I don't understand why."

"I don't," I said, reeling. I don't need anyone to know me that well. "This wasn't voluntary—the Luidaeg did it to me."

His eyes widened at the Luidaeg's name, and he asked, "Why?"

"She said she needed to." If he wanted the details, he could damn well drag them out of me. I didn't feel like sharing.

"I see." He looked at me for a moment, deciding not to press the issue. Smart boy. "So who's the clone with the car?"

In for a penny, in for a pound. "That's May."

"She looks just like you."

"We're sort of related."

"I didn't think you had a sister."

"She's not my sister."

"So who is she?"

"My Fetch."

The world stopped as Connor stared at me, shock and terror warring for dominance of his face. Finally, voice barely audible, he said, "What?"

"She's my Fetch. She showed up just after you called this morning."

He swallowed hard before asking, "Is that why you didn't eat anything at breakfast?"

"Yeah, pretty much."

"You could have said something."

"I was in denial."

"That's no excuse."

"Sorry. Next time Death decides to show up at my door, you'll be the first to know."

He dropped to his knees with a barking sigh. I stepped forward to meet him, and we clung to each other like we could stop the end of the world, me on my tiptoes and Connor kneeling. Spike leaned against me, chirping as Connor buried his face in my hair and shuddered.

"Don't die," he whispered. "Please, don't die . . ."

Funny—I shared the sentiment. I didn't say anything, but I held him and let him hold me. Maybe it wouldn't change anything, but it could help, for a little while.

We let go of each other after a long while. Connor stood, asking, "Where are you going?"

"I have to get the rest of the kids home."

"I'm coming with you."

I paused, thinking about arguing, and then shrugged. If I was going to die and he wanted to be there, I wouldn't stop him. "Fine. I do have one question, though."

"What?"

"Do you want to drive?"

NINETEEN

MAY MOVED TO THE BACKSEAT with surprisingly good grace, pausing to stage whisper, "He's cuter than I remembered!" Connor heard her and turned beet red; May winked at him, grin broadening as I glared. If she hadn't been my personal incarnation of death, I'd have smacked her. As it was, I was strongly tempted.

Connor eyed May, saying, "Toby—"

"I know, Connor." I climbed into the car, fastening my seat belt. Spike jumped up onto the dashboard and chirped, thorns rattling.

"Okay," Connor said, settling in the driver's seat and reaching up to adjust the rearview mirror. He paused before turning to look, disbelieving, into the back seat. "Uh, Toby? When did your car get this big?"

Only the kids I'd originally gone to save were left— Jessica, Andrew, and the children from Tybalt's Court. Most were sleeping, but Raj and Jessica were awake, eyeing him balefully.

"The Luidaeg did it," I said. "We needed the extra seats."

"Uh, yeah, I can see that. Where did you—"

May poked her head back into the front, still grinning. "Look, big guy, I don't mean to stress you out or anything, but you know we're running on a time limit, right? We should probably make these drop-offs while Toby's here to help." In a weird way, she was saying what I would've said in her place. The faster we got the kids home, the sooner they'd be out of the walking blast radius that I'd become.

Connor stiffened and turned his attention to the wheel, pulling out of the parking lot without another word. May withdrew to the backseat, fastening her belt, and there was silence. I didn't mind it; if no one else was talking, I didn't have to. There was nothing for me to say.

We were halfway to San Francisco when I raised my head, blinking away tears, to find us at the base of the Bay Bridge. Connor was staring at the road, hands white-knuckled on the wheel. Maybe he hadn't noticed my crying. Yeah, and maybe I'm the Queen of Faerie. I wiped my cheeks with vicious swipes of my hand, scowling. Damn it. I hate crying almost as much as I hate bleeding. They're both signs of weakness, and I can't afford either one.

I caught a glimpse of the rearview mirror as I lowered my hand. There were half a dozen motorcycles on the freeway behind us, weaving in and out of traffic, never quite letting us out of their sight. That wouldn't have bothered me—there are lots of motorcycle gangs in the Bay Area—but they were following us. And that wasn't possible. When we left the Luidaeg, she cast a don't-look-here spell on the car. She's Maeve's daughter. We should have been so hard to see that we could be in an accident without anyone noticing, and we were being followed. That meant that something was very, very wrong.

Eyes narrowed, I whispered the opening lines of *Romeo and Juliet*. Connor gave me a worried glance. I held up my hand for quiet, the smell of copper and cut grass rising as I concentrated on the bikers. Their illusions wavered for an instant, revealing the outlines of horns and axes, and horses running where motorcycles had been an instant before. I hissed the next line, and their mirror images changed, becoming a line of dark horsemen riding their steeds at unnatural speeds down I-80. Great. California has its weird points, but homicidal faerie horsemen aren't usually among them. Those were Blind Michael's men.

I risked a glance over my shoulder and saw a line of normal motorcycles. My enchantment was only affecting the mirror. "Connor?"

Spike raised its head, following my gaze. Then it hissed, jumping from the dashboard and onto the back of the seat, thorns rattling. That confirmed it: I wasn't seeing things.

"What?" asked Connor.

"Look in the mirror, would you?"

He looked up, and froze. "Oh, dear."

"Yeah." I turned back to the front. Most of the kids were sleeping, stretched out on seats that would have looked more natural in a school bus. At least the outside of the car looked normal. "Watch the road. I'll figure out what to do next."

"Right," he said, and turned his attention back to driving. His shoulders were stiff with obvious anxiety, but he was going to trust me. Good man.

May looked up from braiding Jessica's hair, frowning. "What's going on?"

"Be quiet, I'm thinking."

"Whatever." She shrugged, turning back to Jessica, who was sound asleep and snuggled between May's knees. Andrew was watching them, sucking his thumb and leaning against a catnapping Raj. It would've been cute if the bikers hadn't been closing rapidly. There were seven of them, and now that I was aware of what they really looked like, I could see the flickers in their disguises; they were being eroded by the iron in the bridge and the passage over moving water. Their illusions would probably shatter by the time we reached the other side of the bay, but by then it wouldn't matter; they'd be too close, and they'd take us. I somehow doubted they'd stop just because they were exposed. Blind Michael wasn't likely to care about what the mortals did or didn't see. There were reasons for the Burning Times. If they ever come again, there's going to be a reason for that, too.

"Have we passed the Yerba Buena exit?" I had to stay calm as long as I could; there was no point in starting a panic before I had to.

"A little while ago," said Connor.

Great. Once you pass Yerba Buena, there are no more turnoffs before you reach the city; we were crossing the bridge whether we wanted to or not. "I'm starting to think that people attacking me on this damn bridge is becoming some sort of a trend."

"What?"

"Hang on. I'm thinking." How were we supposed to get out of this one? The last time someone tried to kill me while I was in a car, I drove through downtown like a madwoman until they were too disoriented to catch me. Sure, it got me shot, but I survived. That wasn't an option this time; I was too short to work the pedals, and Connor drove like an aging grandmother afraid of breaking something. What are you supposed to do when you're stuck on a bridge in a car full of kids?

"Titania's *teeth*," I muttered.

"Huh?" May stuck her head over the back of the seat, ignoring Spike's hissing. "Wanna keep it down? Some of the kids are trying to sleep back here."

"Be quiet, May. We're being chased."

"Really?" She turned to look out the back window. "Wow, we are. Hi, guys!" She waved to our pursuers, grinning. "Hi!"

Andrew pulled his thumb out of his mouth and grumbled, "Noisy."

I privately agreed. "What are you doing?" I grabbed her arm, yanking it down. A few of the kids were stirring, rubbing their eyes and making grumbling noises. "They're chasing us!"

"I know—isn't it cool? This is the first time I've been chased!" She leaned on her elbows, still grinning. "What happens if they catch us?"

"We die!" I snapped. "Shut up and let me think!"

"Fine." May folded her arms over her chest, sulking. "Won't let me wave, won't let me drive, why do I even bother . . ."

I stared at her. "What did you just say?"

She blinked. "Why do I bother putting up with you? Cause I really don't know."

"No! Before that!" Spike punctuated my statement with a yowl. I swept it into my arms, ignoring the thorns. "Spike, be quiet."

"Toby?" interjected Connor. "They're gaining."

May and I turned toward him, saying in unison, "Shut *up,* Connor!" It's always good to have backup. After a pause, I added, "And drive faster!" It couldn't hurt to try.

Connor slammed his foot down on the gas. The car lurched forward. Glancing back over the seat, I winced. Blind Michael's men were still gaining. Then again, they weren't dependent on silly things like gasoline or internal combustion. They had magical horses.

"Next time, I get a magical goddamn horse," I muttered, turning back toward May. "You said I wouldn't let you drive."

"Well, you won't! You brought the Selkie instead," she said. "You don't trust me."

"No, I brought the Selkie because you're a lousy driver." I decided to ignore the whole "trust" issue. She was my personal incarnation of death; if she expected me to trust her, she was delusional. "You remember everything I've ever done, right?"

"Well, duh."

"Do you remember the time I had the guy with the gun sneak into the car?"

She blinked. "Yes. Why?"

"Do you think you could do that again?"

"Do what?"

"Drive like that."

There was a pause as she realized what I meant. Then she wailed, "I don't know how to drive like that! I'm not you anymore!"

"So learn," I said, and pressed myself against the door. Spike mewled in protest, pinned against my chest. "Spike, hush. Connor, keep your foot on the gas and scoot over. May, get your ass into the driver's seat."

"What? Why?"

"Toby, this isn't such a good idea—"

"Both of you, just do it. May's driving."

They turned to stare at me, demanding in unison, *"Why?"*

"Because she drives like a manic on crystal meth! Now get moving before I take the wheel and do it myself!"

I didn't think my driving was that much of a threat, but apparently, I was wrong. Connor unfastened his belt and scooted over into the passenger seat, smashing me against the door until I unfastened my seat belt, squirmed free, and balanced myself on his leg. He kept his hands on the steering wheel until May scrambled over the seat and grabbed it, shouting, "Now what?"

"You were driving earlier! Just drive!" I jabbed Connor in the side with my elbow. "Let go of the wheel and buckle up. This is going to get rough."

May was working herself into a panic. "That was just a game!"

"So pretend this is another one!" All the kids were awake now, and several were starting to cry. Trying to sound jovial, I called, "Hey, kids, if you're not wearing a seat belt, put it on!" They'd already been traumatized enough; they didn't need to watch me argue with my Fetch. Then again, neither did Connor.

He fastened his belt, looking at me bleakly. I reached up to grab the oh-shit handle with one hand, offering him the other. When he took it, I squeezed his fingers. "It's gonna be okay."

"Liar," he said.

May fought the wheel, trying to steer. She was being too delicate about it. We'd be lucky if they didn't catch us before we got off the bridge. "Toby!"

I squirmed around to get a better look at the Riders behind us, snapping, "Just drive!"

"Why me?" she wailed.

"Because if you don't, we're all going to die!" There
was something ironic about forcing my Fetch to save my
life, but I could dwell on that later, after we'd survived
the experience.

May stared at me, then nodded and slammed her foot
down on the gas. At least she knew which pedals to use.
The car roared like a wounded beast and leaped forward, accelerating at a distinctly unsafe speed. Finally.

If I even suspected that my driving was half as bad as
hers you'd never get me behind the wheel of a car again.
She rode wild across all four lanes of traffic, weaving
between cars that couldn't see through the Luidaeg's
don't-look-here spell and thus didn't realize we were
there. It was a good thing, too; if they'd been able to see
us, we'd have caused more than a few accidents. More
and more of the children were screaming. I understood
the sentiment.

Connor pulled his hand out of mine and covered his
face, closing his eyes. I glanced at him, trying to pretend
that I wasn't clinging to Spike for dear life. "Coward."

"Your point?" he muttered, not looking up. I sighed.
Fine. If he wanted to be that way, it was no skin off my
nose. I looked to the rearview mirror to check on the
locations of the Riders and smiled. My plan was working; they were still behind us, but our lead was growing because May's driving was too erratic for them to
predict. Drivers—even faerie drivers—usually follow
the rules of the road out of a sense of self-preservation.
May, well . . . May didn't.

I've been driving since I went to work for Devin, and
May knew everything I did. Thing is, watching a sur-
geon on TV doesn't make you a doctor. It just means
you know what surgery looks like. May didn't have my
muscle memory. She'd actually driven a car all of once,
during the relatively simple trip from the Luidaeg's
apartment to Shadowed Hills, and even then she'd
shown a dismaying tendency to drive the wrong way

down one-way streets, ignore traffic lights, and attempt to use the sidewalk as an extra lane. Now . . .

Given free rein on the open highway, May was embracing her inner race car driver. It didn't help that she had no idea how to control her speed, and was thus opting for as fast as the car will go. The children's screaming tapered off as they stared out the windows, awed. They'd probably never been in a car that was trying to break the laws of physics before. I was just afraid they were going to learn what a twelve-car pileup looked like, from the bottom.

Andrew had his nose pressed against the glass, watching wide-eyed as the Riders began closing the distance between us. "Look, Auntie Birdie," he said, "the men are going faster."

"That's nice, Andy," I said, finally letting go of Spike. It climbed over the seat to curl up in Jessica's lap. She was one of the few that was still asleep. I hoped she'd stay that way. If the screams hadn't been enough to wake her, maybe she would.

"They're followin' us."

"Yes, they are." They were getting closer fast, weaving in and out of traffic with a speed my little VW couldn't hope to match. I tried to run down my options and couldn't think of any. We had no place to go. We'd outrun them, or we'd die.

He turned to look at me, frowning. "Why?"

"Because they're mad at me, sweetie. Now hold on tight, okay?"

He smiled at me, nodding. "Okay." I love kids. They're endlessly adaptable, and not as breakable as we think.

My Fetch wasn't handling things nearly as well. She swerved between two trucks with a heart-stopping squeal of the brakes, wailing, "Am I doing this right?"

"You're doing fine! Keep driving!" Maybe I was afraid she'd kill us all, but I was a lot more worried about Blind Michael's men. They weren't the sort who'd negotiate once they'd run us to ground. They might be willing to

lop our heads off and take them home as trophies instead of torturing us, but that was probably about it.

"Aunt Birdie? What's going on?"

I winced at the sound of Jessica's voice. "Honey, just
hold on. We're on the way home."

"Aunt Birdie—"

"Not now, sweetheart!"

"The bridge is ending! The bridge is ending!" May
shouted, slamming her foot down harder. The car sped
up. I hadn't known that was possible. "Now what do I
do?"

"Take the first exit!" I turned to look out the windshield, bracing my hands against the dashboard. "Turn
right and head toward the warehouses when you get off
the bridge!"

May nodded, nearly falling over as she dragged the
wheel to the right. The car wasn't cooperating, and
I couldn't blame it; if she'd been trying to steer me, I
wouldn't have been terribly cooperative either. Connor whimpered, squeezing his eyes more tightly shut as
we swerved off the bridge and down the street, barely
avoiding a collision with a commuter bus. Five of the
Riders managed to change direction and follow us; the
other two missed the turn and went shooting off down
the bridge, trapped in the flow of traffic.

"Two down!" I shouted, jubilant. "Take the first right
and floor it!" Turning, I elbowed Connor. "Look for
things to throw."

He uncovered his face, eyeing me. "What?"

"Look for things to throw out the window. Clothes.
Cans. Whatever."

"Why?"

"Distraction!" The rest of the explanation was lost as
May found the turn and roared around it without slowing down. For one dizzy moment it felt like the car was
going to flip over. I fell back against my seat, accompanied by a chorus of giggles and cheers from the back. At
least some of us were enjoying the ride. Turning my attention back to the windshield, I choked. We were driv-

ing straight for a brick wall, and May wasn't stopping. I caught my breath, and shrieked, "Turn around! Turn around! Turn around!"

She turned and blinked, keeping the gas pedal pressed down hard. "What?"

In unison, Connor and I shouted, *"Watch the road!"*

"Okay ..." May shrugged as she looked back to the road, and then yelped in surprise. "Toby, there's a wall!"

At least one of us was surprised. I slammed my fists down on the dashboard, yelling, "Turn around turn around!"

That got through. She hauled on the wheel, sending us into a wide spin. Andrew tumbled away from the window, slipping out of his seat belt, and bowled Raj over. The two of them landed in a heap on top of one of the smaller Cait Sidhe. She started to howl, surprised, and the rest of the children joined in. The noise startled May enough that she pulled us out of our spin and into a smooth turn.

You can say anything you want about the Volkswagen bug, but never, ever claim that it doesn't have a good turning radius. We somehow avoided slamming into anything, instead winding up pointing toward the mouth of the alley we'd mistakenly tried to use as a getaway route. Problem: the five remaining Riders were lined up across the alley's mouth, blocking our escape.

And May still had her foot on the gas.

What followed was a quick and dirty lesson in the law of relative mass. The Riders were fierce, armed, and possibly deadly; they were riding magical horses that could move as fast or faster than a car and were a lot more maneuverable. These were all things to their advantage. We had a hysterical Selkie, an age-slipped changeling, and a car being driven by someone who had no concept of her own mortality. Guess who had the overall advantage?

We plowed into the Riders at almost full speed, hitting one while two others dove out of the way, losing control of their mounts in the process. The illusions on the two freed horses dissolved, the motorcycles replaced by fae steeds who wheeled and fled.

Only two Riders were left as we pulled out onto the street, and they were following at a cautious distance. "Connor, give me something to throw," I said, rolling down the window.

"Like what?"

"Anything! I don't care!" He stared at me, then bent to remove his shoe and pressed it into my hand. I paused to gauge my aim, and then chucked it out the window.

In a perfect world, I'd have hit something. This isn't a perfect world. The shoe flew wild, landing on the sidewalk. "Damn it. Give me something else."

May interrupted, shouting, "Toby, the sign says 'stop'!"

"Don't stop!"

"But the sign—"

"If you stop, I will *kill you myself!*" I shouted, flinging several empty soda cans and Connor's other shoe into the street. May gave me a panicked look, but didn't slow down. The kids saw what I was doing and cheered. Then they rolled down the back windows, starting to throw anything that wasn't nailed down out of the car. This wasn't the sort of thing I would've normally encouraged, at least in part because it would have caused their parents to kill me, but these were definitely special circumstances. A little lifesaving misbehavior seemed like exactly what we needed.

Spike hissed and fled to the front seat when an overenthusiastic child tried to pull it out of Jessica's lap, having sensibly recognized the rose goblin as something that would cause a lot of damage if thrown. Jessica glared at the kid, removed her one remaining shoe, and pitched it out the window. That was promising; it was the first real action I'd seen her take since we got out of Blind Michael's lands.

Maybe it was the combination of our speed and the objects flying out of the car, or maybe it was just sheer, dumb luck. Whatever the reason, we made it through the intersection just ahead of a turning Metro bus. So did the first Rider. The second Rider didn't. The sound of crashing metal has never been that sweet.

The last Rider was still behind us, and we were running out of things to throw; we needed to lose him. To make matters worse, the excitement was starting to wear off for the children, and it was being replaced by fear. I could hear whimpers starting under their continued giggles. Kids get upset easily. They also recover fast, but that doesn't make it a fair trade.

I threw the last of the cans out the window, demanding, "How are we supposed to get rid of this guy?"

"I don't know!" snapped Connor.

"Then what good are you?" I threw a bad paperback romance out the window, followed by my trash bag from the week before.

"Toby? Toby?"

"Shut *up*, May!"

"Um . . ."

I turned toward her, glaring. "What *is* it?"

She had time to whimper, "Hill," and then we were going down, fast. Very, very fast. I looked in the rearview mirror and saw the last Rider pulling his steed to a halt at the top of the hill, staring. He wasn't dumb enough to follow. Lucky us, we were already committed.

"Turn! Turn!" I shouted. The kids weren't whimpering anymore—most of them were cheering like wild things. The few that had the sense to be scared were screaming, but the screams were almost indistinguishable from the cheers.

San Francisco was built on a series of hills. I guess it seemed like a good idea at the time. Some of them are steep enough that sane people won't drive down them even at a normal pace; they go around instead, using the side streets with gentler inclines. Yet here we were, plummeting down one of the tallest hills in the city at a speed so ludicrous that I was willing to bet we were close to breaking a record. Slowing down would have been suicide. The brakes weren't good enough, and parts of the car simply wouldn't stop.

"Turn where?" wailed May. Connor was staring at the street as it unspooled ahead of us, all the blood drained from his cheeks. He looked terrified. I couldn't blame him.

"Find a smaller hill! Turn!" We could lose some speed by turning. The car probably wasn't going to recover— the damage to the engine had been done—but we might still be able to save ourselves if we could slow down enough.

May wrenched us hard to the left, and this time the car *did* lift up onto two wheels before dropping back to the ground with a bone-jarring thud. The shocks weren't going to like that. The brakes probably weren't too happy about it either.

"I think I'm gonna be sick," said an unhappy voice from the back.

Privately, I agreed. Out loud I said, "Try to wait, okay? Let us stop the car first."

"How do I stop the car?" May demanded.

"Start slowing down!" The hill was tapering off, and we'd stopped gaining speed; there was a chance that we'd be able to decelerate enough to keep from becoming a thin metal sheet at the bottom of the hill. Not a good chance, but a chance.

"How do I slow down?"

"The brakes, hit the brakes!" snapped Connor.

"The what?"

Oh, that was *not* what I wanted to hear. "Take your foot off the gas!"

"Oh!" May nodded and eased off the gas, looking relieved. The car slowed, until we were moving at a speed that had at least a passing resemblance to the legal limit.

"Good," I said. "Now try the other pedal."

Connor held his breath as May fumbled for the brakes, found them, and brought the car to a stop in the middle of the street. She slumped forward, resting her forehead against the wheel, and I leaned over Connor to set the parking brake before we could start rolling again. The kids in the back cheered. Connor shuddered and started breathing.

I eyed him. "Wimp."

"Yes," he agreed. "Are we dead yet?"

"No. The brakes worked."

"I'm gonna be sick," said the voice from the back.

"Me too," said Connor.

"I don't ever want to drive again," moaned May.

"Deal," I said, before adding, "You realize you just saved my life, right?"

"What?" She sat up, staring at me.

"We'd have died if you hadn't taken the wheel." I grinned at her. "Good job."

"I can't save your life! I'm your Fetch!"

"Yeah, I know. Get in the back." I nudged Connor with my elbow. "It's your turn to drive."

He gave me a sharp look. "You're kidding."

"Do I look like I'm kidding?" I shrugged. "I'm still too short to drive. Our other option is May. Do you really want to do that again?"

He looked from my Fetch to me and back, frown deepening in a scowl. Finally, he took off his seat belt, saying, "May, move."

Flashing a grin, May scrambled into the backseat, settling next to Jessica and Spike.

Connor slid into the driver's seat and fastened his seat belt, saying conversationally, "You realize I hate you."

"I know," I said, and smiled. "I'm okay with that."

"I didn't really save your life," said May.

"I'm okay with that, too," I said. "Come on. Let's get these kids home."

Connor sighed and restarted the car. It wasn't riding very smoothly anymore, and I was fairly sure the shocks were shot. Oh, well. There's nothing like a good car chase to start the morning off right. I gave him the directions to Mitch and Stacy's and fell silent, enjoying the quiet. The kids were exhausted, and Connor and May were too busy hating me to talk. It was nice to have the break.

May was right. She didn't save my life, because she *couldn't* save my life; she wasn't the one who was going to take it. A Fetch is an omen of death, not the cause.

Whatever killed me wouldn't be something we could prevent with a little trick driving. I'd finally met an enemy that was bigger than I was. Blind Michael wanted me dead: that's why May was there, and the Riders proved it. We'd gotten away, but whatever he sent after me next would be bigger, meaner, faster, and probably a lot smarter. If I was lucky, I'd be able to get the kids out of the range of fire before it was too late. It was already too late for me.

TWENTY

CONNOR FOUGHT THE CAR TO A STOP as we pulled up in front of Mitch and Stacy's house; the brakes hadn't been working well since our little joyride down the hill. Funny thing, that. Frankly, I was amazed we weren't trying to stop the car by digging our heels into the concrete, Flintstones style.

When we finally stopped moving Connor staggered out of the car, moving to rest his forehead against the nearest tree. "I'm going to die," he moaned.

"No, you're not," said May, climbing into the front seat and then out the driver's side door. "Trust me, I'd know. It's a professional thing."

I unfastened my seat belt, eyeing them. "Guys? Disguises?" The Luidaeg's spell hid us from prying eyes, but I wasn't sure it extended past the boundaries of the car.

"Oh, right." May snapped her fingers and was instantly disguised. She still looked like me, but now she was me-as-human. I'd never seen my human self from the outside before, and somehow, it was more unnerving than looking at my real face. Illusions are personal things, and we don't usually steal them from one another.

Connor groaned and waved a hand, not lifting his head. The air around him shimmered, dissolving the webs between his fingers and roughening the texture of his hair. "Happy now?"

"Yes," I said, leaning over the seat to stroke Jessica's hair away from her forehead. "Come on, puss. Time to go."

Jessica looked at me, then out the window. "That's my house."

"Yes, it is." Andrew had dozed off, curled up with Spike in what would have been a sickeningly cute pose if Spike had been less, well, spiky. "Come on, Andy, wake up," I said, shaking him. Spike opened neon yellow eyes and chirped. "Yeah, I know, I'm bothering you. Now get up."

"Andy doesn't like to wake up," Jessica said.

"I'm noticing that. Can you make him move?"

"Okay." She reached over and yanked Andrew into a sitting position, bracing her knee in the small of his back. He made a mumbling noise and tried to lie back down. "No, Andy. Get up." He protested again, but stopped trying to fight her. Fascinating. People are strange. Jessica was useless for most of the ordeal but as soon as she had to deal with her little brother she was nothing but efficient. I'd have to remember that, just in case another crazed wanna-be god ever kidnapped us.

Raj leaned against the back of the seat, watching Jessica manhandle her baby brother out of the car. "Will you take us home next?" he asked.

"Yeah, we will," I said.

"My parents will be pleased."

"I'm sure they will." I raked my hands through my hair, and paused, realizing that my own disguise wasn't in place. I was pretty sure nobody had seen us yet; the fact that Mitch and Stacy hadn't come charging out of the house told me that much. So now I had a new, simpler problem: how was I supposed to make sure they didn't see me at all?

Stacy could probably have dealt with my sudden second childhood, as long as I brought her kids home—she can be pragmatic about the strangest things—but I didn't think she'd be able to cope with May. Like Connor, she knows that I don't have any sisters; unlike Connor, she couldn't necessarily handle the news of my impending death.

And then there was Karen. I'd seen her ghost. I still didn't know how she had . . . how she . . . no. No more trauma, not yet. I'm a child of Faerie. When all else fails, we lie. Maybe it's not an honorable philosophy, but I've always been willing to bend honor in favor of common sense, and common sense told me that introducing Stacy to my Fetch when her life had already been turned upside down wouldn't be a good idea.

"I'm staying in the car," I announced. I looked out the open driver's-side door, asking May, "You understand why, don't you?"

"I think so," she said, and frowned. "I shouldn't do this."

"I know."

"It's not fair. Don't you think Stacy would want to know?"

"That I'm going to die? How is that going to help, May? She can't change it." I shook my head. "You have my memories. That means you love her, too."

"I do, and you have a point, but . . ." She sighed. "I'm almost sure this is breaking the rules. I shouldn't be helping you."

"Why not?"

"I'm your Fetch."

I shrugged. "So what?"

She nodded, slowly. "All right, but only because I care about Stacy. This is the last time. No more help after this."

"I understand."

May snapped her fingers again. Her clothes shimmered and were replaced by jeans, a button-up cotton shirt, and the battered leather jacket I got from Tybalt—typical "me" attire. Shaking the coat into place, she called, "Andy, Jessie, come on. It's time to go."

Jessica had managed to get Andrew out of the car,

and the two were standing on the sidewalk; Andrew's thumb was back in his mouth. Jessica turned toward May's voice and paused, looking between the two of us. "Aunt Birdie?" she asked, cautiously.

Andrew wasn't as easily confused. He walked over to the open door, leaned in, and grabbed the bottom of my sweater, thumb still in his mouth.

I looked at him, then over to his sister. I couldn't lie to them, mostly because I knew there was no way in hell they'd buy it. "I don't want to worry your mother any more than I have to," I said. "So we're just going to let May be me for a little bit, okay?"

May smiled at the kids, waggling the fingers of one hand in an almost shy wave.

Jessica eyed her and turned back to me, saying, "She's not you."

"I know that, and you know that, but we can pretend, right?"

"Well . . ." she began.

Andrew pulled his thumb out of his mouth. "Okay." Letting go of my sweater, he took May's hand. Jessica watched with panic in her eyes. When she turned back to me, she was shivering.

"I don't want to go without you," she said.

"It's okay, sweetie," I said, leaning out of the car and hugging her. "I know you're scared, but once May takes you to your parents, you'll be safe."

"You promise?"

"I promise. He can't hurt you anymore, because I beat him. You're safe. So go with May now, okay?"

"Okay." She paused, and frowned with an almost frightening intensity. "Aunt Birdie?"

"Yeah?"

"You got us out, and that's good, but now you need to get you out, too." She pulled back and walked to May before I could say anything, intensity smoothing into an unnatural calm as she looked up at my Fetch. "I want to go home now, please."

Andrew nodded. "Home."

"Okay, kids. You got it." May took their hands, glancing at me as she led them toward the front door. I watched until I was sure nothing would leap out of the bushes to attack them and then turned away. I didn't want to see them go inside. My farewells were already said, and there was nothing I could do to take them back.

I looked up when I felt Connor's hand on my shoulder. He was standing next to the car, expression schooled into something almost neutral. "Hey," he said. "You okay?"

Of course I was okay. Isn't *everyone* okay when they've got their death hanging out with them, constantly pointing out that their time is running short? "Peachy," I said, looking away as I blinked back tears.

He frowned. "You can cry, you know. No one's going to judge you for it."

I eyed him. "You know that's not a good idea."

"I was just offering."

"I know. I'm trying to stay mad. Whatever kills me," he flinched, but I continued, "it's going to have to fight for it. I refuse to go down easy."

"You don't have to die!" he protested. "I'll protect you!"

I snorted. "Get real, Connor. You couldn't protect your way out of a paper bag. You're a great guy, but you're not a fighter, and you never have been. You can't save me. If you're lucky, you'll save yourself."

"If I'm lucky? Being lucky means I get to live knowing that I let you die?" His tone was brisk and bitter. "No. I don't think so." Shoulders tense, he turned and walked toward the car.

"Connor—"

"No, don't. It's not worth it. You're going to die, and I'm just the guy who gets to watch, because you won't even let me try to stop it. Whatever my lady wishes." He got into the driver's seat, resting his head against the wheel. Raj looked out the window, frowning, and I shook my head. I couldn't explain.

Damn it. Connor knew as well as I did that I was being practical, not unfair. There's a hierarchy of power in Faerie, and Selkies barely even register. Almost all the magic they have is in their skins. Blind Michael would chew Connor up and throw him aside without slowing down, and I'd go to my grave with another death on my conscience. Was I hurting Connor by refusing to let him help? Yes. Was I doing it because I cared about him too much to make him a speed bump on the road to my own demise?

Yes. Whether he believed me or not, yes. Oak and ash, why can't anything ever stay simple? I stayed where I was, closing my eyes, and didn't even flinch when May put her hands on my shoulders, saying, "I know it's hard, but it'll be over soon."

I couldn't tell whether that was supposed to be a promise or a threat. I opened my eyes and pulled away, muttering, "Great," as I moved toward the car. Spike bounded out of the yard and tagged along at my heels, chirping. "How's Stacy?"

"Happy, but worried about Karen."

"What did you tell her?"

"That Karen was with Lily, and I'd let her know as soon as there was news."

I nodded. "And did she . . . ?"

"Realize I'm not you? No. Why should she? As long as the kids keep quiet, she'll never know." She sighed. "You'd never have gotten away with that if she wasn't so stressed."

"I know," I said, stooping to pick Spike up and cradle it against my shoulder. "We need to get Tybalt's kids to the Court of Cats. Connor's gonna drive."

"Works for me." May shrugged and climbed into the back, nudging Raj. "Move it, kid."

Raj gave her a sharp look and turned to me, demanding, "Are you taking us home *now?*"

"Yes. It's time." I got into the car, closing the door before I said, "Connor?"

He lifted his head off the steering wheel, expression bleak. "Yes?"

"Can you take us to Golden Gate Park, please?"

"Oh, sure. Can I get you anything else while I'm at it? My heart on a stick? The moon and stars for your funeral gown?" He released the parking brake and started the engine.

"Don't be like that."

"Don't be like what? All you've left for me to do is bury you."

"Connor—"

"If you've ever given a damn about me, Toby, just do me a favor and shut up."

I fell silent. There were a lot of things I wanted to say, but I couldn't find the words to make them come out right. Neither of us spoke for the rest of the drive. Even Spike huddled silently in my lap, occasionally rattling its thorns in distress.

The kids were in better spirits. Only the Cait Sidhe were left, and they knew they were going home. The noise didn't bother me—they kept it mostly to themselves, trying not to intrude on the cloud of gloom that covered the front seat, and when they got out of control, Raj settled them down again by means of occasional cuffs and snarls. I didn't intervene.

The Court of Cats is different than the other Courts of Faerie. Tybalt was the current King of the Bay Area, but someday that would change; someday, he'd be replaced, and Raj was the most likely heir. The King of Cats must be dominant in every way. He's the one who gets the greatest share of every kill, first pick of the women, and the finest of all the Cait Sidhe have to offer, but he's also the one who protects the Court. Cats won't obey the weak: to be King, you must be cunning, clever, and strong. Fear matters as much as respect, and if Raj was going to be King, he'd need the loyalty of his peers. That was the glue that would cement his throne.

Tybalt would have to die for Raj to become King. That idea bothered the hell out of me.

May sat quietly in the back, looking almost pensive as she watched the kids giggle and fight. What does Death have to be pensive about? She'd die when I did, that was a start. I wasn't sure it counted, since she only existed to foretell my death, but still.

Connor pulled up in front of Golden Gate Park, starting to turn onto the main road, and the car stopped with a rattling thunk. He tried the ignition a few times, and sighed. "It's dead."

"That's fine, we're here." I opened the door. "Come on, kids. Connor, see if you can push the car out of the road? I don't want to cause an accident."

"I'm coming with you."

"No, you're not."

"Why not?" Connor drew himself up to his full height, glaring at me. He looked pissed, and I couldn't blame him; he expected me to die anytime. He wanted to be there.

Raj kept me from having to answer. He eyed Connor imperiously as he stepped out of the car, saying, "The Court of Cats isn't open ground, and you're not invited."

"That's not fair."

"And?" He shook his head, every inch a Prince of Cats. "You aren't invited. She isn't invited either," he indicated May. "Only her." He looked to me, eyes narrowed. "My uncle's going to want to talk to her."

"Gee, lucky me," I muttered.

"I don't like this," said Connor. "If we can't go, neither should she."

"I agree," said May.

"Good for you two," I said. "Come on, kids. Let's go." They glared as I deposited Spike on the seat and got out of the car, but neither moved to follow. In their own odd ways, they'd both known me long enough to know better.

The children were silent as they left the car, leading me across the street into one of the alleys flanking the park. I released my human disguise once we were out of view of the street—it's rude to enter someone else's Court looking like something you're not—and kept guiding the group along. Shadows began gathering around us, shallowly at first, then growing heavier until they were almost a physical presence. I stumbled to a halt. Someone grabbed my hand, yanking hard, and I fell into the dark. I gasped, struggling for breath in the sudden cold ...

... and staggered into the light. We were at the end of a broad alley, our backs toward the wall. Cats ringed the walls, and more cats filled the alley, perching on fences, crates, and trash cans. Several human-form Cait Sidhe stood or sprawled on heaps of cloth and newspapers on the alley floor. There was a moment of stunned silence, cats and children staring at each other, before the alley erupted in triumphant howls from both sides. They were home.

A gray and white tabby transformed into a man with matching stripes in his hair and ran toward us, sweeping Raj into a hasty embrace as an Abyssinian cat with long, lithe limbs leaped up onto his shoulder. They started talking rapidly in an Arabic-sounding language, the cat yowling comments that both seemed to understand. The other Cait Sidhe swirled around us, laughing in delight as they reclaimed their children.

Folding my arms, I smiled. "Well," I said, quietly, "looks like we win this one."

The sounds of laughter and greeting masked the footsteps. There was no warning; just sudden pain as a hand grabbed my throat and whipped me around, slamming me hard against the wall. I found myself staring into wild, familiar eyes, open wide above a death-mask grin.

"Hi, Toby—miss me?" chirped Julie. Streaks of dirt were smeared down her cheeks, and her tiger-striped hair was matted. That was bad. The Cait Sidhe are obsessive about cleanliness; if she'd let herself go that far, she probably wasn't going to listen to reason. Crazy people rarely do. "Enjoying your second childhood? Let's make it your last!"

She raised her free hand, extending her claws. As a half-blood, Julie didn't inherit many of her long-dead fae parent's physical traits; the claws are an exception, but they could be a deadly one. Sunlight gleamed off them, making them look sharp enough to cut through glass. Her grip on my throat was tight enough that I could barely breathe, much less try to escape. Still grinning, she brought her hand down toward my chest in a hard slashing motion.

TWENTY-ONE

RAJ SLAMMED INTO JULIE FROM THE SIDE, his own claws extended. I saw his face for an instant as he rammed into her, and there was a sharp, feral madness in his eyes. I'd seen that madness before in Tybalt, usually just before something died.

Blood was running down the sides of my throat. I reached up to touch it, almost wonderingly, just before my legs buckled and I fell. Something popped in my right knee. I rolled onto my side, biting back a scream. Maybe I was smaller than normal, but my knees still weren't all that good. The Luidaeg made me younger. She didn't take away my scars.

The other Cait Sidhe had pulled away from the combatants, giving them room to fight without interfering. Raj's teeth were buried in Julie's shoulder, and she was trying to claw his arm off, both of them shrieking. Cats don't fight quietly. The two of them started rolling over each other with the fury of their attacks, moving away from me. I scrambled to my feet, grabbing the nearest heavy object—a two-by-four I could barely lift—and started forward, trying to avoid putting any weight on my right leg.

A hand landed on my shoulder, stopping me. I turned to look, scowling. The man who had greeted Raj was standing behind me, with the Abyssinian cat still perched on his shoulder. "You must not interfere," he said. His eyes were the same clear glass green as Raj's.

I stared at him. "She tried to *kill* me!"

"She failed." He shook his head. "Now my son is fighting and must win on his own."

"That's idiotic." The rules the Cait Sidhe live by sometimes seem positively suicidal. Raj was just a kid. Julie had more than thirty years' experience on him, and a lot of that experience was gained working for Devin, where playing fair was something that happened to other people. There was no way Raj could beat that. "He'll be killed."

"If he can't defeat her, he can't hold the throne while she lives." He tightened his grip on my shoulder, re-straining me. Julie slammed Raj against the wall. "Her blood is mixed. She can't be a Queen for this Court or any other. But she can still stop him from being King."

"And what if she kills him, huh? What then?" Raj squirmed free and lunged, slamming into Julie's stom-ach. She weighed at least fifty pounds more than he did, but gravity was on his side. She went down snarling.

Raj's father shook his head. "If she can kill him, he was never fit to take the throne."

"And you think that *matters* right now?" I demanded. Wrenching myself free, I ran toward the fight. I never made it there. My right knee buckled as soon as I put my weight on it, sending me sprawling. I dropped the board and flung out my arms.

I didn't hit the ground. Tybalt's hands closed on my waist while I was in mid-fall, flipping me upside down as he hoisted me to eye level. He blinked when our eyes met. I blinked back. Finally, he shook his head, expres-sion composing itself back to its usual feline cool.

"My, Toby, you've changed."

"Yeah, well." I tried to shrug. It was impossible to do anything but dangle. "Put me down."

"I . . . yes, of course." He actually reddened slightly as he turned me over and lowered me to my feet. "My apologies." Glancing toward the shrieking whirlwind that was Raj and Julie, he added, "I see you managed to recover my subjects."

"Yeah. Remind me to kill you later."

"Of course," he said, and cracked a smile. "Excuse me a moment, will you?"

"Sure." I leaned against the wall, trying to ignore the pain in my knee and the glare I was getting from Raj's father.

Tybalt moved toward Raj and Julie like a shark moving through the water. I couldn't help feeling sorry for Julie. We were friends for a long time, before an assassin's misfired bullet killed her boyfriend and made her swear to take revenge on me for putting him in the line of fire. I don't like to see her hurt. Still, I didn't look away as he reached down and grabbed her by both wrists, yanking her off the ground. Julie kicked and screamed as he lifted, but didn't manage to break free. Raj hunched down and snarled, but didn't try to interfere. Smart kid.

"We don't attack our guests," Tybalt said calmly, holding Julie at arm's length and giving her a brisk shake. She snapped at him, nearly sinking her teeth into his arm.

Bad idea. Tybalt shook her again, harder this time, and roared. The cats in the alley started to yowl, and the human-form Cait Sidhe joined in, blending their voices with his. I glanced back at Raj's father. He was yowling with the rest. Some things run in the family.

Cait Sidhe are pretty. They're slim and delicate and feline, and sometimes we forget that when we're hold a tabby, we're also holding a lion. Every Court of Cats is a jungle made of concrete and steel, and in his own Court, at least for now, Tybalt was the undisputed King. Julie knew the rules. She had to know how much trouble she was in. She still kept fighting, trying to kick him as he shook her. I guess she was trying to be gloriously defeated.

Julie never was that bright.

She snapped at him again, this time sinking her teeth

into his wrist. That was the last straw. Tybalt's patience visibly dissolved as he snarled and slammed her against the wall. She shrieked at him, and he slammed his foot into her stomach. I winced. The Cait Sidhe aren't particularly fast healers. Their succession fights have been known to turn deadly. And people wonder why Tybalt makes me nervous.

Julie snarled again, but her rage was gone, replaced by resignation; she was just fighting back for show. Tybalt let go of her wrists and wrapped his left hand around her throat, claws barely breaking the surface of her skin.

"Are we done?" he asked, almost gently.

She snapped at the air, hissing, and he slammed her head against the wall with an audible crack. She whimpered, eyes going glassy.

"*Now* are we done?" The gentleness was gone, replaced by anger.

"Yes," she whispered, licking her lips.

"You attacked my guest."

"I did." A trickle of blood was running from the corner of her mouth, and from the way she hit the wall, she'd be lucky if she didn't have a concussion. Tybalt can play a little rough.

"She was here at my invitation and under the protection of your Prince."

"She killed Ross!" Julie coughed, eyes blazing. "She needs to die."

"Maybe," said Tybalt. "This argument is old, and I'm tired of it. Trevor? Gabriel?" A pair of battered tomcats leaped down from the wall, becoming human as they landed. They were massive, like linebackers with pointed ears and fangs; next to them, Tybalt looked almost small. "Our Juliet is tired. Take her to her lair and keep her there."

"Yes, my liege," rumbled Gabriel. He reached down and wrapped one hand around Julie's upper arm. She hissed weakly. It must be nice to be seven feet tall and made of solid muscle, because he didn't bother to hit her; he just hauled her to her feet, keeping his fingers in a vise-grip around her arm. She hung there like a rag doll. "Come on, Julie."

Damn it. She isn't a friend these days, but she used to be. Ignoring the pain in my knee, I straightened. "Tybalt?"

"Yes?" He turned toward me, distractedly licking a smear of blood away from the corner of his mouth. I was pretty sure it wasn't his.

"Don't hurt her."

He blinked, staring at me. I'd managed to break his composure twice in one night; that might be a new record. "But she attacked you."

"I noticed." I rubbed my blood-sticky throat with one hand, wincing. "Just please, for me? Don't hurt her."

"The discipline of my subjects is my business." There was a note of warning in his tone.

"I know. I don't get to dictate. That's why I'm asking."

Raj picked himself up and moved to stand next to me, saying, "Uncle?"

"Yes, Raj?" Tybalt looked at him and smiled. "It's good to see you."

"Toby came in and got us," he said, shivering. There was a scrape down the left side of his face, and blood was matted in his hair.

"I know. I asked her if she would."

"But she did." He looked from me to Tybalt, and said in a rush, "Please don't hurt Julie? Toby doesn't want you to, and I trust her."

"I . . . see." Tybalt looked at me, expression amused. "Are we inspiring mutiny already?"

"Not on purpose," I said.

He studied me for a moment longer, and then said, "Trevor, Gabriel? Keep Juliet from hurting herself further. Bring her water to clean with." He smiled faintly. "Far be it from me to challenge both my Prince and my . . . champion."

The brute squad nodded in unison and carried her into the shadows, vanishing. There's another Court of

Cats, one that exists entirely on the other side of that movable darkness. I've never seen it. I don't think anyone who's not Cait Sidhe ever has.

Raj gave me an anxious look, fighting to keep his balance. His pupils had thinned to hairline slits, almost invisible against his irises. "Are you hurt?"

"Not as badly as you are," I said, frowning.

"It's nothing," he said, waving a hand. And then he fell. Even the resiliency of youth will only go so far. His father was there to catch him before he hit the ground.

"Is he—" I began.

"He'll be fine. He's simply tired," the man said. "My liege?"

"Yes, Samson, take your son and go." Tybalt shook his head, adding, "Toby and I will settle our affairs."

The other parents looked up, their returned charges cradled in their arms as they turned their attention on me. I shivered, trying to hide it. The Court of Cats isn't the most comfortable place to be, even when I'm my normal self. As a wounded child, it was downright scary.

"You may all go," Tybalt said, raising his voice to be heard. "Court is dismissed."

The shadows around us spread wide, and the Cait Sidhe moved through them, vanishing. We were alone in an instant, save for a few bedraggled tabbies who hadn't relinquished their places on the walls. Tybalt looked up, growling a single low note, and they leaped down, racing out of sight.

Tybalt sat down on the edge of an empty milk crate when the last of them was gone, then slumped over with his elbows resting on his knees. He looked at me for a long moment, and I realized with a jolt that he looked genuinely unhappy. Softly, he said, "You brought them home."

"I promised I'd try."

"That's all it's ever taken with you, isn't it?" He laughed, almost bitterly. "Changelings aren't supposed to have honor, you know. Didn't your mother teach you anything?"

"Apparently not," I said, as cheerfully as I could. "A lot of people seem to be pretty annoyed with her about that. Or maybe they're just annoyed with her in general. It's getting to where it's sort of hard to tell."

"Toby . . ."

"Sorry, Tybalt. It's just been a really long day." I sighed, brushing my hair out of my eyes. "And it's not over yet, which isn't making me particularly happy."

"You have the gratitude of my Court, October."

I looked at him sharply. That was dangerously close to thank you. "Do I?"

Tybalt didn't seem to notice his own slip. He just closed his eyes, leaning back until his shoulders hit the wall, and said, softly, "I thought I sent you to die. After what you told me, with your Fetch appearing . . . I thought that you were going to die because of what I asked you to do."

"Hey." I stepped over and put my hand on his shoulder, needing to reach up to do it. "I was already going. Mitch and Stacy's kids are like family. If anything happened, it wouldn't have been your fault."

"That doesn't matter. I'm in your debt."

The thought was alarming. "No, you're not. We're even now."

"You've done more than you owed, and I won't pretend you didn't." He put his hand over mine, covering it completely. Eyes still closed, he said, "All threats of death aside, I had no idea how much it would cost."

"What?" It took me a moment to realize that he meant my sudden regression to elementary school. "Oh. The Luidaeg did it so I could enter Blind Michael's lands. He sort of posted a 'you must be less than this tall to ride this ride' sign at the borders."

"I barely recognized you," he said.

"Yeah, about that. How *did* you recognize me?" The world was dismayingly full of people who didn't bat an eye when they saw me. I'm not vain or anything, but it was nice to think folks might notice my losing all the ground I'd gained since puberty.

He opened his eyes and smiled. It was a little disconcerting to be standing that close to his smile. Thankfully, being physically under the age of ten blunted most of the effect. "No matter what you look like, you still smell like you."

"Oh," I said, faintly.

"Are you done now? Are the children safe?"

"I think so. But a Fetch isn't usually a long-term houseguest. They pretty much show up when the house is about to go away." I pulled my hand out from under his, stepping back. "In that sense, I guess I'm pretty much finished."

"Don't give up hope." He offered another smile. This one was smaller, but no less sincere. "I've seen you manage the impossible before."

"Yeah, well." I glanced away, trying not to focus on his eyes. "Did you find what you were looking for?"

"Not yet." He stood, leaning down to brush my hair back with one gentle hand. "Come see me once you've managed the impossible again. If anyone can ... my Court is open to you."

I felt my cheeks redden. "Tybalt, what—"

"I found my answers. I know you weren't the one who lied to me." He pulled back his hand and vanished into the shadows, gone in an instant.

"Tybalt! Don't you *dare* say cryptic shit and then run out on me!" His exit was made; he didn't reappear.

Bastard.

I turned and limped toward the back of the alley, trusting that Tybalt wouldn't have left me in his Court if the exits were locked. Sure enough, the brick was misty under my fingers; I closed my eyes, stepping through. Movement was getting harder. It felt like my knee was trying to lock up. That was going to make dealing with the bridges in Lily's knowe a lot of fun.

The mist got thicker and colder as I moved through the wall. I filled my hands with it, reweaving my human disguise as I walked. I had no interest in being mistaken for an alien invader just because my mother had the bad grace to pass on her pointed ears. It was late enough in the year that I might be mistaken for a kid who'd started trick-or-treating early, but that didn't appeal either.

Connor was sitting on the sidewalk with his back to the alley wall when I emerged. He stood as he saw me approaching, and I was glad that my illusions were hiding the blood. Selkies don't have an enhanced sense of smell in their human forms; I could fool him, even though I'd never have been able to fool Tybalt.

He waited until I was closer before offering his hand. "I'm sorry. I was a jerk."

"Yes, you were." Never stop a man from admitting his faults. Still, I paused, and said, "I was a jerk, too."

"It's okay. I'm just worried about you."

"You were still a bigger jerk than I was."

"I know." He sighed. "I just . . . we lost you once. I don't want to lose you again."

I sighed, slipping my hand into his. Maybe he was a jerk, but he was a jerk who cared, and that's worth a lot in my book. Besides, it wasn't like it mattered. It would all be over soon.

He looked up, something like hope in his eyes. "Toby . . ."

"We're okay." I smiled wanly. "We need to get to Lily's. Can you just stop being a jerk until we get there? Please?"

"I think I can manage that," he said, and smiled. It was worth it just for that.

I left my hand in his as we walked past the car and toward the gates of Golden Gate Park. The height difference was jarring at first, but the feeling passed, and for a few minutes, everything was all right. May joined us while we were waiting for the crosswalk to be clear, Spike following at her heels, and somehow, that was right, too. The rose goblin ran ahead, and the Fetch followed behind as we walked, hand in hand, into Golden Gate Park.

I told Tybalt the truth, after all. I was almost finished.

TWENTY-TWO

MARCIA LEANED OUT OF HER BOOTH as we approached, beaming. "Toby! Connor! Hey!" I was ready to get annoyed—Connor and Tybalt recognizing me was one thing, but Marcia?—when she looked down, asking, "And who's your little friend?"

The phrase "little friend" pissed me off when I was actually the age I seemed to be, and it hadn't gotten any less annoying as I got older. I was tired, my knees ached, and I didn't have time to be patronized. "Can it, Marcia. Is Lily available?"

"What?" She blinked. "That's not a nice way to talk to your elders, you know."

"You were born in nineteen eighty-three," I said. "If you're my elder, I'll eat my socks. Can we see Lily?"

"Who's stopping you?" She squinted, the faerie ointment around her eyes reflecting the afternoon light in sparkles of turquoise and gold. "You're not what you look like." She looked toward May, still squinting. "Neither is she."

"Marcia, please, just let us in," I said.

Marcia is only a quarter-blooded changeling, and she needs faerie ointment to see our world at all. Ironically enough, the ointment opens her eyes a little wider than most. She not only sees through illusions; sometimes, she sees through realities. I guess that's why Lily likes her. It certainly can't be for the stimulating conversation.

Marcia pulled back, frowning. "I think you'd better leave. I mean, Toby isn't Toby, and your kid's not a kid, and Connor . . . well, Connor's okay, and I think that's Toby's rose goblin, but that's all I can tell. People I don't recognize shouldn't come here. Lily doesn't like it."

"Please refrain from exerting yourself, Marcia," Lily said, stepping up to the edge of the garden; she couldn't come any farther. Each Undine is literally bound to their domain, unable to ever leave it. In exchange, they know everything that happens in their own lands, and control them more intimately than any noble has ever controlled a knowe. I've always wondered whether it's a fair trade, but I've never been able to get up the nerve to ask. "I know our guests."

"Lily," I said. "Hey."

"Hello, October," she said. "I see you found the moon. Connor. It's been too long."

"I know," he said, his hand tightening in mine. "I've been busy."

"Of course." She turned to May. "You would be . . . ?"

"May," said my Fetch, expression grave.

"A good name. Ironic, but good. Whatever will we do when the months of the year are used entirely?" Lily looked back to Marcia. "These are my guests. October Daye, daughter of Amandine, albeit in slightly reduced circumstances; Connor O'Dell of Shadowed Hills; and May, who is, unless I am much mistaken, October's Fetch." Her voice stayed calm, but she looked at me when she said May's name, eyes unreadable.

Marcia stared at me, eyes wide. "You're *Toby?*" she squeaked.

"Is that a problem?" I asked.

"But you're so little!"

"And you're so blonde."

"Marcia, Toby and her friends look very tired, and I'm sure she wants to see her friend."

"Karen," I said. "Is she . . . ?" I let the question trail

off, not sure how to finish it. She wasn't talking like Karen was dead, but we were in a semipublic place. She might just be waiting to get us alone.

"No, October. I'm sorry." Lily shook her head. "I tried everything. I failed."

Oh, root and branch. How was I supposed to tell Stacy that Karen wasn't coming home? Swallowing, I asked, "How did she die?"

Lily frowned, looking bewildered. "Die?"

"Karen. How did she die?"

Marcia blinked. "Somebody died?"

"October, I think perhaps you and your company ought to come with me," said Lily, still frowning. "The sun will be down soon, and it seems we have much to discuss." She turned. Too confused to argue, I followed her, not releasing Connor's hand.

She led us to the base of the moon bridge, then stopped and knelt, putting her hand over my knee. "You're hurt," she said, disapprovingly. "That won't do, but I can't fix it here. Fetch?"

"Huh?" said May, blinking.

The folds of Lily's kimono rustled as she straightened. "Carry her. We must get her into the knowe, and she can't possibly handle the bridge with her knee in that condition."

"But—"

"There will be time to weep and wail and play the Banshee soon enough. For now, carry her. Connor?"

"Yes?"

"Come." She held out her arm, obviously expecting him to take it. Connor glanced at me as he released my hand and slid his arm through hers, letting her lead him up the bridge and out of sight. Spike bounded after them, leaving me alone with May. Peachy.

May looked at me, frowning. "She wants me to carry you."

"I noticed."

"Of all the ludicrous—"

I sighed, holding up my arms. "Come on, May. The

sooner we finish this, the sooner you can carry me off to my eternal reward."

"I'm still not sure I'm allowed to help you."

"Look, I won't tell if you won't. Do you want to piss off Lily?"

She blanched. When she got my memories, she got the full set. "No."

"I didn't think so. So come on and pick me up."

May sighed and knelt. "Oh, fine." Even shifting so she could lift me piggyback-style hurt my knee, and I hated to think what climbing the bridge on my own would've been like. Lily was right—I needed to be carried—but still, being carried by your own Fetch is just embarrassing.

May leaned forward to counterbalance my weight as she mounted the bridge. It worked well enough that we didn't fall backward, but it was slow going. She stopped, grabbing the railing as she panted for breath.

"What have you been eating?" she asked. "Bricks?"

I "accidentally" dug my heels into her sides. "I thought you were indestructible."

"No, I'm unkillable," she said, panting. "I still get tired, and you're heavy."

"Stuff it."

"Such gratitude." She started climbing again. There was a soft popping sound as we reached the top of the bridge, and we were standing at a crossroads with four small cobblestone paths stretching out across a checkerboard expanse of marsh. Only the paths provided a clear route to solid ground. We were in Lily's knowe.

"Cute," May grumbled, starting down the nearest path. We were halfway to land when she slipped.

Riding piggyback doesn't give you much in the way of the ability to catch yourself, and with her arms around my legs, May couldn't catch us. We barely had time to shriek—in perfect unison—before we hit the water. It was lukewarm, like fresh blood.

The thought was enough to make me shove away from May and start thrashing, and the fact that I was in the water at all was enough to make me keep thrashing. I spent fourteen years living with Lily. Neither of us planned it that way; a man named Simon Torquill decided I'd make a lovely koi and had the magic to test the theory. He transformed me and left me in one of the ponds that riddle the Tea Gardens. I haven't been real big on water since that happened. I don't even take baths anymore, just showers. Put me in water and I tend to panic a little.

Okay, more than a little. I kept thrashing, struggling to find the surface. Most koi ponds are shallow, but Lily's ponds aren't exactly what you'd call standard. I don't remember what they were like when I lived there, but I've never found the bottom while I was in my original shape, and I'm not going looking. I tried to scream, and water filled my mouth, choking me.

Great, I thought wildly, *this is how I die. My Fetch drowns me by mistake.*

Hands grabbed my shoulders and wrenched me out of the water, dropping me on something solid before hitting me on the back. I started coughing. Air. There was air in the world. Opening my eyes, I found myself staring up at Connor.

"Are you all right?" he said.

"Y-yeah," I stammered. "Sorry."

"Not your fault. May dropped you." He glared back over his shoulder.

"I didn't mean to!" May was a few feet away, wringing water out of her hair.

"It's okay, Connor. I'm okay," I said, sitting up and looking around. "She didn't mean to drop me. Where's Lily?"

"The pavilion," said Connor, almost smiling.

"Which would be where?"

"Try looking behind you," said May.

I looked over my shoulder. The pavilion was there, just like last time. Lily was seated at the table, mixing herbs in a small mortar. Spike was off to one side, watching and occasionally reaching out to bat at the pestle.

She didn't seem bothered by the rose goblin's antics; she ignored it, placidly continuing to work. And Karen was lying on the cushions behind the table, just where I'd left her.

It took a moment for that to process. When it did, I scrambled to my feet and ran for the pavilion, only to fall again as my knees buckled beneath me. "Maeve's *teeth!*" I snarled. "Lily!"

"Oh, crying for me now, are you?" She looked up, expression unreadable. "What would you ask from me?"

"Lily, you—I—I need to get to Karen! I need to see that she's okay."

"Do you?" She rose, walking down the pavilion steps with a fluidity even Tybalt could only envy. "It seems to me that what you need is to hold still for a time."

"Lily . . ." May and Connor were both standing, but they weren't moving. Turning toward Lily, I said, pleadingly, "Lily, please."

"If I truly loved you, I would refuse," she said, smiling sadly as she came to kneel on the moss in front of me, the mortar still in her hand. "I'd say 'no, you've had enough gifts of me,' and I'd let you heal at your own pace, just this once. Perhaps then your charming twin would leave us in peace, and while you might hate me for a while, you would be here to do it."

"I don't think it works that way," said May. She sounded sorry.

"I know that as well as you do. I've known more of your breed than you'd believe," chided Lily, pulling a chunk of moss off the ground and pressing it into her mortar. "Once you arrive, events must play to their logical conclusions. I hope you don't mind my hating you."

"It's okay," said May, coming to sit beside us. "It comes with the territory."

"Yes. It does. October?"

"Yes?"

"Connor is behind you. What is he doing?"

She sounded curious enough that I turned. Connor was watching me bleakly; he looked like he was losing his best friend. "He's not doing anything, Lily. Why did you—"

Her fists slammed into my knee. I screamed, whipping around to face her. She was empty-handed, looking at me innocently. I started to shout, and stopped as I realized that the pain was gone. I settled for glaring. "That *hurt*."

"Such things often do." She stood, leaving the moss on my leg as she walked back into the pavilion. "Come now, all of you. I am sure you have places to go and deaths to face."

I stood and followed her into the pavilion, letting her makeshift poultice lie where it fell. There was a flash of light as I climbed the steps, and the smell of hibiscus tea filled the air. I staggered, catching myself on the wall, and realized I was clean, dry, and wearing a purple robe embroidered with red heraldic roses. My hair was braided smoothly back.

And I was physically back to the correct age.

"What the—?" I looked up. At least I wasn't the only one confused; May and Connor were staring at me, mouths hanging open.

Lily inclined her head, looking satisfied. "As I thought. This suits you far better, given the circumstances." She knelt, pouring tea into a set of black-and-white patterned cups. "See to the girl; I know you too well to think you'll listen before you know she lives."

"Karen!" Suddenly reminded, I rushed over to drop to my knees and press my ear to Karen's chest. I didn't really stop holding my breath until I heard the steady, muffled beating of her heart. She had a heartbeat. She was alive. "She's alive." I sat up, turning toward the others, and beamed. "She's alive."

"I told you that," said Lily, chidingly. "She's alive and whole, and there is nothing I can do for her. Now come, all three of you, and drink your tea."

"Lily—"

"Come. Sit. Don't argue with me."

What were we supposed to do? We sat. I knelt across

from Lily, with May to my left and Connor to my right. He squeezed my knee under the table; I smiled at him. Lily simply watched us, passing the teacups around the table.

May was the first to receive her cup. She picked it up, sipped, and smiled. "Hey, peppermint."

Connor picked up his own cup, and blinked at her. "This isn't peppermint. It's rosehips and watercress."

"As you say," said Lily, sipping her own tea.

Right. I picked up my cup and took a cautious sip. The liquid hit my tongue, and I choked, flinging my cup away. It shattered against the pavilion floor as I turned to spit out what was already in my mouth. "Blood?" I looked back to Lily, furious. "You served me *blood!*"

"No, I didn't. You served it to yourself, just as May served herself peppermint and Connor served himself rosehips. The difference is what you made of it. Much like your lives, I'd imagine. And now you've broken another of my teacups." She sighed. "Really, October, what am I going to do with you?"

"Is there a reason you people are so damn obscure?" I demanded, standing. The taste of blood makes me cranky under any circumstances. I'd managed to spit out most of it, but I was still getting flickering glimpses of Lily's life, like shadows cast on a distant wall. I didn't want them. "Screw this. Karen and I are leaving."

"Are you, now? She's rather larger than you can easily manage on your own."

"Connor will help." I glanced back toward him. He hadn't moved; he was just watching us with a befuddled look on his face. "Won't you?"

"Oh, sure," he said, sounding dazed. Then he fell over.

"What the—" May started to stand, but her eyes glazed over and she collapsed in mid-motion. Spike hissed and slunk behind me, crouching at my heels.

Lily put down her teacup. "I know you too well," she said. "I knew you wouldn't drink your tea."

"What did you do?" I moved to Connor's side, fumbling for his pulse. It was strong and steady.

"I bought you some time," she said. "You don't have as much as you think. The tea leaves never lie."

"What the hell are you talking about?" I snapped.

"You let me help you. Your bond is mine." She raised a hand, saying, "By sea and wave and shore, by the boon of Maeve, mother of waters, I call you to me. Accept my request and grant what I need in this moment." Her jade eyes seemed darker than usual, and very sad.

"Lily?" I stood, taking a step backward. "What are you doing?"

She shook her head, moving toward me. "By storm and frost and tempest, in the name of Maeve, mother of marshes, I call you to me. The road is ours who are her children, and it shall open when there are no others."

It was getting hard to keep my eyes open. I hadn't drunk the tea, but I tasted it, and that was enough to let her put me under. I dropped to my knees, whispering, "Lily, why?"

"For your own good," she said, and reached down to nudge my eyelids closed. I tried to pull away, but I couldn't move. Not at all.

And then there was nothing.

TWENTY-THREE

KAREN WAS SITTING ON MY CHEST, and some-how, she didn't weigh anything at all. "Aunt Birdie? Are you awake?"

"Karen." *I smiled. The landscape was a blur, like a half-finished watercolor.* "You're awake."

"No, I'm not, and neither are you. You have to come back; it's important. I'm sorry, but it's important that you wake up."

"What's going on?"

"It's time to finish things. You have to come back. You have to—"

Her face blurred, dissolving as someone began shouting. "Wake up, Toby! Damn it, girl, wake up!" The new voice was louder and more strident. Someone was shaking me.

I opened my eyes.

The Luidaeg was holding me by the shoulders. She had reverted to her normal human appearance, with freckles and coveralls and tousled black curls. Even her eyes were human, brown and ordinary. None of that was strange for her. It was the fear in her expression that was new.

"Luidaeg?" I said blearily. My head felt like it was wrapped in cotton. Whatever Lily dosed me with, it was strong.

"Yeah," she said, letting go of my shoulders. "You're at my place."

"What?" I forced myself to sit up, squinting. I was on the Luidaeg's couch, across from the room's single dirt-streaked window. The curtains were open; I'd never seen them that way before. The room was usually lit by flickering bulbs and a sort of undefined glow, letting the shadows breed in the corners and pulse with an odd life of their own. Now, watery sunlight was chasing them away, making the mess on the floor a lot easier to see. The walls were black with grime, and patches of vari-colored mold covered the couch.

A brightly colored, clean-smelling quilt was spread over my legs, so out of place that it was almost jarring.

"How did I get here?" I asked, looking at the Luidaeg.

"Lily sent you on the tidal path." She shook her head, something of her customary smirk creeping into her face. "She seemed to think hanging out with your Fetch was a bad plan."

"Lily!" I threw the quilt off my legs, trying to stand. It didn't work. "She drugged us!"

"Yup," agreed the Luidaeg. "Really got you good. Invoked Mom's name and everything. Do you have any idea how long it's been since I've heard that invocation? That's the Undine equivalent of breaking out the good china."

"But—"

"She wanted you away from your Fetch, and frankly, I think she was right."

I stared at her. "But she drugged us."

"That is no longer news, dumbass. Are you going to ask why she drugged you?"

"All right," I said, narrowing my eyes, "Why?"

"Because, dear October, you're the most passively suicidal person I've ever met, and that's saying something. You'll never open your wrists, but you'll run head-first into hell. You'll have good reasons. You'll have great reasons, even. And part of you will be praying that you won't come out again."

Her words struck a little too close to home. "That's not true," I protested, weakly.

"Isn't it?" She stood, moving to the window and looking out onto the street. "Faeries live forever. Humans don't, but they know they're going to die; it's in their blood. Your blood doesn't know the way, and I think you're trying to teach yourself." She shook her head. "You mean well, but you've never been all that bright."

"What does that have to do with May and Connor?"

"Connor? Nothing. He was just in the way." She looked back to me. "May, on the other hand, is pretty much the crux of the problem. She's here, so you think you're getting what you want. You think you get to die. Well, guess what? You can't. We won't let you."

"Won't let me do *what?*"

"Die."

"That's nuts."

"Is it?" She turned and walked into the kitchen. I levered myself off the couch and followed. I was still wearing the red and purple robe; my knife was tucked into the belt. At least I wasn't unarmed.

The Luidaeg was ramming unwashed dishes into a cabinet when I entered the room, the clattering punctuated by the sound of breaking china. She stopped when she heard my footsteps, but didn't turn. "You're going back, aren't you?"

"Katie's still a horse. Can you fix her?"

"Not while my brother holds her. He didn't let go just because you stole her."

"And Karen—Karen! She's still at Lily's. I have to go back for her."

"No, you don't. She's in my room."

I paused. "She's *here?*"

"That's what I said. Poor kid must be exhausted. She's been asleep since you got here."

"Luidaeg, she's been asleep since Blind Michael came."

She dropped the plate she was holding, whipping around to stare at me. "What?"

"She won't wake up."

"Aw, *fuck*. You mean Lily wasn't being obscure to piss me off?" She stalked into the hall. I followed. I've seen a lot of things since meeting the Luidaeg; some of them were even pleasant. But I'd never seen her bedroom, and considering the condition of the public parts of her apartment, I wasn't sure I wanted to. Still, if Karen was there, I needed to. I put my feet where the Luidaeg put hers as we walked down the hall, trusting her to know where it was safe to step. She stopped at the one door in the hall that was always closed, sighed, and pushed it open. "After you."

I only paused for a moment before stepping through.

The room was dark, filled with shifting shadows too active to be natural. Behind me, the Luidaeg said, "Close your eyes," and snapped her fingers before I had a chance to react. The candles clustered on every available surface burst into flame, flooding the room with light.

When the afterimages faded from my retinas, I blinked, looking around again. The candles filled the room with slow, heavy light that refracted off the six large fish tanks lining the far wall and threw ripples across the ceiling and the polished hardwood floor. Strange fish swam in those tanks, monsters of the deep with poison barbs and razored spines. A pearl-eyed sea dragon the length of my arm swam up to the glass, eyeing me balefully. The air smelled like seawater and brine.

An antique four-poster bed took up most of the wall next to the door. The frame was ornately carved with waves and seaweed and stylized mermaids, and the heavy black velvet curtains were drawn, hiding its contents from view.

"Luidaeg, this is—"

"Yeah, I know. I can't keep up appearances everywhere; a girl has to sleep sometime." She gestured toward the bed. "She's in there."

I stepped over to the bed, opening the curtains. Karen was lying there with sheets drawn up to her waist, unmoving. The blankets and pillows were a deep wine red, seeming almost bloody against her skin. She looked like a sleeping princess from a fairy story, small and wan and lost forever. Kneeling, I put my hand against her cheek and winced. It felt like she was running a fever, but there was no color in her cheeks; she was burning up without a flame, and her eyes were moving behind closed lids. Still dreaming. She'd been asleep for days, and she was still dreaming.

"Why won't she wake up?"

"Hell if I know." The Luidaeg sat on the edge of the bed, nudging Karen in the arm. When this failed to get a response, she nudged again, harder. "She's really out of it."

"I know that. Can you tell me why?"

"Not yet," she said, leaning down and prying Karen's right eye open. She peered into it, apparently looking for something, before leaning back and letting go. Karen's eye closed again, but otherwise, she didn't move. "Huh. How about that."

"What's wrong with her?" I balled my hands into fists, resting them against the bed. I hate feeling helpless almost as much as I hate bleeding.

"Could be a lot of things," she said. "A curse, a hex, bloodworms, food poisoning—you got that knife of yours?"

"What?"

"Your knife. The one I know you carry. Do you have it with you?"

"Yes, but—"

"Good." She held out her hand. "Give it to me."

"Why?" The Luidaeg had a nasty tendency to cut things when she was armed, and frequently, that meant me. I didn't think I could stop her by refusing to hand over my knife, but I had to ask.

She lifted her head. "Do you want to know what's wrong with her?"

"Yes!"

"Then give me the knife. I don't have the patience

for your little games right now. This whole situation is pissing me off."

Wordlessly, I pulled the knife out of my belt and handed it to her. Odd though it might seem, I trust the Luidaeg. I may not always approve of her methods, but I trust her.

She lifted Karen's arm and paused. "I'm not a child killer. You know that, right?"

"I know," I said. "If I thought you were going to hurt her . . ."

"You'd challenge me and lose. You know it, I know it, but you'd still do it. Sometimes your sense of honor confuses the hell out of me." She grinned. "All changelings are crazy."

"Yes, we are. What are you going to do?"

"I'm not going to hurt her; I just need a little blood." She slid the knife across Karen's thumb. Blood beaded to the skin, the scent of it filling the air until it drowned out the salt water. "There we go." Lowering her head, the Luidaeg pressed the cut to her lips in a bizarre parody of kiss it and make it better, and held that position, swallowing. Karen didn't move.

The Luidaeg raised her head after several minutes, licking her lips. "Well, well, well. I see," she said, and stood, dropping Karen's hand. Her eyes had gone white. "I don't believe it."

"What is it?" I asked, rising. "What's wrong with her?"

"I should have killed you when I had the chance," she said, licking her lips again. Her fangs showed when she spoke. "I'd have ripped your heart out of your chest and had it for a toy. It would've been a beautiful death."

"I'm sure," I said, shuddering. The Luidaeg seemed to like me, but that didn't mean anything. "Let's skip that for now."

She shrugged, licking her lips a third time. "It's your funeral. She's an oneiromancer."

"A what?"

"An oneiromancer, a dream-scryer. She sees the future—and probably the present—in her dreams."

"What does that have to do with anything?"

The Luidaeg sighed. "You're not getting it. Look, the brat can read the future in her dreams. That means she doesn't have a very good connection with her body. You with me?"

"Yes . . ." I said. Karen was an oneiromancer? I'd heard of them, but never met one. Fortune-telling is a rare gift, and that's a good thing; people who see the future don't have the best connection to the present. They tend to say too much and wind up dead. Stacy comes from Barrow Wight stock; Mitch is part Nixie. Neither breed is known for seeing the future. Where the hell did this little curveball come from?

"Michael stole the others physically. Karen wasn't in her body when the Riders came, so they took her to him a different way; they took her in her dreams."

"What?" I stared at her. "How?"

"What you and your mother read in the blood is the self; it can be removed. Karen's self isn't anchored like yours or mine because of what she is. That's what he stole."

"Is that why she won't wake up?" *And why I see her when I dream?*

Her expression hardened. "Yes."

"Fine." I stood, squaring my shoulders. "I'm going to get her back."

"You make it sound so *simple.*" She crossed her arms. "It really is just like watching Daddy get ready to ride out and subdue another group of rioting idiots. Sword, shield, suit of shining armor, ingrained stupidity, and you're ready to go."

I blinked. "What are you talking about?"

"Heroes, Toby, heroes. You're all idiots—and don't tell me you're not a hero, because I don't feel like having that argument tonight. You'll need this." She pulled my candle out of the air, dropping it into my left hand as she pressed my knife into the right. "You can get there and back by the light of a candle, after all. Trouble is, you're off the Children's Road. I can't set you on it more than once. Against the rules."

"So how am I supposed to get to Blind Michael?"

"Patience! Dad's balls, they don't teach kids any manners anymore. I should slaughter the lot of you." She shook her head. "There are other roads."

"How do I find them?"

"You've been on one of them before. The Rose Road."

"What?" I frowned. "But I thought—"

"Luna sent you on the Rose Road the first time you came here, and that means you have the right to pass there. I can't open it for you, but she can."

Luna Torquill was one of the last people I wanted to deal with. I put the thought resolutely aside, nodding. "All right. I'll ask her."

"Little problem. It won't be that easy."

"What do you mean?"

"It starts now." She snapped her fingers. My candle lit, burning blue-green. I felt the shock of the blood inside the wax waking up again. "When you leave this room, you're on the road. You can get there and back by the candle's light, but Lily didn't do you any favors; it's going to be harder now. The Rose Road has rules when you use it for more than just a shortcut."

"What are they?"

"When you leave—and you'd better do it soon—don't look back, no matter what you see or hear. You can take any help you find, but you can't ask for it; it has to be offered."

"So they're the same as before. Got it. Anything else?" I asked sourly.

"Actually, yes."

I sighed. "I had to ask, didn't I?"

"I'm serious; this is important," she said. "You have twenty-four hours, no more. If you can't get there and back in that time, you won't get there at all, and the Rose Road will be closed to you forever."

"But—"

"That means more than you think it does. You can't take the Old Road; the Blood Road would kill you; the

Tidal Road is lost for anything bigger than bringing you to me. It's this road or none, and you'd better go." She crossed to a small wardrobe, opening it. "Lily thinks too much about appearances—you *can't* go in what you're wearing. Here." She tossed me a sweater, a pair of black leggings and a belt with an attached sheath. "Get changed and get out."

"Luidaeg, I—"

"Toby, do it." Something in her expression told me not to argue.

Getting the robe off was easy. Getting the sweater on without dropping the candle or setting my hair on fire was hard, but after a few false starts, I managed to get everything in place. I straightened, shoving my knife into the sheath. "Now what?" I asked.

"Now you leave." She pointed to the door. "Go that way. Now."

"Are you—"

"When you reach Shadowed Hills, tell Luna to send the horse-girl to me. I'll try to help." She paused. "If you get yourself killed, I'll hurt you in ways you can't even imagine."

"I—"

"Go!"

I backed away, stopping when my shoulders hit the wall. The Luidaeg folded her arms, glaring until I found the doorknob, fumbled it open, and backed out into the hall. The door slammed shut in my face. The hall seemed to stretch as I made my way to the front door, the shadows growing darker and harder to deny. I gripped my candle and kept walking. If I'd been the only thing at stake, I might have wavered, but it wasn't just me. Stacy didn't deserve to lose her daughter; Quentin didn't deserve to lose his girlfriend. And I was going to get them back.

I was halfway down the hall when the screaming started, hitting a high, endlessly angry note, as pitiless as the sea. I shivered, but didn't look back. I'm not Orpheus. I'm not that easy to trick.

The front door opened when I twisted the knob, and I stepped out into the cold air of the September night. I frowned, muttering, "There was sunlight inside ..." Now time was screwing around with me, too. Just what I needed. I had twenty-four hours to get from downtown San Francisco to Pleasant Hill, break into Blind Michael's lands, rescue Karen, and get out. All without cash or a car, when I wasn't allowed to call for help. Right.

"Piece of cake," I said, and started walking.

The universe doesn't like to be mocked. I was halfway to the main road when I heard engines rev behind me. Mindful of the Luidaeg's words, I didn't look back; I just picked up the pace, scanning for a place to hide. Nothing was really presenting itself—the street was blank, empty of both cover and assistance. The engines got louder, and I broke into a run, forcing myself to keep my eyes fixed firmly ahead.

I made it almost two blocks before the motorcycles surrounded me, engines gunning with a sound that was suspiciously like the nickering of horses. The Riders grinned down at me from behind their visors, confident in their victory. There were three of them and just one of me, and there was nowhere left for me to run.

TWENTY-FOUR

"**O**H, OAK AND ASH," I muttered, stepping backward. My candle apparently didn't work the same way outside of Blind Michael's lands, because it clearly wasn't hiding me. The Riders had me surrounded, and even if I could make it to the Luidaeg's place before they grabbed me, turning around would take me off the Rose Road. I was stuck.

Looking around, I said, "You know your timing sucks, right?"

The Riders laughed, making the hair on the back of my neck stand on end. They knew they had me.

That didn't mean I had to go quietly. I drew my knife, falling into a defensive stance. "Come on, damn you," I snapped. "I don't have time to play. Come on!"

They were starting to look uneasy, glancing to each other and back to me. Blind Michael's Riders weren't used to prey that fought back. I thought about using that confusion against them, but dismissed the idea. They weren't that confused, and I wasn't that good.

"Come *on!*" I shouted. That did it. The engines revved with a sound like hoofbeats, and they were suddenly charging me. I held my ground. If I was lucky, they'd kill me.

The first Rider's elbow hit me in the shoulder, sending me sprawling. My knife skittered out of my hand and into the gutter when I hit the ground, leaving me unarmed. I scrambled to my feet, and the second blow hit me in the side of the head, knocking me back down. I fell hard. When I tried to get up again, I couldn't; my head was spinning, and black spots were blocking large portions of the landscape. I rolled onto my side and curled up, trying to minimize their target area while I waited to see whether my head would clear.

And a half-recognizable voice called, "Close your eyes!" from behind me. I listen to commands from the shadows, especially when I don't have any other choice. I screwed my eyes closed, curling up even more tightly.

I didn't see what came next. Most of the time, I'm glad of that fact. Then there are the times late at night when my mind tries to fill in the pictures that go with the sounds, and I wish I *had* seen what happened. It couldn't have been as bad as the things I can imagine. It couldn't.

Nothing could be that bad.

It began with a rising scream like a Banshee's wail, but wilder and angrier. Then it cut off, replaced by the sound of smashing and the bloody softness of rending flesh. Screams and snarls filled the air. I lifted my head, and ducked again as a chunk of armor spun past me. Right. I couldn't stand, and I couldn't run; I was just going to wait quietly and hope that whatever was attacking the Riders didn't want a side order of changeling for dessert.

The sounds cut off with a final furious roar, and everything was silent. I stayed where I was, eyes squeezed shut. Footsteps approached me, and I heard someone kneel.

"Here," said Tybalt, sounding darkly amused. "Your knife." A familiar hilt was pressed into my fingers. "You can open your eyes now."

I did, raising my aching head until the King of Cats swam into view. His shirt was half-shredded, and he was covered in blood, but he didn't look hurt. "We should go," he said, offering his hand. "The rest of Blind Michael's men won't be very amused."

"How did you—" I shoved the knife into its sheath, taking his hand and using it to lever myself off the ground. The motion made my head spin. Damn it. Just once, I'd like to be attacked without somebody trying to crack my skull.

"The Luidaeg called me," he said. I must have stared, because he flashed a brief, genuine smile. "She said you weren't allowed to ask for help. She, on the other hand, is welcome to ask for whatever she wants."

"Did she actually ask?" I said, checking my candle to make sure it wasn't damaged. The flame was still burning clean and blue, thank Oberon.

"No," he replied. "Does she ever?"

"I guess not," I said. "You just here to save my butt?"

"She seemed to think you might like an escort."

I stared at him, pride fighting a brief, losing battle with my common sense. Did I want to admit that I needed help? Hell, no. Was I going to make it to Shadowed Hills if I didn't? Probably not.

"Yeah," I said, with a sigh. "I could use one."

He chuckled, and the hair on the back of my neck rose in an entirely different way. "Sometimes, you are *entirely* too proud. I'm not trying to get you back into my debt, you realize. You saved the children of my Court. I'm glad to have a chance to help."

"I . . ." I stopped, not sure what to say. Tybalt was my enemy, damn it; we sniped and argued and held each other in debt. We didn't do favors. He shouldn't offer to help me without any strings attached. It wasn't right. And he definitely shouldn't smile while he made the offer. Because if we weren't going to be enemies anymore, I didn't know what we were. Slowly, I asked, "You'll get me there?"

"If I can. You need me. Every minute you waste is a minute you can't afford."

He had me there. "Fine," I said. "You can help me." I was trying to make it seem like I was doing him the favor. It made me feel better, even though we both knew it was a lie.

"Good." He rose and started walking, forcing me to follow or be left behind. My head was spinning, but I found that if I kept my eyes on him, I could move in a straight line. That was a good sign. I wasn't having any trouble walking; that was another good sign. If we kept collecting good signs, I might reach Shadowed Hills alive.

We'd gone almost a mile when Tybalt stopped and sniffed the air, stiffening. I glanced at my candle, reassured to see that it was still burning a clean blue. "Tybalt, what's—"

"Shhh," he hissed. "Something's coming."

"Where?" I peered down the street. There was no one there, but that didn't necessarily mean anything: if Tybalt said something was coming, he meant it. "Tybalt—"

"I think it's time to consider running," he said, grabbing my free hand.

"What?"

"Run!" He bolted, hauling me with him. I stumbled but forced myself to ignore the sickening jouncing of the landscape all around us. Finally I just squeezed my eyes shut and ran blind, letting him guide me through the dark.

I could hear them around us as soon as my eyes were closed. The air came alive with hungry, panting sighs and the shrill cries of the monstrous children from Blind Michael's halls. The Riders weren't working, so the bastard was trying something new. He'd unleashed the only hounds he had—the children nobody had saved.

We ran until my legs buckled under me and I fell, nearly yanking my hand out of Tybalt's. He paused long enough to grab me and swing me up into his arms before he started running again, faster than before. I huddled against him, gasping for air. The sounds of pursuit were getting dimmer: we were outrunning them, at least for now.

"Keep your eyes closed and don't open them, no matter what," he said next to my ear, in a surprisingly steady voice. "We have farther to go this time, and it may hurt.

Do you understand?" I forced myself to nod. If he was in danger it was my fault; I had to do what he asked me to do. It might get us through alive.

"Good," he said. "Now hold your breath."

I barely had time to breathe in before the world turned to ice. I kept my eyes shut, forcing myself to count backward from one hundred. The air kept getting colder as Tybalt ran, reaching temperatures I hadn't known were possible. How cold could shadows get? Ice was forming in my hair, and my lungs were starting to ache. I wasn't sure how long I could hold on.

My grip on Tybalt's arm tightened, and he said, sounding strained, "Hold on. We're almost there—"

The air warmed so suddenly it was like someone had flipped a switch, and Tybalt stumbled as he made the transition from shadows to solid ground. I opened my eyes, blinking ice from my lashes. We were in an alley, and judging by the buildings around us, we were somewhere in Oakland, at least thirty miles from where we'd started. And we were alone. That was an improvement.

"Toby, if you don't mind, I need to put you down," he said. His voice was shaking. I looked up and winced. He looked like a man who'd just run a relay race through hell.

"Of course," I said.

He lowered me to the ground. I sat, sticking my head between my knees. My body was telling me in no uncertain terms that it wanted a chance to stop and be violently ill. I'm usually willing to listen to the things my body tells me, but unfortunately, it doesn't have a very good sense of impending doom. I was alone in an alley with the King of Cats, waiting for Blind Michael's minions to swoop in and kill us. It wasn't a good time to be sick. I ordered my stomach to behave itself, hoping it would listen.

Tybalt padded to the mouth of the alley, head cocked as he scanned the street for signs of danger. I stayed where I was, trying not to pant. My lungs were almost as angry as my stomach; they wanted air, and they wanted it *now*. Still, I was okay with letting Tybalt take care of us. I could let him watch my back. I love Stacy and Connor. I wouldn't trust them to keep me alive. I need people like Tybalt for that.

I paused, stiffening. The Luidaeg knew where I'd taken the kids, and Blind Michael was her brother. How deep did their ties run? Was it deep enough that he'd leave her alone? I knew he wanted me—I had plenty of proof of that—but would he go after her if he thought it would bring his lost children back? The Luidaeg is one of the biggest, meanest people I know. That didn't mean Blind Michael couldn't be bigger. Or meaner.

I didn't hear Tybalt come back until his hand clamped down on my shoulder. If he'd been one of Blind Michael's men, it would've been too late to run. Ah, the joy of total exhaustion. I jumped, and he smiled wearily as he sat beside me, leaving his hand where it was.

"You're hurt," he said, in a disapproving tone.

"I guess," I said. There was a suspicious dampness on the back of my neck. My vision had returned to normal, so I wasn't thinking concussion. Quite. "It's nothing major."

Tybalt took his hand off my shoulder and slid it through my hair. I bit my tongue, holding back a yelp as his fingers found every scrape and abrasion my battered scalp had to offer. "Nothing major?" he asked, pulling his hand away. Blood covered his fingertips. "When the night-haunts come for you, should I tell them to go away because it's nothing major?"

"That's not fair," I said, gritting my teeth against the pain. The blood on his hand wasn't helping. I hate the sight of my own blood.

"Since when has fair had anything to do with us?" he asked, and stood, picking me up in the process. I found myself supported against his chest with my legs pinned under his arm before I had a chance to react.

"Hey!" I protested. "Put me down!"

He blinked, almost smiling. "We need to reach Shadowed Hills before the Hunt finds us. I followed your scent across the city. Do you think Blind Michael's men are any less skilled? I have an advantage—I have a certain familiarity with your scent—but they'll find us."

"So we need to move. I get that." It was hard to move with him holding me like that. If nothing else, it was distracting as all hell.

"We need to move *quickly*."

"That doesn't mean I need to be carried!"

"Doesn't it? Would you rather walk?"

I paused. Shadowed Hills was a thirty minute drive from Oakland, and as far as I knew, Tybalt didn't drive. That meant he was probably planning on getting us there some other way. Even healthy, most of his roads would've worn me out. Wounded and exhausted, well . . .

Right. "Fine. Let's go to Shadowed Hills."

"Good girl," he said, adjusting his grip. "Close your eyes, hold your candle close, and take the deepest breath you can. This time will take a little longer."

"Define 'a little.'"

His smile grew. "Just trust me."

There was nothing I could say to that, and so I simply nodded.

"Close your eyes," he said, and I closed them, clutching my candle. Not dropping me was Tybalt's responsibility; not dropping the candle was mine. I felt him back up, getting a running start, and leap toward what I knew was actually a solid wall.

We never hit the stone. The world turned cold around us, existence reducing itself to the circle of Tybalt's arms and the hot wax dripping on my hands. I kept my eyes screwed shut, holding my breath until I thought I would choke on it. Spots were dancing behind my eyes; I couldn't possibly hold my breath any longer. How long did he expect me to go without air? Of course, he was the one doing the running. How far could he go before he fell down?

I forced myself not to breathe, nestling farther down in his arms and trying to let the rhythm of his body keep me calm. It wasn't working. Everything was dark and cold, and ice was forming in my hair. Lines of frost ran down my lips and cheeks. And Tybalt kept running.

The darkness would never end, and this was worse than stupidity; it was suicide. I couldn't hold my breath any longer even if I wanted to. I let the air out of my lungs in a great rush, preparing to breathe in—

—and we broke out into the light. There was no time to catch myself as Tybalt stumbled and fell. I hit the ground hard, rolling several feet to the right before I opened my eyes.

The air was filled with the glow of pixies and the brighter light of tiny lanterns. It looked like multiple flocks had gathered in the trees above us, all of them twirling in an intricate aerial reel. I blinked, and then grinned as I realized what they were doing. It was almost Moving Day, and they were celebrating as they prepared. On All Hallows' Eve they'd all take wing at once, finding a new place to call home for the dark half of the year. Moving Day is a beautiful sight. My mother used to bring me to the mortal world to watch it.

I stayed on my back until I could breathe again, just watching the pixies. When my lungs stopped aching I sat up, turning to Tybalt with a smile. "Hey, Tybalt, I guess you . . . Tybalt?"

He hadn't moved. I crawled toward him, clutching my candle in one hand, and shook his shoulder. "Tybalt?" There was no reaction. I shook harder and grabbed his wrist, checking for a pulse.

There wasn't one.

He wasn't breathing.

TWENTY-FIVE

"TYBALT! DAMMIT, TYBALT, WAKE UP!" I dropped my candle, grabbing his shoulders with both hands and shaking him. "You can't die! I won't *let* you!"

The ice in my hair was melting down my face in cold lines, but it didn't matter, because Tybalt wasn't breathing. One of my elbows was scraped from falling out of his arms, and that didn't matter, because Tybalt wasn't breathing. I shook him again. "Tybalt, no. You can't . . ."

Couldn't what? Die? Why not? There was nothing stopping him. Couldn't go away and leave me here alone? Maybe.

"Wake up, damn you!" I clamped my hand over his nose and my mouth over his own, trying to force air into his lungs. I couldn't tell whether or not it was making a difference, so I just kept doing it, blowing in and forcing the air out again by beating my fists against his chest. "Wake up!"

It wasn't working. I collapsed against him, burying my face in the crook of his shoulder and sobbing. It wasn't supposed to end like this. I didn't know what I'd expected, but it wasn't supposed to end like this. Tybalt wasn't supposed to die some stupid, pointless death he'd have avoided if it wasn't for me. Raj would inherit early, and it was my fault.

Dozens of pixies dropped out of the trees and landed around us, folding their chiming wings and patting me sympathetically. I ignored them, curling more tightly against Tybalt.

"This isn't fair," I mumbled.

"Oh, I don't know," he rasped. "It seems like a nice bargain to me. I risk life and limb to bring you here, and you beat me up and cry all over me."

"Tybalt!" I shoved myself upright, staring at him. He was watching me, smiling, and while he was pale, he was also breathing. "But you—you were—"

"They tell a lot of stories about cats, don't they?"

"What?"

"They say we have nine lives." He levered himself into a sitting position, giving me time to move away. I did, but not far; I wasn't letting go just yet. "There's a sort of truth in that."

"How?" I asked. Inside, I was screaming and crying and demanding answers. Outside, I could wait. He was alive. That was enough.

"Kings and Queens of Cats are hard to kill. Things that would kill our subjects, or us, before we were crowned, they can take us down, but we come back." He had reached up at some point and was idly toying with a strand of my hair. I didn't pull away. "Only so many times, though. Not nine. It would be more than my life is worth to tell you the real number."

"But—"

"Shhh. Hush. I'm all right; you didn't kill me. Although Juliet would be happy if you did, since it would give her an excuse to kill you." His smile didn't waver. "You have a talent for alienating people, you know that? You don't mean to, but you manage all the same."

"Tybalt, I'm—"

"Don't make excuses; we're better than that." He pulled his hand away from my hair. "Go. We're in the

park that hosts Shadowed Hills. You can still do whatever needs to be done."

"What about you?"

"I'll be fine. Sore, but fine. Now go."

I stood, uncertainly. He started to close his eyes.
"Tybalt?"

"Yes?" A note of irritation crept into his tone as his
right eye finished closing, leaving him squinting at me
out of the left.

"What did you mean before? When you said you
knew I didn't lie to you?"

"Ah." The sound was half exclamation, half sigh. He
closed his left eye, lips curving in a smile. "You've told
me certain untruths, little fish, and it was important that
I know the reasons. Now I know that you didn't know
any better, and we can proceed."

"What—"

"If I tell you, you'll call me a liar, Toby. No. I'm not
trying to play the riddler, but no. If you want these answers, you'll need to find them yourself. I hope you will.
Now go." He yawned. "I'm tired. Coming back from the
dead takes a great deal out of a man."

I stared at him. He saved my life and I got him killed,
and now all he could do was make vague pronounce-
ments and tell me to go away? Fine. I bent to retrieve
my still-burning candle, trying not to look at him. "I
guess I'll see you later."

"I hope so," he said, simply.

More confused than ever, I started walking. I couldn't
look back. The Luidaeg's rules didn't allow it.

Pixies swarmed around me as I trudged up the hill,
chasing each other through a series of complex airborne
acrobatics. I bit back a smile. Pixies aren't very smart—
they're like spider monkeys with wings—but they mean
well, when they're not attacking people at random.
They're tricky, thieving vermin, and that's part of why I
like them so much.

There were no humans in the park. It was too late in

the year and too late at night; sunset emptied the safety out of their world, sending them scurrying home. There were too many shadows for them. After all, dark is when the monsters come. Normally, that doesn't bother me much, but this wasn't a normal situation. I needed to get into the knowe. What little safety I had was in the dubious comfort of the Luidaeg's hospitality, and I'd left her behind to chase her crazy baby brother. I was really batting a thousand.

Getting into Shadowed Hills requires a series of twists and turns that would embarrass some circus performers. If the Torquills have any sense at all, they keep a closed-circuit camera system filming the door at all times. Not for security reasons but for the entertainment value. The pixies scattered as I climbed dutifully through my paces, laughing as they went. Maybe they weren't entirely stupid.

The door in the old oak appeared as I squirmed out from under the hawthorn bushes. I yanked it open, stepping through into Shadowed Hills. And then I stopped, blinking. The oak door usually leads to the entrance hall, and well . . . this wasn't it.

The floor was grass green marble, and the walls were blue, gradating up to a ceiling patterned with puffy white clouds. The furniture was overstuffed and soft looking, with no hard edges. The whole room seemed to be built on a smaller scale than I was used to. I'd found the Children's Hall.

I sank awkwardly into the nearest chair, giving my knees a rest as I considered the room. I hadn't seen the Children's Hall since my own childhood ended, but it was just like I remembered it. There were smudgy fingerprints on the wall, not quite washed away, and I could almost believe that some of them were mine. Childhood is brief, even for the immortal. It gets squandered on wishing to grow up.

The tapping of claws on marble warned me before the rose goblin jumped into my lap. I blinked at it. "Hello." It was smaller and more delicate than Spike, with pink eyes and gray and burgundy thorns. "Can I help you with something?"

"It was looking for you," said Luna, stepping into view. "The pixies said you were coming, but we weren't sure of where you were."

"Luna. Hi." I looked up, offering her a tired smile. "I'm sort of on a quest."

"They mentioned that as well. And that you'd killed poor Tybalt."

"He got better."

"He tends to. It's one of his few virtues." She looked at the candle in my hand. There was no surprise in her eyes; none at all. "So you're going to back to my father's lands, then."

"He still has Karen. He's the only one who can fix Katie."

"Yes, he is." She sighed. "We've tried, but it isn't stopping. If her change progresses much further, she won't be human at all."

"I'm not sure she's human now, Luna. The Luidaeg said to tell you to send Katie to her. She may not be able to do anything, but she can try."

"I don't think that's safe," Luna said.

"I don't know. I have to go." I stood, wincing. The pain in my head was annoying but livable. I didn't have much of a choice about that. "I can't take the Children's Road. You were willing to kill me, Luna. You owe me this."

"Ah," she said, softly. Yellow lines were beginning to streak through her eyes, obscuring the brown. "I should have known it would come to this. We harvest the things we plant in this life, however many years it takes their seeds to grow." A bitter smile creased her lips. "You'd best survive, October Daye, daughter of Amandine, or my husband will never forgive me. I've never wished to be my mother."

"Luna, what—"

"She's put you on the Rose Road, and it's up to me to send you on your way. But you won't come back on that road. Your return will have a different path." Her eyes were almost yellow now, and threads of pink were appearing in her hair. "I'm sorry I lied. I never wanted to. But I couldn't let my father find me. This is the second time his Riders have come since I left his halls, and I didn't stand for any of the children they claimed then. This harvest puts paid to all. She told you there was a time limit?"

I blinked, thrown by what seemed to be a sudden change of subjects. "Twenty-four hours. Get in and out before the candle dies, or don't get out at all."

"Exactly so." She offered me her hand. "Come, my dear. There isn't time to waste. Not now." Every time my eyes left her she changed a little more, shifting more and more toward the woman she'd been when she took Acacia's rose. "Maybe there never has been." With that said, she took my hand in hers, and led me out of the Children's Hall.

We walked through halls and gardens, bedrooms, kitchens, and libraries, until the rooms began to blur together. A hall of portraits; a hall filled with dusty furniture; a country garden; a library filled with books that whispered as we passed. We walked until my head was spinning, never stopping, never looking back. And then a familiar door was in front of us, made of unvarnished wood with a stained glass rose where the eyehole should have been. Luna looked at me, unfamiliar eyes filled with pain, and let go of my hand as she opened the door.

The Garden of Glass Roses was filled with light that slanted down from the windows and passed through the translucent roses to scatter into countless tiny rainbows that glittered on the cobblestone paths and gray stone walls. Luna walked ahead of me, trailing her fingers over the unyielding glass edges of the flowers as she passed and leaving traceries of blood behind. I followed slowly, resolutely refusing to listen to the things her blood was trying to tell me. It was too changed and too confused; it knew nothing of value anymore.

Luna stopped in the far corner of the garden, standing in front of a bush with flowers that were crimson shading into black. Their stems were heavy with thorns, so sharply barbed that they looked like weapons. "Roses are always cruel," she said, almost wistfully. "That's what makes them roses." She reached into the bush, not wincing as the thorns gouged her skin.

"What are you talking about?"

Her expression was serene. "Beauty and cruelty, of course. It's simple." There was a thin snapping sound from inside the bush. She withdrew her hand, now holding a perfect black rosebud. "The Rose Roads are no kinder than the others, but people assume they must be, because they're beautiful. Beauty lies." She kissed the flower, almost casually, despite the way the petals sliced her lips. Blood began to flow freely.

And the rose began to open.

The petals unfurled slowly, slicing her lips and fingers until the air was fragrant with the scent of her blood. Luna smiled, offering me the rose. "Prick your finger on the thorns, and you'll be on your way. Take the rose, bleed for it, and it will take you where you want to go."

Still frowning, I held out my hand. She placed the rose on my palm, where it rested lightly, thorns not even scratching me. "What do I need to do?"

"Just bleed."

"All right." I curled my fingers around the rose, stopping when the pain told me that the thorns had found their mark. "Now what do I ... do ... Luna? What's happening?" The world was suddenly hazy, like I was staring through a fog. The woman with the rose-colored hair stood in the middle of it all, bloody hands clasped to her breast.

"I'm sorry," she whispered. "I'm so sorry, but it's the only way. Go quickly ..."

"Is drugging me a new hobby for you people?" I asked, and fell. Part of me was screaming; the Garden of Glass roses is mostly made of glass and stone and has very few soft places to land. That was only a small part—the rest of me was sinking in rose-scented darkness, falling farther and farther from escape. Luna was crying somewhere behind me in the dark. I wanted to shout at her, but there were no words. There was nothing but darkness and the smell of roses.

And then even that was gone.

TWENTY-SIX

*K*AREN SAT BENEATH THE WILLOWS, *combing the hair of a Kitsune child.* "Hello, Aunt Birdie," she said, looking up. "You're coming back for me."

"I know where you are now," I said, hearing the faint echo of my voice against the wind. I was dreaming. "Who's your friend?"

"This is Hoshibara," Karen said. "She died here."

"Why?" I looked at the girl, who offered me a small, shy smile.

"Blind Michael stole her, but she got away; she wouldn't let him change her. She ran to the woods." Karen pulled her hands away from Hoshibara's hair, hiding them in her lap. "She died, but the night-haunts never got her body. Someone else did." She pointed past me. "See?"

I turned. Hoshibara was there, lying under a willow tree. There was someone—a girl, barely more than a child herself, with yellow eyes and hair that fell to her waist in a riot of pink and red curls. She crept out of the trees with one hand over her mouth, staring at the Kitsune.

Hoshibara lifted her head, looking at the girl; looking at Luna. The movement was weak. There wasn't much movement left in her. "I won't go back," she whispered.

Luna knelt beside her. "You don't have to."

"I don't feel good."

"*You're dying.*"

Hoshibara nodded, expression unsurprised. "Will it hurt?"

"*It doesn't have to.*" *Luna held out her hand, showing Hoshibara the thorn she held.* "*I can make it stop hurting right now. But you have to do something for me.*"

The Kitsune looked at her distrustfully. I couldn't blame her. "*What happens then?*"

"*You die.*"

"*Is there a way for me to not die?*"

Luna shook her head. "*Not unless you go back to him.*"

"*What do I do for you?*"

For the first time, Luna looked nervous. "*You let me take your skin. I found . . . I know how the Selkies did it. Let me be Kitsune. Let me go free.*"

"*All right.*" *Hoshibara raised her hand and clasped it over Luna's. She whimpered once as the thorn cut into her skin. Then she closed her eyes, movement stilling. Luna looked at her for a moment, then leaned down, pressing a kiss against her forehead.*

"*I wish there'd been another way,*" *she whispered, and slammed her hand down over Hoshibara's, binding them together with the thorn. Then she threw back her head and screamed. There was a blast of light so bright that if I'd been watching it with anything other than dream-eyes I wouldn't have been able to face it. When it faded, both Hoshibara and the rose-girl were gone. A dainty teenager stood in their place, slender hands covered in blood. She had chestnut hair and silver-furred tails, and looked like neither one of them. She stood unsteadily, clutching the hem of her suddenly too large dress, and staggered into the woods, vanishing.*

"*She got out,*" *Karen said behind me.* "*Can we?*"

"*Karen—*" *I turned. Karen and Hoshibara were gone. The landscape was dissolving in a pastel smear, and I could smell roses on the wind. I closed my eyes—*

—and opened them to find myself at the edge of Acacia's wood, hidden by a tangle of branches. The sky was black, and my candle was at least four inches shorter. Whatever Luna dosed me with knocked me out for more than a little while, and time was running out.

I stood slowly, leaning against one of the nearby trees. I was back in Blind Michael's lands, and I knew how Luna managed her escape, and why she'd been willing to give me up to keep its secret. "The end justifies the means," I whispered. "Oh, Luna."

The cuts on my fingers were swollen and red and burned if I put too much pressure on them. Cute. "It's poison Toby week, isn't it?" I muttered, looking out over the plains. A thick mist had risen, bleaching the landscape; the lights of Blind Michael's halls flickered dimly in the distance.

There was no time like the present and no time to waste. Shivering, I stepped out of the shelter of the trees and started walking. The steady whiteness of the land around me added an eerie quality to the trip that I could've done without. Boulders looked like looming monsters until I got close enough to see them clearly, while brambles and clumps of grass turned the ground into an obstacle course. I held my candle up to light the way, and it burned the mists back just enough to let me see that I was walking in a straight line. The flame was my compass and the light from Blind Michael's halls was my lighthouse, leading me through the night.

Nothing stopped me as I walked through the mist; the land around me was silent. My candle kept burning slowly down; by the time it was another inch shorter, I was standing in front of the halls, aware of just how exposed I really was. The guards wouldn't miss me for long. I hunched down behind a crumbling wall, eyeing the mist for signs of movement.

The Luidaeg said Blind Michael had taken Karen's "self." Remembering ALH, that phrase made me cold. January's machine pulled the self out of people, left them empty and dead from the shock of separation. I didn't think it was something you could just toss into a cell—he had to be keeping it in something more solid.

A trinket or a toy of some sort, something she couldn't escape from. So what was it?

The butterfly globe he taunted me with. That had to be Karen's self, trapped inside the glass and beating itself to death as it struggled to get free. But where *was* it? He'd had it with him before. He might still have it, or he might have given it to his monstrous children as a toy. Either way, I needed to take it away. Neither place seemed more likely than the other, and I finally settled for the children as the lesser of the two evils. I might survive them and get a second chance if I chose wrong. I couldn't say the same about him.

Crossing Blind Michael's holdings alone in the dark is something I never want to do again. I moved from building to building, freezing and holding my breath at the slightest sound. Nothing came out of the darkness to attack me and somehow that wasn't reassuring. There was no way to know whether I was walking into a trap, and so I just kept going, stopping when I reached the hall with the broken walls. It looked different from the outside, but I recognized it. I always know my prisons.

The outside of the hall was smooth stone. The only way in was the obvious—the broken walls were only ten feet high, and they weren't barred in any way. It wasn't a bad climb. I could make it.

An old water barrel butted up against one wall. I climbed on top of it and stuck my candle between my teeth, careful not to bite down too hard as I started feeling around for handholds. There was one clear path, a series of shallow indentations leading up the side of the wall. It made sense. Kids always find a way out, but in Blind Michael's lands, that didn't mean getting away. They also needed a way back in.

The climb was slow, painful, and one of the most nerve-racking things I've ever done. There was no way to run if anyone found me before I was over the wall; if I got caught, I was as good as dead. The cuts on my hand burned when they pressed against the stone, my knees ached from fighting gravity, and hot wax spattered my cheek and neck every time I moved. But I made it. I reached the top of the wall, my candle still burning a steady blue, and no one sounded the alarm.

The Children's Hall spread beneath me in an unmoving patchwork of stillness and shadows. The children were gone, probably still searching for me back in the "real" world. That was a good sign. A tapestry hung a few feet to my left, anchored to the top of the wall with rusty metal loops. It looked as decayed as everything else in Blind Michael's kingdom, but it would do. Inching along the wall, I grabbed the tapestry, intending to climb carefully down.

The decayed fabric had other ideas. It tore under my hands, and I fell, grabbing for a less tattered section of the cloth. This time I got it right. The tapestry stretched but didn't tear, and I slammed against the wall hard enough to knock the air out of my lungs, nearly biting through my candle in the process. I hung there for a moment, breathing rapidly through my nose. When I was sure I wouldn't fall, I started to descend.

The tapestry ended about three feet above the floor. I let go, landing hard but upright. I'd made it; I was in the hall, and the children weren't, although I knew better than to count on that to last. I needed to keep moving.

There were a few makeshift toys scattered around the floor. Sticks, stones, and some bones I didn't look at too closely; a teddy bear without a head and a doll's head without a body; shards of wood and plastic. None of them looked as if they were used very often, save perhaps as weapons. I searched until my candle had grown shorter still and didn't find anything but garbage. "Damn it, where is she?" I whispered. The darkness didn't answer. Wherever she was, it wasn't here, and it was time to get moving.

The tapestry I'd used to break my fall looked like it would hold me. Putting my candle back between my teeth, I grabbed hold and started climbing. It didn't take as long as it did the first time; fear and failure were hurrying my steps. I hauled myself over the edge of the wall, pulling the tapestry with me and dangling it down the outside of the building. It was proof that I'd been there; that didn't matter as much as not breaking my neck did.

The tapestry made an excellent ladder. I lowered myself down, dropping without a sound onto the water barrel. One down—the easy one—and one to go.

Of course, I'd left the hard part for last.

The night was getting colder. I crept from building to building, stopping outside the one other landmark I was sure of: the stable. The screams that surrounded it before were gone, replaced by nickers and whinnies. The children we hadn't rescued weren't children anymore. I shuddered as I slipped inside, hiding behind a bale of hay. No one was likely to look for me there. What kind of idiot hides in a prison? Damn it all, anyway. How many parents were crying for children they'd never see again? Those kids hadn't done anything wrong—they were just human and in the wrong place at the wrong time. It had to end. I was going to save Karen, and then I was going to kill Blind Michael. Firstborn or not, he'd die for what he'd done.

The sounds of the horses faded into background noise, becoming almost normal, and a new sound began making itself heard beneath the stamp of hooves and the rustling of hay. A sound I didn't want to hear. Sobbing.

I turned to look at the nearest stall. It was barred with brambles and wire like the others, but whatever was behind it hadn't been changed. Not all the way; not yet. I crept closer, whispering, "Hello?"

There was a pause. Then a too familiar voice said, "H-hello."

Oh, oak and ash. "Katie?"

"Yes?" She sounded distracted. I'd have been distracted too, if I'd been kidnapped by a madman intent on turning me into a horse.

"How did you get here?" *I saved you,* I thought, *I know I saved you . . .*

"Quentin said we needed to move. He took me outside and then . . ." There was no emotion in the words; it was like she was reading from a script. Something inside of her had broken. "They brought me here again."

"I'll get you out. Don't worry." I cursed myself for a liar even as I spoke. I failed to keep her safe once; what made me think I could do it now? And then there was Quentin. Where was he? When they came for Katie, had they taken him too?

At least the others were safe in Shadowed Hills; the Riders couldn't enter Luna's domain. But Mitch and Stacy's kids, Tybalt's kids—oh, oak and ash. "Katie, were you the only one?"

"They said I hadn't been bargained for. What did they mean?" A note of hysteria was creeping into her voice. "You said I could go home! What's *happening* to me?!"

Blind Michael had broken my spell. It dulled her pain, and he wanted her to hurt. "It'll be okay. I promise." I'd lied to her already. What was once more?

She didn't answer. "Katie?" I glanced to my candle. At the rate it was shrinking I had six hours left; maybe less. Not enough time. "Katie, I'll be back." There was still no answer, and finally I stood and walked away. There was nothing else I could do.

Good luck always runs out. I shouldn't have been surprised when rough hands grabbed me from behind as I left the stable, yanking me into the shadows. I struggled, trying to break free, and was rewarded with a sharp slap upside the head.

"Hush, mongrel," hissed a voice. "We're taking you to Him."

My candle was burning an angry red, warning me, but it was too late; I was caught. They dragged me through the village, the mists rolling back before us, and into a broad clearing filled with Riders and misshapen children. The children laughed and shouted, dancing around a vast bonfire that painted the sky with lashes of crimson and gold. We kept going, past the shrieks and laughter, until we reached the open space in front of the fire. Then the Riders who held my shoulders released me, fading back into the crowd. I stumbled and looked up, already knowing what was there, already afraid to see it.

Blind Michael was seated on a throne made of ivory, amusement in his sightless face as he turned toward me. "So," he said. "You've returned."

"You cheated," I snapped. One day I'll learn when to hold my tongue. "You said I could free Mitch and Stacy's kids. You didn't tell me you had Karen."

He leaned back. "So did you. You took children I'd not agreed to lose."

"I never said I wouldn't."

"I never said I'd tell you what children I had, or that I wouldn't take back the ones you didn't bargain for. The children you won fairly are yours, the others are mine if I want them." He smiled. I shuddered. There were things in that smile I never wanted to know the names for. "Of course, we could always make another bargain. I enjoyed our last one."

"What do you want?" I asked. "You can't keep me here. I have the Luidaeg's blessing."

"Oh, I know. My subjects were—enthusiastic—in bringing you. I apologize." I somehow doubted anyone was going to be punished for their enthusiasm. "As long as you hold my sister's candle, you may leave at any time. But."

"But?" I echoed. There was a catch. Of course there was a catch.

"You leave without this." He pulled a familiar crystal sphere out of his vest, holding it up to show me the struggling butterfly trapped inside. "Isn't she lovely? She brushed past me in the night, and I took her. How long will she last, I wonder?"

Karen. Oh, root and branch, Karen. "Let her go!"

"Stay with me."

I froze, staring at him. "What?"

He smiled again. "Put down your candle. Stay with me. You don't have time to save her and escape, but if you'll stay of your own free will, I'll let her go."

"Why?"

"Because you tricked me once; that impressed me, but I'm not leaving you free to do it again. Because your existence offends me, daughter of Amandine." He spun the sphere, making the butterfly fan its wings in a frantic attempt to stay upright. "You stay. She goes."

"And Katie?"

"You have no claim to her." He shook his head. "Sacrifice yourself to save one, or lose both. The choice is yours, daughter of Amandine. You haven't got that much time left."

I looked down at my candle. He was right: time was slipping away, and I wasn't sure I could make it out alone, much less with my kids. Damn it. Forgive me, Luidaeg, but you were right. I really did run away to die.

"I see," I said, looking up.

Blind Michael smiled. "Will you make the trade?"

I shivered, taking another look at my candle. It wouldn't burn forever; if I stalled too long I'd be trapped, and Karen would be trapped with me. If I took his bargain, at least one of us would get away.

I didn't mean to fail anyone; I didn't mean to leave Katie behind. At least she'd forget that she'd ever been anything but a horse in a madman's stable, and Quentin was young—he'd have outlived her no matter what happened. Loving a mortal is never wise. You get burned every time. He was just going to have to learn that lesson a little earlier than I did.

I knew I was justifying what I was going to do. I didn't care. There was no other way.

"If I stay," I said, slowly, "you'll let Karen go. No tricks, right?"

"Of course," he said, offended. "My word is my bond. Am I not born of Faerie?"

That was the thing. He *was* born of Faerie, a Faerie so old only the Firstborn remembered it. Our word has always been our bond, and his blood was older than mine. His word would be more binding. "Promise me," I said.

"If I promise, you stay. You will join my Hunt and belong to me, forever."

One last chance. I could still say no; I could run away and come back to save them all, if I truly believed I could still get there and back by a candle's light. The wax was melting faster all the time, running down and coating my fingers. How many miles to Babylon?

Too many.

"If you promise, I'll stay," I said. "You have my word."

"That is all I need." Blind Michael stood, giving a short, mocking bow. "By my mother's blood and my father's bones, I promise," he said, in a singsong voice that echoed back and forth until it filled the world. I shivered where I stood, wanting to run. Too little and too late, by far. I'd given up my chance, and I was going to have to live with the consequences.

"By oak and ash, by rowan and thorn, I promise. By root and branch, by rose and tree, by flowers and blood and water, I promise this to you: your sleeping princess and her siblings shall be free of my lands, and I will never touch them again. My Hunt will not pursue them, my Hunters will not take them. You have my word."

His words were ash and dust; I breathed in their power and felt myself go cold. The children erupted into cheers. He'd done it. The promise was made, and not even Blind Michael could escape his own bindings. Karen would go free and I would stay behind. It was up to Quentin and the others to free Katie. The fight wasn't mine anymore. My fighting was over.

I looked into his face and saw the end of the world. "Your turn," he said.

"I . . ." There was nothing I could say. Like it or not, I'd given my word. *You can get there and back by candle-light,* the Luidaeg said, and she'd been right; the light brought me into Blind Michael's lands and kept me as safe as possible while I was there. It was my road home, and as long as I had it, my promises didn't matter. As long as I didn't let go, there was still a chance.

Wordless, I opened my hand, and I let the candle fall.

The Hunt watched, and Blind Michael watched

through them. When it hit the ground, flame finally going out, he smiled. Victory, damn him forever. Victory was his. I stood as straight as I could, blinking back tears. The land wasn't very welcoming when I was under the Luidaeg's protection, but now, without my candle, it was terrifying.

Dimly, I realized that I wanted my mother.

"I stay," I said.

"Yes," said Blind Michael, "you do." Something hit the back of my knees, knocking me to the ground. I tried to raise my head, but the world had gone dark, filled with the icy whispering of Blind Michael's lost children. Oak and ash, what had I done?

"Here comes a candle to light you to bed," they chanted. I could feel them closing in around me, but I couldn't get my body to obey me and move away.

Luidaeg, forgive me . . . I thought, desperately.

"Here comes a chopper to chop off your head," rumbled Blind Michael. "Take her."

Something heavy hit me on the base of the skull, and the world fell away.

TWENTY-SEVEN

THE WORLD WAS MADE OF MIST and filled with snatches of song. I hummed along, singing when I knew the words. There was nothing else: just the music, the mist, and me. Sometimes people moved past without speaking, but they didn't matter. Nothing mattered as long as the music was there to keep me warm. There was a time when the world was something more than mist and half-remembered songs, but that time was long ago and far away; that time was over. I hurt when I tried to remember, and so I'd stopped trying. I just sat in the darkness and waited. What I was waiting for exactly was the part I didn't know.

There were things to hope for, even in the misty darkness. If I was very lucky and very good, He might come. He was as big as the sky and as bright as the moon. When He walked the mists parted, and I could see the plains that stretched forever under the twilight sky. I would have done anything for Him. I would have died for Him. I think I told Him that once. I remember His hand on my hair, and His voice, as deep and wide as the ocean, rumbling, "You're almost ready." I cried for a long time after that. I didn't know why. Something about promises.

Time passed. I don't know how much, and I didn't

care; time had no real purpose. All that mattered was the mist, and the hope that soon, He would come again.

When the mists cleared enough to remind me that I had a physical shape, I realized someone was dressing me. Something was coming, something as important as the moon I could remember seeing against . . . some other sky. The thought hurt, so I put it aside; something important was coming, and that meant He would be there. Everything would be fine, as long as He was there. I smiled, letting unseen hands pull boots onto my feet. That didn't seem polite, and so I sang, "Ride a cock horse to Banbury Cross, to see a fine lady upon a white horse . . ."

"Yes, yes, of course," said the someone, and stroked my hair, pulling it back and pinning it. The voice was almost familiar, the way the faces I sometimes saw when I slept were almost familiar. "It's almost time to go. I'm going to get you out of here. Don't worry."

". . . with rings on her fingers and bells on her toes," I sang, closing my eyes. It hurt to watch the mist for too long. It would start dissolving if I did, showing me glimpses of a world that wasn't quite right. It wasn't the way the world was supposed to be; it made me want to bite and scream. Something about children and candles.

"How many miles to Babylon?" I muttered. "It's threescore miles and ten."

"Shhh," said the voice. "You need to be quiet. No more rhymes. No more words."

"Can you get there by candlelight?" What was she talking about? Words and the mist were the only things I had.

"Snap *out* of it!" she whispered and slapped me. I froze. Sometimes He hit me when I sang songs He didn't like. I never knew what songs would make Him hit me until they were already sung and it was too late to take them back. Once, when I sang a song about a woman named Janet and the white horse her lover rode, He started hitting me and almost didn't stop. I bled into the mists for hours after that, bright blood like rubies on my fingers.

I didn't like it when He hit me. It hurt. And it confused me, because as much as I hated it, I didn't want Him to stop. When He hit me, the mists cleared enough that I could start grasping concepts beyond the world I knew, things more complex than mist and half-remembered songs. So I cringed at the blows and remembered what caused them, so that I could make Him do it again whenever I wanted Him to. Whenever I was willing to gamble pain for sanity. When He hit me, I hated Him. When He stopped I hated myself for hating Him.

But I always made Him hit me again.

There was no more pain. I opened my eyes. The mist was empty, eddying in slow swirls. "Hello?" The mist caught my voice and threw it back, drowning out the songs. "Hello?"

No one answered. I wrapped my arms around myself, shivering harder. This wasn't right: I was never alone. There was always someone in the mist, ready to chastise or soothe. They never left me alone. Something might hurt me. Something might frighten me. Something might ...

Might ...

Something might wake me up.

"How many miles to Babylon? It's threescore miles and ten ..." I whispered. I remembered someone else saying the same words; a woman with dark hair and eyes like the mist. She put a candle in my hand, she told me the route to follow for my there-and-back-again; she promised the candle would protect me. There was danger, yes, always danger, but there was a road I could follow. I remembered the oily sheen of her skin, the tapered nails that crooked so naturally into claws ...

The Luidaeg.

I gasped, my heart hammering against my ribs. The Luidaeg. She gave me my candle and set me on the road to Blind Michael. I was safe as long as I held the candle and stayed on the path. I was safe until ... oh, root and branch, what had I done? More important, what was I *doing?* I tried to stand and fell, catching myself on the chair.

A voice behind me said, amused, "Well, that worked better than I expected."

I froze, sorting through the possible speakers and discarding them. Finally, I asked, "Acacia?"

"It's me; now hush. I need you to get up." Her hands were firm on my shoulders. "I won't let you fall."

"Where am I?" I could hear her, but I couldn't see her; the mists blocked everything.

"My husband's private hall." She guided me to my feet. "It'll be all right, but you need to move."

"I can't see."

"You're enchanted—he has plans for you, and they don't include escaping." There was a dark amusement in her tone. "Close your eyes."

I did as I was told, and she dragged a soft, damp cloth across my eyelids. I opened my eyes when the pressure faded, squinting against the sudden brightness. The mist was gone. We were in a small room cluttered with broken furniture and heaps of discarded tapestries. The floor was covered with a thick layer of dust, and footprints led to the chair where I'd been sitting. There were no windows; the door was ajar, and had no locks. They'd held me prisoner, and they hadn't even needed iron bars to do it, because I gave myself to them. I was an idiot.

Acacia was kneeling in front of me, a frown pulling the scar on her cheek taunt. She watched me look around, concern evident in her expression. "Can you see me?"

"I can," I said, looking back to her. "What did he do to me?"

"He coated your eyes with faerie ointment brewed to blind, not reveal." Her smile was bitter. "He's not very original, I'm afraid, but what he does, he does well. Including the taking of other people's toys."

"I thought he was a god." I almost gagged on the words.

"I know. He does that to everyone; even those of us who should know better." She ran her hand over my hair and straightened, saying, "We need to go. It's All Hallows' Eve, and he'll be coming for you soon."

"What?" I stared at her. Had it been that long? It couldn't have been ... but the mists had been so thick. For a moment, I was ready to go with her. Then I sobered, shaking my head. The thought of freedom was like a drug, but it didn't change my promises. "I can't."

"I know you gave your word. Do you know what you swore?"

"To stay."

"You never said you'd Ride. My woods are part of his land. Now come with me. I can't free you, but at least you won't be his."

I studied her before offering my hand and letting her lead me out of the room. "Why are you doing this?"

"Because you didn't have to take her my rose, and because his plans for you would be bad for us both. Now hurry."

I fell silent, letting her guide me through the halls. We were halfway down the hall when Acacia gasped and shoved me behind her. I hunched down, trying to make myself small enough to be overlooked. I hadn't seen whatever startled her, but I was sure it wasn't anything friendly. Very little in Blind Michael's lands was friendly.

Armored feet scuffled on the floor, and a voice said, "Lady Acacia? We did not expect to see you here."

"Do you question my right to pass?" she demanded. Her voice was cold and convinced of its own superiority: the kind of voice purebloods use on changeling servants.

It worked just as well on Blind Michael's guards. There was an embarrassed pause, and the voice said, "No, Lady. But we grow near time to Ride, and I thought ..."

"Who said you should think?" she asked. "You're obviously ill-suited to the task. What breed of fool challenges a lady in her lord's halls? And I am *still* his lady until the Ride is done."

What was she talking about? I remembered Blind Michael's hands on my hair and cheeks and was suddenly terribly afraid that I already knew.

"My lady, I—"

He'd have been better off keeping silent—it was too late to stop her. I'd heard Evening do the same thing more than once; it impressed me coming from her, and she usually had reason. Acacia was doing it cold, with nothing to fuel her but fear. That took skill. "I've half a mind to tell my husband you doubt my right to walk his halls! I'm sure he'll be charmed to know his *guards* would even do so much for his safety as guard his *lady* from his *bed!*"

"Please!" The guard was frantic, and even I felt a little sorry for him: I could guess what it would mean to be reported to Blind Michael for something like that. "A thousand apologies!"

There was a pause. When Acacia spoke again her tone was gentler. "Very well. See to it no one else disturbs me; I haven't a mind to dance these steps more than once a night."

"Yes, Lady!" I heard the guard scramble away, footsteps fading. Acacia kept me pressed against the wall for several minutes, waiting. No alarms sounded.

When she finally stepped away from the wall, she gave me a look that was full of sorrow. "So you know."

"Why—"

"Because." Her sorrow faded, twisting into bitterness. "You'd be a better toy. Come quickly." She grabbed my hand and started walking again, faster now. The guard was as good as his word, and no one else tried to stop us. The end of the hall was in sight when Acacia broke into a run, dragging me with her. We were almost there. We were almost out.

Fingers snagged in my hair, yanking me to a painful stop. I fell backward, hitting the floor hard, and found myself looking up into the smirking face of the Piskie from the Children's Hall. She was sitting astride her Centaur mount, one hand wound in his mane; her other hand was still raised, strands of my hair caught between her webbed fingers.

"He said you might try to get away. He said we should watch you special," she said, and looked to Acacia, eyes cold. "You can't hurt us. *He* knows where we are."

"No," said Acacia wearily, hands dropping to her sides. "I can't hurt you."

"Stupid old hag," said the Piskie. The Centaur grabbed my hair this time, hauling me to my feet. I winced but didn't scream. I wasn't giving them the satisfaction. "These are His halls, not yours. You have no power here."

"No, I don't. I gave it up," said Acacia, and looked at me, expression pleading.

What was I supposed to do? I was already damned. So was she, but I didn't need to make her suffer. She'd do that on her own. I went limp, not fighting against my captors or pleading for help as Acacia turned and walked away.

"You're just in time," said the Piskie. "Now we go."

"Go?" I asked, bleakly.

The Centaur nodded, giving me a brisk shake for punctuation. "Now we Ride."

They dragged me through the hall and out the door, into the clearing where I'd made my bargain. About half of Blind Michael's twisted children were there, milling back and forth under the steady gaze of the Riders. There were other, unchanged children as well, lashed together like cattle. Most of them were crying. The Piskie shoved me into the crowd, and I stumbled, barely managing not to fall. No one seemed to have noticed our arrival; it could have passed for a festival atmosphere if not for the screams.

Riders guarded the edge of the clearing, except for the point where it bordered on a long stone wall. There was a break in the wall, less than twenty feet away; the Piskie and her Centaur mount were cantering toward the front of the clearing, and the other children were ignoring me, caught up in their own private anticipations or terrors.

I started inching backward toward the opening. It was almost time for the Ride to begin. I didn't know what happened when Blind Michael took his Riders out into the night, and I didn't want to; Acacia was right. I promised Blind Michael I'd stay in his lands, but I didn't say anything about sitting idly by while he bound me to his eternal service or took me as his lady. I knew enough to know that if I Rode, I'd belong to him forever, and maybe it was splitting hairs, but the idea of spending all of time with the man just didn't appeal. All my kids were safe at home, except for Katie, and if Blind Michael still had her, it was too late. There was no one left for me to save but myself. It was better to run away, even if I died in the attempt. At least I'd have tried. At least I'd die a hero.

I kept my hands down, trying to look nonchalant. A few of Blind Michael's kids would be glad to hurt me, like the Piskie and her Centaur friend, but others might be glad to see *someone* escape. The wall was only a few feet away. If I could get out of the village, I might be able to reach Acacia's woods before the Riders knew I was gone. Once I was in the woods, they couldn't take me. Acacia ruled there. There was still a chance.

Like an idiot, I let myself believe it. Only for an instant . . . but that was long enough to give me hope. I reached the wall, slid myself into the hole, and got ready to run.

And Blind Michael loomed out of the darkness. For a moment I saw him for what he was: one of the Firstborn, a foundation of Faerie, but still a man. Not a god. Then his illusions slammed into me, and he became the mountains and the sky and the world. I could think about escaping, but much as I wanted to, I couldn't move. "Now we Ride," he said.

Oh, root and branch. Oberon help us all.

TWENTY-EIGHT

THREE PALE LADIES WITH EYES AS BLANK
AS STONE stepped forward at Blind Michael's command, dressing me in tatters of green and gold silk and
tying tiny chiming bells in my hair.

Their sisters descended on the other children, decking
them in rags of gray and white. I gritted my teeth, trying to summon up the strength to move. And I couldn't
find it.

When they were satisfied with their work they lifted
me up onto the back of a white mare. Green and gold
ribbons were braided through her mane and tail, matching my gown, and she pawed the ground as I settled on
her back, trying to step out from underneath me. She
looked as terrified as I felt, and I couldn't blame her.
I'm not that familiar with horses, but even I could recognize the horse Katie had become. Her eyes were still
too human.

I'm sorry, I thought, wishing I could say the words
out loud. *I didn't mean to leave you, but they got me, too.*
Small comforts are sometimes all we have. She and I
would suffer together. Forever.

The older children chosen to accompany us slipped
out of the shadows in groups of one and two, dressed
in shredded finery that accented the strange twists and

curves of their bodies. They crossed the field, finding their horses and mounting in silence. Most of them had obviously done it before. How did they get so strange? What was going to happen to me?

The Centaur trotted over to stand by my horse, the web-fingered Piskie riding sidesaddle on his back. They were still nude, but now had ropes of red and gold silk knotted in their hair.

"Today we Ride," said the Piskie, pleasantly. "Some of us will be Riders; some will not. Some will only change a little and return to the hall. This will be my fifth Ride." I didn't answer her. I couldn't. She seemed to take my silence for fear, because she smiled. "You'll Ride only once, but He promises us it will hurt."

Giggling, the Centaur turned and cantered back to the throng of mounted children, taking her with him. They were happy. Lucky them.

And the Riders came. They were mounted on their twisted horses, armed and armored, and the difference between them and the children was as great as the difference between mountains and sand. They were more than lost; they'd gone willingly. One of them raised a horn, sounding three sharp notes, and Acacia rode out of the darkness, sitting as straight as the trees that were her children.

Willow branches were tangled in her hair, and under her cloak, she wore the same yellow and green rags as I'd been dressed in. The look she gave me was full of weary sorrow, but it wasn't entirely without relief. She'd be free after the night's work was done. Her horse was the color of new-cut wood, with a mane and tail that mixed all the reds, greens, and golds of autumn.

She rode to the front of the gathering, stopping with a crack as sharp and sudden as a branch breaking. Looking over us, she asked, "Who rides here?"

"Blind Michael's Hunt, that sweeps the night," called the Riders, in perfect unison.

"Who Rides here?" The stress was subtle, but it was there.

"The children who would join us; the children we have won, bargained for, and stolen."

"Who do you ride for?"

"Blind Michael, who leads and loves us."

"Who do you Ride for?"

"For the Hunt itself. The Hunt and the Ride and the night."

Acacia shuddered, looking disgusted. I was fairly sure that wasn't a part of the script. "Then you Ride tonight, and your lord rides with you." She pulled her horse to rein, merging into the throng, and I saw her look toward me as she added, "May Oberon help you all."

Blind Michael rode out of the same darkness, which suddenly seemed much darker. His armor was made of ivory and bone, polished mirror-bright, and his horse was vast and black with hooves of steel. I tried to tell myself that it was just an illusion, that he was nothing but another Firstborn, but it was too late. The glory of him slammed into me, and I was His.

He pulled His horse to a stop in front of us, smiling benevolently. I wanted to run to Him and bow, begging for His love, His attention—His blessing. Part of me knew it was nothing but an enchantment, but that didn't matter. He was my god, as ancient and terrible as the sky, and I was His to abuse as He saw fit. I still couldn't move, and that tiny, dying part of me was glad. He'd have my fealty soon enough. I didn't have to give it to him before he took it from me.

"My children," He rumbled, "lend me your eyes." His words were my commandments. I closed my eyes, murmuring the incantation they taught me while I waited in the mist. I felt my vision fragment, and when I opened my eyes, I was looking at a remade world. Every member of the Hunt saw through my eyes, and I saw through theirs. Blind Michael was true to His name, but He'd found a way around His lack of sight: He saw through His children. All of us.

"And now, my children, now we Ride," He said, and smiled, spreading the darkness in front of Him like a curtain as He turned His horse and urged it to a gallop. The Riders followed, dragging the captive children. They pushed their way past me, and I found myself falling back toward the rear of the herd. My thoughts cleared as Blind Michael drew farther away, giving my much-abused common sense a chance to scream. He wasn't a god. He was a madman.

I didn't have much control over my own body, but I might have enough to throw myself from the horse. If I fell hard enough, they'd have to leave me; I'd have until he Rode again to try to get away. I tensed, preparing to fall—and a passing Rider placed his hand on my back, urging me onward. It was too late. All my chances to escape were gone, blown out just like my candle. Game over.

The Ride made its way into darkness, flashes of the landscape flickering around us like Christmas lights. We weren't riding in a real place. We were moving between the human world and the Summerlands, occasionally breaking out of the dark and into places I remembered. The docks flashed by, neon and tourists and the smell of salt; a cobwebbed forest filled with shifting faerie lights; the Castro, blaring dance music and the throng of bodies. The scenes shifted quickly, fading before there was time to sort one from the other.

My fractured vision magnified the strangeness of the landscape, the shared perspectives making it feel like I was watching the world through a prism. The individual viewpoints melted together as we Rode, making the world into something deeper and wilder than anything I'd seen before. It wasn't natural yet, but I knew that it would be, when the Ride was done and Blind Michael took me as his bride. Oberon help me. We were nearing the end of our journey; I could feel it in the air, and every step we took brought me a little closer to being His. If I was already lost, why was I still so afraid?

We flickered back into the mortal world, racing down a street I knew: the road through the center of Golden Gate Park, flanked by jogging trails and tangled foliage.

Pixies flashed past, pinpoints of light that did nothing to break the darkness. I'd never seen a night like this before. It was too unreal and half-drawn for the human world, too solid and bitter for Faerie. I'd never seen a night like this . . . but I'd never ridden with a mad First-born before, either. This was Blind Michael's world.

The air got thick and hazy as we ran along the road, and we slowed. I braced myself, waiting for the darkness to return. We'd passed through more than half of the Bay Area; we had to be almost done, ready to finish our descent into the night.

The first Riders were almost to the crossroads when white light blazed ahead of us, reaching past the tops of the dark-tipped trees and drawing a circle around the center of the street. Blind Michael's horse reared in terror. "Halt!" he shouted, and the Ride came to an uneven stop. I had no idea how to make Katie stop, and so she did it on her own, stumbling over her hooves, eyes wide and frightened. I wanted to lean forward to comfort her, but I couldn't. All I could do was stare into the light.

The Riders looked as lost as I felt, pushing and snarling at each other as they queued up behind their lord. They were too frightened for this to be a part of the ritual. This was something new.

A voice from behind the light shouted, "For I will ride the milk-white steed, the nearest to the town! Because I was an earthly knight, they give me that renown!"

It took me a moment to realize why I knew those words. I'd always spoken them myself, or heard them sung, usually in my mother's sweetly discordant voice as she coaxed me to sleep. Knowing the words didn't make them make sense. Why was someone reciting the ballad of Tam Lin? Old Scottish fairy tales aren't typical reading material for Halloween—of course. It was Halloween, the night for Rides and sacrifices, and Tam Lin ended with a faerie Ride on Halloween night. It was meant to be a sacrifice. It turned into a rescue.

Most people believe it's just a story, but it's not, quite;

it happened a long time ago, before the Burning Times began. The Ride that was interrupted that night resulted in the loss of Queen Maeve and heralded the fall of the old Courts. I've never understood why my mother chose that song as her lullaby, our world began dying the night that ballad began. Janet waited for Maeve's Ride at the crossroads, standing in the center of a circle cast for her protection. She was clever, she was careful, and she won the man who betrayed us all. Could the speaker be coming to stop this Ride the way Janet stopped that one? So who were they stopping it for?

"First let pass the black steeds, and then let past the brown," the voice chanted. There was no arguing with that voice. The children around me were raising their heads, shivering and confused. "Quick run to the milk-white steed and pull the Rider *down!*"

Someone grabbed Katie's reins. She reared, startled, and I fell.

I went limp, almost glad that I didn't have enough control to catch myself or fight. Maybe I couldn't run away, but that didn't mean I had to save myself. Death would be better than survival in slavery.

"No, you don't!" said a cheerful voice, grabbing me out of the air. An elbow slammed into my solar plexus, knocking the wind out of me, and we went tumbling through the light, into the circle that it defined. My captor twisted as we fell, making sure to cushion the blow when we hit the ground. Considerate kidnappers—that was a nice change. It was a pity I was too busy screaming to appreciate it. The light burned. It was like being shredded alive and reassembled by countless unseen hands, none of which were being very careful. Other voices were screaming around me, and I squeezed my eyes shut, trying to block out the light. It didn't help.

The eyes of the Ride kept feeding me images, showing the parade of children and Riders quailing from the fury of our mad god. I saw myself falling in the arms of a green-robed figure while smaller shapes held the reins of my horse, fighting her as she bucked to get free.

Other children were falling, pulled down by figures of their own who dragged them into the light and wouldn't let them go.

And I could see the woman standing at the circle's edge, hands held in front of her, palms turned downward. She wasn't tall, but something about her made her seem almost as vast as Blind Michael. Her hair fell in dark curls, like the waves of an angry sea; her eyes were white as foam, and she wore a gray robe stitched with patterns of mingled white and black that made the shared eyes of the Ride turn away. Only Acacia didn't look away: she knew her, named her and showed her to me with a delight that was close to rejoicing. The Luidaeg.

Something woke in me that remembered how to hope, because I recognized her as soon as I knew her name—the sea witch, Blind Michael's sister, who sent me to him in the first place. There were figures in the darkness behind her, but none of them mattered; the Luidaeg would save me if anyone could. I owed her, after all. She needed me alive to pay my debts.

I landed on my captor, shivering as the pain faded. The woman beneath me must have had an easier trip through the light than I did, because she was already stirring. Bully for her. She flipped me over as soon as I was breathing again, keeping her arms around my waist and pinning my legs with her knees.

"Sorry," she said, in an almost familiar voice, "but I'm not letting you go."

"That's okay," I managed. "I don't think you're supposed to." The scene was still playing out behind my closed eyes, and I didn't know who I wanted to win. I wanted to be free, but Blind Michael's spell was strong. He still had my loyalty.

"What is the meaning of this?" demanded Blind Michael. The remaining procession shuddered behind him. Someone in the back whimpered and was silenced. All eyes were on their lord, and on his sister.

"Tonight is All Hallows' Eve, and the faerie-folk Ride," the Luidaeg said. "The Ride has rules, little brother. Did you forget? You can ignore them, but you can't unmake them."

"You have no right," he snarled, and every word was like a knife in my heart. I threw back my head and screamed. I wasn't the only one: all the children that had been pulled from their horses were screaming with me.

"Shhh," hissed the woman above me. "Get past the pain. Grit your teeth and get past it. You can do it—I know you can."

The Luidaeg waited for the screaming to stop before she said, "I have every right, little brother. Every right in both the worlds."

"You aren't allowed to interfere!"

"Not within your realm. We set those rules when we came here, and I've abided by them, even when it hurt to obey them, even when I saw you destroying everything you'd ever loved. I followed the rules. But you're not in your realm now, little brother. You're in mine."

"My passage is allowed! I took *nothing* of yours!" This time his words were blows, not daggers. I whimpered.

"Didn't you?" The Luidaeg's voice was soothing, smoothing away the bruises her brother left behind. "You bargained for one you knew was under my protection; you couldn't even wait for her candle to burn down. You took her while she still belonged to me."

"All children are mine! The children are always mine."

"Amandine's daughter wasn't a child when you took her. She's not yours."

"Mine!" he screamed. This time it wasn't just the fallen that cried out: all the children writhed in pain, some of them falling off their horses as they tried to make it stop.

It hurt enough to fracture the spell that bound me, giving me control of my own body, but not my mind. It couldn't destroy the urge to return to my lord and master. I was too pinned to move, and so I sobbed, beating my fists against my captor's shoulders. I wasn't escaping that easily, and secretly, I was glad.

"Not yours!" the Luidaeg snapped. The wind rose around her, churning her hair until she seemed to be the sea itself taking physical form and come to kick some serious ass. "Never yours. The Ride has rules, Michael, and you broke them first!"

"It's not fair!" There was no fight in his words this time, just the petulance of a man who'd never been denied in all the centuries of his long, long life.

"Family, friends, and blood-tied companions have the power to break a Ride. They broke our mother's Ride, when the Carter woman stole her sacrifice." She didn't sound angry; resigned and almost sorry, but not angry. "They broke hers. They can damn well break yours."

"Who would come for her?" he snarled, rallying.

Behind me, a voice shouted, "Tybalt, King of Cats. My claim precedes yours."

"Cassandra Brown, student physicist," shouted another voice. "Give me back my aunt!"

"Quentin, foster of Shadowed Hills. You *will* give me back my friend and my lady!" I could hear hooves beating the ground in tandem with his words. He was the one who grabbed Katie's reins. Oh, oak and ash. Little hero.

"Connor O'Dell! She's my friend and you can't have her!" Connor has always been that great cliché, a lover, not a fighter, but there was no fear in his voice. He was taking me home or he wasn't going home at all.

They'd come for me? All of them? Titania wept. I didn't know whether I should laugh or cry. Challenging the Firstborn is never wise, not even when you have one of their number on your side, and you can never be really sure whose side the Luidaeg is on. It's usually her own.

I didn't think there was anything left that would surprise me. Then the woman pinning me shouted, "May Daye, Fetch!"

Opening my eyes, I found myself staring into a mirror. "May?" I squeaked. The split vision of the Ride was starting to fade, leaving me looking out of only my own eyes.

Familiar lips split in an unfamiliar smile. "In the too, too solid flesh," she said.

"What the hell is going on?"

"We cast our compass 'round," she said, looking past me. "Now we'll pay for it."

I craned my neck to follow her gaze. Blind Michael had dismounted. He walked to the edge of the circle and stopped, glaring. The Luidaeg was barely three feet away from him, shielded only by the light.

"Little brother, you've lost. Go home," she said, gently. "Take the children you still have, and go. We won't follow. I'll keep Amandine's daughter from chasing you, and when you Ride again in a hundred years, no one will remember this but you and I."

"There are rules," he answered. "I can try to take them back again."

"You can, if you accept that you might lose them, and more, if you try," she said. "Can you accept that fact?"

"I can."

"Oh, Michael. You always were a fool." The Luidaeg shook her head. "Start your games. Any who releases their quarry are lost; the rest are free to go." She turned, her gown eddying around her in a wave, and May braced herself above me.

"May, what—"

"You rode the white horse. Now we're finishing the song." There wasn't time to say anything more. Blind Michael turned toward me, raising his hand.

Transformation burns. I barely had time to realize I was being changed before it was done, and the weight of Blind Michael's magic was forcing my mind to conform to my new shape. May was suddenly huge, pinning me to the ground with a bulk that exceeded my own by a factor of at least three.

I had to get away; I had to flee and fly or she was going to kill me and use my bones to pick her teeth. I knew it as well as I knew the shape of my wings and the feeling of wind over my feathers. I beat myself against her arms, hissing and jabbing at her with my beak. All that mattered was escape, no matter how badly I was hurt in the process.

Connor lunged forward, pinning my wings while May grabbed for my head. I kept struggling, but I was trapped. I couldn't get away.

"And he will turn me in your arms into a swan so wild," the Luidaeg said. Her voice broke through the fog around me, clearing the madness from my mind. I stopped fighting. Connor let go and May folded herself around me, holding me down. "But hold me tight, don't let me go, and I will love your child."

The world changed again. This time I was thin and smooth, with no wings to beat against my captor. I slithered halfway out of her grasp before she grabbed me behind the head, pinning me again. Someone screamed, and I heard Cassandra chanting, "I am not afraid of snakes I am not afraid of—oh God, I think she's poisonous—snakes—"

I broke free and twisted around, sinking my fangs into May's wrist. She winced but didn't let go. "Damn it, Toby, don't bite," she said. "It's rude."

"And he will turn me in your arms into an asp and adder," shouted the Luidaeg. I released May's wrist and turned toward the sound, tongue scenting the air. "But hold me tight within your arms—I am your baby's father!"

Things shifted again. I was suddenly larger than May, tall and vast and angry. She was clinging to my neck, hands clasped beneath my jaw. I roared and tried to claw her off, unable to think of anything but freedom. I had to escape. If I didn't, something terrible would happen; something I didn't understand but knew enough about to fear.

Then Tybalt was in front of me, pressing his hand against my nose. I subsided, growling at him. He merely looked amused, reaching up to scratch my ears as he chided, "Calm yourself, little lioness." May took advantage of my confusion and got a tighter grip around my neck. I started to snarl, but stopped when Tybalt smacked me on the head. All cats belong to their King. For the moment, I was more his than Blind Michael's.

"Good plan, Tybalt," said May, face muffled against my neck.

"I thought so," he said. He started scratching my jaw, and I sat down, wondering confusedly if lions could purr.

"And he will turn me in your arms into the lion's might," said the Luidaeg. I turned toward her, forgetting my fealty to Tybalt. "But fear me not, don't let me go, and we'll see through this night!"

Everything shifted again, and this time I couldn't move; the world was nothing but May trying to fold herself around me, and heat—burning, searing heat. May screamed, and suddenly Connor and Tybalt were there, forcing her not to let me go.

In the distance, Cassandra and Quentin were screaming. They were probably in the same fix as May; if Katie had joined me in the realm of "really hot things," they'd be forcing each other's arms around her. Burns are bad, but somehow I thought letting go might be worse.

"And he will turn me in your arms into a burning sword," the Luidaeg said. Her words cooled me; I still couldn't move, but it felt like the arms around me were holding just a little closer. "Hold me tight, don't let me go; I am your one reward."

The world shifted for the final time, and I was myself, sandwiched between Tybalt, Connor, and May. A moment later, I realized that I was naked. Gee, that was an improvement. "Please let me go," I said.

Tybalt smirked and stood, stepping back. Connor let go as well, turning away, but not before I saw him blush. May removed her cloak and threw it over me, pulling me further into the circle as she stood. Connor and May were covered in scratches and bites, and all three of them were singed, but no one seemed to be badly burned. There were two small punctures in May's wrist where the snake—where I—had bitten her. I hoped Fetches were really immune to physical harm, or we were going to have a whole new problem.

Katie was crying in the distance, and I could hear Cassandra scolding Quentin. I allowed myself a small, tired smile. Looked like I wasn't the only one who was myself again.

"And he will turn me in your arms into a naked knight," the Luidaeg said. Then her tone changed, leaving the lyrics behind. "That's it, little brother; you've lost, and by your own rules, you can't touch them again." Her robe had turned black, making her seem like a hole in the night. Blind Michael looked wraithlike beside her, all white and gleaming ash, with Acacia like a golden ghost beside him.

"Why?" he asked.

"Because you took her while she was mine."

"And the human child?"

"Because everything is connected." She shook her head. "Nothing is free."

"I won't forget this."

"No," she said sadly, and glanced toward me. "You never do, do you?"

I shrugged May's hands away and moved to stand beside the Luidaeg, looking at my former captor. His Hunt was splayed behind him, children and Riders huddled in confusion, while behind me, those that had come to free their children wept with joy. Softly, I said, "I don't forget either. And I never forgive."

The Luidaeg looked down at me and smiled. Blind Michael didn't say another word; he just turned, cloak billowing behind him as he walked back to his horse and mounted again. He led the remains of his Hunt into the night, and they faded away as they rode, dissolving into mist and shadows. Only Acacia stayed behind, watching them go.

"Well met, sister," said the Luidaeg.

"For some of us. It's good to see you," Acacia said, still watching the Riders fade away. When the last of them was gone she turned to me, and smiled. "You did it. You're free."

"I'm as surprised as you are," I said, pulling May's cloak more tightly around myself. "Are you going with him?"

"Yes. I am."

"Why? He was ready to replace you." I wasn't sure what that would have meant for her. I was certain it wouldn't have been good.

"I've taken this Ride too many times; I have no other roads." She shook her head, looking to the Luidaeg. "Blind Michael is my lord and husband. I follow him."

"You don't have to," I said.

"Don't I?" Acacia smiled. "There isn't anything for me in these lands."

"Nothing?" asked the Luidaeg.

"Mother?" said a voice behind me. It was soft, almost afraid. Acacia froze, her gaze going over our heads as she stiffened. I turned, watching as Luna stepped out of the darkness.

She walked over to the Luidaeg's other side, and stopped, pulling back her hood. She looked tired, and there were circles under her eyes that hadn't been there when I'd seen her last. What had she paid to put me on the Rose Road? But her eyes were still brown, and silver-furred fox ears still crowned her head. There were roses in her hair, perhaps in acknowledgment of what she'd been, once upon a yesterday. "Mother," she repeated.

"Luna," Acacia whispered, raising one hand. Her fingers touched the edge of the circle, and she recoiled. "I . . . oh, Luna. I can't reach you."

"I know," Luna said. "You're too much part of Father's kingdom. The circle is warded against his magic."

"I know."

"We could pull you through . . ."

"And what? Change me the way you've changed yourself? Free me from him? Would you hold me when I bit and struck and burned you? Would you cover my nakedness and set me free?"

"Yes." Luna's answer left no room for argument.

Acacia smiled. The expression was bittersweet. "I believe you. I've missed you so much, little rose."

"I missed you, too."

"Come home."

"No."

"I didn't think you would." Her smile softened, saddening. "I hear you've married."

"Yes, I have. He loves me, despite everything." Luna glanced at me. I looked away.

"He's clever. Love matters." Acacia's smile faltered. "I've always loved you."

"Come home."

"No." Acacia stepped back. "Now we've both asked, and both refused. I miss you, my dear one. I'll always miss you, just as I'll always love you. And now I follow your father."

"Mother—"

Acacia shook her head and walked back to her horse, remounting. Luna started to follow, but the Luidaeg put out an arm, stopping her. "No," she said. "You can't go after her."

"But—"

"No." Acacia was already riding away, fading as she gathered speed. The Luidaeg lowered her arm. "We can't save them if they don't want to be saved. It doesn't work that way."

Luna stared at her for a long moment, then whirled with a small, choked cry and hugged me fiercely. I realized with vague surprise that she was crying. "I thought I let him take you forever," she whispered. "After everything he's taken . . . I thought he took you too."

I shivered and leaned against her, closing my eyes. After everything that had happened, I wasn't entirely sure he hadn't.

TWENTY-NINE

THE STRANGENESS BEGAN BLEEDING out of the night, seeping away bit by bit, until the world outside the shining border of the Luidaeg's circle looked like the world I remembered. A brisk wind blew by, carrying the Halloween scents of dried leaves, burning pumpkin, and impending rain. The Luidaeg was still standing on the circle's edge, moving her fingers in small, seemingly random gestures that were probably all that kept us hidden. No one had exactly been focusing on their illusions in the chaos of breaking Blind Michael's Ride.

The kids that had been saved were stumbling around the circle, disoriented and confused by what had happened. Only the ones who had someone capable of claiming them—"friends, family, or blood-tied companions," as the Luidaeg said—had been pulled out of the Ride. Time in Faerie is a funny thing. Some of the kids from the Children's Hall were mixed into the crowd, clinging to their parents or their suddenly grown-up siblings and crying, or laughing, or both. The Centaur who'd spent so much time taunting me was there, his scales and strangeness washed away by the changes he'd gone through. He had his arms around the waist of a tall female Centaur with a strawberry coat. They were sobbing bitterly, and neither looked inclined to let go any-

time soon. His Piskie companion was nowhere in sight. I
was sorry to see that. She'd been as horrible to me as she
could, but it wasn't her fault. A little cruelty didn't mean
she should never get to go home.

Of all the horses that had accompanied Blind Michael's Ride, only Katie had been pulled inside the circle. She'd reverted to her human form after the cycle
of transformations was finished, but that didn't seem to
have done anything to heal her mind. She was curled
into a ball, sobbing. As I watched, Quentin tried to touch
her upper arm, murmuring something that I couldn't
hear. She screamed, loudly and shrilly enough that if not
for the Luidaeg's spell, we would have had every security guard in Golden Gate Park on us in minutes. Luna
winced and finally left my side, hurrying over to guide
Quentin away from his huddled girlfriend.

Katie stopped screaming and balled back up again,
shivering. Poor kid. She was home, but she was still lost.
Maybe we all were. I could still feel Blind Michael at the
back of my mind, a light, fluttering presence trying to
find a way back in. I shuddered.

"When does it end, Luidaeg?" I asked, voice pitched
low.

She glanced over her shoulder at me. "That's your
choice to make, Toby. Go reassure your friends. They've
been a little worried."

"I—"

"We'll talk about it later. Now if you'll excuse me?"
She smiled mirthlessly. "I need to hold this circle a little
longer, and that does take a little bit of focus."

"Right," I said, and stepped away, giving her space.

Connor and Cassandra were working a strange sort of
crowd control, keeping the kids and their parents inside
the ring of light. Every time someone tried to leave, one
of them was right there, guiding them back to the others.
I couldn't blame the parents for wanting to get their kids
home—some of them had probably been missing for
centuries—but a little more time wouldn't hurt anything,
and it might help a lot.

May and Tybalt were standing off to one side, not helping with the organization, but not breaking the circle, either. I walked over to them, clutching May's cloak tightly around myself.

"Hello" seemed too simple and "thank you" was forbidden, so I said the first thing that popped into my head: "You two look awfully cozy."

"Oh, we are," May said. Her sunny good cheer had only been slightly dampened by getting pummeled, bitten, and baked by the person whose death she was supposed to foretell. "We actually turn out to have a lot in common."

"Oh?" I raised an eyebrow.

"Yes," replied Tybalt, flatly. "The urge to smack you until you stop doing stupid things to yourself is at the head of the list."

"Hey, you helped me get to Shadowed Hills."

"And never have I more regretted helping you, believe me. But it had to be done." He scanned my face, expression unreadable. "You're well?"

"Sure. I mean, except for the whole getting myself enslaved by a crazy Firstborn asshole who was planning to marry me at the end of the Ride part, this has almost been a vacation." I shrugged. "How's it been out here?"

"Karen woke up crying," May said, voice suddenly flat. "Said your candle blew out. It's a good thing she was with the Luidaeg. She would've scared the hell out of me."

"He locked the roads after he took you. No one got in, no one got out." Tybalt kept looking at me with that same blank expression. "Every route we tried to reach his lands was blocked. All we could do was wait until the Ride came down and take you on the road."

"So, like, sorry about the whole abandoning you thing," May finished.

I shook my head. "Pretty sure you can't abandon me, May, being as you're my Fetch and everything. But . . . I appreciate what you did." *I appreciate* skirted the absolute edges of propriety, almost crossing the line into *thank you.* If it bothered either of them, they didn't show it. A brief silence fell between us. I glanced around the circle, taking one more look at the small clusters that had formed as grateful parents kept their children close. More and more of them were beginning to don their human disguises, anticipating the moment when the Luidaeg would drop the circle and let them go. As I should probably have expected, Amandine was nowhere to be seen.

"You'd think Mom might have shown up," I said, as lightly as I could manage. "Saving the life of her only daughter and everything. It could've been a bonding experience."

"Sadly, Amandine has disappeared again," said Tybalt, scowling. "Her tower is sealed."

"Because that's a big surprise." Mom has spent more and more time vanishing into the deeper parts of the Summerlands since she decided to go crazy. I have no idea what she does there. It definitely doesn't include sending postcards home.

Connor stepped up beside me, taking my elbow. "If you could all get your disguises on, the Luidaeg says she's about to drop the circle," he said. "Toby, May, Luna wanted me to inform you that you'll be riding back to Shadowed Hills with us. Sylvester wants to see you. Toby, can I see you for a second?"

"Sure," I said, and let him guide me away.

He tugged me to a spot on the far side of the circle, as far away as the ring of light would allow, and released my elbow in order to cup my face in both hands. His eyes were red. He'd clearly been crying.

"I thought—"

"You thought wrong." I reached up, wrapping my fingers around his wrists and holding his hands in place. "Didn't I tell you I'd come home? Sometimes it just takes a little while. And hey, two months isn't even a *patch* on fourteen years."

Connor laughed unsteadily. "Can we not make this a competition?"

"I'd win."

"That's why we can't do it." He leaned forward to rest his forehead against mine, still cupping my face with his hands. "Are you okay? Are you really okay?"

How was I supposed to answer that? No, I wasn't okay. I was a long, long way from okay. I felt violated. I felt like someone had managed to leave stains on the inside of my skin, and my vision kept blurring around the edges, like it was trying to fragment. Blind Michael had something special planned for me, and his hooks were still sunk deep.

I pulled away from him, releasing his hands. "Yeah," I said. "I'm good."

He looked uncertain, but he didn't argue. There was too much to do. Some of the kids hadn't worn a human disguise in so long that they didn't know how to craft one anymore, and the chaos that started as their parents attempted to walk them through the process gave me the room I needed to retreat, well away from anyone who would ask me uncomfortable questions, and start getting my own disguise on. Maybe the long pause had been good for my magic, because it felt like my illusion came together more easily than normal. It only took a few minutes for me to wrap myself in a facade of mortality.

I was one of the last. Almost as soon as my illusion finished settling into place the Luidaeg lowered her hands, and the circle collapsed. The last thin layer of unreality between us and the mortal night fell away with it, and the sounds and smells of a San Francisco Halloween surged in. It should have been a comfort, but it wasn't, and I felt myself go cold.

It didn't feel like home.

"End of the line, kids," said the Luidaeg, stepping up next to me and looking across the crowd. "All of you, go the fuck home. Set the wards and use the spells I taught you. It may take a while, but they'll come clean." Some of the parents started to murmur, and a few cautious, questioning hands were raised. The Luidaeg scowled.

"Do I look like a fucking advice column? Get out of here."

That was enough to convince even the most die-hard worriers that they had better places to be. The crowd started to disperse, scattering in all directions. I looked at the Luidaeg. She was close enough that I could see the hairline cracks in her human shell, the places where the strangeness was bleeding through. For the first time, she wasn't succeeding in hiding her nature, and that was frightening. Blind Michael was stronger than she was.

"Luidaeg?"

She shook her head. "Not yet, Toby. Soon, but not yet. I'm taking the human girl; I might be able to do something for her. Go on back to Shadowed Hills and figure out what you're going to do now."

I chuckled bitterly. "You mean beyond never sleeping again?"

"You got there by the light of the candle, but you didn't get back that way." She leaned forward, voice soft as she said, "He isn't letting go that easily." Then she was standing up straight, turning to stride across the circle with long, ground-eating steps. I stared after her, and when Luna came to take my elbow and guide me toward the parking lot, I didn't fight.

They'd rented a small bus to get everyone to Golden Gate Park and back to Pleasant Hill afterward. Cassandra climbed into the driver's seat, which made a lot of sense; other than myself and Connor, I wasn't certain anyone else in the crowd had a license, and I was in no condition to drive. Half the kids were asleep before we'd even reached the freeway, collapsed bonelessly against their parents.

I wound up between Connor and Tybalt. They kept glaring at each other over the top of my head. I had a pretty good idea of why, but I didn't want to deal with it; I closed my eyes instead, pulling my cloak tight and melting back into the seat. It all felt like the setup for a bad joke. Purebloods, changelings, a Fetch, and the Duchess of Shadowed Hills are in a bus headed for the East Bay . . .

I dozed off somewhere during the trip, and woke when the bus pulled into the parking lot of Paso Nogal Park. That was the cue for everyone to scatter in every direction possible. The parents took their kids and went home, some of them stopping to take my hands and make sounds of meaningless appreciation. I smiled and nodded and pretended I couldn't see the way they avoided meeting my eyes. Luna led those of us who remained into the knowe via a shortcut I'd never seen before, skipping almost all the ludicrous gymnastics. Cheater.

She left us once we were inside, saying she needed to find Sylvester, while Quentin and Cassandra went off to call Mitch and Stacy. Connor followed after Luna, and I realized that I hadn't seen Tybalt since we left the bus. I glanced to May.

"Where's—"

"He said he had a cat thing," she said, and shrugged.

"Right. Now what?"

"Come on this way. Luna said you'd be hungry. And, y'know." She flashed another tired but sunny smile. "Nudity taboos." With that, she was off and walking, navigating the knowe with the sort of casual ease that told me a lot about how much time she'd been spending at Shadowed Hills since I disappeared. This wasn't borrowed familiarity. This was all her.

After about five minutes of walking through the halls, she opened the door to a small, oak-paneled antechamber. A meal of cold cuts, bread, fruit, and cheese had been laid out on the room's single table, and a pile of clean clothes was folded on one of the chairs. Spike was curled up on the pile of clothing, head down on its paws, looking despondent.

"Hey, Spike," I said.

Its head snapped up and it launched itself from the pile of clothes, mewling frantically as it raced toward me. I surprised myself by laughing as I held out my arms, and it jumped into them, still mewling as it rammed the top of its spiky head against my chin, barely managing to avoid puncturing me.

"I missed you, too, baby. I did," I said, stroking it.

"I had a hell of a time getting it to eat," May said. Crossing to the chair, she picked up the bundle of clothes. "These are from home. We figured they'd still fit, although you lost a little more weight than I was counting on. Didn't they feed you?"

"I don't remember," I said.

Getting dressed while trying to deal with a rose goblin that vehemently didn't want to be put down was an exciting experience, but with some creative juggling and a little help from May, I managed it. I felt a lot better once I had some clothes on, and better still when May managed to remove Spike from my shoulder long enough for me to shrug into my jacket. The leather still smelled, faintly and comfortingly, of pennyroyal.

"So now what?" asked May, as she stepped back.

I picked up a slice of bread, eyeing the cold cuts for a moment before starting to slap a sandwich together. "I'm going to eat this, check in with Sylvester, and—"

"She's going back to my grandfather's lands."

The voice was unfortunately familiar. I stiffened, sandwich forgotten as I turned to face the woman standing in the antechamber doorway. "Rayseline."

"October," she replied, almost mockingly. "You're secretly a cockroach, aren't you? Don't worry, you can tell me. It won't make me think any less of you. Really, I don't think that anything could."

"I'm not a cockroach, I'm just hard to kill," I said, putting my half-assembled sandwich back on the table. "Can I help you with something?"

"Just wanted a look at the dead woman walking," she said, and smiled.

Rayseline Torquill would have been scary no matter who she was, and what I'd learned about Luna's side of the family didn't do anything to make her less unnerving. It didn't help that she looked more like her father than her mother, with the Torquill family's characteristic fox-red hair and honey-colored eyes. With her porcelain complexion and delicate features, she projected the illusion of perfect, unquestionable purity and goodness. At least until she opened her mouth.

"Toby?" said May, uncertainly. "She doesn't really mean that, does she?"

I wanted to tell her no, but I wasn't sure that I could lie to my Fetch and make her believe it. I shook my head instead, and Rayseline laughed, sounding utterly delighted.

"Look at that! She can't even admit to it!" She took a step forward, chin dropped so that she was looking at me from beneath lowered brows. She looked like a predator. "He's got claws in her. He's got hands on her. She's going back."

"Toby . . ."

"He kept my knife," I said, as reasonably as I could. "Dare gave me that knife. He doesn't get to keep my knife."

"There are other knives." May grabbed my arm, jerking me a step to the left. Spike rattled in protest, but didn't remove its claws from my shoulder. "There are entire stores that sell just knives. We'll get you a new knife."

"Oh, this isn't about knives, is it, October?" Raysel kept smiling. "My husband cried himself to sleep whispering your name. I hope you die screaming. Better yet, I hope you live that way."

"Toby, don't be stupid. I already broke the rules to save your life. I can't do it again."

"Gosh, little Fetch, did you really?" Raysel's attention swung toward May. "My grandfather takes his time breaking things. Maybe you just didn't want to wait around."

May gasped. Pleasantly, I said, "Raysel, if you don't get out of here, I'm going to punch you in the face."

A brief spasm of rage twisted Raysel's features before smoothing back into her predatory smile. "I should kill you right here, but I won't," she said. "What's ahead will hurt you *ever* so much worse." She turned on her heel and stalked out of the room, leaving us to stare after her.

Voice shaking, May said, "She's wrong, isn't she? You're not going back."

"I have to. He's in my head, May." I turned toward her. Her face was still the twin of mine, but it wasn't a mirror anymore; she'd had weeks to make it her own. She looked worried, frightened, and like herself. That was reassuring. At least she'd had a chance to have a life. "I can feel him. I can almost hear him, sometimes. I don't think I can get away from him without facing him."

"That's stupid. It's stupid, and it's suicidal, and I won't let you."

"I don't think you get a say, hon," I said, gently removing her fingers from my arm. She didn't fight me. She just stood there, watching bleakly, as I took Spike from my shoulder, set it down on the floor, and turned to walk out of the room. She didn't follow.

Spike did. I walked about halfway down the hall, the sound of its claws always clicking a few feet behind me on the marble floor. Finally, I turned to look at it. It promptly sat down, watching me with lambent, narrowed eyes.

"You're not coming," I said.

It stood and walked forward, sitting down right next to my feet.

"You're *not* coming. It's not safe."

The look it gave me was almost disgusted. *If you're going,* said the look, *I can go, too.*

I sighed. "Fine, Spike, whatever you want." I started walking again, steps accompanied by the soft *click-click-click* of the goblin's claws, and tried to hide how pleased I was. I trusted Spike to be safe, and I really hadn't wanted to go alone. There are a lot of ways to die and alone has always seemed like one of the worst. Almost anything else would be better.

We made it out of the knowe and back into the mortal world without seeing anyone else. The door in the oak slammed shut behind us with a hollow finality, and I stopped, staring blankly out across the hillside.

The others might think they'd saved me, but I knew all the way down to my bones that they hadn't. Blind Michael had me too long for that sort of salvation to work. Part of me was his—might always be his, no matter what happened next—and if he was allowed to live, that part would just keep trying to find a way to drag me back to him. I could pretend that nothing was wrong, or I could admit that nothing was right and try to do something about it.

Blind Michael was a monster, and he'd been allowed to go unchallenged for too long. How many kids had he taken and twisted over the centuries? Hundreds? Thousands? Faerie prizes children above almost everything else, and still no one had dared to try stopping him—not since the Luidaeg tried, and failed. Someone had to do it. Someone should have done it a long time ago.

I just wished it didn't have to be me.

There was no warning before the hand dropped onto my shoulder. I stiffened, ready to run, until Sylvester said, "I know where you're going, October."

I turned to look up at him. "How long have you been out here?" I hadn't seen him until he moved. For someone with such red hair, he could blend astonishingly well.

"Since Luna told me they'd brought you home."

"I've been just inside. Why did you come wait out here?"

"Because I know you better than you think I do." He sighed, looking deeply weary. "I know the rest of this conversation. You apologize, I tell you it's all right. You tell me you're going back to Blind Michael's lands and say I can't stop you. Does that sound about right?"

"Yes . . ."

"I wouldn't dream of trying to stop you."

Okay: that was something I hadn't expected to hear. I stared at him, and he smiled. I wanted to ask why he wouldn't try to stop me, but I couldn't find any words. Not a single one.

"I know you too well, Toby," he said, still smiling.

"Sometimes I wish I didn't, believe me. I'd love to have some illusions to cling to—but I don't anymore. I just know you too well."

"I'm sorry," I whispered.

"Don't be. I went off to play the hero myself, once. I'd do it again, if I had to." His smile turned wistful. "I'd do it all again, and I'd do it differently. When certain people wanted to walk away, well . . . it would be different. But we can't change the past, and now I get to watch you ride away. I saw you born. I watched you grow from a confused little girl into one of my finest knights. I shouldn't have to see you die."

I closed my eyes, shuddering. He wasn't trying to talk me out of it, and somehow, that made it worse. "I'm sorry. But this is important."

"That's the only reason I can let you go. Look at me, please." I opened my eyes. He was holding out his sheathed sword with steady hands. "I know where you're going. I won't stop you. But I won't let you go alone."

"Sylvester—"

He kept talking, ignoring my objection. "This was my father's sword. He gave her to me the first time I rode to war; he said she'd never failed him, and that she wouldn't fail me either. If I had a son, she would be his—she would have belonged to Raysel, if Raysel wanted her. But my daughter never understood what it meant to bear your father's sword."

"Sylvester?" This was too much, too fast. I didn't know how to defend myself from it.

"She's not a gift: I want her back. If I have to, I'll reclaim her when I ride to avenge you. But you wouldn't forgive me if I followed you now; you wouldn't let me steal your vengeance, and dear May's presence tells me you won't come home whether I ride with you or not. I can let you go if you take my father's sword."

"Why?"

"Because when I was younger, I was a hero." He leaned down and kissed my forehead as he pressed the sword into my hands. "Go in glory, Toby. If you have to die, do it well. If you can come back to us, come home."

I bit my lip to keep myself from crying. "Sylvester—"

"You can't thank me, and you can't promise to come back, and those are the only things I want to hear." He smiled again, smoothing my hair with one hand. "If he kills you, take him with you. End this. That's all I ask. I love you."

Turning, he walked away into the woods, leaving me alone with Spike and, clutching his father's sword. When I was sure he wouldn't hear me, I whispered, "I love you, too."

I knelt, meeting Spike's eyes. "You stay here. Watch Sylvester. Don't let him cry for me. All right?" It looked at me assessingly before bounding after Sylvester. I straightened. If someone was looking after Sylvester, even a rose goblin, I could go. I could leave him if he wasn't alone. Not that I had much of a choice.

The sword was surprisingly light; I wasn't large, but I could lift it. That was probably part of why Sylvester gave it—her—to me. He knew she'd serve me well, and while he couldn't take vengeance himself, he could make sure his sword did it for him. Clever guy. I could almost make myself forget that he'd mourn for me. Almost, but not quite. Slinging the scabbard over my shoulder, I started down the hill, pausing at the edge of the trees to fill my hands with shadows and wrap myself in a human disguise that hid both my pointed ears and the sword. I shivered as the illusion settled over me, unable to keep from thinking, *This is the last time.* There wasn't time to start regretting things. It was time to go.

Danny was waiting in the parking lot. Sylvester really *had* known that I'd be leaving. One of the Barghests was sitting in the front passenger seat, panting amiably. I slid into the back. Danny looked up and smiled, catching my eyes in the mirror.

"Long time no see, hey, Daye?"

"Hey, Danny." I closed my eyes. "Wake me when we get there, okay?"

"You got it."

We pulled up in front of the Luidaeg's house a little more than an hour later. Danny was true to his word and didn't wake me until we were parked at the front of the Luidaeg's alley. The Barghest followed him out of the car when he climbed out to hug me good-bye, hopping and slobbering on us like the corgi it utterly failed to resemble. I leaned down to scratch its ears, and it washed my face thoroughly with a raspy tongue.

"This one's Iggy," said Danny, proudly. "He's almost house-trained already."

"You must be so proud." I straightened, offering him a small smile. "Open roads, Danny. It's been fun."

"Come see the kennels next weekend, and that's an order," he said, picking Iggy up under one arm and climbing back into the cab. I waved as he drove away, then turned to head for the Luidaeg's door.

It opened before I had the chance to knock. "I expected you hours ago."

"Sorry. I had to get a few things."

The Luidaeg glanced at the scabbard on my shoulder. "Is that Sylvester's sword?"

"Yeah."

"He was always a bit of a sap." She looked to my face, studying me. There were dark circles around her eyes. She was tired, and if I could see it, she was *too* tired. Would she have the strength to do what I needed her to do? "You're planning to do the hero thing, aren't you?"

"I am. Sorry."

"No, you're not." She shrugged. "It's all right; I expect it from my father's children. I just hoped you'd be different. You realize you're asking me to help you kill my brother?"

I nodded. "I do. I'm sorry."

"Why should I?"

"Because someone has to," I said, quietly. "And he broke the rules."

The Luidaeg looked at me for a long moment before she nodded. "You're clever sometimes. You sure as hell don't get that from your mother. Come inside." She turned and walked into the darkness. I followed. What else was I supposed to do?

She led me to the kitchen and opened the fridge, pulling out a jar with a tablespoon's worth of white liquid gleaming like liquid diamonds in the bottom. Putting the jar down on the counter, she pulled a rusty knife out of the sink, saying, "The things I do for you." Then she brought the knife down across her wrist in one hard slashing motion.

I winced. The Luidaeg gritted her teeth and turned her arm upside down, bleeding into the jar until the white was filled with crimson streaks. The liquids didn't seem to blend, but swirled together instead, like a gory candy cane, all diamond and ruby death.

When the jar was halfway full she pulled her arm away and tied a towel around it, cursing under her breath. Not looking at me, she said, "Drink it."

"What will it do?" I took the jar, looking at its contents, and hesitated. Call me paranoid, but the blood of a Firstborn is powerful stuff. I wanted to know before I signed.

"Do? Nothing much." She laughed mercilessly. "Just put you on the Blood Road. It's the last one open to you as you are. And, Toby, you can't back out of this one. No candles. No rescues." The Luidaeg sounded almost pleading. "Change your mind. Leave him alone. Live."

"Is Katie all right?" I kept my eyes on the jar, watching the liquid sparkle.

The Luidaeg was silent for a long while before she said, "No, she's not."

"Will killing him help her?"

"October—"

"Will killing him help her?"

She sighed. "It might. If he dies, his hold on her will loosen, even if it doesn't break entirely. Without the interference, I may be able to repair the damage he did."

"Then I can't change my mind." Was I willing to die for a single human girl?

My daughter's blood was too thin to require she face the Changeling's Choice, and that makes her a single human girl. Yes, I was. For a single human girl, and for all the children that hadn't been saved . . . and for the sake of all the ones who should never be forced to need saving.

"All right, Toby. You have one way out, once you go. If you can kill him, that should be enough to pay the toll, and you'll come back. If you can't . . . the Blood Road has costs."

"Him or me."

She nodded. Her eyes were human brown and deeply shadowed. She looked tired. "Him or you," she confirmed.

I offered her a smile, raised the jar, and drank. The liquid tasted like hot blood and cold salt water, somehow mixed without blending. I was almost expecting the kickback from the Luidaeg's blood, but that didn't really prepare me for it. Nothing could.

The Luidaeg was born before most of the world learned to measure time. She watched the rise and fall of empires while she held her mother's hand and laughed. I didn't get memories—thank Titania, because I might have broken if I had—but I got the sudden crushing feeling of time, endless time slamming into me as the world flashed bloodred and salt white. I tasted blood, but I didn't know whether it was hers or mine or the blood of time itself, burning and bitter on my tongue.

Then time ended and the colors faded into blackness.

And I was falling.

THIRTY

THE FOREST WAS FULL OF SIGHS. There was no wind, but the branches bent against each other, whispering of pain and blood and loss. I was back in Acacia's wood, and that was fine with me; she was the only thing in Blind Michael's lands that I'd be sorry to leave behind. I turned, trying to get my bearings. I'd been standing in the wood when the darkness cleared, already awake. The Blood Road had been the least painful passage of the three. That was probably because it was supposed to have the most painful ending.

Something was wrong. The darkness around the trees had deepened, and the underbrush was wilting. The wood had been the one place in these lands that felt alive, and now it felt like it was dying. "Acacia?" I called. There was no answer.

Oh, root and branch. She helped me before the Ride; she stayed behind to talk to her daughter when the Ride was broken. Blind Michael must have seen her. These were his lands, and he was obviously stronger than she was. The loss of the children would have weakened him. He'd need someone—anyone—to make an example of. Acacia was no innocent, but she wasn't guilty either; not this time.

I pulled the sword off my shoulder and started to

unsheathe it, unwilling to cross the plains without a weapon in my hands. My palms slipped on the pommel, and I looked down. Blood covered my right hand, flowing from a thin cut that had opened, painlessly, across my wrist. There were no signs of clotting; it just kept bleeding.

"The Blood Road," I said, understanding. There would be more cuts, and more still, until I bled to death where I stood. It wasn't what I'd expected, but it wasn't a surprise, either; I was on a time limit. I knew that already. I'd never had forever—forever isn't something changelings get—and now time was running out. Blind Michael still had to die.

Time was short, the night was long, and everything was on his side. Everything but me, and the blood. Blood had shown me the way when it was mixed with wax and bound into a candle; why wouldn't it help me when it was pure? "How many miles to Babylon?" I whispered, rubbing blood across my lips before I took off for the forest's edge, running through the trees and into the mist-shrouded night. The blood knew the way, and so I trusted the blood, not questioning my steps as I ran into the gray. Before I'd run very far, I could see the distant glow of the fire burning in the clearing of Blind Michael's village. The Riders were gathering again. Good. That meant that he'd be there for me to find.

At least the realm wasn't actively hindering me. I stumbled on a few rocks, but that was only to be expected; I was running over ground I couldn't see, and if I hadn't tripped, I'd have thought that I was running into a trap.

I really need to learn to think more.

I could hear the Riders shouting when I was barely halfway across the plains. They sounded pissed, and I couldn't blame them; from their perspective, the Luidaeg and company had interfered with their big holiday parade. Of course, their big holiday parade consisted of kidnapping and brainwashing, but what's a little horrific torture between friends? There was nothing left to distract me and no one left to save. It was almost a relief; sometimes it's nice to get back to basics. I'd kill Blind Michael or die trying. Kill or be killed. Live or die.

A cut had opened on my forehead, and blood ran into my eyes as I ran through the village, heading for the light. No one stopped me, not even when I burst into the clearing, screaming, *"Michael!"*

The whole Court was there, gathered for whatever celebration I was interrupting. It was too much at once. I stumbled, surprised, and two Riders stepped out of the crowd to grab me, pinning my arms to my sides. "Fight me, you bastard!" I kicked wildly, trying to free myself. They just laughed.

Blind Michael was sitting where I'd known he'd be, high on his throne—the small part of me that wished I'd finished the Ride always knew where he was. For that traitorous part of me, he was still my god.

He must have seen that tiny part of my heart shining in my eyes, because he laughed, saying, "So the prodigal returns, as I knew she would. I had enough time to work on her. Let her come to me."

The Riders let go of my arms and fell into line with the others, forming a wide circle around their lord. Probably wise. If I lost, they'd be right there to get the body; if I won, they'd be close enough to take me down. Pessimism really doesn't improve most situations.

I glared at them, spitting blood onto the ground as I walked toward Blind Michael. He was wearing the armor he'd donned for the Ride, but the mirrored sheen was gone, buried under dust and smears of dried blood. His supernatural composure was gone as well, replaced by an expression of angry irritation.

He only held my attention for a moment. Then it was drawn to the chair next to him, where Acacia sat, yellow eyes wide and empty. Her hair was woven into the chair's wicker back, locking her in place.

"What have you done to her?" I demanded.

Blind Michael frowned, brows knitting over ice-white eyes. "Don't speak to me that way." His words held the weight of commandments. I felt another cut open on the inside of my left arm, adding its silent trickle of blood to the rest. "Never speak to me that way."

It was hard to move with him staring down at me like that, but I managed to raise one hand to my mouth, licking fresh blood from my fingers. The pressure of his words and gaze subsided, fading to an annoying buzz at the back of my mind. My power has always come mostly from the blood. Not even he could touch me while I had it.

"I'll speak to you however I like," I said. "Now get down here and fight me."

"Why?" He narrowed his eyes. My vision fragmented, coming from every direction at once as he forced me to look through the eyes of the Hunt. "You're mine. Why should I fight what belongs to me?"

"I'm not yours!" I shouted. There was a brief, stabbing pain as my sight returned to normal. I couldn't trust it to stay that way; he was too close to me.

"You Rode. You're mine."

"I stopped before the end."

"It doesn't matter; you belong to me. Everything here belongs to me." He turned and ran his hand down Acacia's cheek, almost tenderly. There was love there once, before he twisted it out of shape. "How should I scar her this time? Last time she betrayed me, it was her face. What should it be now? She's suffering for you. You have some say in her pain."

"Let her go, Michael."

He turned back toward me, smiling. "Why should I?"

"Because if you do it on your own, I won't have to force you."

He actually laughed. "Oh, little changeling, Amandine's bastard daughter. What makes you think you can make me do *anything?* Perhaps if you'd taken my kindly offer and become my lovely bride, you might have held some sway, but you turned that offer aside. My sister's protections aren't on you now. She can't save you."

"Then I'll save myself." I glared at him, spitting out

another mouthful of blood. "I didn't come here for her."

"No, you came for yourself. Stupid little hero." He reached between the cushions of his throne and pulled out my knife, pressing it against Acacia's unscarred cheek. His smile didn't waver. "It's a wonder any of my father's children—or grandchildren—have survived."

"Give me back my knife and let her go."

"Why should I?" He didn't bother to turn. "Kneel."

I was on my knees before I realized what he'd said. Hitting the ground opened more cuts on my legs and knees. Swell. We were bantering while I bled to death. "Bite me," I snarled, forcing myself to stand. It wasn't easy; my legs kept trying to buckle underneath me.

"Pretty words, but you're not strong enough. Go die somewhere else."

"Make me," I said, gritting my teeth but managing not to fall again. Blood was running into my eyes; I wiped it away with one hand. Then I paused, looking down in disbelief.

My candle was lying near the base of his throne. I hadn't been able to hear it singing to me under all the fresher blood, but as soon as I saw it, I knew it for my own. That made a certain amount of demented sense: they obviously didn't clean up much around here, and once I'd thrown it away, it was just trash. I'd given up its protections—but that was then, and this was now. If I could reach it, I might still be able to get out by a candle's light.

"I'm not going to die," I said.

"Aren't you?" He smirked. "A pity. If you won't die, it's not worth my time to kill you." He turned back to Acacia, drawing my knife down the side of her face. Her eyes stayed glassy and unfocused, even as the blood started running down her cheek.

Blood ran down my fingers and along the length of Sylvester's sword as I leveled it at him, the metal gleaming purple and gold in the firelight. "Leave her alone and *fight* me!" I shouted. "Be a man, you bastard, not a god!

Or are you too *afraid?*" My last word rang through the square like a battle cry. It was a challenge he couldn't ignore after the failure of the Ride.

Blind Michael dropped my knife into Acacia's lap and stood, sightless eyes narrowed. "Do you really think you can challenge me?" he rumbled. "You, who have turned your heritage aside to live as less than nothing? You're a fool, October, daughter of Amandine. Have you forgotten your god?"

"I'm more of an atheist, really," I said.

"I see." He smiled, extending an empty hand toward me. I thought I heard the Riders around us shout in triumph; then they were gone, voices fading as the mists surged up to block the landscape. "But church is such a quiet, welcoming place. There's no pain there, little changeling. No death. No need for swords."

The sword in my hands vanished, swallowed by the mist. I clenched my fingers together, trying to find it, but touched only air. I looked up, furious—and met Blind Michael's empty eyes. His smile didn't waver. I couldn't look away.

"No pain," he whispered. "No death, no need to fight. Come back, little changeling. Come back to me and be with me forever."

The whiteness of his eyes expanded, just like his sister's, and I was drowning. "I'm not yours," I said, forcing the words out one by one. It was getting hard to move or think, and something in the back of my mind was shouting hosannas, ready to leap back into his arms.

How much of me belonged to him? How much of me was ready to betray the rest? I sucked the inside of my cheek, trying to use the blood I knew was there, but I couldn't taste anything; his magic was too strong, and he wouldn't be caught that way twice.

"I don't want this," I whispered, aware of how weak I sounded. He took another step toward me and I dropped to my knees, staring up at him. There was no pain this time. Either I'd lost more blood than I thought, or he was just that strong—and either way, the odds were good that I was screwed.

"Why not?" he asked, pressing his hand against my cheek. My vision was struggling to fragment back into the multiplicity of the Ride. I caught fleeting glimpses through other eyes, watching a changeling bleeding to death as she bowed before her lord and master. "You're lost without me."

Oh, oak and ash, Luidaeg, Sylvester, Quentin, I'm sorry. I thought I was doing the right thing this time. I thought it was important.

"I'm not . . . lost . . ." He was filling the world. There was nothing left but Blind Michael and the mist, and the brief, fractured visions I was stealing from other eyes.

"Oh, but you are," he said. "You're lost. You can't get there or back again; not anymore. Now close your eyes and let me take you home."

Home? Home. It sounded like a wonderful idea; all I had to do was close my eyes, and he'd take care of everything else. He'd make the world everything it was meant to be. I knew I was bleeding. I knew his home was nothing but enchantment and lies. It still sounded right, and I was so tired . . .

I lowered my head, shivering. I'd have the strength to try this once; if I failed, all bets were off. "Yes," I whispered. "Take me home." Blind Michael straightened and removed his hand from my cheek, confident again now that he'd won me back.

That was what I'd been waiting for.

He stepped away and I lunged, scrabbling in the dust. The ground had no texture; it was just mist. Behind me, he laughed. "What are you doing, little changeling? What are you hoping to find?"

My hand hit something and I grabbed it blindly, hoping. There was a brief, stabbing pain in my forehead as the taste of blood filled my mouth, and then my candle was bursting into flame, bright blue and gleaming like a star through the dissolving mist. Jackpot. I stood and turned to face Blind Michael, wiping the blood out of my eyes with my free hand.

Every visible inch of me was covered in blood, running from the nearly countless cuts covering my body. It was getting harder to focus, and not because of anything that he'd done; the Blood Road demands its tolls. "I will not go with you," I hissed.

He looked almost frightened. Good for him. Sylvester's sword was lying in the dust between us; he stepped toward it and I advanced to meet him, the candle held in front of me like a shield. "Do you really think you can threaten me?" he demanded.

It would have been more convincing if his voice hadn't been shaking. "Yes," I said, and smiled. My mouth tasted of blood, and for once, that was a reassuring thing. As long as I could taste the blood, he couldn't catch me.

Blind Michael lunged, going for the sword. He was closer than I was, and so I didn't even try to beat him; I jumped back instead, grabbing my knife from Acacia's lap. "Come on, Michael. It's not even a fair fight. You're older and stronger than I am. Now take me down!"

He clutched Sylvester's sword, expression telegraphing his unease. When was the last time anything truly frightened him? The Riders were whispering in the darkness, but none of them were stepping forward to help him. He was fighting me alone. "You're beneath me," he said, trying to sound confident.

"Doesn't sound like you believe that," I said. Baiting him was fun, but I didn't have time for fun. I relaxed enough to let his borrowed eyes tell him my guard was down, and then lunged.

It's hard to fight what you can't see, and Blind Michael couldn't really see me. He had a hundred borrowed perspectives to use, but he was missing the most important one of all: his own. He swung wildly as I approached, and I didn't even try to block. The sword hit my upper arm, opening a long, shallow cut between my shoulder and elbow. It was a glancing blow—it hurt, but not badly, and it wasn't going to be crippling. Good. My own attack depended on him thinking he could win, if only for a moment. He thought he had the upper hand; I could see it in the way he let his blade dip, not bothering to brace for a parry.

My shoulder hit him in the chest, bowling him over. He hadn't been expecting that. Idiot. I had nothing but a knife, while he was wearing armor and had a sword—where, exactly, was the benefit in attacking him directly? Disarming him was a much better approach.

He hit the ground hard, Sylvester's sword skidding out of his hand. I landed on his chest, bracing my knees against his upper arms and pressing the edge of my knife against his throat. "What does it take to kill a god?" I asked, coldly.

"You can't hurt me," he said.

"Too bad you don't believe that." I bore down, pressing the blade harder against his skin. My blood was falling over everything, making it impossible to tell whether I was really hurting him. "How long since you did your own fighting, Michael? How long since you started hiding behind children?"

"I—"

"How *long?*" I shouted. He stopped struggling, eyes closing, and I looked up to see the Ride staring at me in unified terror. They finally believed that I'd do it. That I was going to kill their lord . . .

And I couldn't. Nothing I did would hurt him enough; nothing. He needed to suffer forever. I shuddered, letting my head droop as I tried to calm myself enough to slit his throat.

Then Acacia's hand was on my shoulder, and a knife was landing in the dust beside me. "Kill him or let him go, Amandine's daughter, but don't torture him," she said. "Make your choice. You haven't got much time."

I looked up. "Acacia—"

She looked down at me, the short tendrils of her hair curling around her face. When I distracted Blind Michael, that must have broken his hold on her, allowing her to rip herself free. "No. You let others make your choices too often. Kill him or let him live, but do it now. No more games."

"I don't know what to *do*."

"You always know. You just don't listen to yourself." She shook her head, turning, and started to walk away. The Riders parted to let her pass, still silent, still staring at me.

Choices. Oh, Oberon's blood, choices.

I put the candle between my teeth, keeping my knife pressed tight against Blind Michael's throat. The flame licked at my cheek, filling the air with the hot smell of singed blood as I reached out and picked up Acacia's knife. I almost dropped it when the metal hit my hand. Iron—it was made of iron. It would have to be; did I really think I could kill one of the Firstborn with silver alone? That was never an option. Not really.

My father was human; I can stand the touch of iron, if only barely. I forced my hand to close around the hilt, looking at Blind Michael through the thin haze of blood clouding my eyes. I was looking for my hatred, but I couldn't find it. I found pity and anger, but no hate. He was insane. He hurt people because he didn't know any better; he hadn't known better for a long time. Did that absolve him of what he'd done? No. Did that make it right for me to torture him?

No. It didn't.

"I'm sorry," I said. "I can't forgive you." I lifted my hand, bringing the two knives together, and slammed them together down into his throat.

Iron slices through faerie flesh like it's nothing but dry leaves and air. That's what iron exists to do: it kills us. Silver can do almost as well, if you use it properly. Acacia's knife was iron, Dare's was silver, and I held them together as I thrust downward.

He screamed when the blades broke his skin; it was a high, childish sound, the last gasp of someone who thought he was invincible. My vision fragmented for an instant, shared between a hundred sets of eyes before the Ride fell as well, clutching their chests, eyes closing.

For that moment, I was Blind Michael; I was broken; I was bleeding; I was dying.

And then there was nothing but blood. The tolls had been paid—I just didn't know who'd paid them or whether it was done in time. Him or me? The age-old question. I slumped forward onto Blind Michael's corpse, eyes closing. It didn't really matter; he was dead, I had won, and I couldn't fight anymore.

No more children would suffer because of him. In the end, I'd proved myself as a child of Oberon's line, no matter how much I tried to deny it; I was a hero, and I was dying like one, and that was all right, because it was how things had to be. I let out a long, slow breath, relaxing at last, while blood ran down my cheeks like heavy crimson tears.

I was done.

The darkness was almost polite as it came for me, wrapping itself around my fading mind. I had time to wonder if the night-haunts would be able to find me in Blind Michael's lands; then there was only darkness and the sweet taste of blood.

I was done.

THIRTY-ONE

THE TASTE OF BLOOD WOKE ME. I opened my
eyes and rolled over, spitting at the ground. It didn't
help. The air around me was light—too light—with a
strange, even brightness. It was a little jarring. I sat up
and looked around, wiping my mouth with the back of
my hand.

I was lying on a bed of moss at the edge of Acacia's
forest, shrouded by the sheltering trees. The branches
above me were putting out new leaves, pale green and
trembling in the air. They were growing. Everything
was growing. The sky between the branches was dark,
but three pale moons shone against the blackness, surrounded by a scattering of stars. The strange new light
was moonlight. The stars didn't form constellations I
knew, but it was comforting to see them; they were a
sign that the long night of this land was changing, if not
coming to an end.

The bushes rustled behind me, and I turned to see
Acacia walking toward me. The branches bent away
from her as she walked, avoiding the hem of her gray
silk gown, and her short-cropped hair was curled into
a nest of tiny knots that rearranged themselves as I
watched. She wasn't wearing her cloak. I stared at her,
openmouthed, as I realized what she'd been hiding. I'd

never seen her without that cloak; she'd changed gowns, but the covering had always remained the same. I could finally see why.

Acacia had opened her wings. They were broad moth's wings, pale green with golden "eyes" at their tops. The edges were tattered from their long confinement, but they'd heal; anything that could last as long as she had would need to be resilient. And they were beautiful.

"You have wings," I said, amazed.

"I do," she said, still smiling.

"But why did you hide them?"

"Because if Michael forgot them, he wouldn't take them like he took everything else." She tilted her face upward, closing her eyes. "I can feel the stars. Even with my eyes closed, I can feel the stars."

"Is he . . . ?" I couldn't think of a polite way to ask if I'd killed her husband, so I stopped.

"Dead? Yes, you killed him." She smiled, eyes still closed. "He's as dead as dead can be. No more midnight rides or stolen children, no more blood on his hands—or on mine."

"Bloody hands." I looked down at my own hands, almost afraid of what I'd see. Dried blood was caked under my nails and in the creases of my knuckles, but the cuts were gone. My skin was whole. "I'm not bleeding."

"You paid the toll."

I started to stand, stopping and wincing as I tried to put weight on my left arm. Looking more closely, I saw that my jacket and sweater were slashed open all the way to the elbow; the cut beneath was long and raw. "Not entirely."

"My husband gave you that. It wasn't part of your fee." She lowered her head, opening her eyes. "Consider it a part of your reward."

"What happens now? Are you free?"

"What does free mean, I wonder?" Acacia shook her head. "I won't leave these lands, if that's what you mean; they've been my home too long. I don't know the world you come from. It would be no home for me."

"Luna's there."

"I know. I'll visit—I can do that, now. I can visit all my children." This time her smile was sweet and wistful. "I've missed them. Luna especially."

"I think she's missed you, too."

"She was always a good girl. She tried to stay. But she was dying here."

I looked at her thoughtfully. There were traces of green in the mingled gold and brown of her hair. I was willing to bet that as the forest restored itself, Acacia would bloom. "She wasn't the only one."

"No; she wasn't." She sighed. "He wasn't always like that. I won't defend what he did or what he became, but there was a time when he was . . ."

"Sane?" I suggested.

Acacia looked at me, expression grave. "Are the fae *ever* sane? We live in a world that isn't there half the time. We claim that windmills are giants, and because we say it, it's true. Our lives become myth and legend, until even we can't tell what we truly are from what we're told we ought to be. How can we live that way and be considered sane? My lord was never sane, but he was my love once. He always will be, somewhere. Wherever it is that the once upon a times go when they die."

I nodded and rose, this time careful not to put any real weight on my left arm. Once I was up I leaned against the nearest tree, taking a slow inventory. My entire body was covered in blood, but the cut on my arm was the only lingering injury. All the other wounds were made by magic and seemed to have faded the same way.

I looked up to see Acacia watching me. "I think you'll live," she said.

"So do I," I replied. "I should probably—"

"Yes, you should." She gestured toward the ground. Sylvester's sword was there, properly sheathed; so were the knives I'd used to kill Blind Michael. "I've readied your things, and I'm sure there are people who need to know you've survived. I would have wagered on your death. I'm sure they've done the same."

Impulsively, I reached for her hands. "Come with me."

"I can't," she said, and smiled. "I have to stay here. The children need me."

Oak and ash, the Riders. "Will they—are they going to be all right?"

"No," she said, simply. "They're going to be Riders, and they'll be here forever. But they'll be better than they were. These are my lands now. The Rides are over, and we'll live another way. I don't know how. But we'll do it."

"Alone?"

"If we have to." She let go of my hands. "You've given us what we needed, October; you've given us our freedom. Now go home and give your family the same gift."

I bent to collect my weapons, pausing before picking up the second knife. I'd killed with it—it was mine now. In the end, I slid both knives into my belt, slinging the sword over my shoulder. "How do I get home?"

"Come here."

Her smile was warm and welcoming. I stepped forward, stopping barely a foot away.

"Trust me, and close your eyes," she said. I did as I was told, and felt her kiss first my eyelids, then my lips. "Good-bye, Toby."

A breeze rose around me and the smell of the air changed, shifting from forest loam to flowers. I opened my eyes, unsurprised to find myself in the Garden of Glass Roses. The light through the windows indicated that it was past noon, although the light in Shadowed Hills can lie. Crystal butterflies flitted from place to place, unconcerned by the sudden appearance of a changeling in their midst. I could tend myself; it was their job to tend the flowers.

"Good-bye, Acacia," I said, and started for the exit. I needed to find Sylvester and the others, and let them know that I was all right. If I was going to be a hero, it was my job to make sure every part of my family was protected, including their hearts.

Damn it, when did I become the hero?

I stepped out into the empty hall, wincing at the sound of my heels on the marble floor. Sliding Sylvester's sword down from my shoulder and clutching it to my chest, I started walking.

Shadowed Hills is large, but some parts of it remain constant; the route to the throne room is one of them. I walked down halls and through antechambers until I was standing in front of the familiar double doors. There wasn't a footman in sight, so I opened the doors myself and stepped inside.

Sylvester, Luna, and May were on the dais at the front of the room. Sylvester was sitting on his throne with Spike in his lap, while Luna sat on the steps in front of him, trying to calm my sobbing Fetch. All four looked up and stared at me when the doors closed. I stared back. What else was I supposed to do?

Luna let go of May and rose, one hand pressed to her mouth. She looked honestly untidy; her shirt was rumpled, and the fur on her tails was uncombed. May stumbled to her feet a moment later, still crying. She looked just as bad when she cried as I do.

None of us moved for a long time. Then, carefully, Sylvester said, "Toby? Is that you?"

"Yes, it is." I held his sword out, the scabbard resting flat on my palms. "I brought your sword back. Thanks for the loan."

I swear I don't remember him moving. Or me moving, for that matter. No one moved, yet somehow we were all standing in the center of the room, everyone trying to hug everyone else at the same time. Spike was twining back and forth between my ankles, and someone was crying. I thought it might be me.

"You're covered in blood," whispered Luna. "There's so much blood."

I forced myself to meet her eyes, saying, "The Luidaeg sent me back on the Blood Road."

She stiffened, eyes widening. "Then ... my father ... is he ... ?"

"Yes, Luna. I'm sorry. He's dead."

"Oh." She turned away, pinching the bridge of her nose. "I see."

"I'm sorry."

"Don't be. No more children. No more regrets." She looked back, smiling through her tears. "I'll cry for him, but I'll smile for them. And for you."

"Good," I said, and looked to my Fetch. She'd backed off when the first frantic embrace ended, watching me warily. "May?"

"Yeah?"

"I'm sorry about going back."

"Yeah, well." She sniffled. "Does everything have to be about you? Dope."

"Yeah," I said, smiling. "I guess I am sort of a dope."

"Okay," she said, and smiled hesitantly. It wasn't my smile. She was already coming up with a smile of her own. I leaned forward and hugged her. After a moment, she hugged back.

Was she proof that I'd die? Okay, well, maybe. But normally a Fetch shows up right before death occurs. I'd faced down and killed a crazy Firstborn after May arrived. I'd done some ludicrously stupid and suicidal things, and I'd survived them. So what if she was proof that I'd die? I'd known that for years, and treating her like a death sentence wasn't fair to either one of us.

Sylvester was watching when I let go of May, eyes bright with something that looked suspiciously like pride. I didn't even pause. I just stepped into his arms, letting him close them around me and seal the world out. There was blood on my hands. I'd killed Blind Michael, and nothing would change that. A lot of people had been hurt; some of the kids were almost certainly scarred for life; and for the moment, that didn't matter. Not if he could still hold me.

"Thank you for surviving," he whispered so softly that I almost couldn't hear.

I raised my head, staring at him. The prohibitions against saying "thank you" are incredibly strong. Thanks imply obligation and fealty. Then again, Sylvester already had mine, on both counts. I smiled at him, answering, "You're welcome." Then I put my head back against his chest and closed my eyes. And stayed there.

Eventually I must have dozed off. It wasn't that surprising; except for my nap in Danny's cab, I couldn't remember the last time I'd slept when not injured or enchanted. I was a little surprised that I hadn't collapsed sooner.

I woke up tucked into a large bed and wearing clean clothes, with Spike curled up in the middle of my chest. My hair was braided, and the blood had been rinsed off of me; the cut on my arm was sore, but it had at least been bandaged. I sat up, ignoring Spike's protests as it hopped off my chest and curled up, glaring, on my pillow. My stomach made a rumbling noise. I had no idea when my last meal had been, and I was starving.

That's why Shadowed Hills has kitchens. I'd almost managed to climb out of the bed when May swept through the door with a tray in her hands, scolding, "Get *back* in that bed! Luna's orders: you have to eat something before I'm allowed to let you get up."

I eyed her. "You're my Fetch. Who says you get to order me around?"

"The Duchess," she cheerfully replied, putting the tray down next to the bed. She was wearing a patchwork skirt and a peasant blouse tie-dyed in clashing stripes of red and purple. The combination was frightening. "Now shut up and eat."

My stomach rumbled again, and I looked at the tray, suddenly happy to do as I was told. The eggs were perfect, the coffee was hot, and the toast was burned just enough to convince me that I wasn't dreaming. Heaven. Spike gnawed on a crust, staying out of the way on my pillow.

Luna arrived as I was finishing and sat down on the edge of the bed, saying without preamble, "I need a favor."

I blinked at her. "Of course."

"The Luidaeg called. I need you to take Quentin to her. It's about Katie."

I froze before nodding, slowly. "Yes, of course." It wasn't done yet. If Katie was still broken, it wasn't done. Oak and ash. Sometimes it feels like the train wreck never ends.

THIRTY-TWO

I**T WAS A MORTAL TAXI DRIVER THIS TIME**, and he didn't speak English. That was okay; Quentin held my hand for the entire drive, his fingers clenched in mine, white-knuckled and shaking. He was terrified, and there were things that needed to be said, but I couldn't say any of them. Saying something makes it real. There was also our human driver to be considered; he claimed not to speak English, but he still might understand enough to pose a problem if we opened our mouths around him.

So I kept my mouth shut, slid my arm around Quentin's shoulders, and just held him. It was all I could do. It could never have been enough. It had stopped being enough when I handed Spike to Luna and got into the cab to take Quentin off to face his fate.

The driver dropped us off at the mouth of the Luidaeg's street and left; Sylvester had already paid the fare. I just hoped he'd used real money. The purebloods can have a sort of creative interpretation of "polite" behavior when it comes to mortals, and cabbies tend to get cranky when they make a big run and wind up with pockets full of dead leaves and ashes.

We stopped on the Luidaeg's doorstep. I looked at Quentin, gauging the strain in his eyes. "Are you going to be all right with this?" I asked.

"No," he said. "I'm pretty sure I'm not. But I have to."

I nodded. More and more, I was coming to appreciate the concept of "have to." "You know she may not be quite right. Not yet." *You understand that she may be broken beyond even the Luidaeg's capacity to fix? That we may bring her back, but never bring her home? Do you understand?*

There were a lot of things I wanted to say, and I couldn't bring myself to say a single one, because saying them would make them real, and no amount of preparing him would change what was waiting for us.

"I know. I do. I'm not giving up hope. But I know."

"All right, Quentin. Just remember that I'm here, okay? I'm not going away again."

He managed a smile, squeezing my hand. "I know. You'd never be that stupid twice."

"Brat," I said fondly and turned to knock on the door.

Inside, the Luidaeg shouted, "It's open!" When you're a legendary sea witch, you don't need to worry much about robbers.

I pushed the door open and led Quentin into the dark, cluttered hall. Quentin stepped easily into the spaces between the debris, moving with the quiet, self-assured grace that comes naturally to the pureblooded Daoine Sidhe. I was easier to track; I was the one who kept tripping and slamming my toes against things in the gloom. The Luidaeg's hall seems to change length to fit her mood, and we walked for quite a while before we saw the other end come into view. Quentin picked up the pace, his hand still locked in mine, and I let him drag me along.

The living room was as cluttered as ever, reeking of marsh and fen and decaying couch stuffing. Quentin paused for a moment, obviously not used to the smell. Then he saw Katie and froze.

She was sitting on the couch with her hands folded in her lap, gazing into the distance. Her hair had been washed and brushed over her shoulders, and her clothes were clean and new. She looked unhurt and human. The Luidaeg was next to her, one half-clawed hand resting on Katie's knee.

"Katie?" said Quentin. Then he smiled, brightly enough that it seemed to clear the shadows out of the room. I relaxed, letting my own smile slip forward. Then I saw the look on the Luidaeg's face, and smiling ceased to be an option. She looked troubled; almost bleak. I stopped, smile fading, and tilted my head to the side in silent question. She nodded, very slightly, and turned to watch Quentin's approach.

Katie didn't acknowledge Quentin's presence, or even seem to know that he was there until he dropped to his knees in front of her and reached for her hand. When he touched her she flinched, cowering against the Luidaeg and whimpering. The Luidaeg lifted one hand to stroke Katie's hair, whispering soothing words in a language that probably died with Atlantis. Katie shivered, returning to silence.

Quentin leaped to his feet and backed away, eyes as wide and shocked as those of a child who's just learned that fire burns. Oh, baby. The fire always burns.

"Can you fix her?" he whispered, blinking back tears. His world was falling down around him; I knew how that felt. I'd have tried to offer him something solid to hang onto, but I knew better. I was too frayed already. I might snap.

The Luidaeg's gaze was mild, but when she spoke, her tone was icy. "Fix her? I suppose. She has the potential to talk, laugh, cry, lie, and betray again, just like every other human. She can live; she's not too broken for that. At least, not yet."

"How?" asked Quentin, with raw longing in his voice. I winced.

The Luidaeg curled a hand over Katie's shoulder, smiling bitterly. "Will you pay for her restoration? There are costs and choices to be made—one choice, actually, but it's yours alone, and making it pays my fee. Can you bargain with the sea witch a second time, little boy?" Katie's breathing calmed as she leaned against the Luidaeg; Quentin might be breaking, but she was broken, and it was our fault, every one of us. Not all the sparks that fly when the mortal lands and Faerie meet are bright ones.

Quentin stared at the Luidaeg, and I fought the urge to yank him away and take him out of the dark place where the sea witch held her Court and made her quiet bargains. She was my friend, but she was also something old and dark, and she could be the death of him. I wanted to take him away from there. I couldn't. As the Luidaeg said, some choices are for one person and one person only; the blood I could still feel on my hands was a testimony to that. I couldn't interfere. I could only watch and bleed with him, if it came to that.

"It's a simple choice." The Luidaeg smoothed Katie's hair with a clawed hand, expression gentle. There was a time when I wouldn't have realized that. "She's not a changeling; she wasn't made to sit on this line. She has to choose one side or the other. Take her to the Summerlands: tend her, keep her, and let her be the last casualty of my baby brother's madness. Keep her, or let her go and never go near her again, because she'd love you if she saw you, and that love would make her remember our world. Keep her or let her go. But choose."

"That's not a choice!" Quentin balled his hands into fists. What was he going to hit? Reality? The laws of nature? Hitting the Luidaeg could be fatal. "That's not even fair!"

"It is what it is," the Luidaeg said with a shrug. "Who told you choices were fair, kid? I gave you the choice that must be given; I'm giving you the chance to decide. What do you want, Quentin? Her life and heart are in your hands, and she's only a Daughter of Eve. The choice isn't hers. The consequences are hers to bear.

"Whatever you want her to be, she'll be. She'll live or die as you command." There was no pity in her tone; none at all. "Just choose, kid. This isn't a game. Choose."

Quentin turned to me, eyes wide and filled with si-

lent hurt. He was still so very young. Faeries—true faeries, not their changeling throwaways—live forever, and
when you have an eternity of adulthood ahead of you,
you linger over childhood. You tend it and keep it close
to your heart, because once it ends, it's over. Quentin
was barely fifteen. He'd never seen the Great Hunt that
came down every twenty-one years, or been present for
the crowning of a King or Queen of Cats, or announced
his maturity before the throne of High King Aethlin. He
was a child, and he should have had decades left to play;
a century of games and joy and edging cautiously toward adulthood.

But he didn't. I could see his childhood dying in his
eyes as he looked at me, silently begging me to answer
for him. I finally understood why the Luidaeg said making the choice would pay her fee. Whether he gave Katie up or not, he was paying with his innocence. There
are choices you have to make for yourself, unless you
want to spend the rest of your life lying awake wondering when the shadows got so dark. If he kept her with
him, he'd be forcing her to belong to him until she died.
There's no going back on that kind of choice: she'd be
his forever, no matter what she might have wanted. But
love ends, and people change, and ordering someone to
love you for as long as they live isn't a good idea.

Katie was young and innocent enough for Blind Michael's lands. Would she survive another kidnapping?

Love is a powerful thing; it makes us all equals by
making us briefly, beautifully human. First love cuts the
deepest and hurts the worst, and when you're caught in
its claws, you can't imagine that it's ever going to end. I
was just a kid the first time I fell in love. I got over it, but
it took time, and that was something Quentin and Katie
didn't have.

"I . . ." Quentin's voice fell gracelessly into the darkness. He was shaking. There was a time when I wouldn't
have credited him with the humanity that required.

"Quentin—" I started. The Luidaeg silenced me with
a look. This wasn't my fight—it never had been.

He had to say the words alone.

He stood frozen for a moment longer, shivering. Then his shoulders slumped in defeat as he said, "I understand," and began walking toward them.

None of us spoke as he knelt by Katie's feet, and for a moment I saw him in all the terrible glory of his adulthood. Beautiful and terrible they are, the lords of our lands; beautiful and terrible beyond measure. But watching Quentin, I realized they also had the potential to be kind. When did that begin? More important, how do we make sure it never, ever ends?

"Katie," he said, and reached for her hands. Maybe it was the slowness of his approach, or the resignation in his tone, but whatever it was, she didn't pull away. "I never meant for you to get hurt. I really didn't." The words belonged entirely to his childhood, begging for forgiveness and unable to see past the punishment. "I thought it could be okay. I thought I could love you without hurting you. I thought we could be different. I'm sorry."

Katie just kept staring away into the distance; wherever she was, it was a place past easy words. Quentin quieted and watched her for a moment, hungrily, like he was trying to memorize every detail. Maybe he was. Forever is a long time. You have to burn the edges of memory onto your heart, or they can fade, and sometimes the second loss is worse than the first one.

"I would've stayed with you," he whispered. "When you got old, when you were sick, I would've stayed. I . . ."

He stopped, shaking his head. "No. I wouldn't, and won't. I loved you. That's enough." He looked to the Luidaeg like he was asking for permission, and she nodded. Crying bitterly all the while, Quentin leaned in and kissed Katie for the last time.

"We are done, we are done, with the coming of the sun," the Luidaeg said, running her hands through Katie's hair. Quentin pulled away, watching her. "Now the morning light appears, and the Faerie Courts draw near for the dancing of our Queens on the still and dew-soaked green. Human child, run fast away; fae-folk come with close of day."

Something old and wild and cold brushed through the darkness of the apartment. I shivered as it brushed past me, remembering my own Changeling's Choice, so long ago, when I rejected Eden for the wilds beyond.

Katie blinked, eyes going wide as the spell wrapped itself around her. "Quentin?" I wondered what she saw when she looked at him; what fiction her mind was using to cover what she knew damn well was really there. Did it matter? He'd given her up. She was no longer Faerie's concern.

Quentin looked to the Luidaeg, and she nodded marginally, giving her consent. Turning back to Katie, he offered her his hands. "Come on. Let me take you home."

"Home—yes, please. I'd like to go home." She stood, letting him lead her to the hall. It was shorter now, and they reached the front door in a matter of moments.

Quentin looked back once, his face like a mask, before they stepped out into the light of day. Mortal day. The sun has no love for our kind. I knew what came next: it was a simple story. He'd walk her to the corner, hail a taxi, take her home, and leave her on her doorstep, as the fae have done with their mortal lovers since time began. For good or ill, she'd never touch the world of Faerie again. She was free. All it cost was Quentin's heart.

I crossed and sat next to the Luidaeg, watching her. She looked back for a long time before turning away and saying, "I tried, Toby. I really did. Believing in both worlds at once was too much for her. It was either our world or hers, and I couldn't be the one to make that choice for her."

"I know," I said. Oddly enough, I did. I couldn't make the choice for Cliff, or for Gillian, and the human world had taken them both. Understanding didn't make it less painful.

"You came back."

"I'm like a bad penny."

"I put you on the Blood Road."

"Yeah, I actually noticed that part."

"My brother . . ."

"Is dead."

"I see." She raised her head, regarding me with solemn, ancient eyes. "There was a time when I'd have ripped your heart out of your chest and eaten it in front of your dying eyes for saying something like that to me."

"I know."

"Only you wouldn't have died. I'd have left you broken and heartless on the moors, bleeding forever as a warning to anyone who touched my family. I'd have destroyed you."

"I know that, too." I wasn't afraid of her. When did I stop being afraid?

"Once."

"But that was a long time ago."

"I know." She paused, looking down at her hands. The dainty claws that tipped her fingers retracted, reshaping themselves into human nails. "How did he die?"

"I killed him with silver and iron and the light of a candle." I shivered as the memories slipped over me, trying to ignore the feeling of blood on my hands. Blood has power; part of me was his forever. The knives had been iron and silver, but that was only the end of the kill, not the means. He died by blood and fire and faith, by roses and the cold flicker of candlelight. My blades were only an afterthought, a sharp reminder that the long, wild chase was over, and it was time to lie down and be still. It was time to close the nursery windows. It was time to grow up.

The Luidaeg's hand on my shoulder brought me back. I froze, blinking up at her, and she smiled. "As it should have been. Silver was his right, and iron will force the bastard to stay dead. Remember that; you can only kill the Firstborn if you use both metals. They're too fae for silver alone, and too strong for iron. Anybody that tells you different is lying. You did good, Toby. If it had to be anyone, I'm glad it was you."

"Oh," I said, and stopped. There was nothing else to say. I've always been proud of my words, and they'd all left me. They'd been doing that a lot lately.

The Luidaeg sighed and put her arms around me, pulling me close. "Come here," she said. "I need to hold someone, and you need to be held. It's a fair trade. Just for a little while, and then we can go on being what we are."

I thought about objecting, but dismissed the idea and nestled against her, enjoying the feeling of security given by knowing someone bigger and stronger than I was would stop anything from hurting me. That's all childhood is, after all: strong arms to hold back the dark, a story to keep the shadows dancing, and a candle to mark the long journey into day. A song to keep the flights of angels at bay. How many miles to Babylon? Sorry. I don't care.

THIRTY-THREE

I RANG THE DOORBELL with one hand, juggling my armload of packages in an effort to keep myself from scattering them across the porch. It wasn't working very well, and having Spike on my left shoulder wasn't helping.

From inside, a shrill voice caroled, "I got it I got it I got iiiiiiit!" The front door slammed open to reveal a panting six year old, exhausted by the effort of beating her siblings to the prize. "Auntie Birdie!"

"Hey, Jessie," I said, kneeling to hug her with my free arm. Spike chirped in annoyance, jumping down to the floor. "How're you doing?" She seemed to have recovered from her time in Blind Michael's lands, at least on the outside; the inside was another matter. Her mother said she woke up screaming almost every night. If I could've killed the bastard again, I would have.

"I guess okay." She squirmed free, rocking back on her heels. "You here for the party?"

"No, I'm selling Amway products." I ruffled her hair. "Goose. Take me to your leader."

"Okay!" She grabbed my hand and hauled me toward the kitchen, shouting, "Kareeeeen! Auntie Birdie's here!"

The family was gathered around the table in the

kitchen. The birthday girl smiled from her seat, raising one hand in a wave. "I know," said Karen. "Hi, Aunt Birdie." Then she broke off, giggling, as Spike jumped up into her lap.

"Hey, baby. Hey, Stace." I put the packages down and hugged my best friend, hard. She shivered and hugged me back.

"I'm so glad you came," she whispered.

"You couldn't keep me away."

All the kids came home, at least for Mitch and Stacy, but that wasn't enough, and it never would be. Losing those children at all—I still can't imagine what I'd have done if someone had taken Gillian away from me like that. As it was, time had taken her from me, and that's at least a little easier to understand.

The first time I came to check on the kids after everything settled, I told Stacy everything. I thought she was going to haul off and hit me when I told her about May, but she surprised me: instead of reacting with anger, she drove me back to Shadowed Hills, walked up to my Fetch, and said hello, just as polite as you please. May saved my life more than once. That made her part of the family, no matter where she'd come from.

"Hey, guys? Ever heard of holding the door?" May came in behind me, her own presents more sensibly tucked into a plastic shopping bag. She was wearing a forest green skirt that fell almost to her ankles and a pink T-shirt that read "Ladies' Sewing Circle and Terrorist Society." "Not that I mind waiting in the cold or anything, but it's manners."

Stacy let go of me and smiled. "Sorry, May."

"Oh, it's no big deal. It gave me a chance to say hello to your neighbors. Who are very friendly, but have the ugliest dog in the world." She put her bag down on the table, circling around to kiss Karen on the forehead. "Hey, sleepyhead."

"Hi, Aunt May."

The kids adapted fast to the idea of having two aunts—for one thing, it meant more presents, and even though she looked like me, it wasn't hard to tell us apart. My Fetch had a style all her own: a style she'd strewn across my entire no-longer-spare bedroom. She showed up on my doorstep three days after Quentin said good-bye to Katie, looking sheepish and carrying the few belongings she'd managed to collect in a cardboard box. What was I supposed to do? She wouldn't have existed if it weren't for me, and so I let her move in. It was nice to have someone to pay half of the rent, even if I wasn't sure exactly what she was doing for work. Sylvester helped her get a legal identity; as far as the state of California was concerned, I'd always had an identical twin sister.

Bet Amandine would be surprised to hear that one.

I sat down and was promptly rewarded by having Andrew crawl into my lap. "Hey."

He pulled his thumb out of his mouth. "Hey."

"You good?"

"M'good." He replaced the thumb.

Andrew was doing better than Jessica; he was sleeping through the nights and had stopped drawing disturbing pictures. His parents said I'd taken care of the monsters, and that was good enough for him. He was still young enough to believe that heroes could make all the problems go away. I miss that feeling.

Tybalt's kids seemed to be doing well. Raj had come to visit several times, much to Quentin's annoyance; he even brought Helen with him once, treating her like she was made of glass. I wondered what his parents thought of that—interracial dating can be sort of a sore spot with some of the purebloods, and Raj was supposed to be King someday. Oh, well. Not my Court, not my problem.

The King of Cats himself hadn't spoken to me since Blind Michael died; it had been almost a month, and there was still no word. That was fine. Things had been too confusing for me toward the end, and there are some complications I just don't need.

Connor hadn't called me either, and that was fine, too.

"So, Karen, you're twelve today?" May flashed a grin. "Congrats."

Karen nodded almost shyly. "Yeah, I am."

"Toby!" Mitch hugged me from behind. "Glad you could make it."

I leaned back, grinning up at him. "I wouldn't miss it. Isn't this a small party?"

"Just family," Karen said. I looked at her, and she smiled. "It seemed right."

"Yeah," I agreed. "It does."

The Luidaeg hadn't been able to tell me where Karen's oneiromancy came from; it shouldn't have been in her bloodline, but it was. Karen seemed to be recovering well, at least. She was quieter than before, but not by much, and she was happy. That was what I cared about. Everything else was just extra.

Luna had been to Blind Michael's lands to visit her mother at least twice that I knew of. Only they weren't Blind Michael's lands anymore; they were Acacia's, and according to Luna, they were blooming. Something good had come out of everything that happened. Try telling that to the parents whose children never came home. The fae parents were few enough, and they could almost understand; there are always risks to living outside the Summerlands. But the human parents would never know, and for that, I was sorry beyond all measure. I succeeded in doing what I set out to do: I brought my children home. Why did it feel like a failure?

Quentin could've answered that for me, if I'd dared to ask. He'd dropped his entire mortal identity, leaving it all behind for her, and he hadn't even tried to create a new one—I guess it would've been cheating. He gave Katie up once—thanks to the Luidaeg's spell, she didn't even remember that he existed, and he wasn't going to push it by trying to be close to her as someone else. That showed a lot of guts and a level of maturity he shouldn't have had to live with yet. He was growing up. Poor kid. Without a mortal existence to occupy him, I was seeing a lot more of him, and hanging out with a teenage boy was certainly proving to be an education. He could almost make baseball seem interesting, for one thing, and I was getting used to finding him asleep on my couch every Saturday morning. The landscape of my world was changing and somehow I didn't mind at all.

Lily cried when I came back to the Tea Gardens. She hadn't expected to see me again, and I couldn't blame her. The Luidaeg was right when she said I was trying to die; I just hadn't been able to see it until it was right on top of me. I still wasn't sure I could fix it, but at least now I knew it was there. That was something. So Lily and I drank our tea and spoke of inconsequential things, and she smiled until I thought her face would crack. I started visiting her once a week after that, and bringing Quentin and May with me, when they'd come. It wasn't fair to play games with the hearts of people who loved me. And they did love me—I had to admit that, or nothing would ever make sense again.

And me? Somewhere along the line, I'd faced the facts I'd been running from for a long time—maybe since before the Tea Gardens. Before everything. I'd finally run out of places to hide from the truth. I'm a hero. That means certain things. I probably won't live to a ripe old age, Sylvester being sort of the exception as heroes go, but I always knew that. I never expected to live forever. Maybe admitting it to myself was all I needed to do. The rest came from there.

It's a long, hard road to Babylon, but you can get there and back by the light of a candle. You just have to light it for yourself.

"Here comes the cake!" shrieked Jessica. Stacy dimmed the lights, and I turned to see Anthony and Cassandra walking into the room, holding opposite sides of a large white sheet cake. Everyone started joyously shouting the words to "Happy Birthday." Even Spike chirped along with the melody. I didn't sing. I looked from face to face instead, watching my kids—watching the people who had become my family—celebrate being alive, being together, and making it through another year.

"Blow out the candles, baby!" urged Stacy. Karen leaned forward and blew. The candles guttered and died, winking out like stars.

They weren't needed anymore.

We were already home.

The fourth Toby Daye novel from

SEANAN MCGUIRE

LATE ECLIPSES

corsair

Read on for a sneak preview.

I OPENED MY EYES TO A WORLD MADE entirely of flowers. Entirely of white flowers, no less, morning glories and white roses and the delicate brocade of Queen Anne's Lace. I blinked. The flowers remained.

"Okay, this is officially weird," I murmured. A faint breeze stirred the flowers overhead, sending loose petals showering down over me. There was no perfume. Even when the wind was blowing, there was no perfume. I relaxed, suddenly understanding the reason for the bizarre change of scene. "Right. I'm dreaming."

"That was *fast*, Auntie Birdie," said an approving voice to my left.

I sat up, shaking petals out of my hair as I turned. "Given how often you people throw me into whacked-out dream sequences these days, it's becoming a survival skill. Why are you in my dreams tonight, Karen? I'm assuming it's not just boredom."

My adopted niece looked at me gravely. She was kneeling in the grass, petals speckling her white-blonde hair and sticking to her cheeks. Her blue flannel pajamas made her look out of place, like she'd been dropped into the wrong movie. Karen is the second daughter of my best friend, Stacy Brown, and oh, right—she's an oneiromancer, an unexpected talent that decided to manifest itself when she was captured by Blind Michael. She sees the future in dreams. She can also use dreams to tell people things she thinks they need to know. Lucky me, I'm a common target.

Good thing I like the kid, or I might get cranky about having my dreams invaded by a twelve-year-old on a semi-regular basis.

"There's something you need to see," she said, and stood, walking away into the flowers. Lacking any other real options, I stood, brushed the flower petals off my jeans, and followed.

She had an easier time making it out of the impromptu bower than I did; she was lower to the ground, and could duck under branches that slapped me straight across the face. Finally, swearing under my breath, I pushed the last spray of gauzy white irises aside and stepped into the open. My breath caught as I saw where we were, and I froze, wondering abstractly if I could actually pass out in a dream.

Amandine's tower stood tall and proud in the dim Summerlands twilight, the stone it was made from seeming to glow faintly from within, like a lighthouse that never needed to be lit. Low stone walls circled the manicured gardens, providing a delineation of the borders without doing a thing to defend the place. Amandine never seemed to feel she needed defending, and when I was living with her, I was still too young to realize what a strange attitude this was in Faerie.

"Karen," I said, slowly, forcing myself to breathe, "what are we doing here?"

"Just watch," she said.

So I watched.

Dream time isn't like real time; I don't know how long we stood there, looking at my mother's garden. Being there, even in a dream, made my chest ache. I spent half my childhood in that garden, trying to be something I wasn't. It's grown wild since Amandine abandoned her tower, and I'm glad. It's the only reason I can bear to go there.

"There," Karen whispered, taking my hand. "Look."

Someone was approaching via the eastern gate. I narrowed my eyes, squinting in that direction, and went cold as I realized that I knew the woman starting down the garden path. Black hair, golden skin, pointed ears, and eyes the bruised-black of the sky between stars. Oleander de Merelands. I automatically tried to push Karen behind me. "Ash and elm," I hissed. "Karen, get down."

"Dream, Auntie Birdie," she said calmly. "Just watch."

Thrumming with tension, I forced myself to stay where I was, watching Oleander like a mouse watches a snake. Not a bad comparison. Oleander de Merelands was half-Peri, half-Tuatha de Dannan, and all hazardous to your health. She was there when Simon Torquill turned me into a fish; she laughed. Even knowing the things they say about her—the rumors of assassinations, the fondness for poisons, the trafficking in dark magic and darker services—that's the thing I can never seem to forget. She laughed. Where Oleander went, trouble followed.

She walked straight past us, not even glancing in our direction. I relaxed slightly. This was a dream; she couldn't see what wasn't really there. She proceeded down the path to the tower door, where she raised her hand and knocked, calmly as you please.

A minute or so later, the door opened, and my mother—Amandine of Faerie, greatest blood-worker of her generation—stepped out onto the tower steps. My breath caught again, for entirely different reasons. I haven't seen my mother in years. Not really. She slipped away while I was in the pond, and I wasn't prepared for the sight of Amandine in her prime.

Her elegantly braided hair was white gold, but unlike Karen's, which looked faintly bleached, it was the simple, natural color of some unnamed precious metal. Her eyes were the same smoky gray-blue as morning fog. They widened slightly when she saw Oleander standing there, before narrowing in outrage.

"What are you doing here?" she demanded. "You are not welcome. I grant you no hospitalities, nor the warmth of my hearth."

"Why, Amy, aren't you the high-nosed bitch these days," Oleander replied, her own voice thick with loathing. "*He* sent me. Someone thought he should know you'd come home again, and now he's wondering after your welfare."

Amandine pursed her lips, studying Oleander. Finally, dismissively, she asked, "Is this what you're reduced to? Playing messenger-girl for the Daoine Sidhe? I thought you held yourself better than this."

"At least I didn't whore myself to the mortal world for a replacement," Oleander spat. "Has he even seen her, Amy? Your little imitation? I can take her for a visit, if you still think you're too good for social calls. Or are you afraid she'll realize what she is? Are you afraid—"

I winced even before Amandine started to move. Oleander didn't know her as well as I did, and didn't recognize the sudden tension in her posture for what it was before it was too late. Amandine lunged, wrapping one hand around Oleander's throat and the other around her wrist before the other woman had a chance to react.

I shouldn't have been able to hear what came next. We were too far away, and she was speaking too softly. But this was a dream, and I was going to hear what Karen wanted me to hear.

"If you come near my daughter, if you touch her, if you *look* at her, I will know, and I will make you pay." Amandine's voice was tightly controlled. She would have sounded almost reasonable, if not for the fury in her expression . . . and the fear in Oleander's. Oak and ash, one of the scariest women in Faerie was looking at my mother like she was the monster in the closet. "Do you understand me, Oleander? I will make you pay in ways you can barely comprehend. I will make it *hurt*, and the pain won't stop just because I do. Do you understand?"

"Bitch," hissed Oleander.

Amandine narrowed her eyes. The smell of her magic—blood and roses—suddenly filled the formerly scentless garden, and Oleander screamed, writhing in her grasp. Amandine didn't move, but she must have been doing *something*, because Oleander kept screaming, a high, keening sound that wasn't meant to come from any human-shaped throat.

The smell of blood and roses faded. Oleander slumped in Amandine's hands. My mother looked down at her dispassionately, not letting go.

"How much of who you are is what you are?" Amandine asked. Her voice was still soft. That was possibly the worst part. "How much do you think it would change? Would you like to find out?"

"No," whispered Oleander.

"I'm afraid I can't hear you. What was that you said?"

Oleander licked her lips. "I said I wouldn't go near your daughter. I'll leave. I'll say you don't want to be disturbed."

"Ah, good." Amandine released her, looking satisfied. Oleander dropped to her knees, gasping, as Amandine stepped back to her original position. "That was what I hoped you said. Your visit has been most enlightening, Oleander. I trust it won't be repeated."

Oleander staggered to her feet, glaring daggers at my mother as she stumbled backward, out of reach. "It won't. I won't come here again."

"Not even if he sends you?"

"There are some things I won't risk for anyone." Oleander took another step back, keeping her eyes on Amandine the whole time. "Keep your little half-breed bitch. The two of you can rot for all I care."

"I'll take that under advisement," said Amandine. Turning her back on Oleander, she walked into the tower and closed the door.

Oleander stayed where she was for a moment, glaring daggers at my mother's wake. Then she turned, storming back down the path and out the gate, into the fields beyond the tower grounds.

I turned to Karen. "Why did you show me that?"

"I don't know." She shrugged helplessly. "I'm still not very good at this. I just sort of do what the dreams tell me I have to. But I didn't show it to you."

"What?" I frowned. "Of course you did. I just saw it."

"No." She looked past me, into the bower of white-on-white flowers where the dream began. "I didn't show you. I just reminded you that you knew it."

It took me a moment to realize what she was saying. Slowly, I turned, and saw myself—my much smaller, much younger self, still new to the Summerlands, still so dazed by the wonders of Faerie that I hadn't started looking for the dangers—crawling out from underneath the branches.

"See?" said Karen. "You already knew."

"I . . . I don't remember this."

"You do now." I felt her hand on my arm, as light as the flower petals still drifting in the air around us. "It's time to wake up, Auntie Birdie."

So I did.

Late afternoon sun streamed through the bedroom window, hitting me full in the face. I opened my eyes, trying to blink with disorientation and squint against the glare at the same time. Not a good combination. One of the cats was curled on the middle of my chest, purring contentedly.

Sunlight. I'd closed my eyes for just a few minutes before falling into Karen's dreamscape, and that was about an hour before dawn. Just a few—

"Crap!" I sat bolt upright, sending the cat—Cagney—tumbling to the bed.

"Afternoon, Sleeping Beauty," said May. I turned toward the sound of her voice. She was standing in the doorway with a coffee mug in one hand, watching me. "Welcome to the land of the living."

"What time is it?" I demanded, raking my hair back with both hands. It was tangled into hopeless knots, matted stiff with sea salt. Crossing the city on a yarrow broom probably hadn't helped. "Why didn't you wake me sooner?"

"You didn't tell me to," she replied, matter-of-factly. Expression turning solemn, she continued, "Also, you didn't twitch when I opened your curtains half an hour ago, so I figured you needed the sleep. It's almost sunset. Marcia's been calling every two hours. Everything's pretty much the way it was last night. No change in Lily's condition."

"She filled you in?" I let my hands drop to my lap.

May nodded. "Yeah. Now get up, get something into your stomach, and get dressed before we're late."

"Late? For what?" Cagney had recovered from her graceless tumble, and strolled down the bed to smack her sister awake. Lacey responded by biting her in the face. I sympathized.

"I repeat, it's almost sunset. On the first of May. That means what?"

"Oh, *no*." I groaned, falling back on the bed. "May, I can't. Karen was in my head last night. She showed me this fucked-up . . . I don't know if it was a memory or what, but it had Mom in it, and Oleander. I need to call and find out what the hell she was getting at."

"Cry me a river. The Torquills expect you to attend the Beltane Ball, and you're attending. You can explain the situation when we get there."

"I hate you sometimes."

"That's fine. We're still going."

The Beltane Ball at Shadowed Hills has been one of the Duchy's biggest social events for centuries. It's a night of dancing, drinking, and welcoming the summer. In short, May's sort of party. My sort of party involves less of a crowd, and a lot more physical violence. "I don't think this is a good idea."

"It's not," she agreed. "But you can't become Countess of Goldengreen, run out of the Queen's Court like your ass is on fire, and then miss the social event of the season. Not if you want to keep the Queen from figuring something's up."

"Fuck," I said, staring up at the ceiling.

"Basically." I heard her sip her coffee. "You okay?"

I laughed bitterly. "I'm peachy."

"There's the manic-depressive sweetheart we all know and love. Get up. You'll feel better after you've had a shower."

"Look, can't you just call Sylvester and tell him I'm not coming?" I threw an arm over my face to block the light. "Tell him I'm busy saving the world. Better yet, how about you just be me for the night? You look the part."

"Uh, one, no way. Two, I look like you, the jig would be up the minute I opened my mouth." She walked over and kicked the bed. "Get up before I get the ice water. You're trying to wallow in your misery, and I'm not putting up with it."

I moved my arm, glaring at her. "I hate you."

"I know. Now come on. We'll go to the Ball, and you can meet my date."

That was news. I sat up, blinking. "You have a date?"

"I do. See, unlike some people, I know a good thing when I see it."

"I'm going to leave that alone," I said, and sat up, scooting to the edge of the bed. My skirt snarled around me, hampering my movement. "I'm up. See? I'm up."

"Good girl. Just for that, you can have a *hot* shower."

"Don't make me kick your ass."

"You can try. Now come on: breakfast, coffee, shower, clothes." She left the room, whistling. I flung a pillow after her. It bounced off the doorframe.

May was in her room when I emerged, clearly choosing retreat as the better part of valor. There was a cup of coffee on the hall table next to the phone. I had to smile a little at that. My Fetch knows me better than anybody else. I guess that should be creepy, but somehow, it's actually reassuring.

I dialed the Tea Gardens and leaned against the wall. I'd been waiting long enough for an answer to give serious thought to panic when Marcia picked up, saying, "Japanese Tea Gardens. How may I help you?"

"It's me, Marcia. How is she?"

"Toby!" The relief in her voice was enough to make me wince. "I'm so glad you called."

"I would have called earlier, but I just woke up." I sipped my coffee, nearly burning my lip. The pain wasn't enough to detract from the relief of the caffeine. "May gave me a status report. Has anything changed?"

"No. Lily isn't any worse. That's good, right?"

I wanted to reassure her. I couldn't do it. "I don't know. Has there been any progress in finding her pearl?"

"Not yet. Everybody's looking."

"Keep looking, and make sure that whoever you have watching Lily knows to ask about it if she wakes up. I have to go to Shadowed Hills and make an appearance at the Beltane Ball before I can come. Call there if you need anything."

"Okay." She sniffled. "I will."

There was nothing to say after that. We exchanged a few vague reassurances before I hung up, still unsettled. Attending a Ball while Lily was sick felt too much like Nero fiddling while Rome burned, but May was right; I didn't have much of a choice, especially not the day after I'd been elevated to Countess. Playing by the political rules was suddenly a lot more important.

Taking another large gulp of coffee, I dialed Mitch and Stacy's. "Almost sunset" meant that everyone would be up; fae kids may be nocturnal, but that doesn't make them immune to the allure of afternoon TV.

"Brown residence," said the solemn, almost too-mature voice of Anthony, the older of the two Brown boys. He was ten on his last birthday.

"Hey, kiddo," I said, relaxing a bit against the wall. "Is your sister up yet?"

"Auntie Birdie!" he crowed, sounding delighted. Then he sobered, the moment of childish exuberance fading as he said, "Karen went back to bed, but she told everybody that if you called, we should say you know everything that she knows, and she doesn't know why it's important. Did she dream with you last night?"

"Yeah, she did," I said, resisting the urge to start swearing. "Look, when she wakes up, tell her to call if she thinks of *anything*, okay? And tell your mom I'll try to come over soon."

"Promise?"

"Double-promise. I miss you guys." The Browns are some of my favorite people in the world, and that goes double for their kids. It just seems like there's never time for the good parts of life these days, like hanging out with my old friends and their kids. It's been one emergency after the other, practically since I got out of the pond.

"We miss you, too, Auntie Birdie," said Anthony gravely.

Much as I wanted to stay on the line and ask him to tell me what he was studying, what his brother and sisters were doing, all the things a good aunt would ask, there wasn't time. I repeated my promise to visit soon and hung up, realizing as I did that I was hungry. Looked like the coffee had been enough to wake up my stomach.

I went to the kitchen and filled a bowl with Lucky Charms and coffee. Cliff used to make gagging noises and pretend to choke when I did that, but it's how I've always liked my cereal. I paused with the spoon halfway to my mouth as I realized that, for the first time in a long time, the thought of Cliff didn't hurt. It made me sad, sure—he wasn't just my lover and the father of my child; he was one of my best friends, and losing friends is never fun—but it was only sadness. No pain. No longing.

Maybe I was starting to move on.

I did feel better after eating, and a shower would prob- ably make me feel almost normal. I left my bowl on the counter, fighting with my dress all the way to the bathroom. I've worn enough formal gowns to know how to move in them, but they were almost all illusionary, making changing out of them nothing more than a matter of dropping the spell. This dress was heavy, dirty, and all too real. Getting it off felt almost like a moral victory.

The apartment has excellent water pressure. I turned the taps as high as they would go before stepping into the shower, letting the spray sting my arms and face. I stayed that way long after I was clean, breathing in the steam. There's something reassuring about standing in the shower; as long as you're there, you can't get dirty.

May was waiting on the couch when I came out of the bathroom. She looked me up and down before asking, "Feel better?"

"Actually, yes."

"Told you so. Now get dressed."

I flipped her off amiably. Her laughter followed me down the hall to my bedroom, where Cagney and Lacey curled up on the bed in the remains of the sunbeam. Lacey lifted her head, eyeing me.

"Don't worry," I said. "You're the lucky ones. You get to stay home." I started for the dresser, pausing with one hand stretched toward the top drawer.

The Queen's habit of transforming my clothes is incredibly irritating, especially since I lack the magical oomph to change them *back*. There are only a few bloodlines in Faerie talented at transforming the inanimate; the Daoine Sidhe aren't among them, which is why we depend on illusions and chicanery to enhance our wardrobes. But if I happened to have a dress formal enough for the occasion . . .

I grabbed the crumpled gown off the floor, holding it up. If I could figure out how to get the grass stains out of the skirt . . . I stuck my head out of the room. "Hey, May, you know anything about cleaning silk?"

She leaned over the back of the couch, eyes widening when she saw what I was holding. "Are you seriously thinking about wearing that?"

"I don't think I should be throwing magic around if I can help it, do you? It's not like I have much to spare." Every changeling has a different amount of power, and pushing past your limits is a good way to fuck yourself up. If I was going to stay at the top of my game, I needed to avoid magic-burn for as long as possible.

May hesitated before getting off the couch and walking toward my room. She bit her index finger, looking torn, and finally said, "I can help. Go get your knife."

I blinked. She met my eyes, nodding marginally. Something in that gesture told me to listen. I stepped past her, heading for the rack by the front door, where my knives still hung. I unsnapped the loop holding my silver knife in place and glanced back to May. "I assume I can use the silver, and not the iron?"

"Yeah," she said, with another nod. "Bleed on the dress."

I raised an eyebrow. "What?"

"Just trust me." She offered a wan smile. "It's a funky Fetch thing."

"Right," I said, slowly. I didn't have any better ideas, and so I nicked the back of my left hand, my stomach doing a slow flip as blood welled to the surface. I hate the sight of my own blood. I glanced at May before wiping my hand on the bodice.

The fabric only darkened for a moment, drinking the blood like dry earth drinks the rain. I tried to jerk my hand back. May grabbed my wrist, forcing me to stay where I was. "Trust me."

"May . . ."

My magic flared before I could finish the sentence, rising with an eagerness that was almost scary. I was pulling less than a quarter of the power I'd need for an illusion, and it was coming nearly on its own. May's magic rose, adding ashes and cotton candy to the mingled scents of copper, fresh-cut grass, and blood.

The Queen's magic snapped into place, filling my mouth with the taste of frozen salt and damp sand. I stared at May. She let go of my hand.

"The spell's fresh enough to argue with. Now tell it what to be."

I stared for a moment more before reaching out with my still-bleeding hand, grabbing for the Queen's spell the way I'd grab for mists or shadows when shaping an illusion. I hit a brief resistance, like the air was pushing back. Then my fingers caught, my magic surging to obscure everything else, and I understood what to do. The Queen taught my clothes to become a gown. I couldn't break her spell—not even blood could give me that kind of power—but as long as I wasn't trying, I could change the definition of "gown."

Visualization is important when you're assembling an illusion, and this was close enough that the same principles applied. I fixed the image of a simpler, *clean* dress in my mind and muttered, "Cinderella dressed in yellow went upstairs to kiss a fellow. Made a mistake, kissed a snake, how many doctors did it take?"

The magic pulled tight before bursting, leaving me with the gritty feeling of sand coating my tongue. My head didn't hurt. May's magic had fueled the spell, not mine; my magic only directed it.

"I didn't know you could do that," I whispered.

May held up the dress. I stared.

The Queen designed a dress too fragile for heavy use and too impractical for anyone expecting to do something more strenuous than a waltz. It wasn't that dress anymore. The fabric had changed from silk to velvet. It was still the color of dried blood, but the material was slashed to reveal a dark rose underskirt, which looked decorative, yet left me able to both conceal and reach my knives.

"Here." May thrust the dress at me. "Go get ready."

I slung the dress over one arm before putting my knife back into its sheath and taking the belt off the rack. "You want to tell me how we did that?"

"Radical transformations stay malleable for a day or so; her spell was fresh enough to transmute. And you bled." She shrugged. "I'm your Fetch. I know when things are possible. Just go with it."

I eyed her, trying to figure out what she wasn't telling me. She smiled guilelessly. I finally sighed. "Be right back."

"I'll be waiting."

I managed to resist the urge to slam the bedroom door, but only because it would have bothered the cats.

Getting into the transmuted gown was a hell of a lot easier than getting out of it had been. Most of the hooks and ties were gone, replaced by buttons; my knife belt went over the interior skirt, the slight bulge it made hidden by a band of gold brocade that rode low and easy on my hips. Maybe it's tacky to go to a formal party armed, but these days, I try not to go anywhere without a way to defend myself. Sylvester would understand. He always did.

I raked a brush through my hair, scowling at my reflection. It scowled obligingly back. One good thing about having hair with no real body: if I brush it out and clip it back, it stays clipped. "The things I do for Faerie, I swear," I muttered, before dropping the brush and calling it good.

May was waiting in the living room. Spike jumped onto the back of the couch when it saw me, rattling its thorns, and chirped as I walked over and started to stroke it. There's an art to petting a rose goblin without injuring yourself. They're basically animate, vaguely cat-shaped rosebushes, and you have to make sure not to move against the grain of the thorns.

"Let's go!" May gestured at the door.

I straightened, only flinching a little as Spike leaped onto my shoulder. "Are you coming?" I asked. It chirped, rubbing a prickly cheek against mine. "Of course you are." Spike likes riding in the car a bit too much. I've had to fetch it from Stacy's twice, after she left without checking for hitchhikers.

"Think of it as a fashion statement," said May. "Ladies used to wear parrots and little monkeys. You wear a rose goblin. It's very chic." She waved her hands. The smell of cotton candy and ashes rose, fading to leave us both looking entirely human. I also appeared to be wearing an outfit identical to hers.

I raised an eyebrow.

"What? You *said* you needed to save your magic for later, and you can't go out looking like you just escaped from a Renaissance Fair." May grinned. "I'm not on the super-saver plan. I'll make myself something when we get there, after I see what my date's wearing."

"Showoff." I grabbed my jacket, slinging it over my arm before opening the door and pushing May out. She huffed as she went. Her giggles sort of spoiled the effect.

She waited on the walkway as I reset the wards. "Are you ready *yet*?" she demanded, with a playful stomp for emphasis.

"As ready as I'm going to get," I replied. "Come on."

Still giggling, May grabbed my elbow and steered me toward the car. One way or another, I was going to the Ball.